ALTAR OF INFLUENCE

THE ORSARIAN WAR

A PRELUDE TO THE DYING LANDS CHRONICLE

JACOB COOPER

DEDICATION

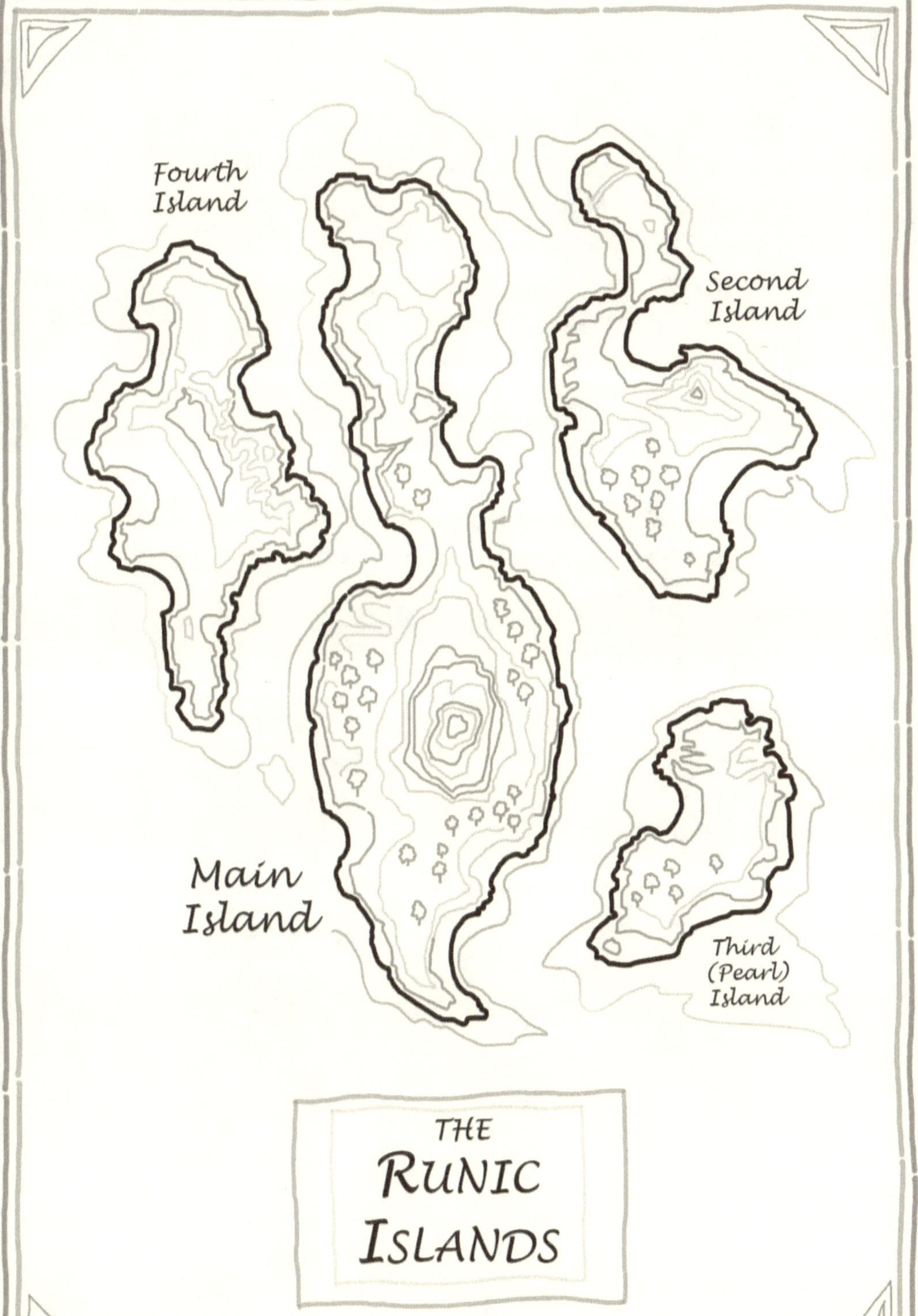

Fourth Island
Second Island
Main Island
Third (Pearl) Island
THE RUNIC ISLANDS

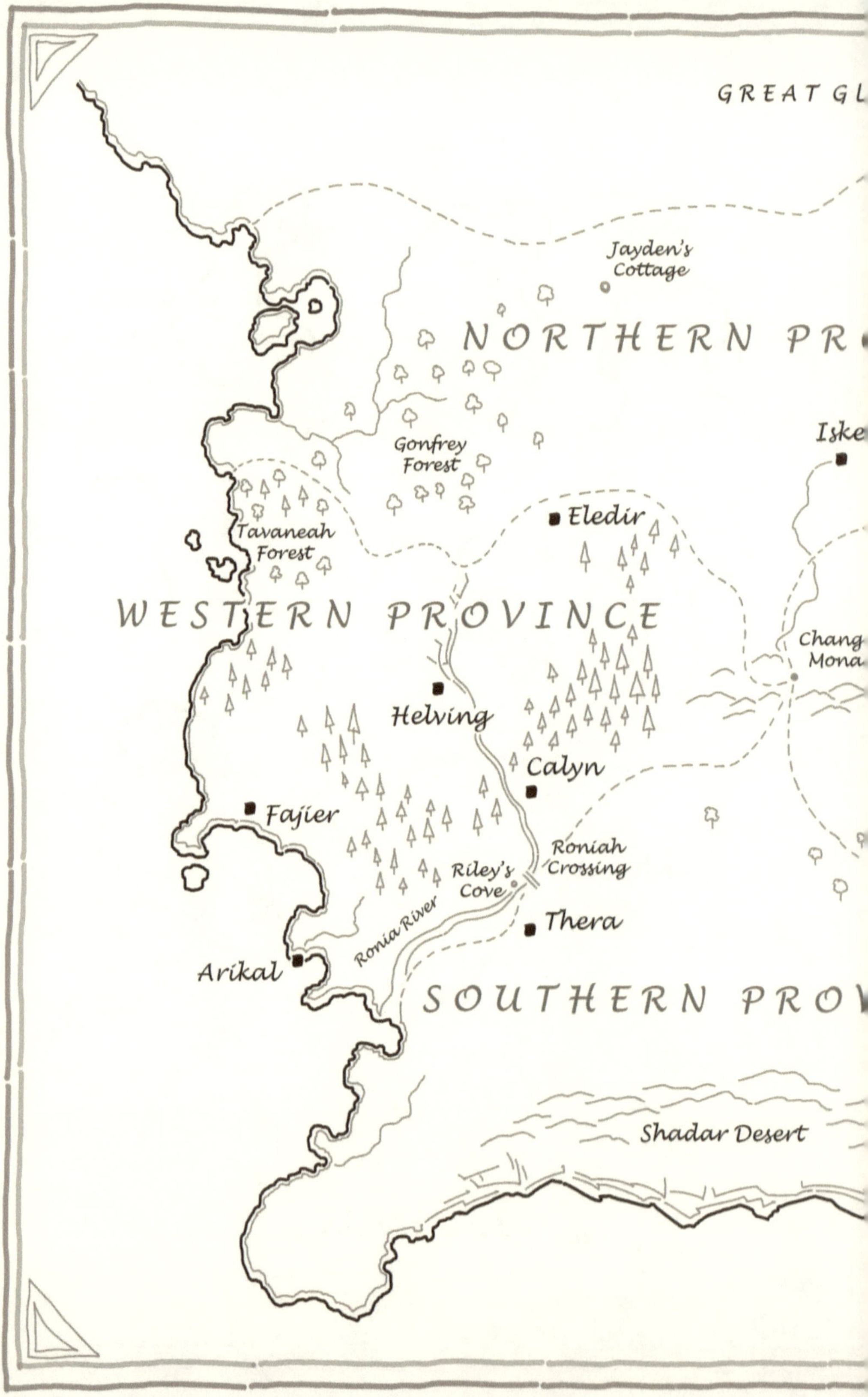

GREAT GL
Jayden's Cottage
NORTHERN PR
Iske
Gonfrey Forest
Eledir
Tavaneah Forest
WESTERN PROVINCE
Chang Mona
Helving
Calyn
Fajier
Roniah Crossing
Riley's Cove
Thera
Ronia River
Arikal
SOUTHERN PRO
Shadar Desert

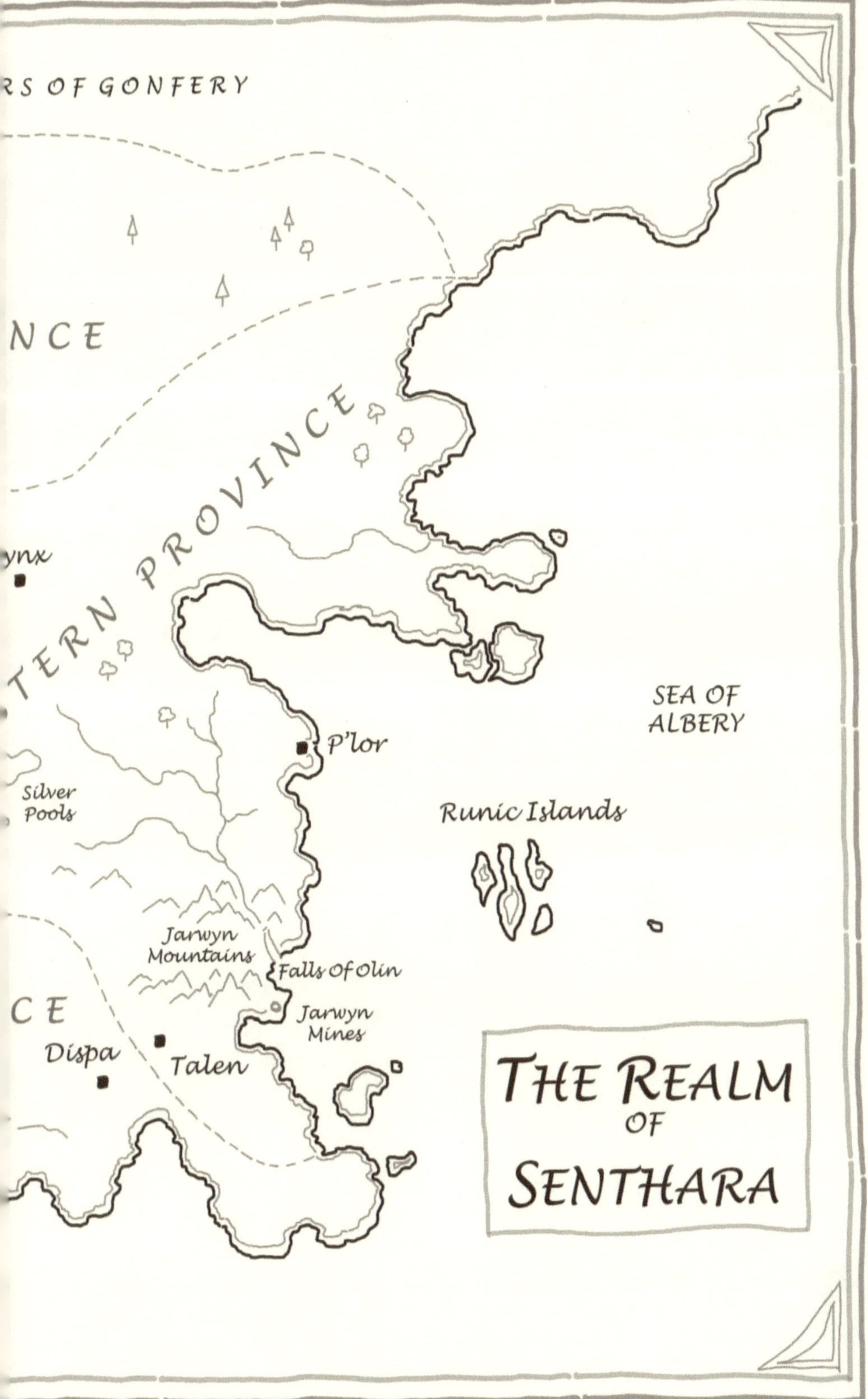
RS OF GONFERY
NCE
TERN PROVINCE
ynx
SEA OF ALBERY
Silver Pools
P'lor
Runic Islands
Jarwyn Mountains
Falls Of Olin
Jarwyn Mines
CE
Dispa
Talen
THE REALM OF SENTHARA

FORWARD

During early test readings of *Circle of Reign*, book 1 of *The Dying Lands Chronicle*, many readers expressed an interest in the story of Thannuel Kerr's early life as well as the Orsarian War, referenced several times in *Circle of Reign*. Although an interesting question, I had not given serious consideration to writing a prequel to the Dying Lands Chronicle, especially before the series was complete. However, the more I pondered on the idea, the more excited I became by the prospect and decided to write a short story, no more than fifty pages, on the Orsarian War. Obviously, I failed miserably. The story took on a life of its own and the book grew to a full-length novel, providing deeper insights, history and richness to the world of Våleira and the overall story of *The Dying Lands Chronicle*.

Although *Altar of Influence* chronologically predates *Circle of Reign* as a story, and readers are free to read the books in whatever order they wish, I wrote *Altar of Influence* with the perspective that a person had previously read *Circle of Reign*. Regardless, I believe the reader will enjoy this story no matter where in *The Dying Lands Chronicle* he or she chooses to pick it up.

~Jacob Cooper

ALTAR OF INFLUENCE

THE ORSARIAN WAR

PROLOGUE

Day 15 of the 3rd Cycle of the Moons of the Low Season
375 Years After Unification (A.U.)

THE THOULDEN-SHA WAITED for the full first moon to rise above the darkening horizon with his knife in hand. Parts of its blade were still coated with blood from the previous cycle's full first moon. It would take many more to resurrect the power of Marishaden.

The chill of the evening air was typical for the low season, even this far south. Only seven leagues west and barely south, the Schadar Desert spread its vast nothingness.

"Ancients above, please don't do this!"

The bound man pleaded more fervently when the sun had disappeared, knowing first moon would rise only minutes from now. His pleas went unheeded.

The remote village of Dispa sat in the southern part of the Eastern Province, where sand dunes rippled the land and rough rock cliffs jutted skyward at random places, creating narrow slot canyons and caves that wove for miles. Soft rock cliffs tapered from a wide base to a slightly narrower top and showcased many layers of sediment, as if a painter had brushed from the bottom up, layer after layer being applied to the landscape, thinning as the brush ran out of paint near the top.

Other villages, larger than the Thoulden-sha's own, all stood within a day's walk. Though only twenty years old, more than a hundred people had believed in the Thoulden-sha's divine calling and accepted him as the Oracle of Mari-shaden. The Marishee, those who believed—his disciples—stood around him and waited to witness another step toward the Resurgence.

Every night, the Marishee quietly spread the news of his calling, announcing his divinity and inviting others to witness the power of the Oracle as he drew the imprisoned pieces of Mari-shaden's Influence from the moons back to the realm of the living. When he completed the Resurgence, the Thoulden-sha would have power to control the events of the world: when the sun rose and set, the tides, the winds, the seasons, the cycling of the lands. It would take decades, but he was patient. Eventually, the blood of more noble bloodlines would be required—a particular bloodline, in fact.

The Kiarra.

For now, however, anyone refusing to cast off his or her heretical genealogy would do.

"Please! I have children! A wife! They need me, please!"

Time fell short. The Thoulden-sha motioned for the bound man to be placed upon the open altar that had been built. The ritual demanded that the sacrifice be completed at the exact moment that a full first moon completely birthed its horizon.

"I beg you!" the man screamed. "For my family's sake! Do not do this! I have some krenshell, not a lot, but the money is yours if you let me go. And my land, my home, all I have!"

The first sliver of bluish-white light crested the horizon and the Marishee began to hum an eerie chorale. The man upon the altar struggled against his bonds, growing desperate.

"Nesyr," a female voice said. The crowd of Marishee parted, lowering the volume of their humming, and the man on the altar—Nesyr—craned his head toward the voice. His face morphed from terror to disbelief.

"Anaveit?"

"Nesyr, do not fear. We know your sacrifice. It is needed," Anaveit said. "I will tell the children one day, when the Resurgence is completed. They will be so proud of your part."

Nesyr looked too shocked to say anything. Tears of pain and betrayal streamed down his cheeks, leaving small streaks of clean on an otherwise dirty face.

"Anaveit—" he began pleadingly.

"The Thoulden-sha has shown me the path to save our world, husband. He is the Oracle. This is the only way."

"Anaveit, no!"

The humming increased as first moon's bottom arc lifted free from the horizon. The knife in the Thoulden-sha's hand fell swift and accurate, and the crowd of Marishee broke into a celebratory melody as Nesyr's blood spilled from the altar to the ground.

The Thoulden-sha looked up to first moon after Nesyr's life had left him and saw it enlarge in the night sky. To an unbeliever, the change would be imperceptible, but not to his eyes.

"Muhktar, my honored First, you may prepare him as the others," he said, not taking his eyes from first moon.

"Yes, my Oracle," Muhktar answered.

"No, he was my husband," Anaveit said. "It is my responsibility."

Muhktar, the first who had accepted the Thoulden-sha as Marishaden's Oracle, hesitated.

"If the Thoulden-sha wishes it," he said.

The Oracle glanced down on Anaveit. Her eyes glimmered, full of belief, exotically beautiful in the moon's luminescence. They almost seemed to invite him—no, they *dared* him—to take her. To love her. This woman—Mari-shaden's will coursed strongly through her. Her body flowed, as if curving with the wind and sands. Yes, he would accept the invitation in her eyes. Anaveit drew close, daring to touch the Oracle, a soft touch on his forearm as she leaned close to his ear. She whispered, "We will raise up seed unto Mari-shaden, a new generation with her Influence running thick in their blood. I have seen it, my Oracle."

A pure generation, born free from the cursed bloodlines. Surely, Mari-shaden had anointed this woman of such will and allure.

"Very well," the Thoulden-sha said, turning to Muhktar. "Anaveit may prepare the body."

As he turned his gaze back toward first moon, he smiled. *I will draw you closer every cycle until your Influence is within reach, Mari-shaden. The blood of those responsible shall flow like the rivers, empowering your true descendants. Then, your power shall walk the world of Våleira, incarnate within me.*

Evrin pondered on the promptings from the forest, leaning heavily on his walking stick with his right hand, his left pressed flush against the light colored bark of a tree. A triarch tree, to be sure. Amnoch and Norvuld, here at his request, remained silent, patiently waiting for Evrin to speak. One did not rush the Keeper of the Living Light.

Spiral branches coated in green moss sprawled outward from the tree under which they stood before jutting upward. The same thick moss covered boulders, tree stumps, fallen branches, and the earth alike all around them. High above, the expansive canopy of triarch frondescence knitted a leafy sky, parsimoniously soaking in the midday sun but allowing pockets of light to penetrate to the ground sporadically. Few other species of trees populated the Tavaniah Forest, the most northwestern part of the Western Province. Mist danced and twirled in the rays of the yellow brilliance before ascending, only to be caught in the canopy above, joining the thin, wispy clouds that lazily hung there in seeming perpetuum.

It had been a half-span plus one—six days—since he had first felt the incongruous pulse of the trees, like an erratic heartbeat drumming awkward polyrhythms. They coursed through him as he tried to decipher their meaning, but an unexpected undertow pulled the tendrils of understanding from him every time he thought he drew closer. It was a strange feeling for the Tavaniah Forest to communicate, one of foreboding. Some threat swelled in strength, one not felt since … he did not know. A millennium of life and the feelings he now perceived were foreign to him, the first of this kind he had ever felt.

And I thought I knew the Lumenatis so well, he thought, once again humbled by the evidence of his imperfect knowledge. *How will the Gyldenal ever be able to restore the Ancients with me at their head?*

Pride. It had nearly destroyed him once, hundreds of years ago, the scar on his left cheek an ever-present reminder, one that he had refused to let heal over the centuries. Now, try as he might to curb it, pride continued to haunt him, prohibiting him from greater knowledge the Lumenatis would otherwise grant him if he were more prepared. He felt the truth of this. To the Lumenatis, the

Influence that promoted and sustained life, *motive* was of key importance.

Ancients forgive me. He did not capture and recycle the shame friction, desiring to feel its rebuke fully.

"I feel … something emerging," Evrin said. "Surfacing."

Was *re*surfacing a more apt description? Evrin's face contorted with concentration, his long gray hair falling in front of his face as he lowered his head. The promptings of the forest were never clear, not spoken through language, but rather feelings, impressions … *influences.*

"Evrin?" Norvuld asked.

The master shipwright's voice interrupted Evrin's concentration.

"I am sorry," the old man said, straightening himself. "I feel … a tide swelling."

"A tide?" Norvuld asked. A sunbeam struck his gray-streaked black hair, making it glisten.

"Not the ocean's tide, I grant you. But yes, one that *is* steadily rising."

There, the undertow again, pulling the revelation from me. He had almost grasped it that time. *Something else is here, something in opposition.*

Amnoch bristled, shifting his weight while bringing his left hand to rest on the pommel of the dark-bladed sword at his hip. The rich blue tunic he wore, embroidered with a simple pattern of laced leather around the neck and trim of the short sleeves, contrasted against their lush green environment. "Perhaps I should build a boat?"

Norvuld turned and gave Amnoch a quizzical glance.

"Or, rather, maybe *you* should build us a boat, Master Norvuld. More your area."

"I'm fairly certain that's not what Evrin is suggesting," Norvuld said.

Evrin smiled kindly. "I know your impatience with figurative language, Amnoch. It is what I feel, however. The Lumenatis—all of the eternal forces, for that matter—do not communicate in the same way humans do. It takes quite a bit of patience to decipher, to be sure."

"Then I am certain I will never be as fluent as you."

"There can be doubt," Norvuld agreed.

The levity, always enjoyed by Evrin, did not dissuade the warning within him. He felt the forest—or the Light within it—struggling to form ... a word? Whatever it tried to communicate had to be of supernal importance if it struggled so mightily to bring specificity to this prompting, to communicate with *language*, with—

It finally came and Evrin's eyes opened wide, stretching the wrinkled skin of his face.

"Amnoch," Evrin spoke, using a more full timbre, the richness of the authoritative voice he had once used when he commanded legions returning to him after so many centuries as the urgency of the Light's prompting found place in him. "You must go to House Kerr. They will have need of you."

The broad-shouldered man with thinning hair looked bewildered. "Me? I'm skilled with steel and a little healing, Evrin, but beyond that—"

"Precisely, Amnoch." Evrin's eyes found Norvuld's. "You, Master Norvuld ... I am not sure how to best guide you in your task, I admit. You must find a way to expand the Light beyond our borders, across the sea."

"I ... "

"I do not know more than this, but I felt strongly about having you two here," Evrin said. "It was the will of the Living Light, I am certain. I see the confusion on your faces, but you will understand. Time is short but not yet expired."

Ancients guide us, Evrin thought, now fully understanding that the world of Våleira was dying. Not simply cycling, but *dying.* Perhaps their world would become as the others, as the Ancients had feared.

The Kiarra Clan must once again rise if Våleira is to survive this … Resurgence. Yes, the forest had fought to convey that exact word, amplifying its meaning with images and feelings, overcoming the resistance that had been so plainly present.

The undertow I felt? A parasite of sorts … within the Living Light? Impeding his connection? It didn't seem possible to Evrin, especially not deep within the Tavaniah where the Light welled deepest.

The Kiarra Clan had dwindled over the centuries, Evrin knew, almost as if the Ancient Dark had a hand in their narrowing progeny, an impediment of some kind upon their expansion as a bloodline. And now … he sensed a direct threat that would confront them, one they might never see coming.

Still, the capacity of their forbearers resides therein, in their blood. It must. Evrin tried to convince himself of this, praying it was true.

If it does not, then we are already lost.

PART ONE

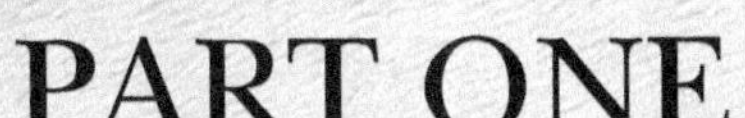

No mystery has plagued the world of Våleira to a greater degree than identity of the Thoulden-sha. Some said of him that he was a farmer, others a blacksmith, others a shipwright. None of the apocryphal accounts give much insight into his to power. Of one thing we are certain: his children still walk among us.

—Prime Vicar Ryall of the New Changrual Order.
Consequences of the Resurgence, 3rd scroll, last line

ONE
~ANTIOUS~
Day 6 of 2nd High 379 A.U.

ANTIOUS ROAN STARED DOWN HIS LANE. It ran two hundred yards long and ended with a series of trees, each cascading higher. Four in a row. At the top of the fourth tree hung a flag, the prize. Two boys crouched at his right and five to the left. Some of his fellow classmates. Each of the eight lanes was clearly marked as he scoped out the distance of the field.

Others stood looking on, waiting for the signal to begin the race. It was field day at Therrium Academy, part of activity span. The current event: the dash and jump for the eleven-year-olds. The ten-year-olds had just finished and the twelve-year-old group would follow. Whoever retrieved the flag from the fourth tree first at the end of the field won the event. Simple enough, and a point of pride for the winner of each age group.

Yesterday had been armed forces day, where members of the Arlethian army hosted a thirteen-station obstacle course and a sparring event to close the day. Tomorrow would be craftsman's day, where various tradesmen would host a series of games and workshops centered around their individual skills.

As Antious bore down and stretched his leg out behind him, preparing for the starting signal, he saw Thannuel and three of his friends looking at him with a sort of sneer on their faces. He thought he saw a bit of *you're going to get what you deserve* in the lordling's look but paid it no mind. Antious was only in the academy because of where he happened to live, not because of his breeding. Generally only the noble born, or those invited because of significant academic prowess, attended Therrium Academy. Antious had neither qualification. His father worked as a night watchman at the academy and mother as a campus janitor, affording him the privilege of living on the campus and attending classes. Somehow, this didn't ingratiate him to his fellow students as they saw students like him as leeches, tagging along for the ride and benefitting from what wasn't rightfully theirs.

The mopping and sweeping of his mother's duties often pained her back, and so he would help her late into the night after classes while his father worked his duty shift. He drew more derision because of this, but that didn't bother him. He could take it.

Antious knew why Thannuel glared at him now, however. It was not the general disdain that he attracted because of his station, but rather that Antious had actually bested Thannuel yesterday during the sparring event. It had been no surprise that Thannuel had won the twelve-year-old class, but Antious rising to win his eleven-year-old class surprised everyone. Antious still brimmed with pride inside at seeing his father's own gratification as he watched his son land a decisive blow, knocking his opponent off the rounded pedestal.

Each pedestal had two semicircle-shaped pieces of wood fastened to its underside, perpendicular to the pedestal, making the rounded standing platform, only large enough for one person, rock back and forth. The game tested balance and dexterity as much as weapon skill. The implement of choice for this event had been the bow staff, each end padded to soften the blows.

"I'd bet the leech couldn't defeat a real opponent!" Oberlin Falda had jeered as he stood at Thannuel's side. House Falda was a minor noble house and Oberlin seemed determined to improve his station by sucking up to the Kerr lordling.

"Yeah! No doubt he won by cheating somehow!" said Chase Gorlan, another one of Thannuel's cronies. "No way he could stand up to Thannuel."

Amid the derision, Antious felt his victory turn sour. He lowered his head, too shy to meet the eyes of those taunting him. He searched among his classmates, hoping for some show of support. No one stepped forward or said a thing.

"Oh, no, is he going to cry?" Oberlin said. "Don't cry, little leech. Just slither back to your swamp."

Several laughs came from the other students. Antious felt himself flush. And then, he felt surprise as a soft hand found his and grabbed it tightly. He looked to see a girl, one of the ten-year-olds, by his side. What was her name? Antious's shock forced out any coherent thought.

"I will take that wager," she said. "I bet Antious can whip your little lordling's—"

"Kalisa!" shouted a soldier, stomping his way quickly to her. Kalisa Korin. Her name finally came to Antious.

I'm dead, Ancients take me.

Antious tried to pull away but Kalisa held his hand firmly. The soldier, a captain in the Arlethian army, came to her side. "Drop the boy's hand, daughter."

"I quite like it, Father." She turned to Antious. "Don't you?"

Antious opened his mouth, but the pervasive shock stopped any reply. He thought he must have quite looked like a fish out of water.

"Do not speak, son," the captain said to Antious. "It will be better for you. You've done well, but do not overstep yourself."

"I'm not trying to, sir, I'm just—"

"I thought I said to *not* speak," Captain Korin snapped.

Antious felt his father's familiar pulse come through the ground, approaching from the rear. He had jumped from the audience stands at seeing his son being confronted by another adult. Antious knew his father would not step in when he someone bullied him, always telling him that he needed to grow from the adversity, that it would strengthen him in the end. But an adult confronting him was likely a little much for his father to contain himself.

"Captain, I'm sure your business with your daughter does not include my son," Marekan Roan said as he approached.

"Actually, their *business* seems quite intertwined," Korin retorted, looking down at his daughter's hand clutching Antious's.

"Harmless, no doubt, my good captain." Marekan's words were jovial, the way he sounded when he wanted to defuse a situation. Perhaps only Antious could hear the stressed overtones in his father's voice, pleading for this small confrontation not to escalate.

Captain Korin stepped closer, speaking softly but firmly. "No son of a night watchman is going to have an interest in my daughter!"

Marekan chuckled. "Seemed the affection was flowing from the opposite direction from where I sat."

At that, the captain sneered and stepped back. "Yes, why not one last contest?" He looked past Antious. "What do you think, young Kerr? Are you up for it?" His friends cheered him on, pushing him forward.

Antious felt a pit in his stomach and looked up at his father. Behind his father's confident smile, he saw concern. He tried to draw strength from his dad, but if this didn't turn out right, things would end up worse than they already were for him. But, refusing to accept the challenge would automatically do that anyway.

He felt Kalisa's grip on his hand tighten and then soft, warm lips brush his cheek. He fluttered with an excitement he hadn't felt before and it continued as she whispered in his ear.

"The higher they hold their heads, the harder they fall."

She released his hand and someone—he couldn't remember who—shoved a bow staff in his hand. He tried to steel his nerves as he stepped onto the circular pedestal, and nearly toppled off in his nervousness. A few laughs sounded, but they were cut short by a shrill young voice shouting, "You can do it, Antious! Put him on his royal—" Again, her father's chiding cut Kalisa short. But her words made him find some courage and he steadied himself.

Thannuel attacked brutishly, no form or poise, just swinging the padded ends of the bow staff repeatedly at Antious's head and body. The eleven-year-old blocked and ducked, shifting his weight back and forth as deftly as possible, barely keeping himself on the wooden pedestal. The first person to get knocked off or put a foot on the earth would lose. Obviously, Thannuel's strategy was to continue his attacks, formless though they were, until he landed a blow and knocked Antious to the ground or unbalanced him enough to take a step off.

A jab from Thannuel hit Antious in the stomach and knocked the wind from him. Tears sprang to his eyes as he bent forward, barely keeping his balance. The "oohs" from the audience were barely audible to him. Glimpsing Thannuel's weight shift, he sensed the next blow would come down on his back as an overhead downward thrust.

In that moment of panic, Kalisa's words came back to him. What had she said? The higher they hold their heads …

He looked up and saw Thannuel's arms raised high over his head, his lower jaw angled up, aligning with his raised shoulders. Before Antious could consider how to properly execute the move, he thrust his staff forward like a spear and its end connected with Thannuel's lower jaw just as his arms swung down. Antious heard his opponent's teeth clatter together as they met with surprising force from the blow. Though Thannuel's strike had hit Antious, it bore no sting, glancing weakly off the left side of his hip. The momentum from his own jab, however, carried him forward and he took a step off his round pedestal to catch himself.

He knew he had lost and threw down his staff in shame, not looking up. Any moment, the crowd would cheer Thannuel's victory and his peers would resume their jeers. But silence persisted. Eventually, Antious looked up and saw Thannuel flat on his backside, holding his jaw. Oberlin and Chase stood over him, stunned.

Captain Korin spoke. "Thannuel is the winner."

Still, no applause. Antious had been so distracted that Thannuel's vibrational signature hadn't even registered. He must have felt it but been too concerned trying to get his breath back.

"What?" Kalisa asked, indignant. "That's not true!"

"The boy's foot hit the ground before Thannuel's did. I saw and felt it," Korin answered his daughter. "As did we all."

Marekan came to his son and hugged him. "Well done, Antious. I am proud of you."

Antious certainly did feel a surge of pride at seeing his future lord on the ground by his hand.

"Now, go help him up," his father said. "Extend your hand to him in sportsmanship."

"Dad!" Antious whispered. "Don't make me—"

"Go on, son."

As Antious glumly sauntered his way over to Thannuel, the audience finally roused itself from its stupor and raised an unenthusiastic cheer. He reached down his open hand toward Thannuel but Chase slapped it away.

"He won!" Oberlin declared. "Thannuel doesn't need your help!"

"Well, from up here, it certainly doesn't look much like he won, now does it?" Antious retorted.

Thannuel's cronies hadn't known what to say. Several students, many he didn't know, crowded around Antious, congratulating and cheering him, slapping him on the back. Kalisa found him and gave him another peck on the cheek, making his heart flutter. No moment in his childhood had made him feel prouder.

That had been yesterday.

Now, seeing the look on Thannuel's and his friends' faces as he readied himself on the starting line of the dash and jump, he knew he'd have to sleep with one eye opened for a while.

The officiator waved his flag and all eight competitors took off down their lane, sprinting furiously toward the four trees that grew in height, one right behind the other. The tallest had the flag at its apex. With wood-dweller speeds, it would take only a few seconds to cross the field and leap into the trees, jumping from branch to branch, ascending the trees until reaching the flag.

A win today would assure his social standing. He would have more friends than he ever had before; and Kalisa! She might even favor him with another kiss, if he were lucky. Those two she landed on his cheek yesterday still felt warm to him. He wasn't sure if he'd ever wash his face again. How had he not noticed her much before? She was stunning to him … or she was now that she had shown interest in him.

Antious came to the end of his lane. He felt the others and knew he and the boy from the third lane were in the lead, neck and neck. The muscles in his legs coiled in preparation to jump to the first tree. His eyes were constantly on the flag in the highest tree, dreaming of how his life would change when he won.

Springing up from the ground, he released his pent-up excitement and coiled leg muscles. He felt his body begin to rise for a brief moment before coming crashing down, his feet never leaving the ground. He hit hard but the ground was wrong. Softer than it should have been. Pushing himself up he found his feet, knees, elbows and hands, the points he had hit the ground with, stuck to the ground.

What the Cursed Heavens?

The more he pulled, the stronger the tug to the earth seemed to be. And then he saw it. Underneath a thin layer of dirt was a dull amber color shining through. He knew what it was from his mother's janitor supply closet. Southern amber wax. Underneath the thick coat of wax was a hard surface, probably a large plank of wood. He could tell it had been hastily put down on the ground and quickly covered.

No point in struggling; someone would have to come dig under it to free him. He grimaced at the thought of being peeled from the ground. Southern amber wax could often take skin off.

Less than half a minute had passed before he heard cheers as the boy from the third lane reached the flag. The race had ended. And Antious lay on all fours, like a dog, waiting to be freed. He heard Thannuel's laughs above the cheers.

Thannuel Kerr ran through the trees on his way home from school. He jumped from tree to tree, sliding down branches on his feet as they wove in and out of one another, intermingling with those of other trees like giants clasping arms. The leather jerkin that lay over his tunic flapped in the wind along with his amber hair as he sprang.

Coming to a large Ayzish tree, Thannuel scaled its straight trunk all the way to the thick canopy of frondescence that covered much of Calyn and the Western Province. He broke through the canopy and stood above it, at the apex of the forest. He ran, feet light on the treetops, and leaped. Like most wood-dwellers, Thannuel felt just as secure here as he did on solid ground. In many ways, he felt more so in the trees.

The forest itself was more than a home to his people; it was part of them. This feeling did not extend to other parts of Senthara that had forests, for the trees in those parts did not speak. Only here, in the West, in Arlethia, were the trees *fluent.*

As he sprinted, faster than most animals could match, the warm high season wind whipped across his face and the sun beat down on him. Ahead, he caught sight of one of the spires of the Kerr Hold, his home. Four of them penetrated above the canopy, vines and ivy wrapping around them. He leaped, grabbing hold of the closest one, and slid down it, landing on one of the many elevated pathways that wove from the courtyard of the magnificent hold up and through the forest, each climaxing at one of the spires.

He landed silently in the courtyard of his hold and a middle-aged man greeted him. "Welcome home, my young Lord."

"How are the hounds, Master Elethol?" Thannuel asked cheerfully.

"Growing every day! Haven't had a litter this large since serving under Master Fulburn at the Iskell kennels. You should visit the kennels more often."

"Perhaps after I see my father. Do you know where he is?"

"Yes," Master Elethol said. "In his stateroom with Lord Hoyt. He said not to be disturbed … unless it was you, of course."

"Lord Hoyt is here?" Thannuel asked. "Is Calder here as well?"

Elethol shook his head. "I don't believe so, Lord Thannuel. Just his father."

Thannuel shrugged. "I'm sure Father will want to hear of my day. It was quite exciting."

At that, Elethol gave him a wary look.

"What? Is he in a foul mood?" Thannuel asked.

"Oh, I think it's best you see for yourself, my young Lord."

Lord Branton Kerr sat opposite Lord Callum Hoyt, Lord of the Southern Province, in his stateroom. Ryant'ah, the Archiver assigned to Hold Kerr, sat in a chair to the side of the two lords, a bit removed. While he was in the room, the Archiver was certainly not part of the meeting; his kind were silent observers, recording all they witnessed and transmitting those observations through a Light scry to an elder of his order, high in the Jarwyn mountains in the Eastern Province. The elder on the other end of the Light scry would then speak what Ryant'ah conveyed as a group of young acolytes chiseled the words into obsidian tablets, later to be added to the chronicles of the Realm.

Autonomous as an order, the Archivers supposedly predated the Senthary and even the Hardacheons, keeping themselves aloof from the shifts and changes of those in power. While their records were open to any who would read them, making a trip to the Jarwyn peaks, where the air was too thin to sustain life for any extended period except for the Archivers themselves, was taken on by very few.

Lords Kerr and Hoyt carried on the furtive conversation without any concern of Ryant'ah being in the room.

"It is likely that if they do continue to grow, they will first expand to your province, Callum."

"I'm aware, Lord Kerr," Lord Hoyt said. "In fact, I've had reports from my advisors that they have already made some inroads."

Lord Kerr raised an eyebrow at this.

"Several families from the village of Talen have simply abandoned their farms and migrated east," Hoyt said. "It's no mystery as to where they have gone. Talen is barely in the Southern Province's border, an easy target for this Thoulden-sha to recruit from."

"And, what does Lord Orion say of this? Has he a solution?" Kerr asked. "Certainly he sees where the problem will lead if unchecked."

Hoyt sighed. "Lord Orion seems disinterested at best. Dispa is so far removed from Erynx and the more populous parts of the Eastern Province that I doubt he even thinks much about it."

Orion's indifference did not surprise Kerr. The man barely spent any time outside of Erynx, the East's state city.

"He is often out of touch," Kerr said.

"That's why I'm here, Lord Kerr," Hoyt said. "I need help but I don't want to make this an official matter bogged down in politics."

"You mean you don't want to involve Prime Lord Wellyn," Kerr replied with a smile.

Hoyt nodded. "I've sent some guards around Talen, but these Marishee seem to skip right past them. Even if they were caught, it's not like they're actually doing anything illegal … not that we can tell, anyway."

"What about observing them in Dispa?"

Hoyt shifted in his chair. "Lord Kerr, if I sent southern forces into the Eastern Province, and Lord Orion found out, there would be the Dark to pay. The Prime Lord would certainly get involved then, and not to my benefit, I'm afraid."

The two sat in silence, Branton watching his old friend.

"But you have, nonetheless, haven't you?" he asked.

Hoyt diverted his eyes, a frown upon his face. "Yes," he whispered.

"And?"

"And they did not return, Branton. That whole area around Dispa, with its maze of slot canyons and caves … who knows, maybe they became lost. Some of those narrow canyons can go for miles, twisting and turning."

"But you don't think so," Kerr intuited.

"I'm not sure what I think, yet. But I am concerned."

Thannuel burst into his father's stateroom. He was definitely in a good mood, his jaw feeling immensely better after this morning's payback on that runt.

Should have known he was good with a bow staff, seeing as how

"Hello, Father!"

"Thannuel, home from school?" his father asked. He sat with Lord Callum Hoyt of the Southern Province, likely negotiating some trade treaty or other state business. "Callum, would you excuse me for a few minutes? My son and I need to have some words."

"Why, of course," Lord Hoyt said. He smiled at Thannuel as he left the chamber. "Good to see you, as always, Thannuel."

"Come here, son," Lord Branton Kerr said, motioning to a chair.

"You should have seen it, Father! Not only did I win the bow staff jousting yesterday but today I won the dash and jump for the twelve-year-old age group! If I win an event tomorrow, I'll be the first anyone can remember winning three different events and—"

"I see," Branton said, interrupting his son. "And, winning … this makes you better than others?"

Thannuel was confused. "I, uh, well … I thought you'd be proud of my performances."

"Performances." Branton echoed his son's word. "Is that what they are?"

Thannuel was utterly bewildered. Something was wrong with his father but he didn't know what.

"Father, are you—"

"You see, son, I had a very interesting visit this morning from one of the night watchmen at the academy, a man named Marekan Roan."

Thannuel felt a ball of ice form in his gut. He glanced toward Ryant'ah, obviously wishing the Archiver was not present.

"At first I was concerned something had happened, that you had been injured perhaps. But that was not the case. Marekan seems to think that the ideals we Kerrs uphold are somewhat lost on you. I assured him he must be mistaken and that I would speak with you. But, he shared a most interesting story, one I am sure *my* son was not a character in."

Branton had a deep vertical line in his forehead that gave a menacing feel as he glowered at his son. Thannuel sank in his chair, feeling much smaller than he actually was.

"It was just a bit of fun, Father." Thannuel could not even look at him.

Branton huffed. "I see. Fun. And how much *fun* was it when you got knocked on your backside by this so-called 'leech'?"

Thannuel shrank further. "But I won! I beat him!"

"After Marekan left, I visited Captain Korin. He's still in the vicinity from hosting the games at the academy yesterday. Seems you did indeed win, albeit on a technicality."

Thannuel shrugged. "It's still a win."

"More importantly, I heard from the captain that you fought like a brute and got put down like a brute."

"That's not true!" Thannuel stammered, suddenly standing up.

"Sit down!" Branton snapped, pounding his fist on the table. Thannuel flinched and did as he was told.

"And then today," his father continued, "you humiliated that boy in front of everyone. For what? To gratify your pride? To keep him low? To embarrass him the way he embarrassed you? To get even in a petty contest that he doesn't even know he's a player in?"

Thannuel just looked down. His shame could not be contained and he knew it showed on his face.

Branton's voice softened but lost none of its regal quality. "This boy, Antious, does not have the luxury of life that you do. Yet, from what I know, he comports himself with more dignity and poise than those who are born into nobility."

"Dad, I know, I'm just—"

"No," his father stopped him. "You will hear me. Nobility is not a birthright, son. It is earned. As a Kerr, you are born with many expectations, not all of them fair. Regardless, they exist and I expect you to earn the nobility you were born to. Instead of being the ringleader in this bullying I would have expected you to be the one defending Antious, standing up for him and putting an arm around him."

Thannuel looked away.

"Look here, boy, in my eyes," Branton commanded. "Tomorrow, you will befriend Antious and apologize to him. You will protect him from others who have acted toward him as you have. You will compel your friends to do the same or cease being their friends. I've already spoken to Oberlin and Chase's parents, and neither they, nor their children, are welcome here at Hold Kerr until this happens. They have given their support."

"What? You can't do that!"

Branton slapped Thannuel, leaving a red mark on his cheek. The sting made him wince.

When he spoke, Branton's voice remained calm. "You will do as I have said tomorrow, Thannuel. You will look Antious in the eye, shake his hand, and apologize. If you choose to defy me and not do this, I bring his family into the hold, making his father one of my Hold Guard and employing his mother wherever I can. Antious will be around you all day, every day, until you befriend him. I think you will find my will quite firm in this, son. Do you understand?"

Thannuel was shocked. His father was mad, obviously. What could he say?

"I see the latter course of action will be necessary," Branton said. "Very well." He stood up to call the herald servant, but Thannuel caught his arm.

"No, Father, that won't be necessary. I'll do it."

Branton sat. "Thannuel, I'm not doing this to punish you, but to elevate you. It is the duty of all lords to lift their people, to seek out the heads that are weighed down and ease their burdens. The *only* time a lord puts himself in front of those he rules is when danger is present. If we wish others to be their best, *we* must be our best. I understand the follies of youth and popularity. Besides, Antious sounds rather tough, from the stories I hear. It may serve you well to have a friend such as him."

"Yes, Father." Thannuel got up to leave, sensing the scolding was over.

"Oh, one more thing, son. You'll be training with Master Amnoch before and after school from now on. Your skills with the battle implements have led to somewhat of an embarrassment on your behalf, I'm afraid. I'm certain you will invite your new friend to join you."

Thannuel cursed quietly as he left his father's meeting chamber.

The following morning the sun seemingly found more ways than usual to pierce the forest's canopy with its golden light. Thannuel awoke, squinting from the orb's invasion, and peered out his window, seeing the morning dew steaming from the shrubs and grass of the hold gardens. Common servants busily pruned the plants, hedges and smaller trees into beautiful designs.

Despite the pleasantness of the morning, Thannuel found no joy in himself, only dread. He muttered as he fumbled into his clothes and moped as he went to the kitchens for breakfast. Drilth Wendham, a recent addition to the hold's staff as a chef, greeted him.

"What'll it be today, young Lord?" she asked. "Perhaps some

mangos and dried grains with cream?”

“I guess,” Thannuel mumbled.

Habit more than appetite drove him to the kitchens this morning. His stomach grumbled with worry as he ate, a blank stare upon his face. At some point as he sat wallowing in his misery, someone sat down beside him at the table without Thannuel first realizing it.

“Lord Hoyt,” Thannuel said with surprise. “Pardon me for not acknowledging you. I thought you had left already.”

“Oh, stop with the formalities, Thannuel.” Hoyt smiled. “I head back to the Southern Province this afternoon. If I may say, you appear to be quite consumed.”

Thannuel sighed and put a hand through his hair. “My father is just so … ”

“Unreasonable?”

“Old! He doesn’t understand!”

“Does he not?” Hoyt asked.

“How can he?”

“Was your father ever your age? An heir to a province? Do you think he was always so regal and refined?”

“He acts like he was always perfect,” Thannuel said.

Hoyt chuckled. “Your father, Thannuel, was a hellion beyond reckoning at your age. Or maybe he was a little older. He deserted the hold once, running away. Did you know that?”

“He what?”

“It’s true,” Hoyt said with a smile, obviously taking pleasure in educating Lord Kerr’s son. “Your grandfather and grandmother were sick with worry, searching everywhere.”

“Where did he go? Why?”

“Why do young boys of your age do anything? You’re trying to find your place and somehow believe no one else can understand.

Eventually, you realize that's far from true, and the problem was a narrow and selfish perspective."

"I'm not selfish," Thannuel objected. "I'm stifled! I can't do anything without reprisal or being judged because I'm 'supposed to be setting a good example'." He said this last bit with unbridled mocking.

"The Schadar Desert," Hoyt said.

"What?"

"That's where your father went when he ran away."

"But … why?" Thannuel asked. "There's nothing there."

"Well, besides the Kearon people, you're right. And, I think that was the point. No one was there, no one to tell him he couldn't do what he wanted, no one to scold him."

"Sounds great!"

"Sure, it does," Hoyt admitted. "And I'm sure it did to him as well, until he almost died."

"My father almost died?"

Hoyt nodded. "He rioted through the Southern Province for a while, living free and far enough from home not to be readily recognized. Eventually he was tempted to explore the desert, but the Schadar is brutal, unforgiving. There's almost no game, and limited water. Only those who live there know how to survive its barrenness."

"What happened?" Thannuel asked.

"Oh, it's quite boring, actually. Someone found Branton, sunburned and dehydrated. They tended to him and left him close enough to a village in the Southern Province to be noticed. It did not take long for word to reach your grandparents that he had been found. My own father saw him returned safely."

"Who saved him?"

Hoyt raised his eyebrows. "We don't know. Your father doesn't remember much. It was no doubt one of the Kearon."

"But, why would they save one of us?"

"I think the point is that one of them did save your father when they had every reason not to."

"There's a *point?*" Thannuel realized Lord Hoyt was actually trying to tell him something.

"For some, growing up among those who have so much is a very harsh environment, perhaps somewhat like the Schadar, in a way. And, though we try to be brave and adventurous, many times, people are burned and starving inside and desperately need someone to save them, though they would never admit it.

"Perhaps your father is only trying to help you save your friend."

"He's not my friend."

"Neither was the Kearon who saved your father."

Thannuel intentionally arrived late to school, missing the morning assembly where all the students gathered to start each day. He would have to face Antious at some point today, but it didn't need to be at the beginning.

It was still activity span, ten days of various competitions and activities. On the field, the students ran from exhibit to exhibit, and from game to game. Craftsman's day was usually set up with a myriad of booths, each sponsored by a different trade with information about what each one involved, and a game of some kind.

Thannuel spied Oberlin and Chase running, but not toward a booth. They moved fast, as if … chasing someone. Thannuel looked ahead of his friends and saw Antious sprinting, weaving between students and booths, trying to lose his pursuers … not being successful.

Thannuel almost turned away, thinking that he would at least not participate. Perhaps that would be enough … just stand by and not make things worse.

I was told to be his friend, not his mother! I don't have to protect him!

Antious drew near to Thannuel, not seeing him until he was close. The younger boy's eyes showed fear and he turned away as fast he could. Only then did Thannuel see the raw skin on Antious's forearms and wrists, no doubt from where the southern amber wax had been stripped. It was a hot day, being well into the high season, and yet Antious wore pants. Thannuel did not doubt that similar wounds were on his knees.

Why aren't his wounds bound? Thannuel wondered. Perhaps they were too tender still. They did glisten in the sun, looking almost wet. He saw no scabs. Realization struck him, understanding that it had likely taken most of the night to peel the wax from Antious. Guilt stung Thannuel.

"Come on, Thannuel!" Oberlin said as he sprinted past. "Help us catch him! Chase stole some salt from the cafeteria for the leech's arms!"

Had Thannuel been this cruel? Was he just now seeing himself the way others did?

It is the duty of all lords to lift their people, to seek out the heads that are weighed down and ease their burdens. The only time a lord puts himself in front of those he rules is when danger is present.

His father's words from the day before played back in his mind, having greater gravity given what Lord Hoyt had revealed to him this morning.

"Dimming Light!" he swore, not relishing what he had to do. Thannuel dashed after Oberlin, catching him in seconds. He grabbed Oberlin's shoulder and kicked his legs, tripping him. His friend hit the ground hard.

"Blasted Night! What's wrong with you?" Oberlin yelled.

"Stay down," Thannuel said.

Chase, the largest of the three friends, saw what had happened and broke off from pursuing Antious.

"I'm not your dog!" Oberlin yelled, starting to get up. Thannuel kicked him in the side, knocking the wind from him.

"I said, stay down."

Chase came barreling toward Thannuel, hostility in his eyes. "What are you doing?"

"What I should have done a long time ago."

"I have no problem beating leeches or nobility!" Chase snapped.

"Please, try," Thannuel taunted.

Chase swung and Thannuel ducked. Another punch missed. Thannuel pushed Chase hard, almost feeling like he had struck Chase open-handed. His friend flew back a little but absorbed the blow.

"I don't want to hurt you," Thannuel said. "We don't need to fight. We're just going to leave Antious alone from now on."

Frustrated and angry, Chase yelled, "I don't take orders from you! You're not a lord yet!"

Chase rushed Thannuel like a wild bull, intending to knock him down. Thannuel didn't move. When Chase was close enough to reach out and grab him, Thannuel jumped, bringing both his knees upward to his chest ... but his knees never made it past his hips. They collided with Chase's face as the crown of the boy's head knocked Thannuel square in the chest. Both fell backward, groaning.

As Thannuel recovered, someone stood over him, blocking the sun.

He could feel others arriving, students and staff alike. The person standing over him extended a hand. Thannuel accepted it and pulled himself up.

"Why did you do that?" Antious asked.

"My father told me to."

"Lord Kerr told you to beat up your friends? What does he tell you to do to your enemies?"

Thannuel grimaced with the pain. "Actually, he told me I have to shake your hand and be your friend. Already that has cost me."

"Well, I'm sorry to be such a burden," Antious said. "And I'm not your friend."

Thannuel arched his back, achieving a few satisfying pops. "Why aren't your wounds bound?"

Antious looked down at his forearms. "Took all night to get it off. My mother sent me to get some triarch wraps from the healer when your sidekicks here found me."

"Does it hurt?" Thannuel looked down at Antious's arms. They glistened in parts, moist scabs starting to form.

"What do you think?"

"I think I was prideful and cruel. And, I'm sorry." He extended his hand toward Antious.

"You know you're going to be suspended for this, right?" Antious said.

"Probably." Thannuel shrugged. "But at least I won't have to listen to my father spout another lecture about standing up for you."

"He told you to stand up for me?"

"Are you going to accept my apology or not, mop boy?"

Antious took Thannuel's hand. "I guess I can't let your Lordship get suspended on my account."

Chase Gorlan still writhed on the ground, holding his face. His lips bled and a few teeth might have been loose. Oberlin lay next to him but had started to get up.

"What are you—" Antious's swift kick to the groin silenced him. In reflex, the bully fell to the ground and assumed the fetal position with his hands between his legs, making pathetic whining noises.

"That's going to be memorable," Thannuel noted.

"Leave him alone!" came a shrill cry.

Thannuel turned to see Kalisa Korin in his face, her sandy blonde hair pulled back tight into a ponytail, not concealing any of her indignant, sharp angled face. He flinched as she beat her fists upon his chest. Other students now encircled them and a couple teachers were pushing their way through the crowd.

"Kalisa, stop!" Antious said. "It's not him!" He grabbed her arm. "It's not him. He helped me."

She looked at him, disbelieving.

"You did this?" she asked Thannuel, motioning to Chase and Oberlin.

"Yeah. Well, most of it, anyway," Thannuel admitted. He looked at Antious. "Do you always have girls do your fighting?"

"Do you remember being put on your backside two days ago, lordling?" Antious fired back.

Thannuel smiled. "I think I'm more afraid of your girl here."

"She's not my girl—" Antious started to protest, but was met with a glare from Kalisa that looked like it stung more than a slap would. "Um, okay, I guess apparently she is, actually."

"You all!" a teacher snapped. "Come with me to the curator's office at once!"

"Oh, by the way," Thannuel said. "You're to accompany me to the hold after we get suspended."

"For what?" Antious asked.

"Training."

"Training?"

"Thanks, but I heard myself the first time."

"He's not going!" Kalisa said, following them as they were hurried along to the curator's office. "It's just a trap, Antious!"

Antious did look skeptical. "Right. Why *would* I come to your hold?"

"You don't have to, I suppose. But my father did request it."

"Just like he told you to beat up your friends?"

"Whatever. Are you going to come or not?" Thannuel asked. "We'll be training with our master of the Hold Guard."

"Master Amnoch?" Antious exclaimed.

"You know him?"

"My dad speaks highly of him, like he's one of the most skilled with steel in the Realm."

Thannuel shrugged as several teachers ushered them along. "I guess. Apparently you embarrassed me by winning that stupid duel and so I have been ordered to train with Master Amnoch. And, I'm supposed to invite you. But you better get your wounds seen to first. It might scar otherwise."

"Maybe I should let it!"

"Yeah, that's a *great* idea."

"Will I get more chances to 'embarrass' you if I come?"

"That was a fluke, mop boy. Don't count on it happening again."

Antious smiled. "I'm all in."

I did, once, know your scent, your face, your eyes, your touch. I know of these memories, that they exist, much the way I know other lands exist but cannot touch them. She has taken those parts of me that feel.

—Attribution unknown.
Discovered amongst the *Erynx Fragments,* circa 134 A.U.

TWO

~MOIRA~

Day 4 of 1st High 381 A.U.

"HOW DO WE KNOW it's actually going to be today?" Moira complained as her mother hastily did her hair. "It's probably going to be like every other time we've gone to meet him. The spoiled lordling won't be there and his father will give some excuse, as always."

"That's the Lord of the Western Province you're speaking about," her mother scolded. "And you've been promised to his son, the *next* Lord of the West. Tell her, dear."

"I believe she's heard it all before." Her father stared into his bowl of meat porridge. The apple and wheat roll had been consumed, but the meat porridge remained. He pushed it with his spoon, as if to check that it still lived. Moira stifled a chuckle. Of all the things Herra Albrung did well, cooking was not one of them. But Moira and her father had promised to never tell her mother this little secret.

Their modest home was well appointed in the village of Wenrho, near the Roniah Crossing, south of Calyn. Moira's father, Rondel, had been thrifty during his career as a healer, saving a third of his krenshell every year, allowing him to build a home off a small stream with a gentle waterfall in view.

"Really, Rondel, if you're not going to be supportive, why not just call the whole thing off?" Herra asked.

"Great idea!" Moira said. "Brilliant, actually!"

"Can I marry Lord Thannuel then?" Moira's younger sister, Molina, asked. "I hear Thannuel has hair the color of leaves in the dimming season and eyes like the Roniah River."

At this, Rondel looked up. "Is that right? And where does my youngest daughter hear such things? You've never met the young lord."

"I've seen him," Molina replied. "We've all seen him."

"Only from afar," Moira corrected. "For all you know his hair is actually the color of bean curd and his eyes are hollow, witless circles."

"His hair is not turd!" Molina shouted back.

"Bean *curd*, brat! Not turd."

Molina looked confused. "What's bean curd?"

"Something that looks a lot like turd," her father said. "But tastes much better, thankfully."

Looking smug, Molina told Moira, "See, you said he has hair

that looks like turd, only it tastes better!"

"I did not!"

"Hold still!" her mother snapped, still trying to make Moira's hair cooperate. Every design she had put it in had refused to hold. "And his eyes are almond-shaped, not circles."

"There's nothing you can do with it, Mother," Moira said, speaking of her hair. "It's too straight and fine. No body at all. Just let it be."

Herra surrendered out of frustration.

"I don't understand why he chose me, Father," Moira said, coming to the table, where he still eyed his porridge suspiciously. "We have nothing of great value to offer the Kerr family, no great alliance or wealth."

"Well, *Thannuel* didn't actually choose you," Rondel said. "And it's not really like that anymore. Arranged marriages are just for lords now more out of tradition than anything else."

"That still doesn't tell me why I'm supposed to marry him," Moira said. "And don't give me some lame reason, like we're the same age. That doesn't work anymore."

"Yeah, why not me?" Molina broke back in.

"Because someone has to take care of your mom and me when we're old," Rondel told his youngest daughter.

"Still waiting," Moira said with the impatience of a fourteen-year-old.

"Oh for Light's sake, just tell her, Rondel," Herra scolded.

Her father pushed the meat porridge aside and folded his hands, arms leaning against the table. His face clouded for a moment before clearing.

"What?" Moira asked, concern in her voice.

"No, it's nothing bad, daughter," he said. "It's just not something I talk about much."

"If you don't spit it out, I'm going to tell her!" Moira's mother snapped.

"It was long ago, before Lady Kerr died," Rondel said. "Thannuel never really knew his mother, see? She died when he was born, when I was still a healer. I was urgently called to Hold Kerr early one morning, before the sun had risen. Your mother was actually only a couple cycles from delivering you at the time.

"Something had gone wrong with the labor and Lady Kerr was feverish. When her water had broken, blood came out as well. A little is not uncommon, but the amount coming from Lady Kerr was dangerous."

Moira listened intently, not believing she had never heard this story in her fourteen years.

"How does water break?" Molina asked, obviously not following. She started stabbing the water in her cup with her finger.

"Hush, child," Herra said, now doing Molina's hair.

"Other healers had been called," Rondel continued, "but none could stop the bleeding. Thannuel was convulsing inside her womb when I arrived. Every second counted. I told Lord Kerr I could only save one, but before he could answer, Lady Kerr screamed to save the baby."

"What happened?" Moira asked, both horrified and riveted.

"I think the end of the story is obvious. But as I went to deliver the young Thannuel, Lady Kerr took my hand. Her grip was strong given her weakness. I can still feel—almost—her fingers around my palm."

He raised his hand, inspecting it.

"'If you can save my son,' she said, 'and keep me alive long enough to look into his eyes, I swear by the Ancients he shall marry your first-born daughter'.

"I tried to assure her that was not necessary, that I required no such motivation to do my duty, but she insisted. 'It is my gift for saving my son's life,' she said. 'Do not deny a dying mother's bequest, please. It is all I can give for my gratitude to you. Let our families be united for your service to mine'."

The room was still after Rondel had finished the story, a peace filling the air.

"Lord Kerr honors his dead wife by keeping her vow," Rondel said.

Branton Kerr nearly had to hogtie his son to keep him from escaping without the walls of the hold. Even then, he had almost done it and would have skirted this meeting again except for Master Amnoch's fast feet. The Master of the Hold Guard had exhibited a little too much enjoyment from throwing Thannuel over his shoulder and casually walking back to the courtyard amid the lordling's kicking and yelling.

"I suppose you're getting all this?" Branton asked Ryant'ah.

The Archiver, normally devoid of showing any emotion as he recorded events of House Kerr, cracked a wicked smile. "With particular interest, my Lord."

"You know, my Lord," Master Amnoch said to Branton as he tossed Thannuel down, "your son is fast but not quick. He has to learn to be nimbler on his feet."

"Something I am sure you will teach him," Branton remarked.

"Have been for almost two years. Doesn't seem to sink in," Amnoch muttered. Looking down at Thannuel he said, "You might want to dust yourself off a bit before she arrives."

"Good idea," Thannuel said. "I'll just go to my room and—"

"We will wait here for the Albrungs," Branton said. "There will be no putting it off any longer, no more games."

When they arrived, the Albrungs walked through the south entrance of the courtyard, having passed through the gardens outside the hold walls, and were greeted by the hold's common servants. The herald servant then announced them.

Why am I so nervous all of a sudden? Thannuel wondered. He feared that his father could see his right leg shaking beneath his pants.

The father came into view and greeted them, followed by the mother. A younger girl, energetic with a huge smile, locked dreamy eyes on Thannuel. She could not have been more than eleven, Thannuel guessed. The intensity of the child's stare made him blush.

That can't be her …

"I told her your hair wasn't turd," the girl said.

Herra Albrung brushed the girl aside, scolding her with a stare.

And then, from behind the father, Moira Albrung emerged.

For the rest of his life, Thannuel would feel embarrassed about his reaction to seeing his future wife for the first time. He was not sure how long he had stared or how many times his father had to nudge him to properly introduce himself before having to do it for him. A thin face with pink lips, thick ebony hair and eyes the color of the greenest fields stared shyly back at him.

"I am pleased to meet you, Lord Thannuel," she said. Even her voice was surreal to him and he blinked faster, trying to form words to respond. Before he could, he heard laughter from around the corner, echoing against the hold walls near the servant quarters.

"Lord Thannuel!" The laugh grew louder and louder, turning to cackling. "Lord Thannuel! Oh, Lord Thannuel, marry me!"

Antious!

"Who let that runt in here?" Thannuel demanded. The laughter continued, sounding almost like crying.

"Well, it is time for our afternoon session," Master Amnoch said.

"Good!" Thannuel said, flush with embarrassment. "I can't wait to beat that mop boy silly!" Turning to Moira he said, "You're welcome to stick around and watch. He won't be laughing for long."

Moira cracked a smile and Thannuel felt his mouth go dry as his heart beat faster.

Yes, we will fight. It will bring about our death—our freedom—faster.

—From "*A Song of Revenance*"
Discovered by Reign Kerr amid relics of an ancient hold,
buried within The Great Glaciers of Gonfrey.
Translated into Sentharian by Ryall.

THREE

~THANNUEL~

Day 7 of 4th Low 382 A.U.

THANNUEL CAUGHT ANTIOUS'S GAZE across the auditorium as the younger boy motioned to a spot next to him. The clamor of hundreds of students engaged in excited conversation echoed around the walls, the excitement more from being allowed a break from their routine classes for the general assembly rather than the assembly itself. Taking Moira's hand, Thannuel left the fifteen-year-old section and led her to the seats next to Antious and Kalisa before the meeting started.

Once Moira and Thannuel's engagement became solidified the previous year, Moira had been allowed to transfer into the academy. The students were supposed to sit with their own classes, organized by age, but little enforcement of this rule occurred during large, multiclass meetings.

A general assembly of the students at Therrium Academy occurred once every four cycles, a quarter year. Usually, a renowned speaker from somewhere in the Realm would come and speak in their area of expertise or specialty of study. Karuyl Vesler, Minister of Terran Studies, had been the most recent guest speaker last quarter.

"I wonder who Banner got this time," Thannuel said, referring to his cousin, Banner Therrium, the family namesake of the academy. Banner had been recently named the school's curator though he was still quite young, being promoted from his previous post as a history professor.

Antious shrugged. "Likely someone just as dull as last time. I see a stuffy-looking man in Changrual robe."

"Minister Vesler wasn't that bad," Thannuel responded.

"You have to say that, knowing you'll be interacting with them all eventually, *your Grace.*"

"Watch it, mop boy, or I'll appoint you minister of dung removal."

"The Prime Lord makes those appointments—or do you intend to take the Granite Throne?" Antious asked.

"Ha! Emeron can have it all to himself; but he'll likely give my recommendation some weight." Thannuel's grin was devilish.

"You didn't invite Moira to our training today, did you? Wouldn't want to see you embarrassed again."

"Shhh!" Moira said. "They're starting."

The ambient noise of conversation died down as Banner

Therrium stepped up to the podium.

"Today," he began, "we are honored to be able to hear from High Vicar Rehum Tarylgen, Preceptor of the Changrual Monastery. You will be expected to take notes and turn them in after the assembly's complete for credit. Please pay attention closely, as we will be taking many of the preceptor's points of discussion into the curriculum for next quarter. Please welcome High Vicar Tarylgen."

A less-than-enthused applause filled the auditorium as Banner shook hands with the high vicar and turned the podium over to him.

"Yes, thank you," he said. "I imagine most of you would not be here if it were your choice. If I were you, I would not want to be here either."

A few random laughs were heard.

"So let me do something different than just lecture you, yes?" the high vicar said. "Let's discuss the different ages of Vǻleira to start, and then we'll explore some questions followed by a demonstration, I think. And you'll forgive me if my comments are a bit more religious in nature rather than secular. I am of the Changrual Order, after all. To start, what age came first?"

The high vicar waited until someone was brave enough to answer.

"The Ancients, of course," a girl in the sixteen-year-old class answered.

"Ah," Tarylgen said. "This is what we are taught mostly, yes. And, to be sure, it's not altogether a wrong answer. Thank you." He drew in a deep breath and looked out across the sea of students. "But what, pray tell, did the Ancients do? Where were they from?"

"They created the world," another said, this time a much younger student.

Some murmurs of disagreement arose.

"I think there might be a different idea than some of your fellow students have. Anyone else?"

"The Ancient Heavens created Våleira, then put the Ancients here to cultivate and perfect it," Kalisa said as she stood up, surprising her friends.

"Perfect!" Tarylgen replied. "Perfect answer, directly from the scrolls."

Antious, obviously not liking the attention she had attracted in their direction, pulled on her hand, encouraging Kalisa to sit down. She glared at him and he seemed to wither a little. She remained standing.

"But was not the world already perfect when the Ancient Heavens created it?" the high vicar asked. "Why would they create an imperfect world?"

No one had an answer for him this time.

"Våleira is much older than most know, I suspect. Most terranists will tell you they really don't have any idea how old the world is, or how long the age of the Ancients prevailed; but evidence suggests that the cycling of the lands did not begin until … when?"

"The Turning Away," Kalisa again answered, still on her feet. "Four thousand years ago."

"And what were they turning from?" Tarylgen asked.

Kalisa sat down.

"Most believe," Tarylgen said, answering his own question, "that they turned away from what allowed them to live for a millennium, from the Lumenatis's influence and way of life. You all know the stories and no doubt find tales of the Lumenatis childish … something you were told at night before bed, yes? After all, who among us hasn't heard the fantastical stories of when our ancestors could fly, or mysteriously be in two places at once, or even read each other's thoughts? In fact, I know what you're thinking right now!

'Why, what a quack this guy is'!"

More laughter, this time a little louder as the students warmed up to the high vicar. Thannuel actually found himself interested.

"But," he went on, "let me revisit something we touched on earlier. I believe we said that the Ancients were *placed* here—and from where is another interesting question—to cultivate and perfect the world, yes? No doubt most of us would take that to mean to tame the world, grow crops, build civilization. While that's not incorrect, perhaps there is a different understanding, a higher understanding, that we might come to.

"Another meaning of 'cultivate and perfect' might be 'prepare and purify'. These are understandings I have come to through long hours of personal study. But, assuming the alternate wording is correct, what would Våleira need to be purified *from?*"

There was no answer, but Thannuel saw Banner bristle slightly in his seat.

He's agitated. Why?

"There are those in the Changrual Order who argue that Våleira was populated before the Ancients, an age where the Ancient Dark roamed freely upon the world."

"The Hardacheon Age?" asked a student from the back.

"It does sound similar to what we know of the Hardacheons, yes? But, the Hardacheon Age was *after* the Ancients. This was *before*. In fact, in this light, it makes the phrase 'The Turning Away' inaccurate; for if the Ancients were simply reverting to what once was upon the world, then would not '*The Returning*' be more apt?"

Banner Therrium stood and approached the podium, softly speaking to the high vicar. He tried to appear calm, but Thannuel could see rigidness in his cousin.

"Yes, well, perhaps this is a little deep for today's lecture," Tarylgen said after Banner had retaken his seat. "Let's move on, shall we?"

The rest of the lecture was topically much more mainstream. High Vicar Tarylgen went through each of the ages known to Senthara: The Ancients, The Hardacheon Age, the current Sentharian Age. He made mention that without contact from other lands and peoples, their understanding of the world was somewhat limited; ironic, even, was that there was more known about the predecessors of this land of Senthara than their own history before coming to Senthara during the invasion.

"However," Tarylgen had said, "we dare not make our location known to others. Anytime in history we have had contact with an outside people, it has been a prelude to war, no matter if we were the aggressors, such as when we invaded Senthara, or if we were the ones defending the land we currently hold, such as the most recent conflict over a century ago. The nature of the world, being that lands cycle, leaves civilizations only three choices when their land becomes fallow: remain in place and likely dwindle to death; search for new lands that are fertile … for the time being; or lastly, invade someone else's fertile lands. There are only three choices. Eventually, we will again be faced with these choices. It is inevitable."

Rehum Tarylgen stopped and looked to be considering heavily his next words.

"But, I forget who my audience is today," he said. "The Western Province, once called Arlethia, has no evidence of ever being populated by another people. The Order finds this remarkable, to be frank, and excitingly curious. Perhaps there are things we can learn from this land to better understand cycling, and, perhaps, even prevent cycling elsewhere."

"So, *where* are you going, again?" Antious asked.

The two boys ran through the forest northwest of Calyn while it rained, dashing in and out of the center of the hollow ringed clouds of the low season. The sun's rays shone through the center of the clouds, casting circles of light on the treed canopy, bordered by thick precipitation. Not much farther north, the rain would be sleet or even snow. Thannuel had loved the contrast of the solar spotlight nestled by thick, dark circles of rain since he was a child.

"My father calls it a political tour," Thannuel said. "Says he wants to show me other parts of the Realm, how other people live, or something like that."

"But what about our training?" Antious asked, obviously disappointed. "How long will you be gone?"

"We're headed to the Eastern Province, so maybe a span and a half. Master Amnoch is coming with us, so you'll just have to duel with your shadow."

"It's no fun beating you all the time, anyway," Antious said as they stopped their running and leaping.

"I'm just taking it easy on you, is all," Thannuel said. He tried to laugh it off, but more often than not, his friend did indeed best him in their sparring. It frustrated Thannuel, and Master Amnoch seemingly more so. "I have to give Amnoch something to complain about, right?"

"Well, have fun without me. I'll try not to make Moira fall in love with me while you're gone."

"Could you handle two girls?"

"Believe me, Thannuel, Kalisa is more than enough to try and keep up with. She's a fireball."

"**D**o you think I should have brought him?" Lord Branton Kerr asked.

"Thannuel?" Master Amnoch shook his head. "No, he's not ready. He's better off at the camp with the servants."

"He was disappointed, I'm sure."

Amnoch seemed indifferent. "It's good for him. Rarely happens with noble people."

"Much more so than you know, Master Amnoch."

The Master of the Hold Guard smiled. He knew Branton to be one of the most grounded people he had ever known, never spoiling his son.

Well, no more than can be helped by a provincial lord, at least.

Amnoch and Branton ran silently across the tops of the crude natural pillars of soft rock toward the humming they heard, somewhere below them. The humming had a haunting melody to it, lacking any real rhythm as it echoed through the cavernous system of the narrows below. A chill in the air seemed to intensify as first moon crested the horizon, as if its light brought coldness rather than warmth.

After several days of visiting different towns and villages in the southern parts of the Eastern Province, they had come to a cluster of villages cradled into a rippling sea of sand dunes. One of them, Dispa, was home to the Thoulden-sha, the leader of the Marishee people, who had grown large enough to cause Lord Hoyt from the Southern Province growing unease.

"Remember," Branton said, "we're only here to observe. We cannot be seen."

Amnoch nodded. He had wanted to leave his lord at their camp with the other Hold Guards who had accompanied them on their trip, concerned about his safety as well as his health, but Branton would not hear of it.

"I promised Lord Hoyt, as a friend, that I would look into this personally," he had said. "Besides, I'm a long way from dead."

Small crevices everywhere in the ground looked like simple cracks but were deceptive. Though only a foot wide or even narrower, they were often the apex of a slot canyon or shaft that descended dozens to hundreds of feet below. After running over yet another crevice, both men stopped.

"There," Amnoch whispered.

Branton nodded in agreement. He had felt it too. Vibrations below them, ever so subtle, like people rocking back and forth on their feet but not taking a full step. So far outside their native forests of Arlethia, their wood-dweller senses received no aid from the intertwined root systems of the sentient trees, but they were still acute enough to feel most things, even if they came through unclearly. From the sound of the humming, Amnoch would not have guessed the Marishee were congregated directly below them, but he knew the caverns could carry sound strangely, even deceptively.

As he followed the crevice, he saw it widen several yards from them. He motioned to Branton, who already moved toward it. The opening, oval in shape, spanned a yard before closing on the other side back to a sliver of a crevice.

Roughly fifty feet below them were a couple hundred people, their outlines barely visible in the dim light. From what Amnoch had seen, the narrow paths that wove throughout these rock gardens occasionally opened up to spaces large enough to fit perhaps eight to ten people; below them, however, was something large enough to be an arena, an expanse that could hold at least a thousand people.

It would have taken hours for the couple hundred there to filter in through the maze of narrow paths, he thought.

Near the center of this arena were a score of large rocks piled together, waist high.

An altar, Amnoch realized.

Moonlight started to creep up the side of the altar, the light piercing an opening that Amnoch could not see. It would take only minutes for the light to bathe the top of the altar. Amnoch cringed at what he feared might happen then.

⌇⌇⌇

The Thoulden-sha looked upon those with him, their swords at their hips, black turbans covering their heads. These were his warriors. They had trained relentlessly for years, honing their skills to take part in the Resurgence.

Many had no previous experience with a blade, including the Thoulden-sha, but Mari-shaden had guided him, showing his mind how to wield a blade in the ancient ways. In turn, he had taught the few with him, those most dedicated to his calling.

None have been more so than Muhktar, the earliest of my disciples. It was fitting, then, that Muhktar had exceled above all others in his skill with steel. *A direct correlation of his unyielding belief.*

Though the blade was necessary for now, he yearned for the day in which these crude tools would become obsolete, when he would have the elements at his command, the way he had seen Those Not Remembered in vision once had controlled them, wresting them from their natural course to serve their wills.

As they had grown, the Marishee required a more private

setting to carry on the work of the Resurgence. Mari-shaden had helped its Oracle divine these caverns and slot canyons, mapping them indelibly in his mind. It was one of the gifts bestowed to him as the Thoulden-sha—a perfect memory, free of flaws and alterations with which time often imbued one's memories.

And yet, despite his bestowals of power from Mari-shaden, the Thoulden-sha had fumbled along for the past seven years, learning how to access its Influence through trial and error. His slow growth had caused many to forsake him, being frustrated by promises that had not produced any fruit.

It would have been better for them to have never believed.

Tonight would bring some solace to his soul and those who were chosen to be with him. He had sent Muhktar, his First, after their quarry. Now, making his way through a cavern, most unwillingly, was one who once believed but had renounced his faith. This would be the beginning of recompense upon the unfaithful.

It is a natural cleansing, Mari-shaden had whispered to him. Its words were only impressions in his mind, feelings. They had become more solid in his mind over the years, and he had begun to think of Mari-shaden as having a female's voice. *Even the Marishee must be purified.*

The man, the symbolic sacrifice, arrived through a small crack in the wall like the eye of a large needle, his head being forced down to clear the small opening by Muhktar and one other with him. His hands were bound behind his back, his face hooded. They removed his hood and the whimpering man screamed when he saw the altar, the light of first moon nearly upon its surface. When first moon had left the horizon completely, the top of the altar would be completely covered in its light that shone through an opening in one of the cliff walls, as if Mari-shaden had prepared it specifically for this purpose.

"All blood must be spilled in full sight of first moon," the

Thoulden-sha spoke. It was the same language before every sacrifice. "Through blood and the dark light of first moon, we find life that transcends, life that extends, life that restores and cleanses the world."

The bound man was forced to the altar when the Thoulden-sha held up his hand suddenly, halting the men who brought him forth. He stood still, listening. It was not there, the call of Mari-shaden that accompanied every sacrifice, the feeling that normally authorized his actions.

Kiarra, the word forming in his mind. *Kiarra watches.*

The Thoulden-sha calmly came to the bound man, his trembling making him unable to stand on his own. Reaching forth the same knife he had used every full first moon for more than one hundred cycles, he cut the rope that bound the man's hands. After, with his face close to the now confused captive, he whispered, "Our mistake, friend. We received incorrect information that you had deserted the Marishee. I am certain this is not the case."

The man's jaw quivered and he knelt before the Thoulden-sha. "Of course, I am faithful. I want nothing more than to witness the Resurgence."

It was a lie, the Thoulden-sha knew. The man had openly spoken out against him a couple span ago, publicly denouncing him. However, as with most men, this fellow's beliefs morphed instantly to whatever served him best at the moment.

Casually, the Thoulden-sha looked up to a bowl-like opening in the rock ceiling. They were almost indistinguishable, nearly blending in perfectly with the night sky. He would not have picked them out had they not moved. Two silhouettes in the shapes of heads and shoulders, pulled back from the opening.

So, you have come to me, Kiarra. Very well. It will be my turn next.

They did nothing wrong," Branton said. "It was suspicious, but in the end, they committed no crime. It's not against the law to meet at night in the narrows."

They made their way back to their camp, stopping every so often to listen and feel, ensuring they were not being followed.

"Not unless kidnapping is now legal," Master Amnoch said, but he knew it was a thin argument and the man who had been taken captive was now too terrified to ever accuse the Thoulden-sha of any wrongdoing. "He sensed us somehow," Amnoch continued. He was extremely bothered by what he had seen, but more by the feeling that had invaded him. His insides still were unsettled. "He *would* have killed that man if he had not known we were there."

"I believe you are right, Master Amnoch. I do. But, without the actual committal of a crime, neither Lord Orion nor Prime Lord Wellyn will do anything."

"In the meantime," Amnoch groused, "this Thoulden-sha will be allowed to continue to build his following."

"Splinter groups have often started their own orthodoxies. Even amongst the Changrual there are different opinions, some so great that they can hardly call themselves of the same order."

"That's not what this is, my Lord."

Branton fell silent. Finally: "I know. Let us hope he makes a mistake along the way that allows us to take action sooner or later."

The feeling inside Amnoch abated by and by. He had never been so close to the Influence of the Dark Mother, but he knew that was what he had felt and wondered if this was what Evrin had felt, at least in part, years ago when he had sent Amnoch to Hold Kerr.

"Sooner is better than later, my Lord."

Why? Why is it we think we can cure death by inflicting it upon those who brought it to our door?

—From *Lamentations of Violence*, High Vicar Morcett

FOUR

~THANNUEL~

Day 19 of 3rd High 383 A.U.

"NO, THE DARK TAKE YOU!" Master Amnoch yelled. "Move your feet!"

Thannuel grimaced in pain as Amnoch landed a quick blow to the backside of his left thigh with a baton. It would match the bruise he had on his right thigh from yesterday. This was afternoon practice, and Master Amnoch seemed to be in a particularly foul mood.

"After four years, you'd think you'd remember to keep your feet light and moving," he scolded and then pointed at Ryant'ah.

"At least your fumbling is being recorded for all your posterity to cackle over!"

"It just feels like dancing, not fighting," Thannuel groused.

"Yes, dancing—you would have done well to take a ballet class. In fact, I may speak to your lord father about this."

Thannuel heard Antious stifling a laugh.

"Shut it, mop boy!" Thannuel snapped.

"My apologies, your *highness*," Antious retorted.

"Both of you shut it," Amnoch commanded. "But Antious has a right to laugh at your expense. At least he keeps himself fluid on his feet. It's as simple as this: you plant your feet, you die. Movement is life. Now, go again."

Thannuel and Antious moved back into position, their swords at the ready, each bearing a triarch leafling between a palm and their sword's hilt. They had moved beyond sparring with bokkens, wooden practice swords, last year, now wielding actual steel blades. Thannuel was a year older, true, but Antious had sprouted to his same height with broad shoulders and a trim waist. This training had done him well over the years, defining his body.

The two boys circled each other, eyes locked, each looking for the other to give away some sign. Their heads stayed the same height as they moved, not bobbing up and down like inexperienced swordsmen. A change in height was a signal to an opponent like a beacon in the night, revealing intent and action.

Antious had given Thannuel more than a few reminders of this, easily blocking and countering a blow, drawing small lines of blood. No scars were present from these mishaps, as triarch leaves were always close at hand.

His once perceived nemesis, Antious had grown on Thannuel, becoming a close friend. It was forced at first, at his father's will, but Thannuel hadn't had to pretend for long. He discovered a fair amount he had in common with Antious, despite their very different upbringings.

Thannuel lunged at his opponent with a speed that few could match, bringing his sword down, but Antious blocked. Anticipating this, Thannuel had already started moving his hips to position a follow-up strike, a swipe to Antious's side. The younger boy sucked in and moved away from the blow, his sword still held at the ready. As Thannuel pivoted around to face Antious, he felt a sting at his hip that he didn't even see coming. The broad side of Antious's sword swatted him.

"Blasted Night!" Master Amnoch swore. "You are the most flat-footed boy in all Arlethia! I swear, ducks are jealous of you!"

"He just stung me, is all," Thannuel muttered.

"Yes, stung you. And had he wanted to, he could have crippled you good, he could have! How do you think he was able to get around you?"

"He moved fast?"

"Two reasons: His feet were constantly in motion and—"

"And I was flat-footed," Thannuel finished.

"I just don't understand why he's so hard on me, Father. I know I've improved greatly over the years. I can mimic Master Amnoch's speed and movements and I get the katas right without much help. And I remember everything—"

"Except to move your feet, apparently," Branton said with a smile.

Thannuel huffed with frustration.

"Listen, Thannuel," his father said, bringing his hand to his son's shoulder. "Master Amnoch prepares everyone as if war is coming. That's actually by my command."

"But why?" Thannuel asked. "No one is even alive now who last saw war in Senthara."

"That may be true, but it doesn't change the need to be vigilant. The more you sweat in peacetime, the less you bleed in war."

"What is that, some Arlethian proverb?" Thannuel quipped.

Branton smiled. "Makes sense, yes?"

"I guess. I have homework to get to and then Moira is coming over. We're going out to Doonalin later tonight."

"Ah, I remember Doonalin as a boy. But cliff jumping, on a school night?" Branton asked.

"No, Father, it's end of span. No classes tomorrow."

"You don't seem to mind Moira's presence much anymore. Amazing the fits you'd throw when we would try to arrange an introduction. You'd complain, sneak out, threaten ... it was like we were feeding you to a wild beast, for Light's sake."

"It kinda felt like that when I was younger, to be honest. It's blasted scary meeting a girl you're supposed to marry when you're so young!"

"And you'll deal with it someday with your own son," Branton said, smiling warmly. "But, I daresay, all your anxiety got swept away when you first saw Moira. I could barely hold the laugh at seeing your astonishment!"

Thannuel looked down at his feet. "Yeah, she's okay, I guess."

Branton's laugh turned to a different sound and he coughed something fierce, covering his mouth with a slightly shaking hand. The fit continued for nearly half a minute.

"Father, are you not well?" Thannuel asked.

The Lord of the Western Province waved him off. "Fine, fine. Listen, son, the real reason Amnoch is hard on you ... " He paused, looking uncertain. "I shouldn't tell you for risk that this goes to your head. Promise me you'll not get ahead of yourself."

Thannuel nodded, feeling curious.

"Amnoch told me you are the most naturally gifted with steel he has ever seen."

Thannuel's brows furrowed. "How can that be? He's never said one word of encouragement to me, and Antious—"

"Ever," Branton repeated. "He won't tell you because he wants to see how far you can progress. While you are a natural, you are not perfect, and so he rides you hard. But, he tells me it is harder to find fault with your form the older you get, so he picks apart what he can. Perfection is his goal with you, son."

"But Antious seems to garnish all his praise," Thannuel said. "And he beats me three of five times."

"Antious is not naturally inclined toward this, as you are. He works harder, so he beats you; but he must work harder than you in order to keep up. Don't assume that talent can carry you alone. Talent is wasted where hard work does not accompany it."

"Another proverb?" Thannuel smiled.

"Will Antious enlist when he is eighteen? Has he thought about my offer to sponsor him?" Branton asked.

"I think so. It's likely a good path for him."

"Amnoch thinks he has the mind for it. He's good with organization and calculation. Major Korin though ... that's a different story."

Thannuel perked up at that. "His daughter still telling him what to do and who she'll marry? She's only fourteen but acts like she's twenty."

"I'm not sure who the parent is between those two," Branton admitted. "Korin is a good man, but a hard one. Tough as granite."

"More like rough as granite."

"He finds fault with others rather than strengths, yes. Serves a soldier well against an enemy to do that, but earns one few friends."

"It's not Antious's fault really. Kalisa chose *him*. He can't lighten up a little?"

"Unlikely when his daughter is involved," Branton said. "Now, when you're out tonight, be careful. A band of Marishee that escaped Lord Hoyt's forces has come up through the Roniah River."

"Marishee? From the Southern Province? I thought they were only in the East."

"Seems a great number have migrated west, through the Southern Province. We're not sure what their goal is, but until recently they've been satisfied to make noise in a remote part of the southern parts of the Eastern Province. Lord Orion doesn't pay them much mind, but their talks of sedition are gaining some ground. They are planning something."

Thannuel was intrigued. "Are they dangerous, Father?"

"Hard to say. There are those who have grievances against the throne, but there are channels for that. The Marishee seem intent to sow disorder. Their talk is starting to have a bit of a bite. Anyway, enough of statecraft. Who is going with you to Doonalin?"

"Just the four of us."

Branton sighed. "And, does Major Korin know his daughter will be attending this night out with Antious and you and Moira?"

"Doubt it."

The coughing returned and Branton did his best to curtail it before it turned into another fit. Thannuel reached forward, putting his hand to his father's back in concern.

"It's nothing, son, just a bit of lung moisture. I'm fine. Just … take a short blade with you tonight, yes?"

Thannuel nodded. "If you wish it, of course."

"I do." Branton tried but failed to hide his concern. "And bring one for Antious as well."

The foursome headed back from the Doonalin Falls long after first moon's zenith. The high season breeze was warm but still gave a chill as their damp clothes dried. Moira hung on Thannuel's arm, as if trying to get warm even though her clothes were the driest. Heights did not agree much with her even though she was extremely agile, even for an Arlethian.

Despite the hour, the streets of Calyn still bustled with excitement as they did every end of span, especially in the high season. Wood-dwellers and Senthary alike intermingled freely. Entertainers performed on every corner, advertising shows at various theaters. One troupe from the Northern Province advertised a play about the Hardacheon people, long before the invasion of the Senthary.

"Can you believe people pay for that mess of fiction?" Thannuel asked.

"Huh?" Antious replied.

"There. That Hardacheon production," Thannuel said, pointing. "How would anyone know what the Hardacheons were like? It's not like we have their records or they were ever found."

"Who says they ever kept records?" Antious asked.

"My point exactly!"

"Relax, lordling, it's just for fun," Kalisa said. "Besides, it's no more foolish than jumping from cliffs a hundred feet high into a narrow pond, is it?"

"Likely less, actually." Moira poked Thannuel's ribs. He jumped at the touch, playfully shouting out.

"Oh! I didn't know you were ticklish there! Is there any place you're not?" Moira asked as she poked and prodded his back, sides and arms. Thannuel rigidly tried not to give any reaction but failed miserably.

"I'm not ticklish anywhere!" he said with a stiff face. The laughs came despite his best efforts to contain them and he returned fire, tickling Moira … or trying to. She was truly not ticklish and Thannuel eventually had to flee from her side to extricate himself from a most embarrassing scene.

"Well done, lordling," Kalisa said. "You've managed to show a weakness that can easily be exploited. Don't your tutors counsel against such revelations?"

"Now, Kalisa, leave the poor chap alone," Antious said. "He's in well over his head."

"I do actually have to be home soon," Kalisa said. "If I'm not back before second moon I'll be grounded until I'm forty."

"Do you actually have to salute your dad?" Antious asked.

She pushed him. "I'm not going to dignify that question with an answer." "Wait," Thannuel said, managing to finally grab both Moira's arms and stopping her assaults. "You do, don't you? Oh, Ancients, what I wouldn't give to see that!"

"I do not—"

"So, Antious, if you do enlist, and *if* you actually get to marry Kalisa—"

"Stop now, Thannuel," Antious pleaded.

"Then is she going to make you salute *her*? 'Anti, the baby needs his diaper changed'." Thannuel did Antious's part in his little role-play by saluting. "'As you command!' 'Oh, and after that, the floors need to be repaired in the bedroom. And then you can drop and give me twenty push-ups for being home late'."

As he mock saluted this time, a swift punch connected with his temple.

"You know, that kind of hurt, actually," he groaned.

"I've got several more if you like," Kalisa answered, her fists balled up.

Thannuel smiled. "Ya know, Antious, I really like her."

"Hands off," his friend said.

"She hits harder than you do. Maybe Master Amnoch will let me train against her instead."

"Wouldn't be a fair fight," Antious said. "She'd have you begging for mercy before three exchanges happened. Trust me."

"Well, she's all yours, then. Good luck."

Antious sighed. "I'll need a bit more than that if we're late getting her home."

They came to a side street, more of an alley.

Thannuel waved. "Through here. It bypasses most of the crowds."

They followed him, continuing their lighthearted banter, until Thannuel felt footsteps behind them. Half a dozen or so. Maybe they too were just looking for a shortcut, but he could tell they were not wood-dwellers from the vibrations. They walked lightly and swiftly, picking up their pace little by little. Thannuel glanced at Antious and their eyes met for a brief moment. His friend sensed the wrongness as well; Thannuel could see it in his eyes. The girls continued chatting, obviously not in tune with the moment in the same way.

Thannuel grabbed Moira's arm, just above the elbow, and started moving her along more quickly. Antious did the same to Kalisa.

"Thannuel?" Moira asked.

Before he could answer, he felt the tremor ahead of them. Two men stepped into their path at the narrowest part of the alley. They were dressed all in black, with loose-fitting pants and turbans that covered their heads and most of their faces. Thannuel felt the six behind him stop about five paces away. A quick glance over his shoulder revealed they were dressed in the same manner as the two blocking their way ahead of them. The sounds of the city were still heard but sounded miles away as they were cocooned between tall buildings on both sides. Scaling buildings was not the same as climbing trees, Arlethian or not.

"Some shortcut," Antious mumbled.

"We have no need for the girls," one spoke, although Thannuel had a hard time telling exactly which one. "Kill them and subdue the boys. The Thoulden-sha has use for them."

Had Thannuel heard right? This was Calyn. Murders and kidnappings did not happen, not here, not—then it hit him. *The Marishee.*

Each drew a sword, shorter in length than a standard sword, easier for concealing. Moira gripped Thannuel's arm tightly. Without thinking, he drew his short blade and felt Antious do the same, realizing that it felt so natural. Their enemies would be slower but nevertheless lethal. Neither he nor Antious had ever trained to face odds of four to one, never practiced any kata or sparring where they were required to protect someone while attacking another. At least they knew the enemy objective: kill Moira and Kalisa, capture him and Antious. He could use that.

Wait for an opening. Do not be anxious. Let your opponent make a mistake. He repeated Master Amnoch's lessons over in his mind. *Above all, move your feet.* "Movement is life."

The Marishee attacked. Thannuel pushed Moira down, out of the scope of one blade and then pulled her up violently by the front of her blouse, spinning her from another attack. Lunging with his short blade, his reach was not near long enough. Thannuel knew this, but it brought one man in black closer in. The man was too careless, not understanding the feint until too late. With an

Arlethian's swiftness, Thannuel spun around into the man, ducking down on a knee and swiping his blade up, catching the man in his thigh. The scream that followed was not alone long as Thannuel jumped forward to another who advanced on Moira. The man brought down his sword with a strong arm, his muscles bulging with the effort. Again, the Kerr heir's natural speed aided him well as he swept Moira's legs from under her, removing her from the sword's arc of travel, and launched his blade upward, catching the man's triceps as his arm came down. He palm-heeled the man's nose, causing a spray of red across his face as the smell of wet iron filled the air.

Thannuel caught the man's sword as he let go of it in reaction to his wounds.

"Antious," was all he had to say and his friend reached out his left hand, his short blade still held in his right toward the black-clad men, and deftly caught the sword's hilt as Thannuel tossed it to him.

Antious attacked, keeping Kalisa behind him as much as possible, bringing down two in quick succession. Thannuel pulled Moira up and noticed her holding her left arm in a cradle position. Of course she was hurt from being tossed around like a rag doll, and Thannuel felt a sting of guilt. But he found no blame in her eyes, only fear.

"Run," Thannuel said, pointing ahead of them. "This will take you out near Hold Therrium. From there, you are only half a league from Hold Kerr. Find my father and Master Amnoch. Go."

The clang and clatter of steel against steel echoed in the alley and would soon attract attention, if it had not already. That was good for them. They only had to survive long enough for the city watch to arrive and this would be over.

Thannuel dodged several other attacks, nearly taking a gash to his leg. *Move your feet, blast you!*

He could tell these men were not trying to kill him, but they didn't have any problem wounding him. They had murderous looks for Moira and Kalisa, however.

"Go now! Antious and I will distract them."

"Not without Kalisa!"

Thannuel punched another in the gut. While the man was too slow to block the attack, he only grunted mildly.

Dimming Light, they're strong!

And then, one of the Marishee managed to get a strong hand on Antious, followed by another. Soon, three men had him and began to run in the direction from which they had come.

Kalisa screamed after Antious, but he quickly disappeared. The one remaining man, the one Thannuel had punched with little effect, backed up slowly. The other end of the alley was completely open now.

"Moira, go! Take Kalisa and go!"

This time the girls listened, taking each other by the hand and dashing away.

"What do you want?" Thannuel shouted.

"Come with me, young lord, and your friend just might live," the man answered from behind his turban. "The Thoulden-sha commands it."

"Where are you taking him?"

"The same place you must go. Come. He will not be harmed if you come."

What could Thannuel do? Antious had been carried from his sight by now and it would be almost impossible to find him in the throngs of people in the city.

"You have orders not to kill me?"

The man in black nodded and lowered his guard slightly, obviously believing Thannuel to be considering the offer.

"That's very unfortunate for you," Thannuel said. He leaped at the man with all his weight and speed, short blade extended forward. The man shouted in surprise and raised his sword to deflect Thannuel's bombardment, but Thannuel tucked into a roll, letting himself pass the man and spring up behind him. His blade found the man's lower back, twice. Wounded, the large man stumbled forward and fell to his knees. Before he died, he did some strange motions with his arms while looking up to the moon, whispering something Thannuel could not make out.

"The Thoulden-sha has no use for just one of you, young Kerr," the dying man said. Then he fell forward to the ground, eyes still open.

Time was not on his side. He looked up the alley where the girls had run, praying they were safe. More abductors could have been in hiding but he would have to trust they were almost to Hold Therrium by now if they were moving at full speed. From there, it would be only minutes before they reached Hold Kerr, again assuming they were moving fast.

Turning his attention down the alley, he ran after Antious. Fear, anxiety, uncertainty, rage, determination—a collage of emotions pulsed through him. He sprang against a building, kicking off its wall the way he would a tree in the forest, and pushed himself higher. The narrowness of the alley benefited him as he flew toward another building and ricocheted off it, again pushing himself higher. This shouldn't be possible for him, not against stone and brick. But a strength welled inside him, one that he found did not lessen. It came to him at his command, seeming to be fed by his emotions.

He crested the tops of the buildings before many moments and jumped from rooftop to rooftop, not sure if he was moving in the right direction, but it felt wrong to stand still. *Movement is life.*

What he wouldn't have given for a triarch leafling and a speaking tree now; but even if he could connect with the forest, he would have quite a difficult time singling out any unique vibrations with the number of people below. It would be a parade of vibrational cacophony. No, sight and speed alone would have to be enough.

Running and jumping from uneven rooftops in the city was akin to jumping from limb to limb in the forest, but his footing felt less certain even though the roofs were wider and flatter than branches in general.

And then, he caught sight of them. A disturbance in the crowd was the tell, disgruntled and surprised shouts coming from people being shoved aside. Antious was strong, but having three strong men holding him was too much for him as it would be for most men.

His friend had been bound in the brief minutes Thannuel had lost sight of them, contending with the last man in the alley, and was hoisted above their shoulders. The time it had taken Antious to be bound was likely a blessing in allowing him to eventually catch up to them.

The men disappeared below a low stone arch with a large elm tree draping itself over the top of it. Thannuel came to a lower building, only a couple stories high, and leaped to the ground. He hit light-footed and was sprinting before both feet were even firmly planted. He made up the ground easily, weaving between people gracefully, many making way for him, having been alerted to something awry by the earlier interruption in the crowd from those he pursued.

"Kidnapping!" he shouted to no one in particular. "The Marishee! Tell the city watch Thannuel Kerr went this way in pursuit!"

He knew the mention of his name would bring urgency to the

situation. The people would react, hopefully intelligently, at knowing their lord's son found himself in some kind of trouble.

This part of the city had stone roads rather than open compact soil, mostly for those that visited from other provinces. In the less tourist-oriented parts of the city, paved roads and paths were less frequent. As Thannuel came to the archway under which his friend had disappeared, the paved road ended and earth found his feet.

Yes! he thought in relief, feeling more at ease on this terrain and increasing his speed. The archway was more of a short tunnel. As he came to the end, a warning vibration rattled his bones as he sensed two men, out of sight, on either side of the tunnel's opening. He slid to his knees and laid his head back, nearly flat to the ground, as his momentum carried him forward past the threshold. The faint silver glimmer of a thin wire caught his eye above him as he slid, one that would have certainly clotheslined him and sent him flying to his backside. He blessed the Ancient Heavens for his Arlethian advantage and sprang up from his knee-slide, taking a defensive posture with short blade in hand. The two Marishee at the threshold of the tunnel cursed, dropping their line and drawing swords. The third held Antious, who squirmed wildly against his bonds, but they held fast.

Thannuel sneered as a feeling of righteous hatred welled inside him.

Antious struggled to free himself, rubbing the skin on his arms raw as he flexed and fought. The Marishee's grip on him held fast, but Antious was determined to make it as difficult as possible for him, maybe creating an advantage for his outnumbered friend.

Obviously unconcerned with Antious's ability to free himself, his immediate captor threw him to the ground and drew his sword, joining his companions to surround Thannuel. Antious rolled and turned his head to see. Each man stood at least a head taller than his friend and was broader in the chest. Speed or not, Thannuel did not have their strength.

"No! Thannuel, run! Don't!" he yelled.

Without taking his eyes from those around him, Thannuel said, "You know I've always had to learn the hard way, Antious."

As he lay on his stomach, focused on Thannuel, Antious could see him calculating, planning. As much as he didn't believe in the Ancients, Antious found himself praying, fervently.

The air burned in Moira's lungs as she ran hand in hand with Kalisa. Her other arm radiated pain at the elbow and she cradled it close to her body.

"We have to go faster!" Kalisa said with desperation. The sharp angles of her face gleamed with perspiration.

Moira barely saw the outline of Hold Therrium as she sprinted past it, her vision turning splotchy. "I'm going as fast as I can."

Kalisa pulled Moira by her good arm. "Well, it's not fast enough!" Her voice was nearly hysterical. "They won't survive!"

Oh, Thannuel, why do you have to be brave? Moira asked in her mind. Only minutes had passed since she and Kalisa escaped their attackers while Thannuel and Antious remained behind, fighting for all their lives.

"We're almost there!" Kalisa said.

Moira dug deep and found the strength. Fear and adrenaline

mixed inside her, giving her the capacity to swallow the pain and run with all that her sixteen-year-old body possessed, her entire being focusing on that single need. *Run, Thannuel, please! For once, don't be brave.* She knew he wouldn't run, blasted arrogance. But it wasn't arrogance. She had seen that melt away in him, replaced by nobler traits, those that had just started to truly manifest in him over the past year.

Whether it was arrogance or some form of foolhardy valor, she wouldn't forgive herself if he or Antious died to save her. Burning in protest at the punishment she forced upon them, her leg muscles knotted and kinked. By the time they made it to Hold Kerr, the strides of both girls were awkward and unnatural, their bodies on the verge of giving out.

"Open the doors!" Moira screamed.

The northern gate of the hold opened and Master Amnoch stood in the threshold with a torch in hand. Other torches flared to life inside the courtyard and on the battlements. The flickering orange light illuminated Amnoch's middle-aged face, the seemingly ever-present dark stubble graying on either side of his chin.

"What is it? I feel tumult in your footfall. What has happened?" His eyes looked past the girls. "Where is Thannuel?"

Kalisa collapsed to the earth on her back, pointing but unable to speak as she heaved for air, her mid-length blonde hair a matted mess of sweat and grime. Moira leaned over, her good arm resting against her leg with her head bowed.

"What's wrong with your arm?" Amnoch asked Moira, his tone deepening with concern.

"The city," Moira said between breaths. "On the way back from Doonalin. Men. Dressed in black. Hurry."

Amnoch's face fell. "Oh, Ancients."

Kalisa got to her hands and knees. "There were eight. Please, hurry! They had Antious and were carrying him away!"

"Where?" Amnoch demanded. "You must be specific!"

"An alley," Moira said. "I don't know where we were exactly. I don't know that part of the city well, but—"

Amnoch grabbed Moira and she whimpered slightly, her eyes widening. "Listen, Moira, I care for you and Kalisa, for Antious. But that boy of yours is my *duty*. This family is my duty. Do you understand? You must be precise."

"I will go with you," she said. "I can show you."

Amnoch looked at her arm. "We haven't much time. This will hurt."

Swiftly but gently, Amnoch took her left arm, rolled it palm up, and brought her hand to meet her shoulder. She cried out as he rotated her arm up until she felt a pop in her elbow.

"It'll be sore, but you should have full range of motion back," he said.

She worked her arm, relieved the throbbing pain had faded.

"Do you have enough strength left to run?" he asked Moira and Kalisa.

They nodded. Moira felt Lord Kerr's approach through the ground.

"What is it, children?" he asked. "What's wrong?"

"Marishee," Amnoch answered. "They have Thannuel and Antious, it seems."

Lord Kerr nodded ponderously, the gravity of the situation heavy upon him. It was not the frantic reaction Moira would have expected from a father. Deep ridges formed in his forehead but he radiated calm, understanding, control.

"Very well. Master Amnoch, bring a healer and ten Hold Guard with you. I shall send for another healer to look after the girls while you retrieve the boys."

"My Lord, I need them to show me the way," Amnoch said. "Time is critical."

"They can barely stand," Lord Kerr said.

"Let me worry about that, my Lord. In the meantime, I'll leave orders to lock down the hold. We don't know what other plans may lurk in the dark this night."

"Very well, Master Amnoch. I will have word by wing sent to the parents. And, Amnoch … be sure you find them."

"Branton," Amnoch spoke softly, "you should prepare yourself." The master of the Hold Guard started to say more but stifled his words.

Lord Kerr stiffened as he sucked in a deep breath through clenched teeth, his eyes moistening. "I know. Just … bring them back. Go."

He thinks we are already too late, Moira realized.

Amnoch simultaneously touched Moira and Kalisa on their backs, holding his hands there for a moment with his eyes closed. Was he praying? The exhaustion within her lessened noticeably and she felt somewhat rejuvenated. Looking at Kalisa, she saw a similar result in her as well as the same question in her eyes.

"What was—" Moira started to ask but was interrupted.

"We must be going," Amnoch said. "Now."

Looking at the Marishee surrounding him, Thannuel cursed himself for not grabbing a sword from the downed men in the alley.

Stupid!

Despite Master Amnoch's admonition to never fight with a

weapon one did not know, he felt the circumstances clearly called for an exception.

He tuned in to the unique vibrational signatures of the Marishee surrounding him. They stood in the Calyn Gardens, a sort of respite from the bustling city. While fairly populated by day, they were desolate at night. But, blessedly, they had trees. *Lots* of trees. He scrambled quickly and found a triarch leaf upon the ground and worked it between the fingers of his left hand, his right still brandishing his short blade. The familiar pulse of the forest, that *heartbeat* of Arlethia, grounded him and he immediately felt collected, focused.

"Come with us," one spoke. "No harm will come to you if you do."

"No harm will come to me regardless. I know your orders. You can't kill me."

The Marishee did not answer for a moment. "True, but that condition was optional for your friend."

The man strode the few paces to Antious, still bound and nearly face down on the ground. He inverted his sword, point down, and raised it directly above Antious.

Thannuel didn't think. The forest's pulse surged inside him. In a blur of motion, he stepped forward and threw his short blade with a velocity that left a trail of vapor in the night air. The Marishee who had stood over Antious fell back, his neck snapped backward from the force of the short blade's velocity. Only the last inch of the short blade's haft was visible, barely protruding from the man's skull.

Thannuel dashed forward, taking the dead man's sword, righting his former lack in judgment. With the sword's pummel, he bashed the protruding end of his short blade's haft in the man's skull like hammer to nail, with more force than he realized he could muster. The knife shot through the other side of the man's head, penetrating enough for Thannuel to easily free the rest of it. He was now armed with sword and short blade, the latter's grip wet with brain matter.

Now next to Antious, he had a moment's thought to throw his friend over his shoulder and dash out of there.

"I'm not sure I could haul your dead-weight-self quickly enough for them not to catch us," Thannuel said aloud, answering his own thoughts.

The two Marishee attacked, their grace and fluidity a cut above their fallen companions. Thannuel moved in response, dodging and ducking, parrying and jabbing. The sword was shorter than he was used to, forcing him to get closer to his opponents. Still under the impression he was not to be killed, he was reckless in his advances, not concerned about his guard. He nearly paid for it with his life as the tip of one blade, swung at an upward angle, grazed his left side. It was extremely painful, given how thin the cut was.

The Marishee must have seen the shock on his face as they removed their turbans, revealing smiles full of malevolence.

"Our identities we hold secret, unless we face certain death," one explained. "Mari-shaden forgives the sin of revealing ourselves to an outsider as long as he dies with us. Our mission has failed. We will never escape with you after being so delayed. Our orders, in this case, are to leave no mouths that can speak."

Thannuel felt nervous, knowing that he had not yet faced these Marishee when they were unencumbered by orders. He had seen a different, higher level of skill now that the situation had changed.

"My father's men will be on their way," Thannuel said. "Leave now and you might keep your lives. You've committed no murder, yet."

"Alas, it is not possible, young Kerr. We die in shame to return from a failed mission. Better to die carrying out the will of Mari-shaden and the Thoulden-sha."

And then no further words came. The attacks were well coordinated between the Marishee, working together as if their minds were linked. Thannuel concentrated, lining up the movements he saw with his eyes with the vibrations he felt in his bones. He felt almost clairvoyant as he danced through the movement.

Blocking an overhead strike with his sword and short blade, forming an X in front of him, Thannuel kicked the attacker hard, thrusting him back several feet. The man recovered quickly and rushed him again. The other Marishee attacked from the side. Without looking away from the advancing man, Thannuel reached out a hand to the side and instinctively blocked the flanking attack. His arm moved from position to position, blocking and countering with what felt natural. He did not think from one movement to the next, but allowed his body to react. In front of him, the Marishee he had just kicked in the stomach again confronted him. Thannuel had to deal with him with his short blade only in his left hand. This was as much a mental exercise as physical, and he feared he was going to break.

He tried to back up, giving himself more space, but the Marishee mimicked him, keeping themselves close and pressing their attacks. Though lacking Arlethian speed, they were fast enough to force Thannuel to block instead of attack. The pressure in his mind increased and his head pulsed with concentration. Sweat began pouring down his back, his face, his sides, stinging his open wound. His movements were sloppier as the contest continued.

"Thannuel, keep moving!" Antious yelled.

My mind is going to fracture! he cried inwardly.

Let it, something answered him. Whether a voice he heard or his mind going mad, he did not know. But he trusted the feeling, sensing it meant him no harm.

Thannuel would never be able to describe how it happened or the process of splitting his mind, but as the pressure again surged inside his brain, he did not stifle it but let it build unabated. Right before his mind snapped, a flash of fear lanced through him, wondering if he was mad to listen to a voice in his head. His mind *broke* into two regions.

Instantly, Thannuel's stress level decreased. He was shocked to find he was only fighting one person.

What happened to the other—

The other opponent, the one he thought had vanished, appeared to his vision as he lost sight of the former.

What form of Dark create is this? he asked himself.

And then he felt it: a tickle in his mind, something just out of focus. The other Marishee, still there, still fighting. As he tried to grab that small tickle, his mind refocused, bringing that to the forefront of his mind, sequestering the other.

I'm still fighting both, he realized, *but able to focus fully on either while not ignoring the other.* A more primal side of Thannuel's mind reacted to the unfocused picture, continuing to defend but not attack. The part of his mind he now focused with, pouring all his concentration into one enemy, easily saw the opening and took it.

His sword came down with inhuman speed, opening the man's chest from his collarbone halfway down his torso. Before his body hit the ground, Thannuel's mind refocused to the remaining Marishee and he quickly cut him down.

Thannuel faintly registered shouts in the distance getting closer. Yells of "make way" were heard and he felt a score of men approaching swiftly.

My father's men and the city watch.

He had just killed men. Many of them. He was not sure how he felt about that. He was not sorry for protecting his friends or himself, but the loss of life did burden him.

He cut Antious's bonds and his friend stood up. He wore a penetrating look on his face.

"You … that was incredible. How did you do that?" Antious asked.

"I'm not sure. It just happened," Thannuel said.

"You fought each with one hand. You weren't dodging and evading, you engaged them completely, one-handed. I … it was the most unbelievable thing I've ever seen."

"I killed them," Thannuel said absently.

"They would have killed you. There's no crime here, Thannuel. Don't believe you are guilty of anything."

Thannuel did not answer.

"Thank you," Antious said. "You saved my life."

"You would have done the same for me," Thannuel said.

Antious was silent. "Yes, I would. That wasn't always the case though." He looked down as if ashamed.

"That doesn't matter now."

"I suppose." Antious looked back up to his friend, meeting his eyes. "I will always come for you, Thannuel. I swear it. Always, no matter what may be in the way. I will come for you."

Thannuel saw the sincerity in Antious's eyes and the strength of his oath. The friends embraced as Lord Kerr's Hold Guard and the city watch flooded the gardens. Among them, Kalisa and Moira. They were safe.

"One thing is certain after tonight," Antious said. "Your father is never going to let you go anywhere without protection again."

Thannuel looked up and saw first moon setting. His eyes fixed on the giant elm tree that hugged the top of the arched tunnel, and caught sight of a figure. Thannuel started and almost cried out, but held his peace. The man had not just arrived, so he must have been there for some time. Had he watched the entire confrontation?

The man had an elderly profile, from what he could make out in the waning moonlight, but was not feeble or decrepit.

Well done, young Kerr, came the voice in his mind again, one he knew not to be his. And then, the figure was gone, jumping from his sight and concealed in the night.

Moira led Amnoch to the alley. On the ground lay four black-clad men. She brought her hand to her mouth at the sight of so much blood. It streamed in the cracks of the cobblestone, rivulets of crimson coursing away from the bodies, the air smelling slightly metallic around her. Several of the city watch surrounded the bodies, investigating the scene. The healer who had come with them from Hold Kerr immediately went to check the bodies, but shook his head after a brief inspection.

"This is where Thannuel was when we escaped," Moira said as they arrived in the alley. "Antious had already been captured and carried away." Her heart stammered with both relief and terror at seeing no sign of Thannuel or Antious.

"Constable!" Amnoch called to one of them. "Lord Kerr's son, Thannuel, have you seen him?"

The constable shook his head. "No. We just heard reports that he was seen headed toward the gardens. Some commotion near the archway, apparently. I have men looking into it now."

Moira watched Amnoch take in the scene, a vein at his temple bulging.

"Master Amnoch!" one of the Hold Guard said.

"Yes, Dahey, what it is?"

"There's supposed to be a fifth man."

"A fifth? You're certain?

Dahey nodded. "You can tell by the blood, see?"

Amnoch followed Dahey's gesture as he outlined the pattern. He was right.

"Are you sure there were eight in total?" Amnoch said, turning to the girls.

Kalisa nodded. "I count people around me. It's a habit my dad put in me."

Amnoch smiled wryly. "Only a military father would teach his daughter that." To the constable, he asked, "The gardens, you said?"

The constable pointed. "That end of the alley will lead you out."

"Come!" Amnoch said.

Moira eyed Master Amnoch as he sprinted down the alley and jumped an impossible height to the building ledges above them. She watched in wonder as he leaped a long distance to another building, demonstrating the same dexterity as if he were sprinting along the forest's canopy. As all wood-dwellers, Moira was naturally nimble, at home among the fluent trees of Arlethia; but the adroitness Master Amnoch displayed seemed impossible.

"How … ?" Kalisa asked.

"Just keep running," Moira said. *Please, Thannuel, be alive.*

Amnoch's foot silently touched the building's roof only momentarily before launching again, expending all the friction and Light within him. The brick cracked under the force of his foot's thrust. Through the triarch leafling fastened to his arm under his sleeve, he drew in more Light from the trees. Moira and Kalisa ran below him, struggling to keep up despite the small bit of Light he had given them when he touched their backs to ease their weariness.

Amnoch. The familiar voice sounded in his mind. Evrin. *You may be right about him, Amnoch.*

It won't matter if he dies! Amnoch said, sending his answer through the forest.

He and the other boy are well, Amnoch.

You are near? Amnoch asked. *Evrin?*

He is not ready.

Neither are we.

Time, Amnoch, is not our ally, to be sure. The tide rises.

How long?

No answer came. In typical fashion, the Keeper of the Living Light left Amnoch with more questions than answers. Only seconds later, he caught sight of the gardens and let himself fall to the ground. A mass of people stood gathered around the arched tunnel that led into the gardens.

"Make way, blast you!" he yelled. "Make a path!"

Several of the city watch were also making their way through the crowds. When Amnoch finally emerged through the masses, Thannuel and Antious were walking toward him, a scene of carnage at their backs. Moira and Kalisa's vibrations announced the young ladies' arrival.

"Hey," Thannuel said, looking at Amnoch with a smile. "What took you so long? Forget to move your feet?"

"Lordling or not, I will beat you senseless!" Amnoch worked his mouth but when further words failed him, he embraced both boys. "Blasted fools."

Moira and Kalisa joined the embrace.

"Are you able to run, my dear?" Branton asked Moira. "I'm sorry that we can't take a carriage, just as a precaution. We'll be safer on foot among the trees."

He doesn't want to be trapped in a carriage if the Marishee attack us, Moira realized. It had only been an hour since their return to the hold with Thannuel and Antious. Amnoch still refused to lift the lockdown, not allowing anyone to come or go without his permission. Major Korin sent word that a contingent of soldiers had been dispatched to Calyn to bolster the city watch's number for the next span and had arrived at the Kerr hold shortly thereafter. After collecting Kalisa and giving her a quick inspection to assure himself she was unharmed, he gave a curt "My Lord" to Branton and departed.

Moira nodded. "I'm not hurt, Lord Kerr. Or, not seriously, anyway. I can run."

They stood just outside the southern gate of Hold Kerr in the gardens where, even at night, the beauty of the manicured grounds was breathtaking.

"My Lord," Master Amnoch spoke, "I really must insist that we not tarry. In fact, I believe—"

""Yes, Master Amnoch, I know. You'd prefer we just hold young Moira for the night, but her parents have already been notified. They are no doubt terrified and need to see their daughter. I highly doubt the Marishee will try anything else."

"Maybe not, my Lord. But prudence demands I try to convince you to at least not go with us. Please, Branton, it would be my honor to see her safely home. You'll be more protected here in the hold should something unseemly happen again."

Moira saw how much Master Amnoch cared for Lord Kerr. There obviously existed a friendship beyond the roles of lord and Master of the Hold Guard as evidenced by Amnoch addressing Lord Kerr by his first given name with no reprimand. This was the second time she had heard Amnoch address him casually tonight, but she had to admit that Lord Branton Kerr seemed to wear his title lightly.

"Should something unseemly happen, Master Amnoch, I'm sure you'll rise to the occasion. And I am not completely worthless with steel."

"But, your condition—"

"Is not a concern, my friend. Trust me."

Amnoch sighed heavily. "At least let me bring some additional Hold Guard."

Branton nodded and Master Amnoch retreated into the hold for only a few moments before returning with four Hold Guard.

"Well, let's be on our way," Lord Kerr said.

They arrived well past half night. Second moon hung more than a hand above the southwest horizon when Moira dropped from the trees in front of her home in Wenrho. Her parents had apparently felt their approach and were waiting outside their home, pale-faced and white-knuckled.

As soon as Moira landed, Rondel and Herra gushed with relief, running and nearly tackling her as they jointly embraced her.

"Oh my child," Rondel said, stroking her hair as he held her tightly. "Oh my child, oh my child." Over his shoulder, Moira saw her younger sister, Molina, looking through the window, hugging a blanket. She did that only when she was nervous or scared.

"I'm okay," Moira silently mouthed to Molina.

Too distraught to speak, Herra just held her daughter and wept, refusing to let Moira go. Moira almost yelped at her mother's crushing embrace, her dislocated elbow still a bit tender after being popped back into place, but she forced back any protest and let herself be held.

"Good father and mother Albrung," Lord Kerr said with gravity in his voice, "you have my deepest apologies for what has happened. My healers have seen to your daughter, and she is, I am very pleased to say, well and whole. Bruised and maybe a little tender, but otherwise fine. She's tougher than she comes off."

Lord Kerr shifted his weight. "Still, I feel fully responsible for any harm or danger coming to your daughter. I owe you a debt, and not for the first time. Please, if I can do anything, I implore you to ask."

Rondel finally let go of Moira and bowed before Lord Kerr.

"My Lord, you owe us nothing." There were tears in his eyes and his lower jaw quivered. "You have returned our daughter to us, safe and whole. I will be eternally grateful that your guards arrived in time."

Master Amnoch looked slightly abashed at that comment.

"Actually," Lord Kerr said, "it was all Thannuel and Antious. They stood against the Marishee, allowing Moira and Kalisa to escape safely."

"They killed them," Moira said, finally extricating herself from her mother.

She knew she was still in some shock and her voice sounded removed, as if she had not spoken the words. She still saw Thannuel's face perfectly in her mind. He had been afraid, but put that aside as he placed himself between her and the Marishee. He protected her. Fought for her. There had been no hesitation, not even in the slightest.

"Of course they killed them!" Amnoch said, ruining the tenderness of the moment. "I've trained those boys good and right, I have! They were afraid of dying only because they knew I would chase them into the next life and kill them again for embarrassing me should they have failed. Blasted poltroons."

Moira almost smiled, but Lord Kerr looked disapprovingly at Master Amnoch.

"Right. I think I'll wait . . . somewhere over there," Amnoch said, lowering his head. He mumbled something inaudible as he left the group and stood out of earshot.

"He feels responsible, in a way," Lord Kerr explained. "You must forgive him."

"But all are well?" Rondel asked. "Your son? Major Korin's daughter? The other boy?"

"Antious," Moira said.

"Thannuel, Kalisa, and Antious are all alive and unharmed. I almost had to order Master Amnoch to hogtie Thannuel to make him stay home. He insisted on coming with us to see your daughter home, but I wouldn't allow it. He hopes you don't take that as any slight to the duty he feels to safeguard Moira as his intended. Again, Rondel, Herra, I apologize most sincerely."

"Lord Kerr, I once saved your son's life," Rondel said. "He has now saved my daughter's." The former healer looked to be struggling for words. Finally he said, "I will understand if you feel that their planned union is no longer necessary. Any perceived debt you may have owed me is certainly fulfilled."

"No!" Moira said sharply, and then brought her hand to her mouth.

It was hard to breathe suddenly and her vision clouded, black splotches streaking across her sight. Her knees almost gave out and she felt faint. She wanted to shout, to scream objections, to cry, but could only shake her head, mouth open, blushing deeply.

Lord Kerr smiled. "I think we're beyond any nonsense like that, Rondel. Have you seen these two together? My son gawks at your daughter when she's not looking."

He does? Moira asked in her mind. She blinked a few times in rapid succession and the black spots cleared.

"Apparently, Moira is somewhat smitten with Thannuel as well," Rondel said through a slight grin.

Herra's face turned from a mixture of fear and relief to a huge smile, and Moira blushed even deeper.

"Then, we shall leave it to them," Lord Kerr said. "Moira, do you desire this union to continue with my son? You are free to speak as you will, my dear."

Do I? she asked herself.

She did, she realized. With all her heart, she did. A feeling of warmth shot through her, from the crown of her head to her toes, bouncing through her body until it collected in her heart. It was more than she could contain, something she had never before felt. What did it mean? Was it the feeling of total commitment to another person? Of knowing that someone else valued her life above his own? Perhaps this was all foolishness on her part and she was only imagining how Thannuel felt.

I love him.

That's what the feeling meant, she decided. She could not even pretend otherwise and it must have been plain as the morning sun upon her face. Her heartbeat quickened but the blushing faded. She was not embarrassed any longer.

"Yes. I want to marry Thannuel."

Herra made a happy-squeal noise as her eyes widened, and Lord Kerr smiled.

"And so you shall, Moira."

Lord Branton Kerr sat at Thannuel's bedside through the night after seeing Moira safely home, weariness not finding him. Thannuel's sleep was fitful, but at least he was safe. A single candle burned on an end table in an oval silver plate with an ornate circular handle having appearance of a leaf. Slow rolling pearls of wax dripped down the candle, pooling over the edge of the silver plate, then the end table, forming the likeness of a cascading waterfall slowly freezing in the low season.

Thank you, Ancients above.

What would he have done had he lost his only son? Thannuel's life had been the only thing that had seen him through the trial of losing his beloved wife so soon after their marriage, near the dawn of their lives together.

I miss you, Iliaya. Every day.

Branton brought his hand to his chest. The ailment within him grew slowly. He could feel it spreading, gradually staking more and more claim over his body. Though the healers claimed plenty of rest and triarch tea should cause it to clear up, it had been roughly four years and the malady had not relented, though the healers' curatives did help with the symptoms.

"Please, by the Light, let me live to see my son flourish," he whispered. "This is all I ask."

Orange light peeked in through the windows, washing out the candle's soft glow. Morning came too fast. Branton arose, put his hand lightly on Thannuel's brow, and pleaded with the Ancient Heavens for the prosperity and longevity of his son's life, for happiness to be his during the walk of his days on Våleira. After a moment, Branton kissed his son gently and left the chambers.

The book is indeed one of the keys to Confluence. We ascribe it to the Luminary of House Kearon, but we know it predated him by several millennia. How it came to be in his possession is not known. Of greater import is how he wielded its Influence. This will occupy the balance of my lecture today.

—Vicar Holden Otheal of the New Changrual Order,
Lectures on the Restoration of Confluence

FIVE
~THANNUEL~
Day 20 of 3rd High 383 A.U.

THANNUEL SAT IN A DAZE AT BREAKFAST, not touching his food. Antious sat beside him, having come to the hold early. Lady Wendham busied herself in the kitchens, scurrying around them as she performed her duties, humming a most annoyingly cheerful melody as she worked.

"I'm not going to school today," Thannuel said in a monotone voice.

Antious just shook his head with a "me, either" look on his face. "Didn't sleep at all."

"Your parents won't care?"

"My mom won't know, she sleeps during most of the day," Antious said. "My dad … well, he understands. Said he'd come check on me later when his shift is over."

The shock of the previous night's encounter had finally caught up to them.

"Kalisa and Moira might be worried if we don't show up, though," Antious said.

"I doubt they'll go, either,"

"I'd say that probably ended things for me and Kalisa. No way her father will let her see me after that. I'm sure I'll be to blame. He already doesn't like me."

Thannuel huffed and actually smiled a little, though his eyes remained unmoved, continuing to stare at nothing.

"I'm sorry, Thannuel," Antious said.

"Sorry? For *what?*"

"They got me. I wasn't fast enough. If I had been, you wouldn't have had to put yourself in—"

"Shut up, mop boy. Ancients above, it wasn't your fault."

Master Amnoch came into the kitchens, a briskness in his step.

"Moping, are we? Like a bunch of women?"

Lady Wendham ceased her humming instantly and gave him a withering look.

"Right, pardon me, Lady Wendham." Turning back to the boys, he corrected himself. "Like a bunch of over-privileged poltroons, then."

Thannuel sighed, his head heavy with his thoughts, not in the mood for Amnoch. To his surprise, the master of the Hold Guard came and sat down next to him and Antious, folding his hands.

"Listen, lads, you did a good thing. Those men would have done the same to you. You protected each other, saved each other."

"We killed them," Thannuel said.

Amnoch pursed his lips, lowering his chin. "Yes. And, it was a good thing you did."

"How can you say that?" Thannuel asked. The tension in his voice betrayed him as tears brimmed upon his eyelids. "How can it be good to kill?"

"I know you're struggling with this, Thannuel, but you need to understand that you *saved* others by your actions. Both of you did."

"*I* needed saving," Antious said spitefully.

"We all need saving at different times," Amnoch responded. "That's not anything to be ashamed of, boy."

"Have you ever killed anyone, Master Amnoch?" Thannuel asked.

He nodded. "I have."

"And? Did you feel it was a *good* thing?"

"While in the moment, it was just something that needed to be done … like cleaning up after a meal, or getting dressed in the morning; but, afterwards, especially the first time, I probably felt a bit like you both do now."

"Does it get easier the next time?" Antious asked.

"Easier the *next* time?" Thannuel asked. "You think there will be a *next* time?"

"It does," Amnoch answered quietly. "Get easier, that is. It shouldn't, but it does."

They sat in silence for more than a minute, Antious and Thannuel staring off into nothing again.

"Her dad totally hates me," Antious said.

"Really?" Thannuel snapped. "That's what you're thinking about right now?"

"Of course he does!" Amnoch chortled. "That's his job!"

Thannuel resisted the small grin working its way onto his face but failed.

"Well," Amnoch said, slamming his hands down on the table as he rose, "If you're not going to school, we'll be having an all-day sparring session. Grab your blades and shields."

"What?" Thannuel protested. "I'm too sore! I can barely move!"

Antious, however, rose instantly and exited to the training section of the hold's courtyard.

"I was wrong," Amnoch admitted. "Only one of you is a poltroon. Now get off your noble posterior."

⚶

Moira sat pondering as she stared out the window in her bedroom at the gentle waterfall that flowed at the edge of their land. The water streamed from the Roniah River down a shallow ravine of large, smooth rocks, most covered in moss, the same that covered the base of the nearby trees. The setting sun glistened off the swift moving water, golden sparkles dancing on its surface and hazy rainbows prancing in the waterfall's mist.

There was something grounding to her about this scene, something that warded off the surreal terror that still haunted her from the night before. She had sat here most of the day. Her parents hadn't bothered her other than to ask if she wanted to go to school, but she just shook her head. Two of Lord Kerr's guards had remained to watch over her family but departed around noon, refusing any refreshment offered them by mother Albrung.

Last night wasn't all bad, she told herself. *I found out some things—some important things.*

But did Thannuel feel the same way she did? *Was* she just being foolish? No. That look on his face, in his eyes, as he defended her— a burning resided there, a yearning, she thought.

But was it for me?

A knock at the front door interrupted her musing.

"I got it!" Molina shouted and sprinted toward the door.

Moira rose to follow her sister, but that competitive drive children have to be the first to answer the door had long left her.

Molina opened the door and said, "Oh. Hello, Lord Turd Hair. I'll get Moira."

Moira rolled her eyes when she got to the door and shoved Molina aside. At the look of the boy in her doorway, a tickling in her stomach roused itself.

"Sorry about that. I think she's lost some of her infatuation with you over the years."

"Infatuation?" Thannuel asked. "And that's the second time she talked about my hair and turd in the same sentence."

"That you know of, anyway. It's a long story. Do you want to come in?"

Thannuel brought his hand to the back of his neck and looked over his shoulder.

"Actually, do you want to come outside? It's a nice evening. You don't have to, I'd understand if you wanted to stay—"

Moira stepped out and closed the door behind her. She hugged him, trying to dissolve into him if she could. Thannuel groaned slightly but returned her hug.

"What's wrong?" she asked. "Are you hurt?"

"No … just sore. Master Amnoch made Antious and me spar all day since we didn't go to school. So much for a day off. He never gives us any slack."

"I'm glad for that," she said.

Thannuel smiled but it came out more as a grimace. "Yeah, I guess I am, too. Sort of. Hey, do you have any idea what a poltroon is?"

Moira looked at him and he must have seen the confusion on her face.

"Forget it. It's something Master Amnoch has taken to calling me of late. I'm sure it's not flattering."

"He was proud of you," Moira said. "I could tell last night, when he and your father spoke to my parents."

"Moira?" her mother called from inside the house. "Don't go far!"

Again, Moira rolled her eyes.

"We don't have to go anywhere, really," Thannuel said.

"No guards?" Moira asked, looking around.

Thannuel sighed. "They're not far."

"I often sit on the roof and watch the sunset."

Thannuel nodded. "Okay."

"My father wouldn't let me go last night," Thannuel said when they were on the roof. "I wanted to go and make sure you were safe, but he wouldn't let me leave. Not after . . . you know. I think he had guards outside my door and window all night. It can feel more like prison than protection sometimes."

Moira felt anxious suddenly.

"Did he tell you anything? I mean ... about when he and Master Amnoch brought me home?"

"What do you mean?" Thannuel asked.

"Um ... " Moira shook her head. *Ancients, why does the sunlight have to hit his hair like that?* Certain she looked foolish, she quickly said, "Forget it. Nothing."

"He did tell me about my mother. He doesn't talk about her much but I wish he would. Guess he thought it was a way to apologize for … I don't know what he felt he needed to apologize for, now that I think about it. He's like that sometimes, thinking anything that goes wrong is ultimately his fault. But, I did feel like I actually got to know my mother a little for the first time."

"Tell me," Moira said.

Thannuel paused for a few moments, as if collecting his thoughts and thinking how to begin. "She was kind. Deep red hair that looked brown except in the sunlight. She was always inviting people to the hold. I guess it was a rare evening not to have a dinner guest. Kind of annoyed my father a little, but he never told her. People throughout the province, no matter their station in life, were guests at her table. She offended some noble houses by inviting the common people of their cities to the hold more than them, apparently. Mother said if they were taking offense because of kindness, they deserved to have their feelings trampled a bit."

Moira was hearing him but not really listening. How could she help it when even his voice now had a mesmerizing quality to it? How had she never noticed that before?

You're so stupid, she chided herself. *You're not supposed to like him this much. Not yet.*

"Even in matters of state," Thannuel continued, "when my father would meet with other provincial lords, she wanted to be part of it instead of retreating with the other ladies. Apparently she had quite the mind for politics. Did you know that she was part of—"

Moira kissed him. To her heart's relief, he kissed her back after only a brief hesitation. His lips were soft and full against hers. Moments seemed like hours and she forced herself to pull back just slightly, letting her cheek rest against his. Her eyes refused to open as she took in his scent, the heat of him next to her, savoring the moment.

"You have no idea how long I've wanted to do that," Thannuel whispered, his breath tickling her ear.

Now Moira pulled back further. "You didn't! I'm the one that had to—"

Thannuel reached his hand up behind her neck, through her hair, and pulled her in, half an inch from his lips. His hand felt strong on her slender neck and she felt him shake, just a little. His nose rubbed gently against hers—playfully, fondly. When his lips touched hers again, that warmth she had felt last night came back to her more fully, all-consuming.

"I'm sorry I hurt you last night," Thannuel said, their foreheads leaning together.

"I love you." Moira shuddered as she said the words.

"Of course you do."

They both laughed and she hit him. Thannuel lay back on the roof and she rested her head on his shoulder, curling into him. The sky had turned orange and red with splashes of purple as the sun gave way to night. Above them, the veins in the triarch leaves glowed ever so faintly.

"Were you scared? Last night?" Moira asked.

She felt Thannuel nod as his chin and cheek rubbed her hair.

"Why?"

He was silent for several moments. Moira moved her head from his shoulder to his chest, listening to his steady heartbeat. His arm moved around her, holding her as they lay together. The soft drone of the waterfall in the distance lulled her to a peaceful state just above sleep. When she was sure Thannuel would not answer her, that the moment between them had faded, he spoke.

"I love you, too."

Moira curled even deeper into him and reached her arm around his chest. No matter how tightly she held him, she could not get close enough. He tensed slightly, but relaxed quickly, as if trying to hide it.

"Oh, sorry," Moira said. "I forgot. Is it bad?"

"After last night with the Marishee and today with Amnoch, I'm not sure I've ever been more sore."

Moira relaxed her grip and scooted away a little.

"No," Thannuel said, pulling her close again. "Stay."

"I don't want to hurt you."

"A little pain is good. Lets me know I'm still alive."

"That sounds like Master Amnoch speaking."

"It is."

"So you think I'm good for causing pain, then? Is that it?"

Thannuel shrugged. "Isn't that the role of a woman in a man's life?"

Moira hammer-fisted him hard in the stomach.

"Ancients!" Thannuel cried out and coughed. "How good of you to illustrate my point. You spend too much time around Kalisa."

"I heard that," Antious said, coming up on the roof.

"So did I," Kalisa said, just behind him.

Thannuel mumbled something Moira couldn't quite make out and she pushed herself up by her arm against his chest. Thannuel grimaced again.

"Wouldn't want me to fail in my *role*, would you?" Moira quipped.

"I wouldn't mind a little less dedication, actually."

When Antious and Kalisa saw them snuggled together, they looked at each other with wicked grins.

"Looks like we're interrupting something, Kalisa," Antious said. "Think we should let them be?"

"Not a chance," Kalisa said. "Can't trust them."

"What are you doing here?" Thannuel asked.

"Kalisa came to the hold while I was still putting away the

sparring gear, but you had slipped out," Antious said. "Thanks for the help, by the way. It was pretty easy to guess where you had gone."

"Perfect timing, really," Moira said. "Thannuel was just explaining the role of a woman in a man's life."

"That right?" Kalisa said. "Oh, do continue."

Thannuel flushed.

"Sure, brave when scary men dressed in black with swords and evil accents threaten you, but nothing to say when confronted by women?" Kalisa said.

Thannuel glanced pleadingly at Antious.

"Don't look at me, your Grace."

"Thanks for the help, mop boy," Thannuel said. "Didn't you swear an oath to me last night?"

"Yeah, well, this isn't part of that," Antious said, that wicked grin still in place.

"Ancients come, I surrender," Thannuel said. "Now, can we please return to the previous position?"

"Oh, you mean like this?" Moira said as she laid her head back down on Thannuel's upper chest. She felt him nuzzle her head as he took in the scent of her hair.

"Yeah," he said, "just like that."

"This is so wrong," Antious said with a snicker. "Let's go."

"Why don't you follow your future lord's example and just lie back?" Kalisa said.

"What?"

"You're so dense sometimes, Antious."

Moira looked up to see Kalisa snuggling into Antious despite his clearly uncomfortable posture. Underneath her, Moira felt Thannuel's chest rumble with a soft laugh. She saw him looking over at Antious and Kalisa as well.

"Do we have to?" Antious asked. "I mean—"

"Shut up, Antious," Kalisa mumbled.

"Yes, Antious, shut up," Moira echoed.

She wanted to listen to Thannuel's heart with her right ear and the sound of the rushing water with her other. She found such peace in the strong, steady pace in his chest, like nothing could ever harm her while his heart still beat.

"Don't leave me," she whispered.

"Never," he answered.

For several minutes, a placid silence held. The peaceful serenity of Wenrho enveloped Moira and she wanted to freeze time, never to move from Thannuel's embrace again.

"You know . . . I love you guys, right?" Antious said. The tone of his voice was subdued to Moira's ears. "Life got a lot better for me after you became part of it."

"He's talking again," Moira said with mock agitation.

"You mean after you put me on my back in that jousting game?" Thannuel asked.

"Yeah, that was kinda the start of it."

"I wish I could have seen that," Moira said.

"No you don't," Thannuel said. "I was not exactly at my best during those years. In fact, I only came into my best when you entered my life two years ago."

"That's disgusting," Antious said.

"And really melodramatic," Kalisa agreed.

"And disgusting," Antious repeated.

"Yeah, I know," Thannuel said.

Moira could hear the smile in his voice and she giggled.

"It *was* rather satisfying seeing you on your royal backside," Kalisa said to Thannuel. "You kind of *really* deserved it."

"I'm sorry, Antious. Really. I'm embarrassed whenever I think of that time in our lives. It's hard for me to imagine I was like that."

"I think you made up for it last night," Antious replied. "But I forgave you a long time ago."

Kalisa huffed with annoyance. "Am I the only one who can't stop thinking about last night? Why were they coming for us?"

"I don't know," Thannuel said.

"They were only there for Thannuel," Antious said. "The rest of us were expendable. That's what they said. Well, right before Thannuel threw a dagger through the skull of the Marishee that came to kill me while I was tied up."

Moira tensed. She hadn't heard all the details after she and Kalisa had escaped, but she knew the Marishee were dead.

"It was incredible," Antious said wistfully. "The way he moved, fighting two at once . . . Master Amnoch wouldn't berate you anymore had he seen that."

"Yes he would," Thannuel said. "He can't help it."

"Well, you are a poltroon," Antious said.

"Seriously, what does that mean?" Thannuel asked.

"Okay," Kalisa said, "but why? Why did they attack us and why did they want Thannuel?"

No one answered. Thannuel finally spoke.

"The Marishee mentioned someone called the Thoulden-sha. My father hasn't told me much about the Marishee but I think this Thoulden-sha is their leader." He paused for a moment. "I saw someone," Thannuel said quietly, "in the elm tree above the archway to the Calyn Gardens. Heard him . . . in my mind. Not like a thought, but an actual voice."

"I knew there was something severely wrong with you," Kalisa said.

Moira chuckled.

"Hey!" Thannuel said, poking her in the ribs. "You're supposed to stand up for me, right?"

"It was funny."

"Ah, forget it," Thannuel said. "I can't explain it."

"So, you're seeing ghosts and hearing voices?" Antious asked.

"Whatever he or it was, he helped me. I didn't feel threatened by him."

"I didn't see or hear anyone," Antious said, "but feel free to continue to listen to the voices in your head."

"I think I'll meet with this Thoulden-sha someday," Thannuel said.

"Why?" Moira asked, closing a fist around his shirt.

"He essentially invited me. I would hate to be rude."

The worst of us have we fettered in chains at their behest. Their capacity overflows. They have changed. I can see it. It is the same change I see in myself. The Ancient Heavens for strength I petition. I may choose the fetters for myself before long.

—From the writings of Kelon ol'Eihrin,
discovered in an ancient fort by Reign Kerr, translated into Sentharian by
Prime Vicar Ryall of the New Changrual Order

SIX

~AMNOCH~

Day 21 of 3rd High 383 A.U.

MASTER AMNOCH SPIED THE MAN as he moved from the crowd. One of his arms was crudely bandaged and his face had dark purple discoloration under his eyes with a dried crust of blood across his nose. His injuries matched up with Thannuel's description.

That has to be him, Amnoch told himself.

Through the triarch leafling in his hand, he drew in the strength of the trees around him, their venerable Light filling him. Touching the hilt of his sword, he transferred enough to the Jarwynian blade to make it vibrate in a low hum only one familiar with it could hear.

There had been eight Marishee, but only seven bodies found. This eighth man's efforts to blend in were terribly obvious; even for someone who was not a wood-dweller, his movements tense and unnatural. Less conspicuous clothing had replaced the thin black robes he and his dead Marishee brethren had worn in an effort to blend in as he tried to escape. Unfortunately for him, it didn't help.

Two days since the attack, Amnoch feared he might not find the lone survivor, though he remained convinced the man was still in the city. Calyn had been swarmed by Arlethian soldiers after the attack, standing guard at every possible exit. With hundreds of soldiers and the city watch looking for an injured person not of the Western Province, the task shouldn't have been overly challenging. This, ironically, had also been the problem.

Amnoch proposed his plan to Lord Kerr, asking him to have the soldiers withdraw, at least to a significant degree.

"When hunting, my Lord," Amnoch had said, "the prey has to feel safe. Otherwise, it may never leave its refuge."

"You will capture him, then?" Lord Kerr asked. "Assuming you can flush him out?"

At first Amnoch thought to simply kill the remaining Marishee, but Evrin's constant admonitions for him to be slower to wield his blade as a solution took root—this time.

"No, my Lord, but I believe I should follow him, let him lead me back to whatever hole the little asp crawled out from. Might provide us more insight into the Marishee whereabouts."

Lord Kerr had agreed after some thought. "Rumors of a

Marishee sedition have steadily increased. Prime Lord Wellyn is growing troubled, and a little frustrated with Lord Orion, truth be told. He would appreciate any additional insight we can provide, I am sure."

As will the Gyldenal, Amnoch said silently.

Amnoch had to trail the man closer than he wanted to in the city and risk being seen so he didn't lose him. Thousands of people thronged Calyn's city center as was typical of any given day. With a plethora of vibrations flooding the ground, deciphering any one person's vibrational signature, other than those immediately around him, proved impossible. For the time being, he would have to rely on line of sight alone. If the surviving Marishee spotted Amnoch … *well, then Evrin's admonitions be damned,* he thought and habitually felt for the haft of his sheathed blade, its faint vibrating hum a comfort to him.

When this last of the Marishee assassins made it outside the city without seeing Amnoch, the Master of the Hold Guard smiled.

"Now slither quickly, little asp. Slither home."

Amnoch followed the man for days. The Marishee survivor did not run—or slither, for that matter—but made his way slowly and cautiously back to Dispa. Nothing about his route was typical, obviously trying to shake off anyone who might be following him. The evasion tactics were wise and Amnoch recognized that the man did, in fact, have some decent sense about him, not trusting his eyes alone.

Poor bastard. Doesn't even have a chance despite his caution, Amnoch thought, the image of a shadow lion hunting a turtle coming to his mind. It was a ridiculous comparison, however appropriate.

Reconnaissance was his mission. He had to remind himself of that several times when the urge to dispatch the man and return home became too strong within him.

The more of their locations we know, the better.

Lord Hoyt's spies—those that actually returned—reported the Marishee now populated all the narrows, a series of large rock outcroppings northeast of the Schadar Desert with slot canyons that wove and delved for miles in intricate patterns. While technically part of the Eastern Province, the dunes and narrows around Dispa felt more like they belonged to the Schadar Desert.

As Amnoch's quarry entered the Eastern Province, he changed his travel northeast for a day before heading directly south. That was a good sign, Amnoch knew, taking it to mean the man didn't believe he was being followed.

Poor bastard.

Amnoch knew the attack on Thannuel came as reprisal for him and Lord Kerr spying on the Thoulden-sha the previous year. They had been spotted as they peered down upon the gathering of Marishee through a crevice atop the narrows outside Dispa. The arena that had opened below them could hold more than a thousand people, sprawling wide as if the sand and wind had hollowed the natural dome-like expanse for just such a purpose. The memory of a bound man being brought to the altar in the middle of that expanse came to him, the bluish-white light of first moon bathing it more with each passing minute. The bound man, however, had been unexpectedly released before the sacrifice was completed.

The Thoulden-sha knew we were there, watching ... somehow, Amnoch remembered.

When the Thoulden-sha had looked up, uncannily alerted to his and Lord Kerr's presence, Amnoch's blood had run cold. He felt the Influence of the Ancient Dark, intimately, perhaps in only the way a member of the Gyldenal could.

Evrin, Amnoch recalled. *He speaks of a parasite in the Light more often of late.*

It was nothing Amnoch understood, often being frustrated with figurative and symbolic language, but that feeling from the Thoulden-sha—it was unmistakably hostile and invasive, like being openly seen by a predator, targeted. Amnoch could not shake the thought that the Thoulden-sha himself was this parasite; or, at least, related to it somehow.

Now, some four thousand years since The Turning Away, the old clan bloodlines were diluted. Yet, Evrin was convinced that something resided within the Kerr line—something important, a direct threat to the Ancient Dark. If so, there was some sense as to why Thannuel had been targeted, but making sense of this was not at all comforting.

The farmlands and plains of the Eastern province turned more and more barren the further south Amnoch traveled. His Arlethian senses were attuned to this man's vibrational pulse now, knowing when he moved without having to see him as long as he stayed within a half-mile or so. With the land increasingly barren from cover and the ground softer with loose sand, remaining both unseen and in touch with the man's vibrational signature proved challenging.

Amnoch tore the long sleeves from his shirt, revealing block-like muscled arms, and fashioned them into a head covering. That was something he didn't understand: why could he utilize the Light to both heal and destroy, but not grow back the hair on top of his head? The few strands left were no protection from the searing sun.

The provisions in his pack ran a little thin but he could manage, so long as he held the stored Light within him, its Influence sustaining and regenerative. But if he had to use it this far outside Arlethia with neither access to fluent trees to draw upon nor enough food to replenish his strength, he could be left too malnourished to recuperate. His sword of Jarwynian create—therein was Living Light; but once the specialized ore had been infused, the Influence could not be withdrawn again, only expelled. Using Lumenati Influence did have consequences. He would be cautious.

Recon, return, report. That is your mission.

Amnoch yearned for the day when the Gyldenal's silent fight—that calamitous battle against the Dark Mother's Influence—would be made bare for all Våleira to see.

Let it come.

He let his Marishee prey get much further ahead than he normally would, but Amnoch would make up the distance when night fell. Too great was the danger of being seen amid the naked landscape during the day, and he was tired of traveling low to the ground like a dog. The tracks in the sand would be easily discernable and, by all appearances, the man did not believe he was being pursued. No counter-tracking tactics would be employed.

Not far off from his position stood an outcropping about twenty feet high, the rock bone-white like all formations in these parts. As he approached, he saw that the outcropping was actually two formations cascading closely together, thicker at the bottom and tapering toward the top. Two islands in a sea of hot sepia. He would shelter in their shadows until night came.

Small plants jutted from cracks in the rocks with dark red berries between their thin, spiky fronds. The berries themselves were hollow on the top end with seeds plainly visible on the inside.

"Ah, here to tempt me, are you? I don't think so."

Opening his satchel, he took out a water skin and drained a few swallows. The plant's fronds wept a clear, rheumy fluid that Amnoch knew to be poisonous, as were the berries themselves. If he could reach between the spiky fronds without getting cut, extract a berry without smudging the delicate flesh and releasing the poisonous oil, the seeds themselves were highly nutritious. Many a traveler had survived these sterile parts by the yahla plant; many more had perished from convulsions so powerful ribs were often broken as the poison did its work. The victims of the yahla plants were petrified, it was said, and assimilated into these outcroppings. Amnoch had to admit these smaller groupings of rock were seemingly random, severely out of place. Some reports from the Ministry of Terran Studies claimed they in fact grew every year, if only a few inches. He had accumulated many stories about these barren parts of the Realm during his long years that spanned enough for three lifetimes.

Ghost stories, they are. Amnoch spat. *Next thing you know we'll be told that the rock formations are the bones of the Haxlium.*

"Well, are you the bones of giants?" he asked the white stone, hitting it with his fist. He wasn't sure if he even believed in the Haxlium at all, much less that these rocks were their leftover bones.

With his short blade, he plucked a few yahla berries free and carefully extracted the seeds. They were bitter but would extend his provisions by a meal. A handful would provide energy for many hours of exertion.

"Not as smart as all that, are you?" he said, looking at the yahla fronds still weeping their mucus.

Nightfall cast her blanket over the sun, shrouding the world in its own shadow. As first moon rose and the stars awoke in the night sky, the sands glinted a silvery gleam in the faint light.

Time to be going, then.

As he stepped off the rock and onto the sand, something moved under his foot.

SEVEN

~THANNUEL~

Day 24 of 3rd High 383 A.U.

THANNUEL PARRIED ANTIOUS'S THRUST with a light touch, just enough to change the sword's trajectory, and spun around with an elbow strike aimed for Antious's ear. His friend blocked the blow, placing an outward-faced palm between Thannuel's elbow and his face just in time. Closing his hand around Thannuel's elbow, Antious pulled the arm forward, drawing Thannuel off balance. The knee to Thannuel's ribs came too fast and he crumpled over, gasping for breath.

Antious threw down his sparring blade. "What's wrong with you?"

"Nothing!" Thannuel said harshly. "You just caught me open."

"That's a blasted lie. You're not trying!"

"I am trying. It's just … my head's not right. It's not the same."

"Why? Because if you fought like this a half-span ago, we'd both be dead now. Probably Moira and Kalisa, too."

"I know," Thannuel said a bit milder. "It's just, I mean . . . I wish Amnoch were here."

"That would make you fight harder? I'm happy to verbally assault you as he does, your Grace."

"What do you want from me, Antious?"

"I want you to fight, the Dark take you! Like you did against the Marishee! I want to know how you did it! Could you always do that? Have you been toying with Amnoch and me this whole time? Or is this a joke on me between you and Amnoch?"

"Antious, I'm just as frustrated. I don't know what's going on."

"You're fighting like . . . like . . ."

"Like what? Say it."

Antious held his silence, breathing slow, long breaths through his nose, his mouth scrunched into a bitter expression.

"Like some spoiled Lord's son who knows he doesn't have to try in life! If I didn't know you and saw you fighting like this, I wouldn't believe the rumors. You've heard them, right? The whole academy is saying you killed dozens of men—"

"They're saying that about you, too, Antious. Doesn't it bother you?"

"Which part? The killing or the numbers?"

"The part that's true."

"No! It doesn't bother me that I killed them! It doesn't bother me that you did! Seriously, what the fallen Ancients is wrong with you? We were protecting ourselves, Thannuel, not to mention Kalisa and Moira!" Antious paused. "Wait a minute. If Moira's kisses are affecting you this badly I'll . . . do . . . something. I'm just not sure what yet."

Thannuel half-smiled and looked away. "That's not it, mop boy."

Antious stared at him with an expression that demanded more. Thannuel leaned back against a support pillar in the courtyard. He could smell Lady Wendham's cooking coming from the kitchens, and his stomach growled a small yearning. She might have been the best thing to happen to Hold Kerr in some time.

"I can't figure it out," he finally said. "My mind ... it split, Antious. I'm telling you, I felt it divide. One side was more instinctive and reactive while the other was ... like, more focused or something."

"If you're telling me your head is broken, that's not news."

"I think it's how I was able to fight those last two at the end. They had been holding back until then and they were definitely well trained. You could see it, couldn't you?"

Antious nodded, still scowling. "No need to brag."

"I'm not. I'm frustrated because I don't understand what happened to me, Antious."

"Simple. Your head broke and now you're hearing voices."

"It was this old man in the elm tree, I'm telling you. I wouldn't make this up. Burning Heavens, Antious, I think he might have been an Ancient for all I know."

"The Ancients weren't real, Thannuel, and they're not coming back." Antious finally relaxed. "I just don't understand what happened with you, but I want to! I want to fight like you did. Ancients, Thannuel, I don't think I've seen Master Amnoch move like you did."

"I doubt that. He'd have either of us disarmed in three moves."

Antious shook his head. "Not if you fight like you did, I promise you."

Thannuel ran one hand through his hair. "You want to know what's actually bothering me?"

"Moira doesn't think you kiss well?"

Thannuel looked up, his hand still in his hair. "Did she say something to Kalisa?"

"Nah. Well, not that she told me, anyway. That girl is a steel trap with secrets."

"Are you saying Moira did say something to Kalisa but you just don't know what it was?"

"We're to the point where you tell me what is going on in your royal cranium. Stop delaying."

Thannuel harrumphed softly. "I . . . can't do it again. Whatever happened with my mind, I can't make it happen again."

"Do you think it was the situation? The danger that brought it out?"

"Maybe." Thannuel shrugged. "Probably. But if I knew what it was or how it happened, I could learn to control it, right? I mean, what good is it if I can't use it when needed?"

"If you don't know how it happened, then you can't teach me, can you? Are you sure you're not just keeping this a secret? Using this convenient inability to do it again as a way to hide it from me?"

"Antious, despite being a moron at times, you are my best friend. Do you understand that? I wouldn't hide anything from you."

Antious rubbed his head and sat down. "Yeah, I know. And you're apparently a lot stronger than I thought. You know when you threw that short blade at the guy's head, I actually heard his neck snap? It sounded like a branch torn off a tree."

Thannuel remembered the surge of power at that moment greater than anything he had ever felt in his life. One of the Marishee stood above his bound friend, raising a sword to impale him. The throw had been complete reflex without any thought. Even the hilt entered the man's head, passing almost completely through. The memory sickened him, to think he had caused death with such strength, so easily. Perhaps it was good he could not reproduce the effect.

"I tried asking Master Amnoch about it all before he left, but he was distracted with finding the last of the Marishee."

"You should have killed him," Antious said.

"I was too busy chasing after your captured waste, mop boy. Anyway, I think Master Amnoch was avoiding me, the more I think about it."

"That's because he's wise."

"My father wants to know if you've thought about the military and his offer to sponsor you. He thinks you'll do very well. So do I."

Antious shrugged. "Maybe. It would be nice to get paid to call you 'my Lord' since I'll have to do it before long anyway."

"You really do want a beating, don't you?" Thannuel straightened and brought his sword to bear. "I'll oblige you."

"Talking all fancy-like won't help you, high-born."

"Nor will sitting there." Thannuel wacked Antious on the arm with the flat of his blade.

Antious jumped to his feet. "Dimming finally!"

Thannuel and Moira walked hand in hand down the streets of Calyn, this time keeping to the more populated thoroughfares. A warm drizzle kicked up the smell of earth, foliage, and cobblestone in the humid air.

"Did Antious really do that to you?" Moira asked, reaching up to touch Thannuel's blackened eye.

"Yeah . . . he kind of got a little frustrated, thinking I was taking it easy on him," Thannuel said. "He's actually a lot better than he thinks he is."

"Were you?"

"What?"

"Taking it easy on him?"

"No, I can't afford to."

"Does it hurt? Your eye?"

"Not too bad."

"At least you can blame it on the Marishee." Moira's tease came with a smile and Thannuel brightened.

"I love seeing you smile."

"It's natural when I'm with you."

"Antious is right. We are disgusting."

"We are?"

Thannuel chuckled. "Definitely."

They walked in companionable silence for a time, passing from the merchant district into the financial district. The buildings stood grander here but still as part of the forest, wrapped by vines and sprawling branches. One building, however, stood out, its construction more rigid and blockish than the rest.

"What's that one?" Moira asked.

"It's a branch of the Bank of Thera," Thannuel answered. "The Southern Province's holdings have spread far throughout the Realm."

"Why is it here?"

"Well, they're in every province, really. Besides, my father and Lord Hoyt are friends. The South and West probably do more economic trade together than the other two provinces combined. Did you know the Southern Province makes up nearly fifty percent of Senthara's economic output? The North barely makes up nine percent, even with Iskele, but Iskele really is just a consuming populace, not producing much. Not surprising by the North's lack of usable resources. If it weren't for the seat of the prime lord being there, I don't think there would be even that much output."

Moira looked at him with raised eyebrows. "Therrium Academy actually taught you something?"

"My father says it's my mother's side coming out in me. She not only had a mind for politics but also economics, it seems. I'll have to eventually deal with this kind of stuff."

"But for now, don't bore me, okay?"

"That bores you?"

"Oh, Ancients, that can't be a serious question."

"All right, what do you want to talk about, my Lady?"

"I'm not a Lady."

"Will be soon."

"How soon?"

Thannuel stopped and turned to his intended. "You want to marry me? Truly? Not just out of obligation?"

Moira kissed him on the cheek. "Isn't it obvious?"

"We're being disgusting again, aren't we?"

She leaned closer, stopping just before her lips met his. "Do you want me to stop?"

Warm chills went up Thannuel's neck. "Um, no?"

"Good answer."

Just as Thannuel leaned his head down to meet Moira's lips, a commotion snared his attention, the vibrations rippling through the ground. A young man, not much older looking than Thannuel and a bit scrawny, stumbled out from the Bank of Thera and fell on his face in the street.

"Don't be coming back!" a well-dressed man shouted from the door before slamming it shut behind him.

"Wait here," Thannuel said to Moira.

He approached the young man and helped him to his feet. Dirt covered his shirt and stained his pants at the knees. He shrugged Thannuel off, pointlessly trying to brush the dirt away.

"I don't need your help!"

"Easy," Thannuel said. "Just lending a hand. What's going on?"

"It's not your business. And looks like you've been in a fine scrape yourself."

"You're right," Thannuel said calmly. "But maybe I can help."

He looked at Thannuel discerningly, then said, "What can you do? You're probably just some high-born louse."

He doesn't know who I am, Thannuel realized and thought better of telling him. *Why should it matter? Being a lord's son doesn't make me more or less willing to help.*

"Maybe, but just tell me what happened."

The young man dusted himself off. "Came here to get a loan for my dad's fishing business. He's sick, see? Traveled a long way but they said I'm too young and have no collateral." He looked a little abashed. "I didn't take it well but they were condescending! Talking down to me, you know? Actually, you wouldn't know by the look of you."

Thannuel raised an eyebrow. "Maybe more than you think. What did you do?"

He turned red. "Yelled at him. Told him if he cared more about people than his krenshell he might actually stop being so ugly."

"And he threw you out because of that?"

The young man's blush deepened. "No. He threw me out

because I told him to go kiss a hog."

Thannuel gave him a disbelieving look.

"Okay, I might have been a bit more vulgar than that, but I didn't want to offend your *noble* ears."

"Ah. That does make a little more sense." Thannuel paused. "How much krenshell are you looking for?"

"Two full silvers."

"It's not a huge sum but what would they be used for?"

"You're awfully interested for just randomly meeting me. Who are you?"

Thannuel shrugged. "Humor me."

He sighed, resigned. "It doesn't matter now. Every lender has turned me down. My dad's ship is old. Needs repairs. He's too ill to do it himself and we've not the money to hire help."

"Seems reasonable. Wouldn't they take the ship as collateral?"

"Well," the young man said, kicking at the street, "it's kind of a small ship, and might already have a lien against it."

"Might?" Thannuel pried.

He didn't answer.

"Look, I don't know you, and you're right, it's not my business. But that doesn't mean I can't help." Thannuel reached into his pocket. "I don't have any silvers, but I do have three full gold krenshell." He held out his palm with the money.

The young man's eyes lit up. "That's three cycles worth of food!"

"I will lend this to you," Thannuel said, "and you will pay me back someday, however you can."

Thannuel saw his eyes lighting up.

"Where are you from?" Thannuel asked.

"Faljier."

"You are a long way from home. Do you accept?"

"It's not a trick?" Suspicion was awash across his face.

"No, just one condition. Well, four actually. You must use the krenshell as I instruct, agree?"

The young man furrowed his thick black eyebrows. "What kind of conditions?"

"Hold out your hand. The first is for your father. You will hire a healer on your way home to see to him personally. The second is for food and clothing for your family. You have siblings? A mother?"

He just nodded.

"The third," Thannuel continued, "you may use for repairs to your father's ship."

"But, the cost to fix it is only two full silvers."

"The surplus is for you to pay off the lien against your father's ship, or as much of it as you can."

With a quivering jaw, the young man accepted the money. "Why?" he asked. "Why do this? Who are you?"

"Someone who is glad to be alive. What's your name?"

"Shane."

"Well, Shane, you accept my terms, yes?"

Shane nodded. "But you won't even tell me who you are. How will I repay you?"

"I'm sure the time will come when you will find a way."

"Ancients bless you, whoever you are," Shane said.

Thannuel walked back to Moira and took her soft hand in his.

"What was that about?" she asked.

Thannuel shrugged nonchalantly. "Don't know, really. Just someone who needed a hand."

Though the Gyldenal has preserved many of the Axioms of Light, they are often elusive, often only manifesting themselves in our times of greatest need; still, this is inconsistent, we find. The Light seems to choose when it allows itself to be harvested. The Ancient Dark, however, seems to have no inhibitions.

—Jayden, the wolf shepherd, as recounted by Mith'iah,
an archiver of the Jarwyn Mountains

EIGHT
~AMNOCH~
Day 24 of 3rd High 383 A.U.

REFLEX TOOK AMNOCH BACK A PACE off the sand, his lungs icing over.

What the burning Heavens?

He stood there, several heartbeats passing as he focused his senses, listening. Feeling. The gentle breeze still carried the sun's warmth as it pushed the makeshift headscarf off his neck. Through the air, a swirl of sands sailed lazily.

It could have been the sands just shifting under his feet, couldn't it? Or a rock just under the surface that moved under his weight? Why was he so shaken?

Now who's the poltroon?

He shook his head and scaled the clustered rocks to the peak, carefully avoiding the yahla plants. As he suspected, the Marishee survivor was nowhere in sight, but his tracks showed up in the sand almost like freshly plowed ground. The shallow ridge in the otherwise smooth terrain would make for easy trailing. And Amnoch would be able to run. Really run.

"About time," he said aloud. "That slow pace was killing me, it was."

The Master of the Hold Guard for House Kerr jumped down to the sand, the descent not more than twenty feet. He landed silently and was relieved that nothing felt unnatural under his feet this time. With sand spraying in his wake, he sprinted beside his mark's tracks at a wood-dweller's velocity.

After an hour of running, the tracks in the sand lightened, becoming shallower, before splitting into multiple sets of tracks heading off in different directions.

Amnoch stopped. What was this? Dumfounded, he stared at the tracks as if he could demand answers from them. Sand beat against his naked arms as the wind picked up, the air more tepid now. Which tracks were those of his quarry? He looked behind him to study the tracks more closely, hoping to compare those with the three diverging sets in front of him.

They were gone. His tracks and the Marishee's. Smooth, undisturbed sand flecked by random silver glimmers reflecting the moonlight confronted him. Whipping his head around, Amnoch glared at the three sets of tracks. They were still present.

Focus, think of nothing but this moment. The ancient axiom of Light drew his mind together, culminating his senses to a precision not known to those unfamiliar with the Gyldenal. The welling friction of apprehension he captured and redirected to enhance his vision. Looking forward, he spied what he thought to be the end of one line of tracks.

No, it moved. Extended. New tracks appeared in the sand under some invisible force. As his mind focused through the disbelief, he *did* feel something through the ground. Faint. Less vibration than even a wood-dweller. It would have been impossible to feel without the aid of the axiom, especially outside the Arlethian forests. Finding the heads of the other two trails, he saw their tracks extending as well.

I know this kind. Cankered souls roaming the depths. Ice formed in the hollow regions of his stomach.

Amnoch drew his dark blade.

"All things are matter," he whispered. "Seen or unseen, still matter, still mortal." As he infused more of his stored Light into the sword, its faint humming increased.

The sands underneath him rippled and rolled, becoming unstable as if he were on water. Amnoch ran forward, only his Arlethian dexterity keeping him upright as the desert roiled beneath him.

"Show yourself!"

In front of him, the sand arose and took form, clothing the desert wraith beneath it. Sand rolled off the humanoid shape as the wind exhumed more to replace it, the flowing sand giving an airy outline to the hollow wraith. The eyes lay hollow. Where the mouth would have been, a disfigured ovoid emptiness expanded. At the end of the arms, the falling sands outlined what appeared to be talons. Desert wraiths were said to swim in the sands like sharks in the oceans, not bothering men except in rare instances.

You're in trouble, he told himself.

"You are far from home, Arlethian." The wind carried the wraith's words all around Amnoch, echoing louder and softer.

"What have you to do with the Marishee? Why protect him?"

"Our concerns are beyond those of men, Arlethian."

"Then let me pass!"

"I cannot, for your concerns go beyond those of men, also."

"There need be no strife between us, *Shaung ol'Eihrin.*"

"We do not answer to this name any longer!"

"You were once of the *Lumenatis,* that Light that I serve. You do not serve the Ancient Dark. I ask you, in the memory of that which you once were, let me pass!"

The desert wraith stood silent as the wind wove between the falling sands, giving the illusion of a silken cloak upon its shoulders. Pinprick vibrations softly registered with each grain that fell. The ovoid gap posing as a mouth narrowed vertically.

Two more wraiths arose, surrounding Amnoch. He brought his sword to bear, praying the words would come should he need them, but the ancient axioms often eluded him.

"If you meant me harm, why not kill me before I sensed you?" Amnoch asked. "Why this game? And why protect the Marishee? What are they to you?"

No response came.

"Answer me!"

"They are nothing to us but a means to an end, Arlethian."

"But . . . the tracks. I don't understand."

"There are few of us left, Arlethian. We are desolation. We are abandonment. We are apostasy. We are wrath. We are solitude. We are dejection. We are anguish. We are wretchedness. We are bitterness. We are despair. We are woe."

"The sorrows of the world consumed your clan during The Turning Away," Amnoch said. "You took them upon you, I know, and carried the burdens of all for a time in an effort to ease pain and suffering. You still share the world's sorrows. It was your clan's gift, to lift burdens. You were noble. I seek to end that sorrow, to restore the Ancients, as do all my kind."

"We are woe."

"I have Light!" Amnoch said, striding one step forward. "I have hope. I carry it with me, even now, *ol'Eihrin.* Let me pass. Aid me and the Gyldenal to bring—"

"The Gyldenal?" the desert wraith said with an otherworldly laugh. There was derision there but also pain. "We three are all that are left. The weakening of the Living Light has nearly brought about our extinction."

"The Thoulden-sha and Marishee seek to destroy the *Lumenatis, ol'Eihrin!* They serve Noxmyra. The Keeper of the Living Light has seen it. If you die with the fading of the Light, then we are on the same side! Help me!"

"We are desolation. We are abandonment. We are apostasy. We are wrath. We are solitude. We are dejection. We are anguish. We are wretchedness. We are bitterness. We are despair. We are woe."

"What do you want?" Amnoch screamed.

"To die."

With terrible realization, Amnoch understood. "You . . . are the last."

"We are woe."

"You cannot die until the *Lumenatis* is extinguished, so you . . . you aid those who fight against it —"

"We are woe."

"In order to die."

Amnoch replayed their words in his mind. *We are woe. We* are *woe.* Sustained by the *Lumenatis,* their torment had raged for millennia until all the entropy they subsumed manifested physically, cankering their outward appearance until it reflected all they internally bore, being reborn as wraiths.

"There has to be another way." Amnoch said. "Or if you seek death to end your suffering, I offer you my sword."

"We cannot die by mortal means, Arlethian. You bring us nothing, only pain and continued misery by your existence. We see your current. It is an affront to us. All who serve the *Lumenatis* must perish, that we might also perish."

The desert wraiths' mouths opened wider, sucking in a torrent of sand as screeches bellowed from them. Alien vibrations careened in his ears, ricocheted within his chest. Amnoch tried to step back but found himself sinking. The sand rushed in faster than he could raise his legs and soon his ankles were submerged.

You're in trouble, he again told himself.

"Wait," a soft voice called out. Immediately, the screeching and sinking halted.

Over a small hill, walked a woman. Not a specter, an actual woman. Her step was confident, obviously familiar with the terrain. Extricating himself from the sand, Amnoch held his tongue as she approached, memorizing the unique vibrational signature of her gait. She wore a turban, typical of the fashion in these parts, if more ornate, and thin translucent clothing that left little to the imagination of what lay beneath. Her eyes were exotic beyond anything Amnoch had ever seen in his one hundred and seventy years, the deep green of emeralds encased by smooth almond skin. Behind the diaphanous veil covering her mouth, he saw her smile.

"You have met my pets, I see." The words from her lips were like cool satin over burned skin.

"Who are you?" Amnoch asked.

"One of those you seek. Come, I will take you to him." She held out a delicate hand.

"I don't think so."

"But you must. We must all be cleansed of the heretical bloodlines. The Thoulden-sha can help you. He will cleanse all Våleira."

"I'm here to cleanse the world of him, banshee. I would see his blood run down my sword."

"So certain, are you?" She let her outstretched hand fall, even that simple movement tantalizingly graceful. "Tell me your name, heathen, that I may tell my Oracle who it was that my wraiths dragged down into the desert's depths."

"You first."

She smiled again. Ancients, but she was beautiful.

"Very well. I am Anaveit. I am the first wife of Mari-shaden's Oracle, having given my first husband to the Altar of Influence for the sake of the Resurgence."

"And how is it the desert wraiths seem to obey you?"

"Your name, heathen."

"Master Amnoch, of House Kerr."

Anaveit looked at him curiously. "Kiarra? But you don't feel like one of them."

Amnoch immediately recognized the usage of the ancient Kerr name, something only the Gyldenal should have record of.

"I serve House Kerr, but I am not of their blood."

"No, you are something less refined." Anaveit looked up at first moon. "More of a blunt instrument, it seems."

"You won't find my blade blunt, banshee."

"Why kill me, Amnoch, servant of House Kerr?"

"I think it would brighten my day a bit, for starters."

"So honest. I see it in you. You will try to kill me. Am I such a threat?"

Amnoch looked at the wraiths, the sand still falling over their unnaturally still forms. "That depends. How many people have you and your pets killed?"

"Does it matter? They aid in the Resurgence of Mari-shaden. The blood of heretical bloodlines is required. He is waiting. Will you come?"

"*Shaung ol'Eihrin,* you are still of the *Lumenatis!* You cannot serve this creature of the Ancient Dark. I beseech you to remember who you were."

"She promises an end."

"Not an end, noble *ol'Eihrin,* just another beginning. The Living Light is fading, yes, but there are those that are still strong, still vibrant. Will you seek their end? Will you turn from your noble heritage of yoking yourselves with the sorrows of others to instead releasing pain and sorrow upon the world?"

"We are woe."

"Yes, you have become such, but for the sake of others! Without you, Våleira would have spun into an irrevocable degeneracy long ago. This banshee and those like her seek that for the world! They seek death for all of the *Lumenatis.* As your numbers have dwindled, so has suffering in the world increased. Do you not see? Your very existence blesses others, no matter what you have become. It is all connected. You must see!"

"We are but remnants and shadows of what you speak, Arlethian. We seek an end to the woe. We seek our death."

"You see, Amnoch, servant of House Kerr," Anaveit spoke, "their interests and those of the Marishee align." She unfastened her veil, revealing her face completely, and looked on Amnoch. He felt as though she were seeing all of him, combing through the very core of his sentience.

"You will make a welcome addition to the holy garment of the Thoulden-sha's Honored First. I will personally see to your body, do not worry." Her look turned predacious. "Kill him. Slowly."

The mouths of all three desert wraiths stretched wide. Ominous.

All things are matter. Seen or unseen, still matter. Mortal.

The sand below Amnoch again began to shift but he was better prepared this time. Jumping with friction-enhanced strength, he cleared the swirling sands and flipped backwards. He took his own admonishment that he heaped upon Thannuel and Antious and kept his feet moving lightly across the desert floor. The wraiths dove into the sand, moving toward him, the ground bulging and rippling as they swam, like serpents just beneath the surface. Diving into a forward roll, Amnoch attacked. He swiped his Jarwynian blade through the sand, attempting to cleave one of the wraiths lengthwise. His sword came free from the sand, bare of any ichor. Looking behind him, he saw that the slithering ripples continued unabated, the one that just passed him turning around.

From his left, Amnoch felt the change in the ground too late, the vibrations sloppy compared to the clarity felt in the Western Province.

"Burning Heavens!"

His left arm streamed blood as the desert wraith swept past him, tearing flesh. The surprise and fear friction coalesced within him and he captured it, dulling the pain of the wound. Just as another slithering ripple reached him, Amnoch thrust his blade in the ground at its head.

"Welkaira!"

A shock wave shot out from his sword and he saw the path of slithering sand reverse direction violently before becoming still.

"Felt that, did you?"

"We cannot be killed by mortal means, Arlethian," it spoke, invisible to Amnoch's sight.

"The Light I carry is not of mortal means, *ol'Eihrin*. You may kill me, but you will suffer first. Come, let me add to your woe."

The ground became quiet under him, the faint pulses of the wraiths vanishing. One rose in front of him, clothing itself again in the sands that shimmered silver under the light of first moon. A terrible beauty rested within the wraith's ethereal presence.

"We are woe."

"I carry *hope*."

Though it stood unmoved, Amnoch swore he could tell the wraith was pondering.

"But you are not hope," it finally said.

"Kill him!" Anaveit shrilled.

Woe, Amnoch thought. *What can kill woe?*

Dejection. Apostasy. Bitterness. Anguish.

Hope. But hope alone would not be enough, Amnoch realized, though it was the beginning. He would have to trust it was enough.

"Listen to me, *Shaung ol'Eihrin*, I beg of you. Find that remnant, that small shard of your former selves, and heed my words. If my life brings you less torment, then I offer it to you, freely; but you have not seen the hope that is budding anew. There is a boy, one of the old blood of *il'Kiarra,* whom I believe may have the capacity to restore the Ancients. He is young and headstrong, and does not know what he may yet become. *He* is hope, I promise you. He is becoming honor. He is becoming valor. Search me and see! I know you can discern my words."

"You are truth."

"If he does restore the Ancients, does this not take away the misery of the world? Does this not also end your watch over the calamity of men?"

"You are truth."

"If the Dark Mother does succeed and the Resurgence is completed, Those Not Remembered will again flourish and you will die with the Light. And your suffering will end, yes; but I offer you redemption from your suffering through *life*, not death."

Silence.

Amnoch persisted. "Your yoke will be loosened no matter who prevails, but the way of the *Lumenatis* grants you life! Be free of your woes *and* live. Are you so determined to become extinct? If you find fault in my words, *ol'Eihrin,* pull me under to the fathomless abyss." Amnoch thrust his sword into the ground, still humming with *Lumenati* Influence, and let it go. "I will not stop you."

"You are truth."

"He is false!" Anaveit screamed. "His heretical blood must flow!" Her green eyes darkened with hatred.

The other two desert wraiths materialized under cloaks of sand.

"You must kill him!" Anaveit's voice trembled. "The Thouldensha commands it! Mari-shaden's Oracle commands it!"

"She is subjection," they said in unison. "One of us."

The wraiths turned toward Anaveit.

"What are you doing?" She stepped back. "Kill him!" Gone was the confident demeanor.

"You are subjection, one of us, meant to share our yoke."

The winds plucked up the sands, howling as they spun, discordant against the wraith's screeching.

"No! You must kill him!"

"One of us," the wraiths shrieked.

Anaveit turned to run but the sands caught her before she could take a single step, the whirling vortex lifting her into the air. Her screams came as the coarse sand tore the clothing from her body, shredding it until no thread remained. The friction of horror Amnoch felt at the sight before him flowed unhindered. Suspending her naked in the air, the sand ripped into Anaveit's flesh at terrible velocity, forcing its way into her pores, removing layer after layer until her muscles and tendons lay exposed. Like a ravging fire, the sands eviscerated her organs from existence in moments, the harsh sediment pulverizing them as she writhed with unnatural jerking and twisting. Anaveit's wails mercifully ceased when her bare vocals chords were eroded away. Still shining like emeralds and glistening with malice, her eyes were the last of all her bodily tissue to be eviscerated. The bare skeleton fell to the earth with a dull clatter as the vortex of wind and sand dissipated.

"What … what have you done?" Amnoch asked, his breath short.

Beside Anaveit's pile of bones, Amnoch saw an impression form in the sand, then another. The first felt like a hand on the ground, the second a knee, like someone crawling. Though distinctly weaker, the vibrational signature was unmistakable. Anaveit. Another shallow impression formed under her invisible presence, the pulse in the ground heavy with pain and sorrow. A becalmed serenity prevailed upon the surreal night.

"What have you done to her?"

"She is subjection, one of us," the closest desert wraith answered. "She will now share our burden until we are free."

The wraiths faced Amnoch and the friction of apprehension shot through him. This time, he captured it, tense.

"We will no longer meddle in the affairs of men, Arlethian. You will either prevail or fail. Our freedom comes either way."

"Fight with us!" Amnoch implored.

"We are abandonment. We will remain aloof until that last day comes, when our release is assured."

"What of her?" Amnoch asked.

"She is one of us. She feels as we do, knows our burden, yoked as we are yoked."

"She suffers?"

"With us, without end, until that last day."

Amnoch swallowed hard and felt another heavily laden impression in the sand near Anaveit's skeleton. His eyes briefly flicked in her direction, then back to the wraith.

"You may go no further, Arlethian. Return to your hope. We pray he grows to what you seek."

"He will."

"You are misguided belief, Amnoch, servant of House Kerr, but still truth."

The flowing sands around the desert wraiths fell to the ground and did not rise again. Near Anaveit's bones, he sensed what felt like a small struggle. Amid the scurrying, small waves of sand clashed for several seconds before falling still again. Anaveit's vibrations disappeared as she was pulled under.

Amnoch sank to his knees, breathing heavily. His limbs shook with nervous energy, the adrenaline he had held in check released.

Ancients take me.

To his left, one wraith reappeared. Amnoch retrieved his sword, still sheathed in the sand, and stumbled to his feet.

"We are despair," it said. "This gift we leave with you, taking upon us the despair of what you have seen this night."

"What?"

The wraith's mouth opened wide.

"Wait!" Amnoch pleaded, but the wraith did not heed him. His mind seared with pain, as if being pummeled into fine splinters, and he felt the blackness of unconsciousness close in.

Amnoch awoke to the blinding sunlight. Bringing an arm up to shield his eyes, he sat up and took note of his surroundings: the familiar sight of two cascading outcroppings of white rock and yahla plants. His left arm burned slightly.

"What in the endless Night?" he said as he saw the wound, like something had slashed him.

Claw marks?

The gash was deep. When had that happened? Testing his arm, he found it free of any limited agility, but the confusion stayed with him. He didn't recall falling asleep. He didn't recall being attacked. As his mind toiled, he looked up to the spiky fronds protruding from the cracks. Had he ingested some poison from the yahla plants accidentally? Perhaps his stored Light had healed him after he passed out.

He stood up, slightly woozy, and took a tentative step. He brought a hand to his head and squeezed his eyes shut. The pain in his head . . . yes, it must have been accidental poisoning. Feeling for the stored Light within him, he found it nearly spent. *Best to save what's left*, he thought. He looked at his wounded arm again. If an animal had attacked him while he was passed out, it would have smelled the poison in his blood and left, wouldn't it have? The poison that nearly killed him instead saved him. Yes, it made sense . . . sort of.

The Marishee! he remembered.

Scanning the desert around him, he found neither sign of the man nor tracks in the sand. He knew there was no way to find his mark now. The man would be too far ahead to feel his vibrational signature and with no tracks to follow . . ..

"Blasted fool, you are!"

Squinting at the sun and ignoring the throbbing in his head, Amnoch turned northwest and began to walk home, wondering how he would explain this to Lord Kerr. He wasn't even sure what there was to explain.

"Yes, my Lord, you heard right. My sloppiness caused me to get poisoned, fall prey to some desert predator while sleeping it off, and lose the Marishee survivor. All in all a riveting success."

Something felt as if it were missing, though . . . some *part* of him. Turning south, he looked across the barren desert, searching one last time for . . . what?

A whisper came to him, something in the hot breeze. The words were almost inaudible. He listened. Felt. Focused through the pain in his head.

"You are . . . truth?"

After a moment, he shook his head. "You are a dimming fool, is what you are."

Turning back toward Arlethia, Amnoch ran, spurred by some warning inside him that would not relent, a warning that said he was not welcome to tarry longer. That same ethereal whisper found him again, floating upon the wind as if from beyond a thin veil, a supernal partition of worlds.

"We are all but remnants and shadows, Amnoch, servant of House Kerr."

Yes, I submitted. Ancients forgive me, but I could not tear my mind from that song! I wanted it, needed it. My very soul's continuance depended upon that melody weaving itself into me, creating a new tapestry of the Dark.

—Uncovered writings of Rehum Tarylgen, discovered by Holden Otheal

NINE

~THE THOULDEN-SHA~
Day 2 of 4th High 383 A.U.

THE THOULDEN-SHA COULD NOT CONTAIN his anger when only one of the eight he had sent returned from the West. The sole survivor, Galibrath, was wounded badly in his triceps. *And where is Anaveit?*

"It took you nine days to return and without the Kiarra boy?" The Thoulden-sha's words echoed through the narrow passageways, their timbre ominous as the sound reverberated louder.

"Please, my Oracle, we were outmatched! The boy and his friend were more skilled than we could have known. I myself barely escaped out of the West—"

"I care not for your excuses!" the Thoulden-sha thundered. "Because of your failure, we will be forced to move faster, before we are fully prepared. *You* have brought all the Marishee into great peril."

Around him, several hundred Marishee disciples stood, including the First among them, drabbed in tan, a contrast to the more typical black and gray garb worn by the Marishee. The wounded man knelt before the Oracle of Mari-shaden.

"I will go back with another group," Galibrath said, quivering. "We will succeed this time. We will not underestimate our prey again, I swear it!"

"You have failed, and you know the price Mari-shaden demands."

Galibrath glanced toward the altar, the same that he had watched so many unbelievers' blood flow over.

"We need an advantage," Galibrath said. "These wood-dwellers are too fast for us to fight without greater numbers; but with greater numbers we sacrifice stealth. Perhaps if we infiltrated slowly with more Marishee, then we—"

"I do not require counsel from those who fail me!"

The Thoulden-sha's face contorted, as if in pain, as he focused his fury upon Galibrath. The kneeling man tried to speak, probably to offer another excuse, but the Thoulden-sha did not let another word escape the derelict's mouth. With the Influence of Mari-shaden, limited though it was, he felt through the man's anatomy, finding his throat and airways. With a twist of his mind, he crushed them, causing Galibrath's eyes to bulge in surprise and pain. Mutters arose from the other Marishee who stood close enough to see clearly what had happened.

As the Thoulden-sha stared vehemently at the gasping man, now clutching at his throat, a sneer worked its way onto his face and Galibrath's nose began to bleed. A strange noise came from the dying man as whispered screams escaped his collapsed throat. His eyes rolled up into the back of their sockets until only milky white orbs remained. Sickening cracks were heard, like a miniature earthquake, as the Thoulden-sha used his Influence to send fault lines through Galibrath's cranium. The man slumped forward, dead.

Muhktar came forth and inspected the corpse.

"It is acceptable," he said. "I will prepare the body."

Shaking with the effort, the Thoulden-sha used the last remnants of his strength to address the Marishee as Muhktar dragged Galibrath away. He did his best not to appear haggard or short of breath.

"Only those worthy will survive to see the Resurgence of Marishaden. Galibrath learned what it was to be *unworthy*."

After he spoke his warning, the Thoulden-sha retreated to a cave that he had made his secret dwelling, nearly collapsing from the effort he had displayed. His disciples must not see how limited his powers truly were; they must only see strength.

The jagged walls he felt as he stumbled along extended up over a hundred feet before opening narrowly to the sky above. Every touch, every peak and valley, every contour of the natural stonewalls was familiar to him. Without this web of narrow passages and slot canyons the temperature could be intolerable, especially during the high season; however, it was almost always chilly inside this comforting maze, where direct sunlight never shone.

When he reached the cave and entered, ensuring he was fully out of sight, he did collapse. His whole body ached and burned with a fever. It angered him that so much physical and mental strength had to be utilized to bring an end to just one unworthy person.

Without the blood of Kiarra, I will never harness enough of Mari-shaden's Influence.

As sleep forced its way upon him, dread of the escalated schedule of events ahead weighed heavy upon him.

Continue your progression, he heard Mari-shaden whisper to his heart. *Upon the altar you will eventually retrieve all my Influence from the moons. In time, I shall bring Marishee as nearly countless as the stars to this land by your hand.*

Helsya only exists in our dreams, I fear. Perhaps . . . perhaps our dreams are part of the curse levied by the Lumenatis, not the soothings of the Ancient Dark.

—Scratchings discovered upon the walls of the Kail
in the Northern Province by Master Amnoch

TEN

~MAYNARD~

Day 12 of 2nd Dimming 388 A.U.

MAYNARD SLEPT IN THE HIBERNATION CHAMBER of the Kail with his other Helsyan brethren. A stone slab was all that was required to sleep upon, almost an open-air sepulcher. The Kail, an ancestral home for his kind since The Turning Away, was in the Northern Province near what was presently Hold Wellyn. The ruling house of the Senthary had built their home near the Kail after wresting control of his race from their previous masters during the

Sentharian invasion almost four hundred years ago, keeping themselves near their most closely guarded secret. Whoever had the Stone of Orlack, the *urlenthi*, he would obey without question.

But not by choice.

During the past three years and seven cycles—the tracking of time was not lost during hibernation—Maynard had traveled in the land of dreams, in a world of things that would never be; a world where he and his people were not marred from the crowns of their heads to the soles of their feet with unintelligible symbols and patterns seemingly carved into their pasty, nacreous skin from the womb; a world where the mothers who bore them lived beyond childbirth and reared them into maturity. In his dream, he was not a monster, not a being of the Ancient Dark, not a creature whose sole purpose of existence was to bring an end to the existence of others. It was the same dream upon his mind every time the *urlenthi* allowed him to hibernate, one he felt was almost a memory passed on from his ancestors.

Eighteen: all that remained of his once great people. Being the oldest of those whom lived, he'd been appointed the leader of this clandestine brotherhood of assassins by Prime Lord Wellyn eleven years ago, after the previous Helsyan leader died. The death of a fell reaper—their more common, informal name—was an event that went unnoticed by the world. It was never in the open, where others could witness; never by the hand of another, for reapers were never prey; not by disease or illness, for reapers were immune to the ailments of most men due to the Dark Mother's Influence. Rather, the end of a Helsyan came simply by old age, living well past a century.

The *urlenthi* commanded Akis, the last Helsyan leader, to breed with a woman before he died, ensuring their number stayed at eighteen after he was gone. A male Helsyan was born, as always, and the mother died during childbirth, as always. The youth, Rembbran, was only forty-four seasons—eleven years; but like most of his race, ten years saw him fully grown. The Helsyan boy slumbered in hibernation on a stone slab a couple yards from Maynard.

The past year, the Helsyan leader's rest had been shallower, more fitful. He could sense it in his brethren as well. Something was coming, something almost familiar; it did feel ominous, but he was not sure that was a bad thing—for him.

"Awake."

The word powerfully pulled him from his slumber, demanding his attention. He sat up, his body neither aching nor sore. The dust of his robe swarmed through the air at the disturbance.

Before him stood Prime Lord Parlan Wellyn; and over his tunic lay the sigil of House Wellyn, a four-pointed star flare, emblazoned on a round gold amulet. Recessed on the backside of the amulet was a faintly luminescent, milky-white mineral: the Stone of Orlack, the *urlenthi.*

There was a mission required of him or one of his brethren that demanded furtiveness, a mission that could not be failed—the only reason a Helsyan was Charged.

"I will give you a *dahlrak*, Maynard," Wellyn spoke. "A Charge that I require carried out with the utmost haste."

The anticipation of a *dahlrak* being extended to him made his mouth water. It was what his race lived for, to execute a Charge under the *urlenthi's* will.

"As the stone commands, I obey," Maynard answered, unable to keep the near-seething from his voice.

"There is one in the southern parts of the Eastern Province," Wellyn said, "in or around the village of Dispa, a man known as the Thoulden-sha. He has ceded from the Realm, taking several thousand of my people with him."

The Prime Lord stopped, as if remembering he did not need to explain the reasons for a *dahlrak*.

Wellyn held up a piece of paper, a rolled parchment. Maynard instinctively flared the gills that ran up the bridge of his nose, taking in the parchment's scent.

"This was delivered to me yesterday," Wellyn explained. "It contains, among other things, a message from this Thoulden-sha, declaring his claim to lead those who have followed him as an independent nation. I believed he would have had someone else write the message on his behalf, but my advisers believe he composed the message by his own hand. It would be fitting for one as arrogant as he appears to be, I suppose."

"What do you wish of me?" Maynard asked.

"I Charge you with tracking this scent and destroying he who scrawled it. I *give* him to you by this *dahlrak*."

Maynard, with his blighted appearance, felt the *dahlrak's* endowment of power come upon him, through him, quickening his naturally powerful frame, granting him velocity that only wood-dwellers of the West were believed to possess, and strength that a dozen men—not even the Prime Lord's Khansian Guard—could match. His nervous system deadened, making pain more tolerable; eyesight and hearing sharpened, but his sense of smell—that sense all fell reapers had that could perceive the emotions of others— remained the same, requiring no enhancement. The gill-like slits on the bridge of his nose could discern, within the degrees of the emotional scent emitted, gender and even the motive behind the scent. Prime Lord Wellyn, for example, felt anger coupled with annoyance. A strand of concern about him being perceived as a weak leader because of this Thoulden-sha's rebellion laced the air, but it was dissipating.

Above all, Maynard felt the *urge*, the compulsion of the Charge he had been given, swirling inside him like a storm that would never be sated without the death of the one given him.

"When?" he asked.

"Leave now," Wellyn said. "Once you get near Dispa, you should be able to pick up his scent ... assuming the Thoulden-sha wrote this message."

"There is defiance in the odor, my Liege. A hint of ... daring, tempting."

"He wants me to respond?"

Maynard's nose gills flared. "I would say he expects it."

"He will not be expecting *you*, I am certain."

"No one ever does, my Liege."

Left unsaid by Maynard was something else he smelled from the parchment, something he found curious. The odor was undeniably present, strong even ... but not identifiable. Fear, however—that scent most tantalizing and succulent to a Helsyan—was not present.

Not yet, Maynard thought.

Three days later, after making his way south, crossing over almost the entire Eastern Province, Maynard came to the general location of Dispa. Rolling sand dunes presented themselves and seemed to shimmer in the moonlight. Interrupting the rippling landscape were formations of rock, jutting into the air maybe a hundred feet at the pinnacles. He could see open mouths, thin inlets, at the base of the closest formation.

The narrows, as they are called, he thought.

The wind brought him the scent he sought, and he salivated as the urge of the *dahlrak* propelled him forward, following the odoriferous trail. He came to one of the inlets. It was indeed narrow, wide enough for two people in parts, constricting to be slim enough for only a child as it wove.

Not this one.

Walking a few steps to the right, he saw another trailhead. He took in the air, flaring his nose gills. The scent was strong, directly ahead. Maynard nearly dashed full bore into the high-walled, slender path when a new smell came to him.

He knows I'm here, Maynard thought with surprise. *He is ... waiting for me.* Further, Maynard realized the Thoulden-sha had at least an inkling of what he was.

How?

The Thoulden-sha stepped into view. Though it was night, he could see the man wore a black turban that covered his head and most of his face.

"Welcome, brother."

"You know me?" Maynard asked.

"I recognize the power that aids you, brother," the Thoulden-sha said. "The power of Mari-shaden."

"Your gibberish means nothing to me!"

"Come closer, Helsyan. Come and see."

"How do you know of me? Of my kind?" Maynard asked.

"Mari-shaden has shown me a vision by the blood of infidels upon my altar, a vision in which I saw you coming. We are nearly kin, you and I. Come closer and see."

The Charge given to Maynard suddenly felt slippery, its potency lessening.

No!

Determined to taste this man's fear and fulfill his *dahlrak,* Maynard closed the distance of roughly twenty feet in a blur, bringing his sword over his head to cleave the man in two. But in the instant before he struck, when his eyes locked with the Thoulden-sha's, the *dahlrak's* presence fled from him. It was a different feeling than fulfilling a Charge: no euphoria was present. But, neither was the urge any longer, the urge that would turn to unbearable pain by refusing or failing to carry out a *dahlrak*. Or, so they believed. For no reaper had ever failed in his mission.

"Those of Mari-shaden have no need to destroy one another," the Thoulden-sha said.

As Maynard stared into his former prey's eyes, an understanding pierced him.

"The Dark cannot fight itself," he said.

The Thoulden-sha let down the part of his turban that covered his mouth. Maynard saw a smile there.

"Tell your false master," he said, "that he will soon be consumed by the Influence of Mari-shaden if he does not renounce his rule and subject himself to me. He, and all of Senthara, must join the Marishee."

Maynard listened. "I cannot command the Stone."

"You are commanded only by Mari-shaden," the Thoulden-sha answered. "Though your master wields control over you now, when the Resurgence is complete, I shall shatter that hold. Then, brother, you shall fight the cursed bloodlines of the Ancients by my side, free from all the burdens placed upon you. That bit of knowledge is for you alone."

There was power in this man's words. They resonated with his dreams, like a storyweaver singing in harmony with his fiddle.

"But my *dahlrak* cannot go unfulfilled," Maynard said. "It is—"

"Gone. I have taken it from you, swallowed it up in Mari-shaden. You will not suffer."

Maynard felt uncertainty, even … a small line of anxiety in this man's presence.

"Free me!" Maynard said. "Break the *urlenthi's* control over us!"

"I cannot. Not yet. Not until the Resurgence is complete will I have the fullness of Mari-shaden's Influence. For now, you must return to your false master."

Maynard looked to the side. "I cannot lie to the Prime Lord. I will have to report that I could not carry out his orders. He will send more; if not my kind, then others."

The Thoulden-sha smiled again. "Arlethians."

Maynard sneered. The rift between his race and the Arlethians seemed ageless, a hereditary hatred.

"Worry not, brother," the Thoulden-sha comforted. "We look forward to their arrival."

Anaveit chose new wives for the Thoulden-sha—those she declared worthy—from every village and settlement conquered by the Marishee. The expansion of their state was brilliant, focusing more on ideology than physical borders, using weaponry that cannot be countered by the sword and spear.

—Echoes of Shadenism: The Birth and Death of the Marishee

ELEVEN
~PARLAN WELLYN~
Day 27 of 2nd Dimming 388 A.U.

ISKELL STOOD AS A CITY OF MIGHT. Prime Lord Parlan Wellyn thought of it more as a fortress than actual city when compared to other state cities of the Realm. Battlements, ramparts and towers not only surrounded Hold Wellyn, but most of the city as a whole, looking as if it expected to be besieged at any moment despite the relative peace the Sentharian people had enjoyed for roughly a century.

But Iskell was not just a state city, it served as the capital of the

Realm, where House Wellyn had ruled for nearly four centuries after defeating House Kearon and her allies, winning the right to rule the Senthary. House Kearon and her allies had long been forgotten, forced to exist in the fringes of the Realm, no citizenry or status. Most lived in the Schadar Desert, eking out an existence that could not actually be called *living.* It was said throughout the Realm of the Kearon that they existed but did not live.

Within the walls of Wellyn's council hall, all four provincial lords sat around a long stone table. Sjoni'ah, the seemingly ever-present Archiver who had been assigned to House Wellyn decades earlier, stood at his place behind the Prime Lord. A man in the robes of the Changrual also occupied the hall.

The pressing nature of the meeting was only exacerbated by the failure of Maynard to eliminate the Thoulden-sha. Wellyn had wanted to cut the head of the serpent off, hopefully leaving the body of the rebellion to die. He had no understanding of how Maynard's Charge had been dismissed by this man who defied him, but if he could counter the Influence of the *urlenthi*—something never to have happened, to his knowledge—then the Thoulden-sha could neutralize the Realm's most powerful weapon. This thought made him feel impotent, a feeling the Prime Lord would not tolerate.

"Thank you for coming," Prime Lord Wellyn said in opening. "I believe you all know why you have been called here. I have asked High Vicar Rehum Tarylgen, preceptor of the Changrual Monastery, to join us, hoping he may have insights beyond the political."

"Clearly this is a matter for Lord Orion," Lord Hoyt said. "This is happening in the Eastern Province. The South is threatened now because of his indifference."

"Threatened?" Lord Orion asked. "I'd hardly call a couple thousand desert dwellers a threat, dear man."

"Sedition threatens us all," Branton offered. "I have seen these

Marishee when they were about to sacrifice another man in secrecy. They attacked my son, in our own province. For them to now declare independence from the Realm is a sure sign of their boldness. I do not see peace for the Realm if they are allowed to continue."

"Even more to the point, I cannot allow sedition of any kind in the Realm," Wellyn said. "It cannot be tolerated."

"The Granite Throne cannot appear weak," Lord Gonfrey of the Northern Province agreed. He spoke without moving his mouth.

"Again, this is Lord Orion's problem," Hoyt said. "His failure to secure his own province has put us all at risk."

"Try governing a province twice that of your province's size and thrice as populated!" Orion snapped. "Besides, they have not done anything wrong, save for setting up a different orthodoxy." Glancing at the High Vicar, he said, "I apologize, preceptor. I don't mean to diminish the seriousness of the spiritual depravity these Marishee have shown. You are, of course, aware of my province's devotion to the Changrual Order."

Rehum Tarylgen nodded but did not say anything.

"I want a quick resolution to this 'depravity', as you have put it, Lord Orion," Wellyn said. "But it is not simply a problem of the East. Lord Kerr's son was nearly taken, his intended nearly killed. This Thoulden-sha heretic has recruited from all provinces, most heavily from the Southern Province. As if this were not enough, he has declared himself the ruler of an independent nation within the Eastern Province of my Realm."

Wellyn remained silent for a time, allowing his words to permeate.

"The Order insists on a revival of devotion," Tarylgen said. "Hairline fractures of faith often lead to chasms of division among people of all create. Only strict adherence to the Ancient Heavens and the scrolls can heal hearts that have torn themselves asunder."

Lord Gonfrey rolled his eyes while Lord Orion nodded.

"I will send a battalion of two and a half thousand men," Wellyn announced, arising from his chair with chin in hand. "Five hundred from each province plus an equal complement of my own Khansian Guards. They will mass at the military academy in Erynx and from there depart."

"Very good, your Grace," Orion said. "I shall assign High Lord Marshall Hawkes to lead the assault."

"No, you will not, Lord Orion," Wellyn countered. "You lost any moral authority you might have otherwise had in this matter by allowing sedition in your own province!"

"My Lord," Branton said. "May I perhaps make a suggestion as to a leader for this Battalion?"

"Please, speak freely," Wellyn granted, obviously holding no contempt for the Lord of the Western Province.

"I believe your Grace intends to resolve the matter with as little bloodshed as possible. To that end, appointing a military man, an officer, to lead the battalion may not be the wisest course of action. You need someone that can command a military force but also negotiate on behalf of the Realm; someone the Thoulden-sha will take seriously."

"Branton," Wellyn replied, "I have no intention of sending one of my provincial lords into harm's way, Arlethian or not."

"Not me personally, my Lord. I was thinking, perhaps, my son, Thannuel."

"He's barely a man!" Lord Orion said. "Your Grace, I know of the boy's skill with steel, but he has never done anything like this. He is not skilled in politics and has never led a military force."

"I agree with Lord Orion, strange as that feels," Lord Hoyt said.

"As a *boy* of sixteen," Kerr said, glaring at Orion, "Thannuel defeated eight of the Marishee, along with his friend, Antious Roan, who is now a corporal in the Arlethian army. However, he is a man now at twenty-one and married. He has become a skilled leader, running most of the hold and attending to the majority of the matters of state at my side. My own Master of the Hold Guard, extremely accomplished with steel, can no longer beat Thannuel in swordplay.

"I feel it is important that the Thoulden-sha deal with someone who is not anxious to swing his blade but knows is a serious threat if it came to that."

Lord Kerr paused. "If my Lord will permit me, I insist that my son be allowed this obligation. He will not fail."

Are you still in there, Tyjil? I feel you tinkering with my head.

—Recorded by Ethan, a Khansian Guard,
as he stood his post outside of Tyjil's quarters

TWELVE
~THANNUEL~

Day 10 of 3rd Dimming 388 A.U.

"WHAT KIND OF EMISSARY, claiming to come on peaceful terms, has an army at his back?" the Thoulden-sha asked.

Several of his guards, dressed in loose black and gray clothing with a red sash across their mid-section, attended him. The black turbans upon their heads were an all too eerie reminder of his encounter with several Marishee in Calyn years ago ... but his friends were far from here now. Safe.

One guard, however, was robed completely in tan and light brown clothing, from his turban to his boots, almost blending into the hold's walls. The cloth was heavier in appearance than what the other Marishee wore. Even the scabbard that held his sword matched in color. For reasons he could not explain, this troubled Thannuel.

"Are you here to start a civil war, young Kerr?"

Thannuel remained calm. It *was* true, he had marched to the southeast part of the Eastern Province at the head of two thousand, five hundred soldiers, five hundred of them Arlethians. He and the Thoulden-sha met in an impressively built hold, although small in comparison to most noble houses. Nestled against a cliff face, the back of the hold opened to a delta of stone arteries that wound deep into an erratic maze of narrows. Thannuel felt a cool breeze occasionally, something odd for a structure with no noticeable windows or openings. Angled slits were in the walls and ceiling in certain places but not for light.

Vents, he realized. The air from them was unusually cool for this part of the Realm. *How did they—*

"The narrows," the Thoulden-sha answered Thannuel's thoughts. "The air in them rarely sees the sunlight, remaining cool. It is one of the blessings of Mari-shaden to understand how to wield the world's elements. You, of course, would not understand."

Or maybe just some halfway decent engineering, Thannuel silently countered, but he was actually impressed.

They sat together on thick round cushions atop a floor of sandstone, symbols of an ornate create expertly carved into the surface, forming intricate shapes and designs that flowed from the floor, up several pillars and continued their sprawling pattern upon the domed ceiling, appearing to be one grand design as it ebbed and flowed, separated and reconnected.

"It is the story of the Mari-shaden," the Oracle explained, obviously noting Thannuel's interest as his eyes followed the symbols. "Those Not Remembered were the originators of this world, *not* your Ancients. Mari-shaden has shown this truth to me."

"Strange name, don't you think?" Thannuel asked. "Those *Not* Remembered? Kind of a contradiction in terms since we are sitting here talking about them."

The Thoulden-sha smiled. "It is your heretical Changrual Order's name for them, not mine. Their true name is sacred and not worthy to be known, much less spoken, by those who have not thrown off their blasphemous genealogy."

"Huh."

Despite his outward expression of indifferent curiosity, Thannuel was indeed drawn to one grouping of glyphs in the center of the floor. They were more prominent than the others. Thirteen with one additional symbol, the most deeply carved, above them.

"What are those?" he asked. "What do they represent or say?"

"They are those who are most important in Mari-shaden's Resurgence."

"And … you're the top symbol, I'm guessing?"

Hesitation. Then, "I will not disburse sacred knowledge to those not yet worthy of it, young Kerr."

"Well, you know, if you still have a hammer and chisel lying around I'd love to add my name somewhere."

The Thoulden-sha's eyes darkened.

"Maybe on the wall in your chambers? Or, the ceiling, perhaps, right above your bed?"

The man in tan stepped forward with hostile intent, but the Thoulden-sha stopped him. "No, Muhktar."

A wave of … *something* seemed to press against Thannuel when the man took a step forward, as if his movement had displaced a physical force that had been separating them, shoving it into Thannuel.

"I think we should come to the business at hand," the

Thoulden-sha said. "Are you here to assassinate me, sparking civil war?"

Thannuel smiled coyly and said, "Now, I believe civil war is what you tried to stir up five years ago by your attempted abduction of me and the murder of my friends and intended."

"Rogue disciples, I assure you," the Thoulden-sha replied, waving a hand dismissively. "As you know, I had no knowledge of their actions. I sent envoys to your father, apologizing for that unfortunate … misunderstanding. Seems you were able to mete out a proper punishment for them."

Thannuel couldn't help but feel that the Thoulden-sha meant they had been punished for failing to capture him rather than for the purported unauthorized attempt. But, he did not wish to debate the differing versions of history.

"Prime Lord Wellyn desires a peaceful resolution," he said. "There is no need for bloodshed. He has authorized me to grant pardons to all those who renounce their allegiance to this rebellion and the false nation you have attempted to establish. No harm or punishment will fall upon your disciples if you disband now. He has also agreed to give you a formal forum in Iskell to express your grievances and promises to engage in good faith negotiations."

"Ah, the false leader in the north is threatened by the growth of my rule," the Thoulden-sha said. Thannuel thought he could see a satisfied smile behind the turban that covered his mouth. "He fears the truth I spread among the people, the truth of Mari-shaden's return to the world; he fears the *Resurgence.*"

Thannuel remained on message, not allowing himself to be dragged into a religious conversation in which he had no foundation. "The Prime Lord wishes the best life for all within the Realm. He urges you to end the sedition that has grabbed your heart and allow your people to return to full fellowship within the Realm, as law-abiding citizens, not as insurrectionists."

"It is neither I nor my disciples who are insurrectionists, heathen!" the Thoulden-sha snapped. "We seek to restore the rightful power that was stripped from the world by *your* ancestors!"

"Are we not all descendants of the Ancients?" Thannuel asked.

"The Marishee have been freed from that cursed lineage, our blood changed by Mari-shaden's Influence. We are above this world and its people, having become the descendants of Those Not Remembered."

After saying this he made a gesture with his hands, forming a circle with both hands then bringing it to the center of his chest. Finally, he opened his hands, palms up, as his arms spread.

Thannuel did not have time for meaningless discussions. He would rather be teaching pigs to sing.

"So, just get on with it, then," Thannuel said with mock impatience. "Restore the power of Marin Shroeder, or whoever. What are you waiting for?"

"The time has not yet arrived, infidel. But soon, very soon, you shall see Mari-shaden's power walking upon this land again. Yes, even the whole world. Already you can see evidence of the Resurgence everywhere … if you have eyes to see."

"Well, that sounds like a threat to me, Thoulden-sha," Thannuel said as he stood up, dusting off his hands. "You've heard what the Prime Lord is offering. If you do not accept by tomorrow evening, it will be seen as open aggression against the Granite Throne by you and your followers and you will be attacked. I cannot be clearer. You have seen the forces at my command outside your walls."

"Have you seen mine?"

Thannuel did not answer. The scouts he had sent around the hold earlier had only caught sight of a dozen or so armed guards. There were many others—civilians by the look of it—who populated different areas of the hold.

"You have not, have you?"

The Kerr heir shrugged and started to walk out.

"I warn you, infidel," the Thoulden-sha said, "we are more prepared than you could possibly know."

"We'll take our chances."

"Ah, there's the indifferent arrogance I knew I would see. Perhaps," the Thoulden-sha said to Thannuel's back as he exited the hold, "we shall finish what we started five years ago."

Thannuel stopped and turned his head, looking over his shoulder. "Now you admit that it was you. I'm sure you understand that's not shocking, but attempting to harm me will only result—"

"Who said anything about *you*?"

"Send a bird to Hold Kerr," Thannuel commanded after returning to his camp. He had resisted sprinting from the Thoulden-sha's hold as a sign of control, or unconcern; but his heart raced as he walked back. The distance somehow seemed much longer than it had before. And his head—it pounded something fierce. He had never experienced a headache before but figured this must be one.

"Your fastest bird, master keeper. Inquire as to the safety of Lady Moira. Have Master Amnoch place her under constant watch."

"I'll send a falcon, my Lord."

"How long will it take for the message to reach my father?"

"This far out … I'd say two days, but maybe three."

Thannuel cursed and then nodded. "Make it happen. Now."

Fallen Ancients, please watch over her.

oira Kerr loved to walk the paths north of the Kerr Hold. She was not quite used to the lavish surroundings of her new family's home and these early morning walks helped her remember that the simple things in life often brought the most peace. In fact, her favorite time of the morning was now, just after second moon had set, when only the stars cast their light in the sky.

The veins in the leaves of the triarch trees radiated their faint luminescence in the forested canopy hundreds of feet above. Going to the nearest triarch, she placed her hand upon the bark, palm flush, and just listened. Memories came to her of when her sister, Molina, and she would lie on their roof at night, staring up at the sparkling canopy, and imagine constellations in the glowing triarch leaf veins. When the wind would blow, rustling the leaves, the images were washed away and they would start over again once the breeze calmed. The soft sound of the waterfall near their house was comforting, often lulling her to sleep as a child. She missed that a great deal now, especially with Thannuel away.

Perhaps I should visit Kalisa, Moira thought. She had seen her parents and Molina recently and their village of Wenrho was at least half a day's travel. Kalisa was barely an hour away, even for a casual pace. Antious's platoon was not assigned to accompany Thannuel on his diplomatic mission. If Kalisa's father were away, Antious would actually be allowed in the house and the three of them could have their evening meal together.

I'm sure Antious tried to get himself assigned to Thannuel's detail, foolish boy.

She smiled. Antious was not a boy anymore, not the same shy though often rash teenager she had first met years ago after her engagement to Thannuel had been officially announced.

That night, she remembered. *The Doonalin Falls … it changed him.*

Gone was any lightheartedness in Antious, giving himself fully to training with Master Amnoch, much more than even Thannuel. She knew Antious blamed himself for being captured, forcing Thannuel to pursue him and put himself back into a life-threatening situation on Antious's behalf after he had defeated his own assailants. This, according to Kalisa, was something Antious had a hard time forgiving himself for, for not being stronger and faster, having to rely on someone else to save him.

It had changed all of them, if she were truthful with herself. It was the first time her life had truly been in danger; and not just any danger, but that of someone else intentionally trying to *kill* her. Some women would have been shaken from that experience, realizing the true peril that could come with marrying into a noble house, never mind the *ruling* house of the West. After seeing how Thannuel had put her first, protecting her above himself and even Antious—something she would have never asked of him—her love for Thannuel had blossomed completely. She could not have stayed away even if she had wanted to.

She decided she would visit Kalisa. Somehow, it would make her feel closer to Thannuel, even if he was hundreds of miles away. If nothing else, they could at least laugh together at the foibles of the men they loved.

Moira felt the vibration too late. A hand reached out from the thick-trunked tree she touched as she reminisced, grabbing her long ebony hair and pulling her head back, hard. Other vibrations rang out loudly as others, men by the timbre of the pulses through the ground, surrounded and grabbed her arms. She squirmed vigorously, but before she could scream, another hand clamped down over her mouth followed by the touch of something cold at her neck. She instantly became still, breathing heavily through her nose.

Looking sidelong at her captors, the terror of returning from the Doonalin Falls five years ago came rushing back to her, images of narrow alleys and men in black, looking exactly like the men she now stared at; except her beloved Thannuel was not with her now, not here to defend her. A tear streamed down the left side of her face as she screamed into the man's hand.

It seemed the ramifications of the Thoulden-sha's declaration of sovereignty had far-reaching tentacles. She felt foolish for not taking precautions, for allowing something like this to befall her a second time. The Marishee had obviously been waiting for her, perhaps in place for hours before she began her stroll. She confirmed with sight what she had felt from the ground before she was bound, gagged, and a hood thrown over her head.

Three, two of medium build, one taller and slender.

Moira and Thannuel had been married only a year. Everyone told her that being married to a Provincial Lord, or the heir to that position, would be taxing at times. She had felt prepared for the stresses of marrying into a noble family, but wondered if those who spoke those warnings had abduction in mind.

She tried to keep her wits about her. *If they have not killed me yet, they want me alive.*

This gave her renewed courage to fight. Moira struggled against her bonds but it was useless. Still, she was determined to make as much of a scene as possible, disturbing the brush and environment enough to leave signs of her struggle. Thrashing wildly with her legs, she felt bark from a nearby triarch come loose and the smaller twigs of bushes snap under her kicks. Someone would come looking for her eventually. If not Thannuel, then others.

Her jaw was clenched so tight that her teeth cut through the gag. It loosened and she pushed it out with her tongue.

"Just wait until Amnoch and Antious find you!" she screamed.

"There will be no mercy unless you let me go now!"

A strike to her stomach knocked the wind out of her followed by a cold, dull pain that erupted on the left side of her head before all went black.

Master Amnoch had been worried since midday and was nearly certain something was wrong. The safety of all those who dwelled within the walls of Hold Kerr was his responsibility, with a primary focus upon the Lord of the Western Province. But the young Lady Kerr had not returned from her usual morning walk in the woods north of the hold and evening was not far off. Casual inquiries amongst the hold's servants had not yielding anything of note, only that Moira had gone on her typical morning excursion. The whirlpool-shaped clouds of the dimming season were turning a collage of orange, pink, purple, and red as the sun hung low in the sky, lazily settling into the western horizon.

Lord Branton Kerr had asked after Moira as well. His lordship got around less and less now, generally needing to rest, as his nights were fitful. This cough had been with him for years and he could not overcome it. Amnoch had secretly tried to heal his lord one night as Branton slept, but the Light was fickle at times, especially in healings, sometimes choosing to not allow itself to be harnessed. Amnoch had not become fluent enough in the Living Light to understand why this was, but others who had had centuries' worth of experience still admitted ignorance in many areas pertaining to the Lumenatis.

The later in the day it became, the more Amnoch saw Branton pace.

Perhaps she just took the day, Amnoch thought. *Went to her sister's, to visit her father. She's a grown woman and her husband is away. Yes, she probably went to see family.*

"She would have said something," Branton remarked, looking at Amnoch, as if knowing his thoughts. They stood in the grand courtyard of the hold at the foot of one of the many elevated pathways.

"Maybe," Amnoch said, but he knew Branton was right.

"Send a messenger to her sister and father," Branton commanded. "In the meantime, take a few men and begin to scour the woods. The kennel master has some new breed in from the Iskell kennels, supposed to be great trackers."

Master Amnoch nodded. "Yes, my Lord."

"Oh, and Amnoch, send a messenger to find Antious. I have a feeling he will want to know. But keep it quiet."

"Master Amnoch!" Antious yelled as he entered the hold from one of the elevated pathways, appearing to almost be sliding down it from the canopy above. He purposely hit the ground hard, announcing his presence through his vibrational signature. It was akin to yelling for a wood-dweller. "*Amnoch!*"

"Easy, son."

Antious whirled to find Lord Kerr behind him. He immediately bowed to one knee.

"Stand up, corporal," Branton said. "I am glad you are here. How long have you been sprinting? You have a wind-blown cast about you and your hair is matted straight back with sweat."

"My Lord, I am sorry to have lost composure and to appear

disheveled before you. I came as soon as I heard."

"Nonsense. You fill that uniform out well, Antious."

"He's still a runt," Master Amnoch said, approaching from behind Branton. "I'll need you to be composed, boy, not tripping all over yourself. That's not exactly what I meant when I taught you to keep your feet in motion, now is it?"

"How long has she been missing?" Antious asked.

Amnoch answered. "Last time anyone saw her was after second moon, before sunrise."

"Dimming Light, the sun has less than half a hand left!"

"And you're wasting that daylight by asking questions. The Hold Guard have assembled."

Antious nodded. "Let's do what we're here to do."

Four teams were assembled from among the Hold Guard, each consisting of three men and two hounds. Each hound was given time to familiarize itself with Moira's scent, a dress and pillow having been retrieved from her rooms. Other messengers were sent into Calyn to ask after Moira at popular establishments.

"All of you know your routes," Amnoch said. "We must be swift. It's been a long time since Hold Kerr has had a Lady Matron. We're not going to lose another before her time." Turning to Antious he said, "You're with my party."

Antious nodded and drew his steel.

The teams split up, one in each direction. Master Amnoch took his team to the south. He had almost taken the north route, knowing that's where Moira was last headed; but if there were foul play, she would likely be taken from the Western Province and that meant south, over the Roniah.

It's the busiest and most direct route out, he thought. *It's what I would do.*

Amnoch knelt and put his fingertips into the soil.

"What are you doing?" Antious asked impatiently.

"Listening. Something you might try a little more of."

The hounds sniffed shrubbery and the ground, wagging their tales and quickly moving from one point of interest to the next.

"We have to keep moving," Antious said. "We're wasting time."

"No, we're not. And put that thing away," Amnoch said, looking at Antious's sword. "Only draw it when you need to."

Antious bit his tongue and sheathed his sword.

"Let's stick to the river bank," Amnoch said, standing up. "If Moira has been abducted, we'll likely find her at one of the crossings."

He was right. As his team searched, tracing the banks of the river south, the hounds howled and sped off, not waiting for their masters.

Dimming Light, they're fast!

Amnoch, Antious and the two Hold Guard chased the hounds, catching them and keeping their pace. A half-mile ahead, four men dressed as merchants with long robes were loading a small river craft with all manner of objects. A fifth fellow, obviously the boat's captain, was at the helm.

"Hold!" Master Amnoch shouted. The men looked up and one put a smile on his face.

"Good evening, master," the smiling merchant said as Amnoch's team arrived. "Have you come to see our wares? We have just finished in Calyn and are now headed to Thera."

"Where is she?" Amnoch demanded.

The merchant looked confused. "She? Who?"

"Moira Kerr," Amnoch growled.

Antious started slowly moving around the merchants, taking up an offensive position. Amnoch saw the man he spoke to notice the action.

Good move, but go easy, boy, Amnoch thought, impressed with Antious's situational awareness.

"Kerr?" The merchant looked to his companions, as if searching for help in understanding what was being asked of him. "I am sorry, master, I do not know of whom you speak. But we have some wonderful—"

Master Amnoch looked hard at the merchants' wares as the man went on about their inventory and what he might be interested in.

"Why dock here?" Amnoch asked, looking around. "Riley's Cove seems a more suitable port. There's nothing here. It's odd, to say the least."

"We were indeed traveling to Riley's Cove when our captain here happened upon us," the merchant said. "It was a stroke of luck as we are all weary from a long day at the Calyn markets.

"But master, whoever you seek is not here," the merchant continued. "We pray you will have fortune in your search."

"If she's not here," Amnoch said, "you won't mind if we take a closer look."

"Of course not," the man said. "Please, be sure to inspect our latest clothing items, woven from the best wool of the East. For men such as yourselves, you want something that is warm during the coming cycles but also is light, letting your body breathe."

Amnoch inspected everything on the riverbank that had not been loaded on to the riverboat; Antious stood motionless in his position, looking tense. He opened wooden crates, too small for Moira—assuming she was still in one piece—but only found clothes, spices, and supplies—mostly trinkets and cheap goods.

"Yes, that is a very fine line of spices," the merchant said. "Especially this one." He retrieved a jar from the crate and opened its lid. "Ah, it is wonderful, yes?" He waved his hand over the open container toward his nose. "Please, see for yourself. Perhaps your wife—"

"The boat," Amnoch said. "We'll be inspecting that next."

A moment of nervousness flashed in the man's eyes but was gone almost instantly.

"Of course," he said, holding his hand out to the ramp that connected the boat to the shore. "But please, be careful. We have many expensive things and our families depend upon us."

Amnoch ordered the dogs over first. They sniffed and searched everywhere: the deck, the rails, the captain at the helm. A few crates had been loaded on the boat, but the dogs showed no interest until one of them kept coming back to a certain chest. It was designed with ornate carvings and inlays of silver and a blue metal Amnoch did not recognize. The hound put his paws up on it, sniffing more intently. The second hound came to the chest now, inspecting it closely.

"Ah, yes, of course. They are intrigued by the scent of our fresh produce. Did you know," the merchant said, "that we just acquired these fruits today? From your own Arlethian orchards and vineyards. Perhaps some for you and your men, yes?"

The hounds started whining as they pawed at the chest, sniffing more intently. Amnoch studied the merchant and saw perspiration begin to form on his forehead.

Why are you tense? he asked silently.

Coming to the chest, he opened it and was met with the sight of … fruit. Grapes, apples, peaches, cherries. A strange red star-shaped breed he was not familiar with.

Are they truly just hungry? he thought, looking at the hounds. They continued to scratch at the sides of the chest. As he was about to shut the lid, he saw it: a streak of ebony that did not belong, a lock of hair resting on a clump of deep purple grapes. He had almost missed it. In truth, Amnoch was impressed. Trying to mask Moira's scent by hiding her under a load of fruit was at least well thought out, he had to admit.

Master Amnoch began to draw in the Living Light from the forest and, with his hand on the hilt of his Jarwynian forged sword, began to channel a portion of the Light into it. A low hum came to his ears, barely audible.

"You know, master merchant," Amnoch said as he gently let down the lid. "I have a confession to make. Those robes you wear don't hide your Marishee swords quite as well as you think."

Five days later, Thannuel finally received word by wing. Moira had indeed been taken, but was recovered alive. Other than a lump on her head, she was fine. Kalisa and her family were with her now at the hold.

It was obvious the Thoulden-sha had planned to use her against him, forcing him to withdraw his forces. His father's last line in the missive actually made him smile despite the rage welling inside him.

Master Amnoch wishes you to know that Moira's assailants died flat-footed.

"And so ends this game," Thannuel said as he lowered the parchment.

The storming of the Thoulden-sha's hold met little resistance, most of Marishee simply surrendering; but their ultimate target had not been found. Immediately after securing the hold, Thannuel had ordered it demolished.

"Leave no stone standing atop another."

Turning to a field marshal, a man of House Gonfrey not much older than he was, Thannuel said, "After you have completely razed the hold, send detachments into the narrows after me. The Thoulden-sha must have fled there."

He pursued the Thoulden-sha through the maze of passageways behind the now demolished hold, listening and feeling as he went. Though there were no triarch trees in Dispa or anywhere outside of the Western Province, Thannuel still held a triarch leafling in his hand as he ran.

Some of the paths were so narrow that he had to turn sideways, scraping his back and stomach as he passed through; others only continued after crawling through a low tunnel. Jumping up and bracing himself between two walls that were barely shoulder-width apart, Thannuel closed his eyes to feel more sensitively. The pounding in his head was massive, the same that had begun five days ago when he first met with the Thoulden-sha. He hadn't mentioned it to any of the seven healers that had been assigned to his battalion, not wishing to bother them over something so trivial.

But, it did not feel so trivial now. The more he tried to feel after the Thoulden-sha, the more his head screamed with pain. He let himself down and continued forward, his left eye closed and his right squinting from the throbbing. His breathing became labored as he traveled deeper into the slot canyons and the pain increased, but he persisted, knowing he must find the Thoulden-sha if they were to have continued peace in the Realm.

Eventually, he came to a grand opening spacious enough to

hold hundreds, maybe even thousands. A couple feet off the ground, the walls were covered with an unusually thick layer of dust, the same light soil that frosted the ground, indicating that this open-ceiling cave had indeed had many visitors, many pairs of feet that disturbed the ground sediment. Then he remembered the arena his father had told him that he and Amnoch had peered down into six years ago.

But they had said that in the center of the space was—

He saw the altar before he could finish his thought. It was stained brown and crimson, almost none of the natural bone white and yellow sand color of the visible rocks. As he stared at it, he thought he could hear cries of anguish coming from the altar, voices of those lost to the Fathomless Abyss upon its cold, rough surface. Blood was the mortar that held this abomination together.

Thannuel's tension increased, as did the pain in his head—a warning in the air, wrongness. He looked up, his eyes trying to focus through the pain, and made out caves of varying depths and heights in the surrounding walls of the arena, the lowest about his height from the ground, others much higher.

Fool!

He had thought the Marishee that had put down their arms in the hold were the extent of the Thoulden-sha's forces. He knew in his mind what he would see next before his eyes physically registered it. Scores of Marishee—maybe as many as a hundred—dressed in the same black he had encountered them in five years earlier, emerged from the caves that dotted around and above him. Coming from around the corner of a tributary corridor, the Thoulden-sha calmly walked forward with the man clad in tan just behind him. The Thoulden-sha seemed to almost float, his feet barely touching the ground. Thannuel haggardly drew his blade and fought to keep his footing. The steel felt so heavy in his hand.

"You do not look well, young Lord Kerr."

The pounding in Thannuel's head became unbearable and he dropped to a knee, bringing the heel of his left hand to his left temple.

"Tell me of your distress. Perhaps I can ease it for you."

Thannuel grunted, pushing against his temple as the veins throbbed with pressure. As the pain began to cause delirium, Thannuel screamed out and rocked back from his knee to his backside. His back arched and he screamed again.

"It is your blood, the blood of the Kiarra Clan, that is trying to free itself from your body, from your very arteries. It urges you to this altar of Influence that I, the Oracle of Mari-shaden, may undo what your ancestors have wrongly brought upon this world. Come, Lord Thannuel, let me ease your burden."

The Thoulden-sha held out his hand. "Please. Come."

There were not many times in Thannuel's life that he had truly not known what to do; fewer were the times that he felt truly afraid—pure, unadulterated fear. At no time, however, had he felt both at once.

Endless Night! My head!

As Thannuel dropped his sword and brought his other hand to his head, he thought perhaps it was just the natural thing to do when you felt as if your head would literally explode, regardless of the futility of the action.

"Take my hand, Thannuel. Let me end this suffering for you. I offer you this redemption."

As the Thoulden-sha extended his hand closer, Thannuel caught sight of a glistening through his squinting on his enemy's brow.

He's sweating; he's ... doing this to me!

With the realization came even more fear but also anger, and with the anger and fear came strength. His skull seemed to be reinforced, his veins and arteries thickening. It was the oddest sensation he had experienced, but it nevertheless felt good, *empowering,* like a reservoir had just opened to him.

Like the night of the Doonalin Falls ...

With his newfound strength, Thannuel pushed back on the oppressive force upon him, whittling it down until it felt light enough to cast aside. Slowly, he forced himself to get up and found the hilt of his sword. The Thoulden-sha's attack redoubled as Thannuel felt the tentacles of his renewed attack reaching and clawing for the hold they had lost.

"I think I'm going to pass on your offer, Thoulden-sha," Thannuel said.

With a burst of power from the reservoir inside him, the heir of Arlethia broke the last of the mental shackles with which he had been bound and the Thoulden-sha's face swam with disbelief.

"But, I do think I'll attend to your altar in the same manner as I did your hold."

"No! Attack! Attack!" the Thoulden-sha shrieked.

Marishee began to descend from their perches, falling to the ground and springing toward Thannuel with swords raised. The Thoulden-sha disappeared behind the curtain of disciples that enclosed him, covering his escape.

Immediately, Thannuel split his mind in half, preparing to engage the enemy, hoping to cut through them in time to arrest the Thoulden-sha's retreat.

The first Marishee that arrived did not have time to react as Thannuel's wood-dweller speed brought his sword up, tracing it along the man's abdomen and chest. While Thannuel had meant to kill him, he had not intended to cleave the man's torso in two lengthwise. His sword came free at the man's collarbone, just to the left of his neck.

Three more came at him at once, bringing their steel down in an overhead thrust. Thannuel timed his block perfectly, waiting until the first enemy blade interrupted the arc of the other two. He only had to block the first, which did the job of blocking the others for him. Shoving the swords violently to the right with his own, he threw two of them off balance. In the split second they tried to regain their balance, they were cut down. The third man attempted to bring his weapon back to bear, but Thannuel moved in too close for the sword to be effective and swept his legs from under him, followed by an efficient stab to the heart.

More stepped forward, a swarm of arms and swords, desperately swinging and slashing. He ducked and spun, opening the stomach of one and thrusting his sword through the soft palate of the chin of another. The sword was retracted and the next Marishee warrior engaged before blood had time to begin flowing from the wound.

Without the aid of the Arlethian forest's sentient trees and interwoven root system, the horde of vibrations that sang to him was too chaotic to distinguish. He was forced to rely mostly on his eyes and ears to decipher enemy movements as he tried to dull his natural wood-dweller senses. His speed, however, was one trait not dependent upon being in his native forests.

"Part," came a voice, uncannily cutting through the cacophony of battle. "I will have him."

The Marishee ceased their advances on Thannuel and did part, opening a corridor of sight to … the man clad in tan. Muhktar, Thannuel recalled.

"Do you know what this is?" Muhktar asked, gesturing to his clothing. His voice had a chorus effect, sounding as if several people had spoken at once.

"It is the garment of the Oracle, given to his First."

"First what?" Thannuel asked, not allowing his alertness to diminish.

Muhktar smiled. "So much you do not know, Kiarra. The sacrifices upon this altar are clothed upon me, a divine gift from Mari-shaden."

Sacrifices? Clothed upon—

Thannuel's jaw quivered and lips sneered as he understood. He fought the rising bile within him.

"I speak with their voices, know the desires of their hearts that will never be."

Pure rage was something Thannuel Kerr was not accustomed to feeling; but as he now faced what he was sure was evil in quintessence, an open portal of the Ancient Dark, he could find no other emotion.

"I will take great pleasure in liberating them from you!"

"Most importantly, Kiarra, I have a portion of their strength that resides within me, granted to me by this holy garment. Mari-shaden willing, the Thoulden-sha will soon add your heretical flesh to these robes. You cannot prevail."

Do not be goaded, he heard Amnoch's words play in his mind. *You cannot overcome what faces you until you understand what faces you.*

"You mean the same Thoulden-sha who is fleeing from here, escaping *alone?*"

Muhktar drew his sword from its sheath of tanned flesh. Through the ground, though muted, Thannuel could feel the swift-footed approach of others. He smiled.

"In moments, my forces will arrive, swarming this arena and surrounding all of you," he said. "I give you this one chance to surrender now."

He imagined what it must have looked like, one man

demanding the surrender of a hundred. A small chuckle escaped, not able to contain himself.

"Lies," said the discordant voices within Muhktar.

"See for yourself," Thannuel said, slowly raising a finger upward toward the wide crevice at the top of the slot canyon. Scores of silhouetted profiles looked down upon the arena.

"Those are Arlethians, Muhktar. At my word, they will rain down upon you and the Marishee with relentless wrath."

Audible echoes were now heard bounding through the narrows leading into the arena, the heavier footfall and shuffle of Sentharian soldiers. Thannuel saw the consternation of the Marishee as they realized their ambush had failed and that they were encompassed now on all sides.

Muhktar wailed, the sound coming from him an inhuman chorus, and ran toward Thannuel. He launched off the altar into the air with surprising speed. Thannuel raised his sword, meeting the downward thrust of Muhktar's blade head on. The force of the collision was unexpected and Thannuel was driven down to one knee. Before he could counter, Muhktar's knee found his face, splitting his lips. Thannuel saw stars and black spots, blinded from the explosion of pain. Rolling backward, he barely escaped the next attack from Muhktar that would have ended him, seeing the sparks from his opponent's sword as it struck the rocky ground.

That rage within him, bordering on hatred, started to dissipate along with the pain. Clarity came to him and a small boost of strength, as it had when he stifled the Thoulden-sha's mental attack only minutes before.

How?

He kipped hard, landing nimbly on the balls of his feet, knees slightly bent. He was ready.

Muhktar advanced again, faster than should be possible, but

Thannuel sprang into motion with speed faster still. With his mind still partitioned, he attacked, letting the first part of his mind have command over his physical movements, blocking and countering. The strength of Muhktar's blows jarred Thannuel and his blade chipped in several places as he blocked and advanced, but it held. He delivered a fast jab to Muhktar's midsection then spun low with his leg extended and swept Muhktar's legs from under him. But the man adorned in the flesh of innocents was upon his feet again, appearing not even dazed.

The second part of Thannuel's mind, with the fullness of thought processes at its command, analyzed and strategized, calmly assessing what was before him. He *saw* emotions welling within him: surprise at the force of Muhktar's strikes, rage for the Thouldensha's actions against Moira, sorrow and regret for the lives of those lost upon that altar, concern for his men in this confrontation with him. And as he *saw* these emotions with this half of his mind, he knew a truth that came to him innately: *this is power.* He had been using it somehow, yoking this energy, this …

Friction. The word came to him, un-beckoned but *right.* He felt it in the core of sentience and realized he had used this *friction* throughout his life at various times, times when miraculous feats had been performed that he had no explanation for.

Urged on by the frenzy of battle, the Marishee ceased being bystanders and launched into action, turning on the Sentharian soldiers at their backs. From above, the Arlethians dropped down through the open crevice, landing with a near-perfect silence upon the hard earth. They sprang into the fray, lethality in their wake.

There was no turning back now, no way out for the Marishee. They had chosen this course.

Muhktar rushed Thannuel again. The man did not stop when he came within striking distance but continued forward. Thannuel, preparing to parry a sword blow, was momentarily confused and Muhktar hit him, the two becoming tangled together as Thannuel fell backwards, his sword knocked from his hand, but not the triarch leafling. Immediately upon hitting the ground, Thannuel felt his face taking the punishment of Muhktar's fists as if it were a blacksmith's anvil. Thannuel tried to raise his arms but there were pinned under Muhktar's knees.

Dimming Light, he's too strong! Thannuel's mind screamed as he tried to free himself.

Three more blows came and the skin of Thannuel's left check split. Blood stung his eye and Muhktar laughed with the voices of many. He fought to keep his mind split as the two halves were losing distinction, starting to meld back to one. Fear was seen by the second part of his mind, an emotion inky in form and black in appearance, moving with a fast current in his mind. New fear came upon him as he thought about trying to reach out with his mind and *touch* it.

It's power, his mind told him. *Friction. You must channel it.*

Screaming with frustration, he forced his mind to reach out a figurative finger and plunge it into the fear. A surge came to him as he mentally touched it; wild and untamed, feral even, it sought *direction.*

Muhktar felt lighter suddenly, or his pinned arms felt stronger, Thannuel was not sure which. With a renewed effort, the Arlethian lifted his arms, throwing Muhktar off of him. Thannuel scrambled to his knees but Muhktar was already rushing him again.

Before executing the lethal strike, he saw the move in the second half of his mind while the first half made it come to life, moving his body and limbs with precision. Plunging deeper into the fear friction, he thrust his right arm forward while rotating his hips, the heel of his palm meeting Muhktar's solar plexus at the exact instant his arm achieved maximum extension. He could almost see the energy in slow motion as it rippled through Muhktar's body like a focused beam. A sickening crack was heard, even amid the sounds of battle, as a bloody piece of carnage shot out of Muhktar's back, ripping through both layers of skin—his own and the demonic robe clad upon him—and ricocheted with a dull clatter off a distant sandstone wall.

The man, the Thoulden-sha's First, slumped forward upon Thannuel's arm, lifeless. The remaining Marishee, less than a score, surrendered instantly. As he went to retrieve his sword, he saw fragments of steel scattered around the vicinity where he and Muhktar had fought. The damage to his blade was much greater upon inspecting it than he had realized.

Thannuel opened his fist to grab his sword and the triarch leafling fell free to the ground.

It's dead, he realized. Triarch leaflings could last several span before wilting, but this one, barely a span and a half from its tree, had lost all its color, turning brittle. *Fifteen days and already dead?*

The Thoulden-sha was not to be found. Nowhere in the ravines he had fled through, or in the surrounding villages. Thannuel and his men searched for a half span, but he was gone.

Lord Orion arrived during their five-day search, finally taking enough interest in these matters despite them happening within his province. The vastness of the Eastern Province left him generally unconcerned with the events on the fringes.

"Respectfully, my Lord," Thannuel said as he was debriefed, "I believe this sedition could have been ended long ago."

"Perhaps," Lord Orion said dismissively, the jowls of his face jiggling. "But little actual harm was done."

Deciding to leave comments of his confrontation with the Marishee five years ago and Moira's recent endangerment out of his response, he said, "I have learned that with every full first moon for over a decade the Thoulden-sha sacrificed an innocent person. Nearly two hundred of your citizens. I wonder if my Lord considers that 'little actual harm'."

Grady Orion did not answer for several moments. "But you have lost him? The Marishee leader?"

"He fled, cowardly leaving his followers to fend for themselves," Thannuel said, not bothering to hide his annoyance at Lord Orion's insinuation. "But, I have a gift for you, Lord Orion. A token to remember this event by."

Thannuel took a small wooden box from his bag. "I took the liberty of having one of my own soldiers carve the sigil of your house on the lid. Apparently, he has quite a skill in this area. I think he did an excellent job."

Lord Orion took the small box, somewhat hesitantly. "I do say, the mane of the horse is rather exquisitely done. Which of your men has this talent?"

"The carving is beautiful, but that's not the actual gift. Open it."

Orion's eyes grew as he stared at the box's content and threw it down. "What is this?"

Thannuel bent down and picked up Muhktar's vertebra, dusting it off. "This, *my Lord,* is a reminder of the consequences of indifference!" He shoved it back in the box, snapped the lid shut, and thrust it into Orion's chest. "A memento from the Thoulden-sha's first disciple. I hope you never forget what happened here, in *your province,* where 'little actual harm' occurred!"

"Regardless, he is gone and his rebellion put down," Orion said with a chuckle, trying to lighten the mood. "No doubt he will be in hiding the rest of his life."

Thannuel hoped that was true. He turned away as he spoke. "I am not certain, Lord Orion. He was ... driven. A zealot. I think he actually believes in his delusions."

But they were not mere delusions, Thannuel knew. *He had command over some Dark Influence,* Thannuel admitted to himself. *It had nearly ended me. And Muhktar ...*

Never had Thannuel faced something so ... *dark* in his life. It still frightened him. Although he had overcome him, using this *friction*, he could not replicate what he had done, nor see his emotions in his mind any longer. While he had tapped into some kind of power—*could it have been Influence?*—he knew, even in the moment of its use, that he had been lucky. He had no more command over this ability than did a passing cloud over the mountain in its path.

"They called me Kiarra," Thannuel mumbled to himself. "Both of them."

At first he had thought that it was their desert accents, calling him Kerr; but as he thought back on it—

"Lord Thannuel?" Orion said.

The Kiarra Clan, he remembered the Thoulden-sha saying. *The blood ... of the Kiarra Clan.*

Someday, perhaps, he would have the Archivers bring his genealogy to him for deeper study. For now, however, he could not stand being in Dispa another moment.

"I bid you farewell, my Lord," he said, not glancing at Lord Orion. "I'm going home to my wife."

As Thannuel and his men began their march home later that night, first moon arose. Its bluish-white light completely covered the celestial orb, the cycle's waxing completed this very night. He marveled how large the moon appeared in the open skies of the Eastern Province as he walked across the soft sand dunes. The lunar rays glistened silver over the desert landscape, giving the ironic appearance of frost. If he couldn't feel the day's heat being released from the sand as he trudged along, he might have believed the land to indeed be frozen by sight alone. The white soft-rock formations that emerged high into the air at random points across Dispa's desert-scape masqueraded as desolate, icy islands in this sea of arenaceous, stagnant waves.

Not very far south lay the Schadar, and Thannuel thought of what Lord Hoyt had revealed to him years ago. What was in the Schadar that could tempt his father to abscond there in his youth? Only the miscreants of society dwelled there, the Kearon, somehow surviving on Senthara's wasteland for centuries after their defeat by House Wellyn.

Thannuel's attention was drawn back to the moon. Though he couldn't explain it, there was something … ominous, something that bespoke of a foreboding. It was nearly a feeling of being … trapped? But, the feeling did not last, fading from his mind as quickly as it had come.

Tides. Tides of Entropy I see, reaching to from the far parts of the world. Senthara has become an island amid the rising Night.

—Evrin, Keeper of the Living Light

THIRTEEN

~THE THOULDEN-SHA~

Day 19 of 2nd Dimming 392 A.U.

THE CROCODILE SLITHERED THROUGH THE MUD, barely noticeable to the untrained eye. But the Thoulden-sha had watched this predator in action for years, almost becoming its prey more than once. In fact, the Thoulden-sha now employed a trick that he had seen the crocodile use against other prey many times, having buried himself in the slimy mud of a river delta that fed into the ocean. His current position was right next to the large lizard's nest, where six eggs waited to be tended.

Normally, he would have been concerned about his scent, but that would be masked by the awful smell of the wet earth that covered him from head to toe. The beast was nearly seventeen feet long, from snout to tail, and no doubt weighed as much as several boulders. The Thoulden-sha dreaded being stepped on, but he'd picked his hiding spot carefully.

Four years had passed since he was driven out from his home, since he'd been ousted from being the leader of his people. He had narrowly escaped the wrath of Prime Lord Wellyn; but more specifically, of Thannuel Kerr.

A descendent of the Kiarra Clan has once again defeated those of Mari-shaden.

He had been arrogant, too quick to bring about the Resurgence. He should have waited until he contained more of Mari-shaden's Influence. But, it was done. And though he clearly remembered the direction back to Senthara, there was no vessel that could ferry him there.

The small ship he had secured with the secret help of a believer in P'lor had long ago been wrecked in a storm. Only the power of Mari-shaden had sustained him as he drifted for days before being washed up on this very shore.

Without an altar and infidels to sacrifice, Mari-shaden's Influence had not grown inside him. In fact, it had dimmed considerably, taking immense effort to focus and utilize the Influence. So great was the draw on his strength when he called upon the power of Mari-shaden that he avoided it as much as possible. He felt as if his heart were in a drought, thirsting for increase. Nevertheless, *her* voice—the Thoulden-sha was now certain that Mari-shaden was female—calmed and aided him in his time of loneliness, tutoring him by visions and insights. He thought of her in a motherly way after these long years under her care.

If I cannot harness more power, at least I will have the knowledge for when the Resurgence process will once again resume.

He was not sure if he would enjoy crocodile meat, but the animal food supply had been dwindling noticeably. There was room for only one predator in this marsh-like part of the world. At the very least, its skin and bones would be useful.

He felt a depression of several inches in the mud next to his left thigh, then another next to his hip on the right. Tensing, he sucked in slowly, as if trying to make himself thinner. As he felt the next depression, this one next to his left arm, the Thoulden-sha thrust his arms up with a two-handed grip on his short blade. The knife was dull and cankered from the lack of proper care over the years, but still sharp enough for this task.

The mammoth of a lizard squirmed in pain, lifting its head and running forward, toward its nest. With the blade still penetrating, he sliced downward as the crocodile ran, extending the wound until its stomach opened and spilled its girth upon the mud. The Thoulden-sha extricated himself from the mud with all haste before the thing could collapse on top of him.

Lying next to its eggs, the crocodile lay still with a trail of blood and entrails behind it, mixing with the mud. Not wishing to take any chances, the Thoulden-sha quickly approached from behind and buried his short blade between the crocodile's raised eyes, scrambling its small brain.

Using a smooth rock, the now diminished oracle scraped the blade against the stone, putting an edge on the rusted blade. He had always loved the sound of steel against stone, ever since working in the Jarwyn mines as a teen. That was long before his calling came upon him.

After cleaning the reptile as best he could, he went to work on skinning it when something caught his eye: movement upon the surface of the ocean, something ... were they whales surfacing for air? No, the things were too tall and did not dive, but remained floating. Constant speed. Too dark to be ships, even though they moved like ships. But then he saw it: a sail, black as a thundercloud against the blue horizon, caught the breeze. It *was* a fleet of some create; a *large* fleet.

Go to them, Mari-shaden whispered. *I will raise up new Marishee around you.*

He began to gather driftwood and branches, hurriedly cobbling them together.

After anchoring the frigate some hundred yards offshore, Admiral Gendaeri threw the long sea bag with all his belongings in the world into a shore boat. The amber color of second moon reflected off the water, like a candle's flame flickering in the wind. He was the last to leave the black-hulled ship and joined his sea bag along with the other few sailors in the shore boat, a small skiff. They waited for his command.

"Row," he said.

Gendaeri watched the shore grow larger, second by second. In the harbor, his fleet of some hundred ships was anchored. These needed to last until they discovered a new home. They had stripped almost two-thirds of the forests in Orsari in building this armada, including the larger transport vessels that would follow once a foothold was established in new fertile land.

In the distance, miles inland, he saw the dark outline of a city he once loved. Thulfera had once seemed majestic to him, built of ores and stone, ornamented by gems. Even the streets had been lined with sapphires and emeralds. Now, however, it felt more like a mass grave for his people, who dwindled toward extinction.

Some shore boats from other vessels in his search fleet had already come ashore, being met by anxious crowds of his people. There were perhaps a few hundred on the long, deep beach, which was illuminated by numerous large torches, all elevated roughly forty feet in the air by massive rock foundations. Flammable rocks were alight upon the large, shallow basins of the torches, like large dishes from which the Haxlium giants of old might have eaten. They were lit every night while his fleet was out, beacons shining their light to guide his dark marauders home.

Gendaeri could see the news had already been relayed. The Underlander had not blessed their mission with success and the responsibility as newly appointed admiral of the Orsarian Fleet weighed heavily upon his shoulders. He stomped his feet on the skiff's floorboards once. This brought no relief, so the admiral persisted, slamming a booted foot down over and over until a satisfying crack was heard in one of the boards.

"Admiral, no!" Pelnith said. "We'll take on water."

Failing to appreciate the wisdom of his first officer, Gendaeri grabbed the man's head, his fist clenching a grip of dark hair, and slammed Pelnith's forehead into the stern thwart.

"It's just the floorboards, you imbecile! Not the hull! Perhaps you did not learn your proper place after challenging me for command," Gendaeri snapped.

Pelnith, still reeling from the blow to his head, seemed utterly confused to find himself in the water when his senses returned, as if he did not feel Gendaeri violently throw him overboard.

"Try not to take on water on your swim to shore," Gendaeri said.

Dead fish of strange create lined the beach, the shore break waves pushing them farther up as the tide rose. Large bodies with heads too narrow, a sinewy lanyard of some kind attached to a single eye socket that dangled in front of their heads. Some guessed that they were a deep-water species that had been stirred up by the changes coming upon them. Apparently, the changes—more aptly disturbances—were not just land based. At least the fish tasted somewhat appealing when cooked with hog fat and spiced with emerbi cloves. Of course, emerbi bushes were rarely found of late and hogs were leaner than they had ever been. They had fresh water inland, but the soil seemed to not benefit from it, somehow refusing the water's nourishment. Seeds refused to germinate and what produce they could harvest, while still edible, was more bitter and stiff than what was natural.

The lands of Orsari were cycling. Slowly but definitively. They had known for over a decade and had been searching for a new home for nearly half that time. Våleira's oceans seemed to have no end, however. Previous voyages had traced the coastlines in all directions, but the land was fallow everywhere they landed. They found little plant life and even less animal life, the cycling of those lands being far more advanced than theirs ... for now.

Overland parties searched for many cycles, crossing plains and mountains alike until they reached another part of the ocean. In growing desperation, the land parties had hoped to eventually run into other people, perhaps those whose lands were still fertile, and seek help.

This did happen. Once.

A group of people that lived in the mountains far south of their home, the Ma'arnu, had been discovered and help was sought. They appeared to be simple goat herders and hunters, snaring small animals and fowl for food, showing extreme skill with net casting. When the Ma'arnu people came, it was not the type of help the Orsarians had been expecting to receive. Only their advanced ingenuity had saved them from the Ma'arnu surprise attack, but with their victory they gained the herds of the Ma'arnu, giving the Orsarians much needed provisions that had sustained them.

Since then, Gendaeri's people had taken on a new tactic, a darker pursuit, turning their focus to one of conquest rather than simple survival. They painted their ships and sails black, and took the name of *dark marauders* upon their warriors. But, thus far, no land or people had presented themselves to be conquered.

As Gendaeri set foot on the land, his legs wobbled.

The land feels more unstable than ships at sail on the open sea.

As his equilibrium adjusted, someone shouted, "Look! Northwest!"

Gendaeri swiveled his head, following the gaze of those around him. A single sail came from around an arched atoll crowned with scores of seagulls three quarters of a mile out to sea. It was plain to see, even with the dimmer light of second moon.

"One of ours?" Gendaeri asked, knowing the answer.

"No," one of his deckhands answered. "The sail is white."

Such a small vessel … it had to be a short-range boat.

"Maybe one of our fishing boats, then," Gendaeri said.

"Too small, and still the sails are not black."

Pelnith had finally made his way ashore, looking extremely displeased but did not glare or make any hostile move against his admiral. Instead, he came to Gendaeri's side and reassumed his role as first officer.

"Find out from the other ships' crews if anyone saw this boat following us," he ordered the deckhands nearby. "Report back immediately."

The men scurried off, running across the beach to the other shore boats that had landed. Gendaeri, though tense, resisted giving an order to make ready for a surprise attack, but the boat was alone. A lookout from atop a bluff on the north side of this inlet signaled that all was clear.

"Pelnith," a deckhand called as he returned from speaking with one of the crewmembers. "One man, a lookout, remembers seeing something that he now recognizes as the boat that approaches two days past from the crow's nest. He thought it was just driftwood from afar and didn't see it the next day."

Pelnith wrinkled his nose as he raised his upper lip, obviously unsure how to respond to this information.

"So ... shall I execute the lookout?" the deckhand offered.

"Not yet," Pelnith said.

Something is off, Gendaeri thought. *Why would a lone sea craft be approaching a fleet?*

And approaching the small boat was, its course clear. It intended to make anchor in the midst of their fleet, if it even had an anchor.

"No crew, just a single sailor," Pelnith reported. He held his hand at his eyebrows, squinting against the sun. No matter the annoyance this man caused Gendaeri occasionally, the admiral could not deny his first officer's exceedingly sharp eyesight.

Perhaps he will occupy the crow's nest as part of his penance. But the admiral thought better of it, admitting Pelnith had indeed fulfilled his penance.

"The ship itself ... " Pelnith paused and then took his hand down from his head. He looked right at Gendaeri. "Admiral, the boat should not be moving."

"It is in disrepair?" Gendaeri asked.

Pelnith shook his head. "It's not even really a boat, more of a raft. But ... " He squinted harder. "There appears to be no hull, Admiral. Just logs lashed together in a square, like a border but no floor. Just open to the water. The mast is tied to two other narrow logs leaned together and each lashed to one of the base logs."

Gendaeri relaxed, knowing this drifter was no threat and probably had been marooned somewhere. He had probably just seen their fleet passing by and followed.

"Logs float," Gendaeri said. "There's nothing disconcerting there."

"It's not that, Admiral. It's ... the sail."

"What of it?"

"There's no wind. The sail is limp. Drooping. But ... the craft is still moving. In fact, it looks more like a ... yes, like a flag than a sail."

"The current is taking it." But Gendaeri countered his own thought as he continued to observe. At this time of day, the currents would be almost directly opposite the vector from which this imposter approached.

"I think," Pelnith said, "that he wishes to be seen."

When the raft got close enough, the waves propelled it ashore. It seemed to slide up the sand as if a smooth rock gracefully sliding across a frozen lake. A heavily bearded man in ragged, muddy clothes stepped from the feeble craft onto the golden beach that would have appeared to be a paradise in normal times. Gendaeri almost viewed it as toxic now.

The man made no further steps.

"He waits to be invited, Admiral," Pelnith said.

"No," Gendaeri said as he studied the man. His chin was high, arms relaxed at his sides, showing no sign of timidity. There was an air of authority about him, one Gendaeri had recognized in other leaders that had preceded him. "No, he is waiting for us to come to him."

Gendaeri drew one of his scimitars.

Several approached the Thoulden-sha, leveling shortened swords at him. They were shouting something, commands no doubt. But the Thoulden-sha did not make eye contact with any of them. He listened intently to their speech, concentrating. Wind from the ocean whipped against him, chilling him and teasing the giant flames of the torches farther up the beach.

Another two men arrived on the scene and those immediately around him made way. As they spoke to the two newcomers, the Thoulden-sha noticed the change in timbre of the voices, one of deference. The cadence was also different, slower, as they spoke, probably asking for direction on what to do about him.

The taller of the two men, dark skinned with black hair and the smell of the ocean on him, walked to within a foot of the Thoulden-sha's face. Still, he did not make eye contact.

The man, obviously a leader of these people, spoke. He held a slightly curved sword in his hand. The sound of his words was smooth, only occasionally interrupted by hard phonetic breaks.

The Thoulden-sha did not respond. Again the man spoke, using his hands and arms more, trying to accentuate his meaning. Repeating the words over in his mind, the Thoulden-sha analyzed the syllables, the breaks, the cadence.

When he did not make any response again, the man confronting him became agitated and spoke harsher. Again, the words and manner of speech were analyzed, and the Thoulden-sha began to recognize several repeating sounds.

Knowing his refusal to make eye contact or respond would be seen as arrogant at best, and likely even hostile, the Thoulden-sha looked up toward second moon and inhaled through his nose. He closed his eyes for a brief moment and held the inhaled air. The light of second moon was not as potent, containing less of Mari-shaden's power, but nonetheless sufficient to deal with these lesser mortals. He knew he would have only one opportunity.

"Fo-eliant! Oul Fo-eliant!" one of the first men who had greeted him shouted, making threatening gestures with his curved sword. He wore no recognizable emblems of rank.

He wants to me raise my arms, the Thoulden-sha realized. *Very well.*

Gathering the small bit of Influence granted him, he reached into the man and found his will, his free thought, and overran it, trampling it like a horse upon an ant. Then he raised his arms, and the man mimicked his movements.

"Ishanta! Fon oul ishanta brezenga!" he shouted as he brought his sword to his neck.

Mari-shaden's oracle allowed the man to speak. He wanted the others to hear his pleas, the fear in his voice.

"Fon feresn ishanta! Lorith fon—"

The screams turned to gurgles as the Thoulden-sha commanded the man to slide the edge of his steel across his throat, slowly. When he had made one complete pass, the Thoulden-sha cocked his head and squinted slightly, and the man pulled his blade back the other way as blood pumped out of his open wound like a geyser. Mutters of concern and confusion erupted, his friends obviously telling him to stop; but they did not know he wasn't there anymore, his will swallowed up in Mari-shaden. The dying man looked like he was playing a fiddle, his vocal chords the strings resonating against the steel bow. It was truly music to his ears as the man involuntarily tried to breathe.

After the third pass, the Thoulden-sha had nothing left to hold onto within the man, his death complete, and the body collapsed to the sand. Others around him stood shocked, but it wore off quickly as three others started to charge in, screaming as they raised their blades. Each of them stopped suddenly in their steps, as if frozen. The Thoulden-sha grimaced with the effort, holding them in their positions. He did not have much strength left.

The taller man, the leader who had spoken to him, raised his free hand slowly and put down his sword with the other. Both hands were raised now and he lowered his head slightly.

Submission, the Thoulden-sha knew. Not complete submission, he saw in the leader's eyes, but enough fear to make him submit for now.

Calmly, he reached down and grabbed the dead man's sword. It glistened black with the man's blood, still warm on the cold steel. He supposed it was a sacrifice and would count, the blood being eradiated with the Influence of Mari-shaden. Bringing it to his mouth, the oracle licked the blade, taking the blood into his body.

He trembled slightly as the euphoria of lunar-eradiated blood once again flowed in his veins, ending his four-year drought and feeling Mari-shaden draw closer. Turning to the leader, he locked his eyes with his and pushed his way into the man's mind. His prey immediately went rigid. He was stronger, this one, more sound in his mental fortitude. But, as was expected, it did not take long before Gendaeri's mind unraveled to him like a scroll. That was the first thing he gleaned from the man, his name.

Admiral Gendaeri ... of the Orsarian Fleet.

Traveling through his mind like lightning racing amongst the clouds, the Thoulden-sha saw the tribulation of the Orsarian people, their desperate but unsuccessful searches, their dwindling numbers and fading hope. Finally, he found what he was looking for: language. Within four minutes he had mapped their syntax and grammar, matching images in Gendaeri's mind with the correct vocabulary. It was not all that different from the ability Mari-shaden had given him to map the narrows outside Dispa.

The structure of the language was simple, formulaic even. He intuited several aspects of the language that he knew Gendaeri did not grasp, making connections that a scholar would take years of study to arrive at.

When it was done, he released his mental hold on Gendaeri as well as the other three men who had tried to attack him. Gendaeri's eyes were red and he looked haggard. He stumbled, trying to remain on his feet.

"Build me an altar, Gendaeri," the Thoulden-sha said in Orsari. "And I will show you how your Underlander has provided you an oracle, even one to divine a path of salvation through the darkness you now face."

PART TWO

BROKEN THINGS

It is postulated, and largely accepted, amongst the Changrual, that certain factions of the Ancients feared the joy of life more so than the pain of death. Thus, their actions in turning from the Light are explained logically, rather than relying on some form of otherworldly sensationalism. Notable dissents to this opinion exist, of course—Vicar Danier, objecting on the basis of false premise, namely that the Ancients were never worthy of our reverence, and thus could not fall; Vicar Holister, objecting on the grounds of the immortal shift theory, believing that the Ancients altered themselves to a more refined state that we cannot perceive, and thus never died, having fully embraced life; and Vicar Fürad, objecting because that is what he does. Still, the latter's brilliance in persuasive argument cannot be overstated, in that he convinces you of the error of your belief so profoundly but leaves only a void in its place, never suggesting alternate theories. In this, he never advances critical thought other than the art of critical thought itself.

—Exposition and Argument, Volume 2, Years 113-157 A.U.

FOURTEEN

~ELKINAL~

Day 8 of 2nd Rising 393 A.U.

ELKINAL SPLIT THE OYSTER SHELL with his short blade and peered inside to find the small luminescent pearl. The brilliant white gem shone beautifully in the setting sun, almost giving it a purple luster, matching the dusk sky.

"Ah, there you are, my sweet." He took it from its shelled womb and held it in the palm of his hand.

"Ser! Come see!" he called to his daughter. She stood a stone's cast from him and, like him, in calf-deep water harvesting oysters, both for food and for the rare treasures they sometimes bestowed.

Serisa made her way to him.

"It's beautiful," she remarked. "How many is that now?"

"Two today; three in the past half span," Elkinal answered. "That'll feed us for a whole cycle once the merchant ship comes back."

"When is the next ship?"

"Two days or so."

Serisa put her hand to her forehead to block the sun that pressed upon the western horizon as she looked toward the mainland and the silhouette of the Jarwyn Mountains.

"Good," she said. "I'm tired of oysters and mussels and coconuts. I'm ready for some fresh meat and bread. Do you think they'll have any apples?"

"Not this early in the year," her father said. "It likely won't be until third or even fourth high that they start to come in. They've just seeded in the Eastern Province's orchards no doubt."

He could tell his daughter was disappointed by the face she made, even though her sandy blonde hair blocked most of her face as the wind blew. The Runic Islands produced all manner of island fruits: passion, guava, bananas, and pineapple. His daughter, though, tired easily of them.

"But maybe," he continued, "they will have grapes from the West."

Serisa perked up when she heard this. "Do you think so?"

Elkinal shrugged. "It's possible. The temperature in some parts of the Western Province remains warm enough for grapes almost year round."

Serisa made a happy squeal noise and clapped her hands with hope.

"What's this ruckus I'm hearing over here?"

Elkinal turned to see his brother, Lomand, approaching. Lomand's large arms bulged with the muscles forged through a lifetime of casting and hauling in nets from the ocean, much like Elkinal's own frame. Both participated every year in the sea sprint competition, a swim race starting on Fourth Island, south around the southern peninsula of Main Island, north on the east side of Pearl Island and ending on the north shore of Second Island. Lomand had won three years straight, but the year previous to Lomand's first victory, Elkinal had won and set a new time record that had yet to be broken. While not biological brothers, they enjoyed the bond of brotherhood as much as any blood siblings. Lomand was dark skinned with tight curly black hair while Elkinal was a bronze skin tone with shaggy sun-bleached blond hair. Lomand's family had taken Elkinal in when he was still very young after his parents' fishing vessel was lost during a storm.

"Uncle, Father thinks they might have grapes on the next ship!" Serisa exclaimed as she jumped up and down.

"Grapes? And what would my fourteen-year-old niece do with grapes? Try to make her own wine, maybe? Hmmm?" Lomand chuckled as he teased her.

"No! That's what Drailin does!" she shot back.

"Speaking of your cousin, where is he?" Elkinal asked.

"I left him just around the tail." Lomand gestured toward a thin piece of land that jutted out into the ocean like a miniature peninsula. Pearl Island's shape loosely resembled a turtle with a tail at the southeast shore. The only way to get to the west side of the tail was to take a long hike through a dense forest, or swim around it—the more common choice for the kids. "Likely the blasted boy is just sitting there, not working. I swear, Elkinal, I don't know how you do it. I'm lucky to get two full sentences from that boy all day long."

"The teenage years are tough for all of us, especially the kids," Elkinal answered his brother. "Right, Ser?"

She shrugged. "I don't know."

"Of course you don't," her father said. "Now, go find your cousin. We need to get back to Main Island before nightfall."

They were on Third Island, sometimes called Pearl Island by virtue of all the oysters, the smallest of the four Runic Islands. No one lived here, but many came to fish and hunt from the other three islands. Main Island was the largest with a high mountain that often broke into the cloud layers and was covered with snow during the low season. Its population swelled to as much as eight thousand during the rising and high seasons, but only a few thousand permanent residents lived there year round. Second and Fourth islands barely had a thousand permanent residents between them both, although they each saw their populations double during the warmer seasons as well. From where they stood, they could see Second Island off to the north. It was so close that a stranger might believe it to be one island with Third.

"Likely the merchant ship won't be alone when she pulls into the harbor," Elkinal said as he watched Ser hop off to find Drailin.

"Yeah, I know. We've already started seeing some mainlanders arrive." Lomand spat. "Don't know why they just can't stay where they are."

"It's good for us, good for our small economy. Lord Orion will likely even visit at some point this season or next."

"Come to check on his little piece of paradise," Lomand muttered.

Though technically part of the Eastern Province, those who lived on the Runic Islands prided themselves in being almost a separate people unto themselves. Some Runic families traced their roots back to the invasion of the Senthary to Senthara, settling here and not continuing to the mainland. The shores of the Eastern Province were only a day's travel by ship, but many Runics never even set foot on the mainland during their lifetime.

"I don't mind so much," Elkinal said. He still had the pearl in his hand.

"No, not when you have goods to trade. How many ships do you suppose will come with the merchant ship?"

"Hard to say, but I might guess three or four."

"Dimming Light, that many?"

Elkinal put the pearl in the pouch on his belt. "Don't know, brother. Maybe none. Hard to say."

"El, look!" Lomand said, pulling his brother's arm and turning him around. "Speaking of ships, are they early? And there's a lot more than three or four!"

Elkinal gazed toward the horizon where his brother pointed. It looked like a whole fleet approached them. Did Senthara even have this many ships? The mainlanders were coming in droves much earlier this year, but then something seemed off to Elkinal as he saw the number of ships in his view continue to grow. He turned around and looked at the outline of the Jarwyn peaks behind him—to the west—then back to the approaching ships.

"They're coming from the wrong direction!"

"What?" Lomand asked. "What do you—"

"The east! They're coming from the east!"

It finally hit Lomand. "Fallen Ancients! They can't be from Senthara!"

Adrenaline started pumping through Elkinal and his jaw quivered. The whole eastern horizon was blocked by this foreign armada.

Hours! We only have hours!

He ran after Serisa, yelling her name, Lomand right behind him. His daughter had already made it around the bend and he knew she couldn't hear him amidst the crashing waves, but Elkinal continued to yell for her, turning his voice hoarse. As he ran, he cut deep footprints in the wet sand and his calves burned. Finally, Ser and Drailin appeared from around the tail and looked utterly perplexed at seeing their fathers dashing toward them like madmen.

"The ships!" Lomand screamed and pointed in exaggerated gestures. "The ships!"

The cousins looked east and saw them. It only took a second before they started to run, frantic looks on their faces. Within a minute, they were regrouped.

"Who are they?" Serisa asked, out of breath.

"We don't know and it doesn't matter," Elkinal replied. "Quickly, we must get to Main Island!"

Their small boat was a quarter mile north, close to where they oystered. By the time they made it back to Main Island, they might have an hour before the first ships of the approaching fleet landed. Elkinal did not doubt that others on the island had already seen them and had raised the alarm, but little good it would do. They would need to evacuate to P'lor, the closest harbor in the Eastern Province. It would be a desperate retreat, but word must reach Prime Lord Wellyn of this event. No, more than an *event*, Elkinal knew. This was the beginning of an invasion.

The sun sank below the horizon and complete darkness was only minutes away. As they got beyond the shore break in their skiff, Elkinal saw several frigates land on the beach of Second Island. These smaller, faster ships must have scouted ahead and had gone unnoticed by him. Black hulls and black sails.

"Row!" Lomand yelled.

"Dad!" Ser screamed and pointed. A ship the color of night bore down on them like a ghost from the Fathomless Abyss.

Silent. How is it so silent?

Elkinal saw the keel cut through the rough water, creating wake and small whitecaps, but heard no sound coming from the vessel. Men appeared on the port side staring down at them. Shouts in some odd language were heard bearing the timbre of command, followed by grappling hooks being tossed over the side of the black ship. They hit the floor of the skiff with a heavy dull sound and the rope they were attached to immediately went taut, securing them against the inner wall of their small vessel's starboard side. The two brothers tried to dislodge the grappling hooks—Elkinal grunted loudly with the effort—but the tension was too great and held them in place. A strong tug followed and Elkinal knew they were being dragged sideways across the water to the frigate.

"Knife!" Lomand shouted. He started desperately trying to cut through the line, as did Elkinal. Slashing the line with all his might proved futile, like a bad dream in which even the simplest acts proved maddeningly impossible. Reaching a hand out, Elkinal felt the rope and surprise washed over him.

"Metal!" he yelled to Lomand. "It's a metal rope of some create!"

The spear hit Lomand in his stomach and penetrated out his back. He slumped forward, silent, his face coming to rest on the wooden shaft that impaled him.

"No!" Drailin yelled. "Father! *Father!*"

The boy tried to hold him up but Lomand was dead.

"Dad!" Ser called again. She was crying. "Dad! Watch out!"

The violent jerk of the skiff moving sideways as it was pulled toward the larger frigate mercifully caused the spear meant for Elkinal's chest to hit his shoulder instead. Pain shot through him as the heavy weapon impaled him and the force of the blow, combined with the pull of the grappling hooks, threw him overboard. The cold salt water stung his wound and filled his nose and mouth. Failing to resurface, though he frantically tried to, added to his terror and he eventually took an involuntary breath. The waters of the Sea of Albery burned his airways as they flowed to his lungs. Another unintended though painful breath followed, filling his lungs as if they were water skins. Serisa and Drailin's screams became muffled, fading to nothing as he sank into the depths.

"**D**ad!" Serisa screamed. She reached over the side of their small fishing boat, her hand splashing frantically in the water. "Take my hand! *Dad!*"

Another pull on the grappling lines from the invaders' ship nearly sent her overboard as more than half her weight already leaned over the side. Her stomach slammed hard into the port gunwale, saving her from falling into the ocean but knocking the wind from her. Drailin pulled her back.

"Ser! Are you all right?" he asked.

There was blood on her knees from scraping the forward thwart when she slammed against the gunwale, but she was otherwise intact. Finally, she coughed as air found her lungs.

"Uncle?" she asked.

Drailin shook his head.

A loud bang was felt as the two ships met. Serisa shook from the jolt but also with fear. The shaking in her arms proved too hard to control and she looked back at Drailin, whose jaw quivered.

"We can make it," he said.

"What?"

In answer, her cousin pointed with his eyes to the beach. They were likely three hundred feet from shore, the outline barely visible in the fading light. If they waited until first moon rose, the riptides might be too strong for them to make it to shore.

"I don't know," Serisa said. She looked back to the water, praying her father would resurface.

"Ser, we don't have a choice. We're both strong swimmers. We can make it!"

She felt the boat start to come free from the water's surface. Looking up, Serisa saw the silhouettes of men growing larger. They were being hoisted up to the deck level of the enemy ship. That made her decision for her.

Looking back to her cousin, she nodded. Drailin turned his head back to his father.

"Goodbye, Father." The boy had tears streaming down his face as he told Serisa, "I can't remember the last time I told him I loved him."

"Tell him now," Serisa said.

Drailin shut his eyes tighter, as if to command the tears to stop. Then, in less than a heartbeat's time, he said, "I love you," and dove from the boat.

"Bye, Uncle. Find my father in the Light."

She dove into the dark water.

"Heave!" Gendaeri commanded. "Heave!"

His men, haggard after so many long, desperate journeys but infused with adrenaline at finding these islands, pulled the grappling lines vigorously. The small boat with the two children came toward his scouting frigate. Gendaeri heard the cries of fright from the children, a boy and girl. He judged them to be adolescents, likely only a few years from adulthood. The boy they had use for on the oars and other hard labor.

Let our enemies' hands blister instead of our own.

The girl … well, they had uses for her as well. It had been quite a long journey for his men and their carnality could only be stemmed for so long.

Soon, the shores of these isles would run red, tainting the waters crimson. In the setting sun, he could see mountains less than a day's sail. They were staggering in height, signaling land they so desperately searched for. The fact that it was so close to these thriving islands brought hope to his heart that the continent he saw was also still fertile. So far, their strange prophet, this Dark Diviner, had been accurate in his directions, claiming to have seen and touched fertile land in his visions. He had come to them from the sea, under his own power, supposedly sent by the Underlander himself. The weaponry he had guided them to create, the advanced techniques in shipbuilding, all had quickly made believers of his people. Even Gendaeri had to admit he was cautiously impressed.

My skepticism might actually turn to seeds of belief.

Though this was technically the Orsarians' fifth voyage in search of a new home, it was the first expedition under the Dark

Diviner's guidance. This impressed Gendaeri, something not easily accomplished.

Yes, he thought, *these islands will make a suitable rally point for the rest of the forces.*

The remnants of his invasion force, some hundred ships, were only hours behind him. Roughly thirty thousand Orsarian dark marauders would soon join him on these shores in preparation for the conquest of victory. And, on the capitol ship—the most magnificent vessel ever constructed by his people—the Dark Diviner.

Once these islands were secured, the rest of his armed forces would follow, bringing their complement to more than a hundred and forty thousand dark marauders. That would only be thirty to forty days, depending on the winds. But in the meantime, they would be vulnerable. They must secure all the islands swiftly, and he had given strict orders upon this matter. If even one person escaped to the mainland, it could be devastating to their strategy.

Even now, the other advance teams were surrounding the other islands, doing as he was, destroying all vessels and capturing or killing their crews. He trusted his dark marauders and knew his plan would be executed with all speed and efficiency. Gendaeri's pride swelled within him as he envisioned himself being hailed as his people's savior.

The thud of the small fishing boat striking his frigate's hull brought his mind back to the present. His men shouted curses as two splashes were heard.

"They've gone overboard!" Pelnith shouted. The first officer pointed over the port bow. "Water lamps!"

At his command, a score of thick translucent glass globes with fire inside, each the size of a coconut, were cast into the water.

"There!" a deckhand shouted.

Gendaeri came to the port railing and saw their two would-be-captives frantically swimming away. Their speed through the water was impressive.

"Net cannon!" he ordered.

A small cannon with a reel attached to its side was brought and rested on the railing where Gendaeri stood, one of the many inventions the Dark Diviner had revealed once an altar had been built on the beaches of Orsari.

"Fire!"

The crack of a small explosion chased the spreading net as it spiraled through the air, wider and wider. It landed on the two fleeing children and the weighted edges of the net immediately sank, ensnaring them fully.

"Reel them in!" Pelnith shouted.

Their captives flailed and screamed with panic as they were dragged through the water, toward the frigate. The ship's men jeered derisively at them. They had learned from their own hard experience that there is no sharing of the land, only conquest. At one time, before they had become marauders with dark ships, the admiral supposed this kind of behavior would have been deplorable to his people. As he heard the teens wail in the heavy net, he couldn't imagine why he would have ever felt that way.

That's right, squirm. Fear! Gendaeri taunted in his mind. *You have every reason to be afraid.*

The waves washed up over him repeatedly, finally waking him. He coughed violently, expelling the brine from his lungs, followed by vomiting. Elkinal rolled to his side and let the seawater flow out of him onto the black shore. It washed away with the next wave, moonlight dancing across its small crest. The pain in Elkinal's shoulder shocked him, but it felt no worse than the soreness in his chest and acid-like burn in his nose and throat. His mind drifted to nothing as the shore break waves continued to gently wash up to his waist and retreat, lulling him to sleep.

The sound of gulls soon roused him. Slowly, he split his eyelids open with his fingers, wiping away salty encrustations that had glued them closed, and swiped at the small hermit crabs huddled on his torn pants. The morning sun was bright. A drop of water hit his forehead, followed by another. It felt like a hammer against his throbbing head until he realized it was rain. To the east, the sun shone unabated. Squinting his eyes as he scanned the rest of the sky, Elkinal saw dark clouds almost upon him from the south. The salt water had left his throat dried and swollen. Knowing how fast the rains could come and go, he forced himself to his feet and tore a large leaf from a plant where the beach met the beginning of a forest. He rolled it into a funnel shape and lay back on the sand, inserting the thin end of the leaf-funnel into his mouth and waited.

The clouds arrived over him and released their downpour. Elkinal was once again soaked in moments and the rain captured by his funnel felt strange on his tongue and throat. When a decent mouthful had been accumulated, he swallowed, washing away the briny taste. In less than ten minutes, the clouds had moved on in their travels to Second Island.

As his eyes followed the clouds, taking his gaze north, he spied the black ships. They were beached on both Pearl and Second Island, the closest one about a quarter mile from him. He could have been spotted at any moment and thanked the Ancient Heavens they hadn't yet seen him. Slowly, Elkinal made his way off the beach and into the cover of the forest.

Serisa, Drailin. His mind began to replay the events of the past night. The pain in his heart over his brother's death kept him trapped there. In time, he would grieve him—but not now.

Somewhere, on one of these black ships, were his daughter and nephew—assuming they were still alive.

There must be at least a dozen ships on this shore alone!

Infiltrating them one by one would take incredible stealth and patience, but he did not know what other alternative existed. He would not hide while his home was invaded, while Ser and Drailin may still live. The wound in his shoulder burned, but the adrenaline numbed him. He would deal with the consequences later.

Crawling with his elbows, he dragged his body from the forest and back on to the black sand beach. Elkinal reasoned that with no population living on Pearl Island, the ships beached here would be the lightest defended. He saw much larger ships anchored off shore in Second Island's harbor, and believed there must be many more around Main Island.

As he reached the edge of the beach where the waves began to meet him, he grabbed a rock in each hand, stones heavy enough to sink him if he let them and disappeared beneath the next shore break, back into ocean's depth.

Matter itself matters little, left inert. Once infused by an eternal force, matter comes to matter greatly.

FIFTEEN

~AILSA~

Day 9 of 2nd Rising 393 A.U.

AILSA FELT THE SAND AND BRUSH of the beach under her as she was dragged inland. It had been a trap that she had seen too late, the rope snagging her leg and yanking her to the ground. She couldn't even sit up to reach forward and grab the line by which she was being towed, so great was the force that reeled her in. Several seconds flew by before she had realized what had even happened. She kicked and cursed, twisting her body and clawing at the sand, at bushes and trees as she passed them, but she could find no hold. The feeling of small lacerations and bruises along her legs and backside careened through her as she was hauled over the rough terrain.

"Ailsa!"

Her brother, Collin. Ailsa looked to the left and saw him being dragged as well, his image disappearing and reappearing as the foliage between them thickened and thinned.

They got us both? The others?

Frantically, Ailsa scanned left and right, then arched her head to see behind her until a rock, embedded in the ground, clubbed her from beneath as she flew over it, and all went dark.

Voices. Jumbled voices, speaking unintelligibly. They found her ears then left her thoughts just as quickly. She was floating, swaying in the darkness. She felt something was not right but the small part of her conscious mind could not explain it. There was a dull throbbing somewhere … her feet? No, her head, but why did the throbbing feel like it was coming from *below* her?

My eyes, she thought. *So … heavy.*

The scream jolted her awake, lucidity flushing out the grogginess in less than a heartbeat. As her eyes shot open, the world was upside down and the throbbing in her head turned to full pounding, tidal waves thrashing against her over and over. To her left, was Collin, also upside down. Beyond him, a row of people strung up, like her and Collin, like hogs after slaughter … though the slaughter for them seemed to be just getting started.

"Collin!" she hissed. "Collin! Wake up!"

He hung there, gently swaying, blood crusted through his blond hair that had streamed from his nose, up his face. Whether that was caused from the force of being dragged at high speed or from hanging upside down, she was not sure. A rope ensnared her ankles and she realized then that her hands were bound.

Another scream came and Ailsa turned left, bending her torso to let her see. In the waxing light of first moon, she could make out three men kneeling before one of the captives, a short man. She thought it almost looked like Kuthipara, the same who owned a small glide board shop. Ailsa had bought several glide boards from him over the past few years.

His body was tense, writhing. One of the men—he looked to be touching Kuthipara, near his neck or shoulder—suddenly yanked his hand back. A long slender blade was unsheathed from Kuthipara while another of the kneeling men placed a bucket under Kuthipara's head. The third kneeling man held him still as the blood drained from the puncture, making a small sound, similar to rain on a palmetto leaf, as it pooled into the bucket.

Some of the captives were awake, pleading and fighting against their bonds; others were still unconscious.

Merciful tides! Where are you, Ewan?

She was part of a very small resistance force. They had no idea what they were doing other than whatever they could. She knew they could not change anything on their own, but maybe they could survive long enough for help to arrive.

Help from whom? The mainland doesn't even know yet.

Any weapons they had managed to find were of crude create, mostly adapted fishing equipment and short blades. Ailsa had not so much as struck anyone before her home had been invaded. The invaders, however, seemed to have no shortage of ingenious ways of harming her people.

"Wake up!" she hissed again to Collin. Moving her body, she tried to get some momentum to knock herself into him.

Another scream, this time a female. A girl, barely out of her adolescence. There were only four more before they got to Collin. The rushing adrenaline within Ailsa drowned out the throbbing of her head, though the pain was still present.

Merciful tides, Ewan! Please!

Even if their group had managed to track her and Collin, what could they do? They were not fighters, not soldiers. Ewan himself was sixty, though you couldn't tell it.

Collin's eyes crept open and he moaned softly. Although it felt like several eternities passed before Ailsa saw him understand the situation, it was truly only a few moments.

"Ailsa!" he cried out.

"I'm here," she whispered.

Collin looked to his right, meeting her eyes, horror upon his face. Another scream came and Collin turned to see the gruesome actions playing out before him. He turned back to Ailsa, shaking his head.

"My hands are bound."

"I know," she answered. "Mine, too."

"Ewan? Lorne?"

Ailsa shook her head. "They're not here."

She saw her brother calculate, his eyes light with a dim glimmer of hope. Then, she saw the glimmer fade as he thought through what she had already surmised. There would be no rescue.

Ailsa heard the dripping blood from the current victim become shallower as the supply petered out to a light dribble. The invaders came to the next captive. The man begged fiercely, wriggling with abject desperation as the tip of a long, narrow blade was brought to the skin under his collarbone. The man went rigid as the blade entered him at an angle toward his heart, but no scream.

"Ailsa, I … "

There was nothing to say, nothing that could be done. Tears leaked from her eyes and her bottom lip tightened. The last man before Collin was mercifully asleep when they came to him, but yelled briefly as the blade cut through him before once again falling back to sleep, this time forever. His blood sprayed on the bucket and the sand below him.

They came to Collin.

"No!" Ailsa screamed. "No! Ancients, please!"

Living Light, deliver us! she pleaded inwardly. *Show me a way! Show me how!*

Collin made no sound, no pleading. As the tip of the knife was lined up, one of the other men held his torso and back. Collin turned his head and looked at his sister.

"You know, turtles were always my favorite sea animal."

Ailsa didn't understand what he was saying, such a random thing to say, especially now. Had his mind broken from the stress? Was he still there? Inside?

"Wh-what?" she asked, her lip trembling uncontrollably.

Collin smiled, if only mildly. "Look away, sister. I love you."

The sobs from Ailsa stopped her reply. She wanted to tell him the same, how she loved him as her younger brother, to not be afraid, that they would find each other in the Light and—

Collin suddenly arched his back and violently curled forward, bashing the brow of his head into the man with the knife. The man cried out in surprise and pain, bringing a hand to his eye. It came away bloody and he yelled what must have been a curse. The other two, still kneeling, started to get up. Collin lurched forward again and bit one of them on the face. The man screamed while the third man started punching Collin, his head, his stomach, but Collin refused to let go. The man's screaming became louder as Collin grunted in triumph, ripping the man's left cheek free. Reeling, the disfigured invader backed up hurriedly, screaming as he tripped over himself and fell.

The second man, the only one Collin had not harmed, wrapped his arms around Ailsa's squirming brother from behind, out of range of gnashing teeth and bashing heads. The man with the knife laughed, blinking his eye where blood from the broken skin of his eyebrow flowed.

"Is good," he said.

Ailsa was terrified but more stunned to hear this monster speak in her own tongue. He brought the blade back to Collin.

"Is good," the man said again, this time with his free hand on Collin's face, gently touching it. "Dark Diviner teach us about you. Say, strong blood good for Orsarians, blood like yours. Say, make this island his altar. Make dark marauders strong, conquer land."

Collin, still struggling, spat in his face.

The smile of the knife-wielding man—*Orsarian?*—became tight. The hand on Collin's face moved to his neck and grabbed the hair at the back of his head firmly.

"No!" Ailsa screamed, her voice cracking.

She heard the knife thrust into her brother, saw his face go pale with pain as his neck muscles constricted.

"Collin!"

A rush of footfall found her ears, shadows of others coming into view as shouts and curses erupted. A figure ran from the brush in front of her, holding a rock and slamming it down on the man who had stabbed her brother. The man's skull caved in. Ailsa could not take her eyes off Collin. Even in the darkness, she saw his pallor change as his life flowed out of him.

"Cut her down!" shouted a voice, a *familiar* voice.

Kneeling before her, she saw the kind face of Ewan, his seemingly ever-present gray and dirty blond scruff giving her a quick, sad smile.

"We've got you, Ailsa. Hang on."

The remaining shouts and sounds of fighting died in a few moments, Lorne and Blare now coming into her view. Ewan held her as they cut her bonds, letting her down to the ground slowly. Shouts in another language were heard, not far off and approaching fast.

"We have to go!" Lorne said.

"Collin," Ailsa said. Her voice sounded monotone to her.

Ewan's eyes saddened and he shook his head. "We have to leave, Ail. I'm sorry."

"Now!" Lorne said tightly. "They are *coming*!"

"I know you're hurt, but you have to run, Ailsa," Ewan said. "We have our glide boards and a plan but we need to get out of here, *right now.*"

It was as if she were in a dream. She nodded slightly and ran into the brush after her friends, leaving the part of her that had died along with Collin behind forever.

The Orsarians occupied all the islands. Ailsa hid on Fourth Island with the four others of her group in a cluster of palm frond bushes and waited for night to come. More and more people were being rounded up from villages and moved farther inland. She knew the fate that awaited them, sickening her as she thought of her brother, the massacre from the night before. She and those with her remained hidden, wanting but unable to help.

The waves on the west coast of Fourth Island were always best for wave gliding, something she had done since she was old enough to swim. She loved feeling the water with her hand as the waves barreled around her, and the spray of the salt water against her face when the wave's lip met the surface of the ocean. She had been on a wave two days ago, the best of the season so far, when foreign ships had come into view, approaching from both the south and north.

Each of her four friends had their glide boards with them along with a small, rolled up wind sail that could be unfurled and mounted if desired. The sail was wrapped around a small wooden mast, roughly six feet tall, and secured by a thin rope that would hoist the sail as a mooring and keep it taut. Carrying the extra weight would make it harder to get out beyond the shore break, but they would need the wind sails for their journey if they hoped to reach P'lor. It was a day's distance by ship. Ailsa did not know how long it would take on her glide board, sail hoisted or not. Regardless, they would have to paddle out for several miles, even in the dark, before daring to raise the sails.

Even if the invaders had not destroyed all the boats available, it would be impossible to get beyond the patrols. Black ships scouted the north-south running shorelines on the island relentlessly, searching for those attempting to do exactly what she and her friends meant to accomplish.

"There's only one blind spot I can see," Ewan said. The oldest of the group, he'd been gliding waves since before Ailsa was born. Now only twenty-four, she hoped she would be able to live to see sixty as Ewan had.

"When two ships cross, they are unlikely to look behind each other," he continued. "We need to be in the water, duck-diving the waves, right before this happens. They'll likely be looking at each other, making sure not to come too close as they pass … I hope. Then, after they pass each other, we must cut through the path behind their sterns. The closer we are to their sterns, the better. The wake will make for a tough swim, but we all can do it."

"Even if they don't see us paddling out, they'll see us after once we pass them," Lorne, Ewan's son, said.

Ewan shrugged. "We have to take that chance. I'd rather die out there than here."

Ailsa knew he meant dying *like Collin* when he said "here".

"Besides," he continued, "it's unlikely they'll be looking west. Their attention should be east, toward the shorelines."

Ailsa agreed with Ewan, but her hands still shook from anxiety at what they were about to attempt.

Blare and Fennel, her other two friends, were silent. Ailsa could see their apprehension as well, especially Fennel. She was not as strong a swimmer as the rest of them.

They all drank heavily from their water skins that were filled at the small stream on the north end of the island, draining them completely.

"Now, listen," Ewan continued. "Assuming, by the Light's grace, we make it beyond the patrols, there are still dangers. Hoist your sails and keep a westward bearing. Use the Jarwyn peaks as a navigation point but stay north of them.

"The night will be easier, but once the adrenaline wears off and morning comes, you'll be thirsty and hungry. Each of you can last a day or two without food, but when expending as much energy as we'll be using, your bodies will crave nourishment. Above all, it will want water. You will have none to drink. You *must not* drink the seawater.

"The sun will beat upon us as well. Try to stay to the shadow of your sail. If you don't have to paddle, don't. The splashing could bring unwanted attention from sharks."

Everyone nodded.

"Remember," Ewan said, "if we don't survive, then Senthara may not survive. We must get to P'lor as fast as possible. If we're lucky, and the winds favor us, we could make it to land by tomorrow night. Help each other, but at least one must survive."

The sun set and the time arrived. Two black-hulled patrol boats approached each other, three more farther off. First moon had not yet risen, but would crest the horizon within the hour.

Ailsa rushed the beach, her glide board and rolled sail under one arm, and jumped into the surf. Four other splashes sounded right next to her. She shook with adrenaline as she started to paddle and kick.

Calm yourself! she pleaded with her body, but it did not heed her. She dove under a wave and resurfaced, continuing to paddle fiercely. The saltwater stung her eyes but she paid it no mind. After her rescue, she had not cared if she had lived or died, too distraught and numb from the death of Collin. But now, that indifference had faded and she *wanted* to live.

Faster!

The ships had nearly passed each other. She was so close to one that she could almost touch its hull. It towered over her, as a sea monster glaring down. She paddled deeper, preparing herself for the wake of the ships and to shoot through the breach behind the sterns, when she lost her grip upon her sail. Ailsa reached out and tried to grab it, but the first waves of the wake hit her and threw her off her glide board. The sail drifted out of reach and began to unwind, floating on the ocean's surface.

Quickly, she got back on her glide board and began to paddle after her fleeing sail.

"Ailsa!" Ewan whispered, his voice nearly drowned out by the surf. "Ailsa! Let it go!"

But she couldn't. She might as well turn around or die now without it.

From the patrol boat heading north, the one closest to her, Ailsa saw glowing spheres tossed into the water around her and her friends. They glowed orange and yellow, balls of fire within them.

Someone shouted, and the south-heading ship suddenly threw its own fire-filled spheres into the water, illuminating more of the ocean's surface.

"Go!" Ewan cried.

Ailsa reached her sail and slid off her board. She kicked her strong legs, keeping herself afloat while she rolled her sail back up around the mast. The narrow mooring line floated nearby and she grabbed it, wrapping it around her wrist for the time being, and continued to frantically roll her sail around the mast. More shouts from the patrol boats arose, becoming more excited as they spotted her and her friends.

Ewan, Lorne, Blare, and Fennel swam hard through the breach, moving fast atop their glide boards. Spears rained down from the stern of the south-facing ship, all missing as they cut through the water. But one thrown from the north ship hit Fennel in her leg and she rolled off her board, screaming. Blare stopped, trying to grab her and haul her onto his board, but was struck full in the middle of his back by a two-pronged spear. He crumpled and fell into the ocean, not resurfacing.

The horror of the scene paralyzed Ailsa. She searched for Ewan and Lorne and spotted them west of the breach. They had *made* it through! The excitement of the moment ended abruptly as she heard a small boom from the starboard stern of the south ship, followed by a weighted net sailing through the air. It ensnared the fleeing father and son, and they wailed in the net like a pair of seals, trying to free themselves. A rope attached to the net led back to the ship.

No! They'll be captured! Ailsa screamed in her mind, knowing what awaited them.

But they were not reeled in. Instead, Ailsa saw the line that led back to the ship go slack and fall to the water. The weight of the net dragged Ewan and Lorne down, even while they hugged their glide boards.

Ailsa flipped her glide board over so that the bowed bottom arched above the water's surface and let go of the sail and mast. She ducked under the board, using it as a shield, and started to kick—slowly, gently, keeping her legs under the water. When she needed air, Ailsa brought her lips to the center of her board, the highest point of the gentle arch of the bowed wood, and drew in quick breaths before quietly pulling her head back under.

It was full dark now. She prayed these invaders had not seen her, or been able to track her, as they pursued her friends, and then felt sick for even being grateful that they had been targeted and not her. But, it had been her sail that got away from her and been seen as it unraveled. They had risked everything to save her and she caused their deaths. The sudden guilt felt like a millstone around her neck.

She drew another shallow breath. When she ducked back under the surface, still hiding beneath her overturned glide board, she saw a shimmer ahead of her: one of the many fire spheres the invaders had thrown into the ocean. The fear that preyed upon her almost made her jerk her board, turning away from the light as fast as she could, but she didn't. Instead, the rational part of her mind took over and she allowed herself to drift toward it, placing the wide nose of her board under the globe so the light did not penetrate down.

From just beneath the water, Ailsa thought she heard another shout.

Have they seen me?

An answer quickly came as her board jolted in her hands, reverberating from something striking it. To her left, a spear cut the water, tiny air bubbles escaping from its surface as it sank. Ailsa did not move. Even if she were above water, she would have been holding her breath. She allowed herself to drift with the current in no particular direction, hoping they would believe her board to simply be drifting aimlessly.

Her lungs burned from being under so long and begged for release. As calmly as she could, she surfaced under her board and drew in another breath, her lips barely breaking the surface.

The fire sphere eventually separated from atop the nose of her board. Mercifully, it drifted away from her and she began again to gently kick, putting more distance between herself and the light. When she felt far enough away, she surfaced completely, slowly looking around. She was still east of the patrol ships, but they were sailing away and would not be able to see her now in the night.

After kicking and paddling for an hour, Ailsa began to cry. Loudly and uncontrolled. There was no one to hear her. She lay on her glide board face down with her arms and legs dangling, sobbing until no more tears came.

She was dead, just like everyone she knew. She could not swim to the mainland, not without her sail, before dying of dehydration or exhaustion. Thoughts of turning back were useless because she did not know which way 'back' was. The light of morning, still hours away, would likely not help depending on where the current took her. Perhaps sharks would find her before dehydration or starvation did.

She paddled for hours more, her hands severely pruned, not knowing her direction of travel. Her neck hurt from careening it up as she lay prone on the glide board, trying to catch an outline of the Jarwyn Mountains in the dark night. The stars and waxing light of second moon were all she had for illumination.

As she paddled, the tender skin of her armpits blistered against the edges of the glide board. Salt water stung the irritated skin, but she paddled on, numb to the pain.

Something bumped the underside of her board. Though startled, Ailsa became deathly still, terror gripping her.

Oh, please, merciful tides! Not like this!

Again, something bumped her board from beneath her, while at the same time she felt a grazing against her left calf. Ailsa jumped, pulling all her limbs up on her board as she shifted to sit on her rear end, pulling her knees to her chest.

"Please, please, please," she muttered. "Not like this. Not like this."

But what had grazed against her leg was not soft or smooth, not like a shark or scaly like a fish of any create. It was hard and textured, slick but with the feeling of algae. Almost like a rock … like …

A turtle!

If she were wrong, it wouldn't matter.

I'm dead.

Lying prone on her stomach once again, Ailsa put her hands back down in the water. Timid at first, her last tendrils of hope soon prevailed and she thrust her hands out, feeling in all directions. It did not take long for her to feel another turtle—if that's what they were. She tried to grab it, but it was gone before she even had a chance. Another ran into her board, and she scrambled desperately to find a hold, her nails scratching its hard shell.

"Hold dimming still, Light curse you!"

Ahead of her, breaking the dark line of the water's surface, Ailsa saw a rounded rock-like image bobbing. It was gone and then back again, just floating there. The moonlight glistened off its wet surface. And then, a beautiful sight filled her night-adjusted vision as the turtle's head crested the water. Long and slow, it raised its head, taking in the night air and … it looked to be waiting.

You don't have to ask me twice! she thought and paddled over to it. *How do I hold on to you?*

In all the excitement of the night, she had completely forgotten about the mooring line, still wrapped around her right wrist and forearm. Quickly unraveling it, she shimmied up her board a bit, maneuvering it just above the turtle, and gently wrapped the line under the base of the turtle's neck, in front of the forward flippers.

"Okay," she whispered. "I'm all yours."

The large turtle submerged and Ailsa gripped the thin rope tightly. She and her glide board began to move. If wonderment should have enraptured her at the auspicious arrival of her savior, it didn't. She knew he would come for her. Deep down, she had known.

I don't know where you're taking me, Collin, but I don't really care.

Ailsa lashed the two ends of the rope together and hooked them onto the small mast coupling that sat a couple feet back from the board's nose, put her head down on her left cheek, and drifted to sleep.

I held it once, the book. The answer. My scar is the only reminder that my faint memory is real.

—Evrin, Keeper of the Living Light

SIXTEEN

~ANTIOUS~

Day 11 of 2nd Rising 393 A.U.

LIEUTENANT ANTIOUS ROAN FOUND HIMSELF SURROUNDED. Ten soldiers menacingly bore down on him, some even his own kind—wood-dwellers. Sweat dripped through his nearly shorn blond hair onto his neck, his body tense with anticipation. He wished for the soil of the Western Province, where the intertwined root systems of the forest would aid him better in feeling his surroundings rather than the hard compact soil of Erynx, the Eastern Province's state city. Sweat dripped down his brow as he concentrated on the shallower vibrational pulses of his attackers.

A throwing knife flew through the air toward him. Antious had felt the vibration of the thrower's leg hit the ground as he adjusted his stance in preparation to hurl the knife, and the short blade's vector was instantly known to him. He arced his sword through the air, deflecting the throw. Before he had time to bring his sword back to a position of defense, two wood-dweller soldiers moved in and swung their dulled practice blades with blurring speed. Though no blade of those participating in Antious's advancement test held a fine enough edge to cut skin, the threat of blunt force trauma gave enough motivation to treat every attack seriously. All advancement examinations were traditionally performed here, at the Erynx Military Academy.

Antious parried the blows masterfully, matching the dizzying speed of his attackers. Another soldier, not a wood-dweller, circled behind him and managed a strike at the back of Antious's thigh. In a real battle, the enemy's blade would have crippled Antious. He grunted in pain and anger, knowing that would count against him.

For all his skill, Antious received heavy scrutiny as he had recently jumped from the enlisted ranks to that of an officer, a move not often done in the Arlethian army. In the wake of his promotion, he left his former fellow enlisted comrades feeling abandoned and found an icy welcome from the officer corps he had joined.

The things I do for love! he thought.

Ignoring the pulsing pain of the budding bruise on his thigh, Antious jumped backward, doing a backflip over the man at his rear just as the two in front of him moved in more forcefully. The three collided, causing a tangle of arms and legs. Antious made what would be a killing blow to each of the three before they could gather their wits and the arbiter called out, signaling their simulated deaths. They would stay where they fell for the remainder of the test. One of the wood-dwellers who had fallen swore. Seven remained, two of which were Arlethians.

Don't underestimate the Senthary soldiers, he heard his mind warn him.

The seven formed a circle around him, each in a battle stance. Antious focused inward and tried to discern each of their vibrational signatures, like trying to distinguish seven unique voices all speaking at once. The vibrations were sharper and more muted through the harder soil of Erynx, but still there was enough distinction among the soldiers and his training took over, mentally noting which signature belonged to which soldier. Antious identified the most zealous-feeling signal and prepared himself, not losing his concentration on the others. Just as the eager man took a step forward, the arbiter called for a brief cessation. The soldier, a field marshal, looked frustrated at being commanded to halt.

General Korin, the supreme commander of all Arlethian armed forces under Lord Kerr, leaned over to the arbiter and whispered something. Antious felt a sinking feeling in his stomach. The general rarely attended an advancement test and Antious knew his attendance here was not out of support or even benign curiosity. To the right of General Korin stood Kalisa, the younger of his two daughters and the most beautiful woman in the Realm to Antious Roan. His eyes met hers briefly and he saw her pride shining through with only a hint of concern. Students of the academy and several score soldiers, including those of his platoon, were present.

Ancients! Don't let me let her down.

If he passed the advancement test, he would be promoted to the rank of captain in the Arlethian army and, he hoped, one step closer to winning over his commanding officer's approval to marry his daughter.

"A change has been made," the arbiter announced. All ten of the soldiers on the field gazed in confusion at Antious, who shrugged and returned their looks with a questioning glance of his own. "We will proceed with a small hindrance upon the lieutenant."

The arbiter motioned to a young man, a third-year student at the military academy, who stepped forward and pulled out a long piece of cloth from his pocket.

"Lieutenant, we shall be pleased to have you conclude your test blindfolded," the arbiter said. "Tulley, you may proceed."

The student, Tulley, made his way through the seven soldiers still standing, pulled the blindfold over Antious's eyes and tied it in the back.

"It was the general's idea," Tulley whispered as he walked away. "Not right, but I couldn't argue. I'm sorry."

"Father, what are you doing?" Antious heard Kalisa ask in protest. "This isn't done until the test for lieutenant colonel!"

"Enough, Kalisa!" the general answered. "Six years as an enlisted soldier should have given him enough experience to handle it. He is not just a mere lieutenant straight out of the academy."

Before Kalisa could voice further protest, General Korin said, "You may continue, arbiter."

A whistle sounded and the test resumed. Not being granted sight of his opponents gave a somewhat dizzy feeling to Antious as he focused only on the vibrational signatures coursing through the ground. He could feel the men's hesitation and pictured confused looks on their faces, but that soon passed as their movements became less hesitant and more focused, feeling the familiar signals of battle stances being assumed.

Wait, he told himself. *Let them come. Be patient ... patient ...*

Two sets of loud footsteps shot toward him. Antious instantly knew them to be Senthary soldiers. One swung his sword from the left at Antious's head but he parried and, instead of striking back, did a reverse leg sweep and sent the man to his backside. With the pommel of his sword's handle, Antious hammer-fisted the man in his solar plexus and he heard a wince as the air left his opponent's lungs. He felt the second man, now behind him as Antious knelt, ready himself to swing down in a hammer blow. Raising his sword behind him and covering his back, Antious blocked the blow and came to his feet. Two more soldiers charged him, making his current odds three to one. Mentally marking where the downed man lay gasping for breath so as not to trip over him, Antious surprised the two new arrivals by charging them instead of assuming a defensive stance. The speed of a wood-dweller was unmatchable by the Senthary, even hard to follow for most eyes in close quarters. Antious raised both his elbows to chin height, pointing them outward with his triceps parallel to the ground and caught both men in the face before they could block the attack. He was careful to raise his elbows up at the last moment so as not to hit his comrades in the throat, that being the normal strike he would have employed if in true combat—a killing blow. The arbiter called out their simulated deaths and they lay still on the ground, both trying to stop the flow of blood from their noses. The third man, still remaining, flanked Antious and struck with what felt like a very weak blow. Antious easily blocked but his counter strike found nothing but air. Confusion didn't have enough time to root itself before a blow he did not sense took him in the torso and knocked him down. His sword fled from his hand in surprise.

Crouched! He was crouched when he attacked, you fool! As soon as Antious had countered with a useless swing well over the soldier's head, the man launched upward and into Antious, a nearly silent attack to sense, even for a wood-dweller.

Now on top of Antious, the soldier secured a chokehold and applied pressure to the veins on the side of his neck. The lieutenant tried to shift his hips and unbalance the soldier but he was strong.

"Finish him!" he heard the onlookers shouting out. Other

cheers and goading were heard but Antious didn't distinguish them as his vision darkened behind the blindfold.

He twisted and raised his hips again, trying to dislodge the soldier but to no avail. The man was too strong.

Elbows, he reminded himself. *One of the weakest joints when not bent.*

Antious brought his arms above his head against the ground and thrust them forward with all his might, driving his curled arms into the inside of the soldier's elbows, forcing them to involuntarily bend and give way. Suddenly off balance, the man's hold broke and his face came forward. Antious was prepared and curled his head forward, forcing his chin to his sternum. The bridge of the soldier's nose met the crown of Antious's head and blossomed with blood. He screamed and brought his hands to his face. Dislodging him now was easy. Antious found his sword, having mentally noted its distance by its vibrational signature when it hit the ground, and brought it down on the man's torso with minimal force. The arbiter called out his simulated death.

Seven gone. Three left. Of the three that still stood, two were wood-dwellers and posed a real threat. Advancement exams were only administered once a year. If he failed, he would have to wait until next year to try again. Worse, it would provide Kalisa's father yet another reason to disapprove of their courtship. The sinking feeling in his stomach became greater and he doubted himself. This was his greatest weakness, Kalisa often told him, that he could not see the leadership potential in himself that she and others so often saw. Thannuel, his best friend from childhood, often teased him that he would someday be a general, even if he didn't want it.

"It's just in you, Antious," Thannuel would say.

All that's in me now is uncertainty.

The faint smell of grain was in the air as a warm southerly wind blew from the plains of the Eastern Province. A foreign vibration came to Antious's attention, from the east: a horse, galloping hard. The beast was beleaguered, Antious could tell, and had likely been running for many hours.

This could be an intentional distraction, he thought, chiding himself to stay focused and alert. He would not have put it past General Korin to add yet another unexpected element to his trial. But the more he listened, felt, the less he thought the horse's arrival was part of the test. He heard a few mutters as the horse and its rider came closer, and Antious could discern that the group itself was the rider's intended destination based on the current vector.

The arbiter called for a cessation and, breathing a sigh of relief, Antious removed the blindfold. The men on the ground where they were killed off during the test began to stand up. Some leveled menacing glares at Antious for their injuries, but he felt no guilt, knowing they would have done the same to him if they had the opportunity. Advancement exams weren't meant to be lethal, but that did not mean they weren't brutal at times.

The rider dismounted, breathless. His demeanor bespoke an urgency and someone brought him a water skin.

"Who is the commanding officer?" the rider asked with heavy breaths.

General Korin stepped forward. "This is the military academy. High Lord Marshal Fortisan leads the academy, but he is away currently. I am General Korin of the Arlethian army and the highest-ranking officer present. What business do you have?"

"General," the rider said, "I am Tolber, a harbormaster at P'lor. The islands have been invaded!"

There was a brief moment when Antious thought he was supposed to answer the rider while still operating at a higher stress level due to his exam. He was in reaction mode. Just as he opened his mouth, Korin spoke, sparing Antious an embarrassing moment.

"You are certain?" Korin's voice contained a dangerous edge, as if warning Tolber against continuing to perpetuate any prank.

"Early this morning, one of our patrol frigates found a woman floating in the harbor on nothing more than a shaped wooden plank … a glide board, I am told. She was unconscious and badly sunburned, her face and lips cracked from exposure. It took us hours to rouse her, seeping water into her mouth and tending to her burns."

"Get to the point!" Korin snapped.

Tolber continued: "She claims to be from the Runic Islands, having made her way across the ocean on her glide board, aided by a turtle."

The look the general gave Tolber bespoke his incredulity.

"She said she barely escaped off Fourth Island a day and half ago, after others with her were killed by patrol boats painted black. The stories she tells … General, I'm convinced an invading force has overrun the islands. This is all I know."

"How can you be certain?" Korin asked.

"I'm not, sir, but that's not my problem. I've delivered the message. What to do now is your problem."

Tolber turned his horse around, and began to ride back to P'lor.

General Korin snapped commands to several officers and sent a messenger to Lord Orion, Provincial Lord of the East.

"We will march to Iskell at once," Korin said to his men. "The rest of you … "—he looked at the students present—" … will return to your barracks and await instructions from your infantry marshals."

Antious joined his men in formation and prepared to move out.

"Not you, Lieutenant Roan," Korin said. "Take your platoon to Calyn and advise Lord Kerr of the situation with all haste."

"Yes, sir!"

Korin moved in so that only he could hear his next words. "Your advancement exam is *not* complete, *Lieutenant.*"

Antious swallowed, choosing silence as his response as he stood at attention.

"Dismissed!" Korin shouted only a nose from Antious's ear.

Antious saluted. "Yes, sir!"

He stole one more longing glance at Kalisa before ordering his platoon to move out.

I was no one before I met you; now you are no one as well. If you tell, no one will believe you.

SEVENTEEN
~ELKINAL~
Day 11 of 2nd Rising 393 A.U.

ELKINAL SLOWLY APPROACHED THE STERN of the first vessel anchored near Second Island through the water. The swim from Pearl to Second was normally an easy one for him, but after two days of near complete exposure to the sea, Elkinal was dehydrated and waterlogged. Only smaller frigates were beached on Pearl Island, making his incursion among them much easier.

All eight frigates had been beached on a cove where the shelf of land disappeared suddenly a few yards after the shore break. The sudden depth of the water made for a natural docking point for smaller ships, especially these black-hulled ships the invaders had sailed in on. The bows were secured on the beach while the sterns were completely afloat. He remembered how shallowly the keels had cut into the water and wondered if that had something to do with their near soundless approach.

The trench was a series of beautiful underwater cliffs, one of Elkinal and Serisa's favorite places to swim. Sea life normally only found much farther off shore manifested itself abundantly in the trench, only a few yards from land. And the water: the deepest blue imaginable. Serisa had often said how surprised she was to see her world when she surfaced, feeling as if she had been transported to a different one entirely when snorkeling at the submerged cliffs. These memories were what kept hope in his heart, that he would find his daughter and nephew yet alive.

The eight frigates docked at the trench on Pearl Island were lightly crewed, some having none at all. Elkinal had easily searched them, scaling rope ladders and nets to the decks. No lookouts were posted, for the enemy had discovered quickly that this island was uninhabited and therefore feared no attack. There would be no reprisals from his people on the other three islands either; they were not warriors or trained in battle. Most were fishers and craftsmen, with a few retired nobility sprinkled among them.

He did not find Serisa and Drailin on the frigates, even though they had been taken by one of them. No doubt they had been transferred to a larger ship, like one he now approached off Second Island. This one was massive: three masts, a quarterdeck as long as one of the frigates he had searched, and a stern that towered higher than any building or tree he had seen in his lifetime, though admittedly he had never been to the mainland. Wellyn's palace in Iskell was said to be surpassed in grandiosity only by the entire Western Province's state city of Calyn, whose spires pierced the clouds. Three horizontal levels of square ports lay stacked above the ship's hull, some covered, others open with dark, open-mouthed log-like structures protruding. They were probably black but it was too hard to tell in the night, barely seeing their outline. Elkinal didn't know what they were, but an uneasy feeling settled upon him as he studied them from the water below.

He came to the aft hull and began searching for a ladder or net with his pruned hands. There was none. He heard the chorus of voices above him, men laughing and shouting. He couldn't make out their language, but thought the tenor was one of mocking or jeering.

He continued searching the hull, making his way to the starboard side of the ship. The wood was smooth, coated in some kind of pitch. There would be almost no friction from the water as this floating city cut through the ocean. If Elkinal weren't so stressed and focused on finding his daughter, he might have been impressed.

Finally, he came to a wooden ladder of sorts, built into the starboard side of the hull itself and slightly out of reach. To the right, a chain hung just above the surface of the water and Elkinal grabbed it. Its thick links rattled slightly and he cursed himself for not being more careful. Any noise could mean his end.

He pushed his feet against the hull, straightening his legs, and awkwardly walked up the blackened wood. When he reached the ladder, he straightened himself and carefully let the massive chain go. His muscles quivered simultaneously with fatigue and adrenaline.

Calm yourself.

Through a piece of rope tied around his waist, he carried a scimitar against his back. He'd found the medium-length curved sword on the sixth ship he searched below deck, and he'd fastened a piece of shroud rope to serve as a belt. He had no experience in sword fighting and hoped he would not have to use it. But, it did not seem all that complicated: sharp edge out toward your opponent and stick him before he sticks you.

He crested the deck and looked through the banister railing. Lanterns and curious glass globes alight with fire inside illuminated parts of the deck. Mercifully, much of the quarterdeck was cloaked in shadow. Below the quarterdeck he would find most of the living quarters, especially those of the officers. Once he got below he could make his way mid-ship, where he guessed any prisoners would be held.

Wet and dripping, Elkinal stayed in the shadows as he made his way aft. He saw light approaching and hunkered down behind some barrels. Elkinal feared the passing guard would hear his heart thudding against his chest like a kettledrum. He tried not to stare at the lantern from his hiding place, preserving his night vision.

The guard passed.

Below deck, Elkinal made his way cautiously past quarters, most crude and giving off the stench of stale body odor. It was obvious these people had been on a voyage of long duration. A mug of water sat on a table in one of the rooms, and a roll of hardened bread. He greedily drank the water and shoved the roll into his mouth. The bread crunched as he chewed.

Voices became louder as he made his way forward to mid-ship through a narrow hallway. Lanterns were strewn head high every few paces on both sides. The jeering he had heard earlier came from below deck, directly ahead of him. He swallowed and forced himself to breathe steadily. A door met him at the end of a hallway. Just as he was about to gently push, a hand grabbed his shoulder from behind and he felt the scimitar yanked from the rope around his waist. He spun and faced a man with olive skin and black hair.

Elkinal charged the man. The hallway left little room to maneuver. The dark-skinned man brought the scimitar up with an uppercut motion and Elkinal barely blocked it with his left arm, shifting his body to the side. His back hit the wall and he used it as a counterpoint as he latched onto the man's sword arm and wrenched his wrist outward. The man yelped in pain and let go of the sword but wriggled his arm free. A knee found Elkinal's stomach, knocking the wind from him, followed by a double hammer-fist upon his back. He fell face first to the floor and thought for certain the commotion would bring others. Reaching out with both arms, he locked his hands around the man's ankles and jumped to his feet with all his might, thrusting his powerful legs upward. His opponent yelped in surprise as the wooden planks found his backside hard.

Elkinal wobbled a bit, back on his feet, his vision marred by black spots. He grabbed a lantern from its hold and slammed it down on his attacker's head, the glass breaking and oil from its base washing out on the man's head. It caught flame and the man screamed, writhing upon the floor.

Elkinal needed to shut the man up, quickly. Finding the scimitar, the peaceful islander stabbed the man in his chest, being sure to go under the rib cage toward the heart. The screams stopped almost instantly.

Elkinal's hands shook and he suddenly felt sick. He had little in his stomach other than the water and hardened bread he had consumed moments before, but it came up regardless. Taking another's life had never once entered his mind as a possibility before his home was invaded. He knew he might be called upon to do it in order to save his family but did not know if he could when the moment came. He was almost ashamed at how easily he had done it. No hesitation. No remorse. The physical aftermath, the retching, was more from the adrenaline than any revulsion. He knew he could do it again.

Returning to the door at the end of the hallway, from behind which came the raucous noise that proved loud enough to drown out his brawl, he pushed it open enough to see through a crack. A dining room, tables pushed to the sides. A crowd of a score, maybe more, stood around two men circling each other. Both had short blades. One was Drailin. His nephew had bruises on his face, purple and red. His left eye was swollen shut with crusted blood around it. These were not new wounds. He fought not another prisoner, but one of the enemy sailors.

The men around him, all olive skinned with black hair, spat and threw rotten food at Drailin as he stepped warily in a defense stance. The lad was big for his age, resembling his father, Lomand; but Elkinal could see the fear on his face. And then, he saw Serisa, arms chained above her head on a far wall, facing out. The look on his daughter's face was one of despair, of being broken. Her clothing was ragged and torn, and she herself bore several bruises. Her arms, shoulders, neck. Sandy blonde hair hung disheveled past her shoulders, part of it crusted with blood.

Elkinal's anger flared, but he held himself in check. Drailin's sparring partner lunged toward him, but the boy moved aside and swung his own short blade. He missed, but managed a kick to the man's back, throwing him off balance. The man whirled around, throwing his arm in a wide arc and caught Drailin on the forearm. The crowd cheered and Elkinal saw his daughter wince.

A thin line of blood came from the cut and Drailin stepped back. Seeing the boy stagger, Drailin's opponent rushed forward and landed a two-footed flying kick in his chest. Drailin fell to the ground, his short blade flying free from his grasp. Instantly, the man was on him, choking him. Drailin flailed his arms, clawing at the man's face. The boy managed to get a finger in the man's mouth and pulled his cheek from the inside. Before the skin tore, he relented and released his chokehold on Drailin's neck.

Drailin landed several blows on the man's face and the crowd booed, throwing more trash and rotten food. Elkinal's grip on his scimitar tightened and his mind searched for an answer of how to proceed. Drailin was likely to get himself killed if this continued much longer. As if in answer to his fears, Elkinal saw his nephew get taken by surprise as the man he fought jumped on his back with an arm around his neck.

No! he thought as the man's other arm, holding his short blade, came up. Having no vision behind him, there was no way Drailin could see the attack to block it. But then, something unexpected happened. The man threw his short blade, making sure Drailin could not reach it, and brought that arm under the arm already across Drailin's neck, locking the hold.

He's not trying to kill him, Elkinal realized. *Why?*

Drailin lost consciousness as blood and oxygen were cut off from his brain. He slumped to the floor and the crowd went wild. The victor raised his arms in triumph and Serisa started to squirm in her shackles. She called for Drailin but he didn't rise.

The man who had beaten Elkinal's nephew accepted a key and walked to where Serisa was chained to the wall. She lashed out at him and the crowd laughed, pulling back in mock fear. The man unchained her shackles at the wall, but not around her wrists, and started to lead her away amid howls and lewd gestures from his companions.

Elkinal finally understood and his anger turned to rage. This was obviously a nightly ritual for the crew. They posed Drailin as Serisa's protector in this devious sport of theirs. If one defeated Drailin … well the prize was obvious.

Ancients help me!

A few dragged Drailin's unconscious body back to a cell and splashed a bucket of water on his face. Elkinal watched as his daughter was pulled down a corridor at the opposite side of the large room, toward the front of the ship on the port side.

There must be another way through! He could not fight his way to his daughter, not against such odds. He retreated back up the stairs to the quarterdeck and peered across the ship. Few were on the ship's deck; most were probably below for the entertainment.

Staying to the shadows, Elkinal made his way port and found a trapdoor he assumed to be forward of the dining room, the small arena, just below deck. Slowly lifting the hatch, he saw a thin hallway below, much the same as the one where he had just killed someone in the starboard aft section of the ship. Holding his breath, he let himself down through the trap door as silently as he could, and crouched. He was tense, ready. No one.

Stepping lightly, he made his way astern. The familiar ambience of men in the dining room found his ears and he grappled with the urge to rush in and strike down as many as he could before they overtook him.

And then he heard it: muffled cries that he knew to be his daughter's, in a room just ahead to his right. The sound of a gruff voice yelling commands or curses, Elkinal could not be sure which. The door was locked. Breaking it down would cause too much noise. Sweat made lines down his face as he thought. He would have to gamble.

His fist struck the door three times and he again held his breath. An answer came, one of a foreign tongue.

Living Light! Open the door, please!

He knocked again. An agitated answer came and Elkinal heard footsteps approaching the threshold. For good measure, he mumbled something inaudible and knocked once more.

As soon as he heard the latch unlock, he threw his weight against the door, forcing it open, pushing with his legs against the opposite wall of the narrow hallway. The man yelled out, but tripped as he stumbled backwards. Elkinal shut the door, quickly locking it.

"Dad!" Serisa cried out between tears and gasps. Her clothes were ripped even more than before, barely covering her, and a fresh bruise was puffy on her face.

Elkinal turned murderous. "You know, I'm rather fond of splitting open oysters and searching for their treasure." He knew the man down on the ground could not understand him, but the blade at his throat kept him still. "Sometimes, there's nothing there but the meat. But sometimes, rare but often enough, I find a pearl." Elkinal took the pearl from his pouch he had found three days ago and held it between his fingers.

The man looked curiously at him and eyed the pearl with interest. Slowly, he looked at Serisa and then back at the pearl. He raised a hand, palm up, and nodded.

"No," Elkinal said with a half-smile. "I'm not buying her from you with this. She's worth far more than this trifle."

Turning to Serisa, he asked, "Are you all right?"

She nodded with a whimper.

"You think you can hold this sword at his throat?"

Her shaking hands, slow movements ... her timidity ... so unnatural for his bright-eyed daughter. They were dimmer now— her eyes. Seeing this brewed a storm inside him, a fatherly torrent of righteous indignation. Elkinal reached for his daughter's hand and she jumped slightly.

"Serisa, I am your father," he said gently. "You are safe now."

Her lower lip quivered as her eyes glanced back toward the man on the ground.

"He's nothing," Elkinal said. "Look at me, not him."

Her eyes came back to his. The dam that had held back all her emotional vulnerabilities was cracking.

"You don't have to be brave anymore, Ser. That's my job now. But I do know something that might make you feel a little better."

Again, Elkinal motioned for her to hold the sword and he saw her fortitude take over, the strength that he knew she had despite these men trying to break her. Serisa stood and with two hands, held the blade at her abuser's throat. Its point pricked him and drew a drop of blood. The man recoiled.

"No, it's okay," Elkinal said, making a calming gesture to the man but still feeling the rage of righteous indignation upon him. When he settled, Elkinal pounced, pinning one knee on the man's chest and grabbing his face with a powerful hand. With the other hand, he forced the pearl into the man's mouth, pushing it down his throat and then clenching it shut. Keeping his hand over the man's mouth as he tried to scream, Elkinal pinched his nose closed. The man struggled but Elkinal did not let up until he had swallowed the pearl completely.

"Now, as I was saying," Elkinal said, taking the curved sword back from his daughter. "Oystering is one of my favorite things. I'm pretty good at it. Let's find out what treasure lies inside you, shall we?"

The rapist finally understood. A strong kick to the man's throat crushed his larynx, making his screams no more than airy whines. Standing on both arms, clamping them down, Elkinal sank the tip of the scimitar into the man's navel and carefully sawed up. The sternum required a bit of extra effort, but he got through it. The man's writhing stopped at about the time his diaphragm was destroyed.

After pulling apart the dead man's rib cage, opening it much like an oyster, Elkinal ripped and tore, fished and reached, knowing he would find what he sought but also knowing it was not what he truly hoped to find. Somewhere, in the carnage, Elkinal searched for his daughter's dignity, for her lost innocence. Tears fell to his bloodied hands as he worked, tears of regret and failure for not being able to protect that which he should have, that which every father was charged to safeguard at all costs by the Ancient Heavens. Redemption: that was what he meant to exhume from the ruin of this man as he thrashed in his organs and ichor.

A hand touched his shoulder. It shocked Elkinal and he tried to pull away, but the hand tightened around his wet shirt.

"Daddy?"

Serisa's voice struck like lightning to his heart.

"Daddy, it's okay," she said.

At the base of the trachea, he saw the pearl, a piece of white barely visible through the tissue and blood that covered it. He retrieved it and held it between his thumb and forefinger. Wiping it clean with his soiled hands, Elkinal stared at the pearl, searching its surface diligently, desperately looking—

"Dad, Drailin ... we have to get to him."

He realized then he would never find it, never be able to give it back to her. He only sought to restore his daughter, to make her whole again; but it would not be. Still on his knees, he leaned his head toward Serisa's young, tender hand. She reached her other hand to his head, through his hair, and gently pulled him to her.

His body heaved as his head lay against Serisa's lap, salty tears washing away the blood splatter on his face.

Forgive me! Forgive me! Forgive me! he wailed inside, but the words could not form on his lips between his silent cries. It only lasted a minute before the sobs subsided, but the echoes of this night would never leave him.

"All right," he finally said with a choked, hoarse voice. "All right, let's get Lomand's boy."

Elkinal led Serisa back through the hallway by the hand, toward the stairway he had sneaked down by the port bow. The staircase split, offering a choice of ascending to the main deck or further below deck. Only the faintest glow of light escaped from the lower level. While he had intended to simply retrace his steps, staying to the shadows, Elkinal thought he saw something in a glimmer of light on the lower deck that startled him.

"Get back!" he whispered, forcing Serisa and himself flat against the wall, shielding them from sight by hiding behind the ascending stairway.

"What is it?" Serisa asked. Elkinal felt her tremble under his arm that was extended across her body.

He didn't answer for a few moments, intently listening. "I thought I saw ... " Leaning forward, he peered down the stairway, slowly bringing his head around the wall that split the stairway in half.

The glimmer came again and shadows extended across the floor and walked up the walls. He jerked his head back, holding his breath. He felt Serisa tense, his arm still across her body. She tugged on him, trying to pull him back to her. Turning his head, he saw the terror in her wide eyes as she shook her head, pleading.

Wait, he said to himself. *The glimmer, the shadows ...*

Elkinal took his daughter's hand in his, interlocking their fingers and gripped the blood-coated sword more firmly with his other hand. Taking a deep breath and standing up straight, he started down the staircase swiftly with Serisa in tow.

He landed at the lower deck with wobbly knees, tense and ready. When no one attacked or raised an alarm at their appearance, Elkinal slowly let out his pent-up breath. On the walls were several torches, emitting their orange glow and casting ever-changing shadows as the wind caressed the dancing flames.

The wind ... why is their wind below deck?

The quarters they were in were tight with a low ceiling and even lower beams that ran from port to starboard, staggered every ten feet or so. He grabbed a torch from its sconce and slowly moved it through the air, waiting for his eyes to adjust.

There were lanterns on the deck above us. Why use open flame on this deck?

A few steps forward and Elkinal's left foot caught on something, something that blocked it. He brought the torch lower, his vision finally starting to adjust to the dark setting, and stared. Before him was one of the fat, dark log-like things. As he knelt down to inspect it more closely, the torch flickered, frightening him for a split second.

A breeze. It ran off the left the side of his face, coming from the port. He knew what he would see even before he turned into the wind: an open square port, the likes of which he had seen from the water below the starboard side. In the dim light, he could make out the outlines of roughly a dozen more of these strange windows, each with its own black tube.

"Dad, let's go," Serisa urged.

"I need to see this, Ser."

"Why?"

He had a good answer, just not one he could articulate currently. Running his hand up the cylindrical thing, he was surprised by how cold it was to the touch.

"It's metal," he mumbled. Extending the torch to his daughter, he said, "Hold this for a minute."

Elkinal put himself squarely behind the metal tube and found it mounted upon a wooden casing with wheels. A small hole was in the top of the shaft with a twine-like rope protruding. Squatting, he tried to lift the contraption, wrapping his arms under the rounded backside. After getting it maybe an inch off the ground, he almost lost his grip, his palms slick with sweat.

"Dad!"

He let it down as silently as he could, still intrigued but stumped. Serisa gave him the torch back. Then he saw it: a pile of black, round balls stacked in a pyramid form to the right of the heavy mystery object. A single black ball was heavy, but he managed lifting it just fine. It was also metal, the size of two or three coconuts. Other, smaller rock-like things were also present, varying in size from a large pearl to an orange. He spun quickly, looking to the wall behind him and saw a row of barrels, each tied down with a rope, securing it against the wall. Black sand-like residue culminated on some of the lids of the barrels.

I wonder …

Elkinal set down his sword and pried the lid off the closest barrel with his short blade. Black sand, thicker and larger granules than the sand on Pearl Island, filled the barrel. The smell was pungent and his nose wrinkled.

"Why are they storing sand?" Serisa asked.

He hated the timidity now in his daughter's voice, pained tones that used to be joyful.

"I don't really think this is sand, Ser."

Elkinal scooped some of the substance into his hand—it was lighter than sand—and placed it on the floor in front of him.

Merciful tides, I hope this is less foolish than I think it is.

"Get back, Ser." Elkinal brought the torch down to the pile of black grit.

"I don't think that's a good—"

Serisa's protest was cut short by a bright flare accompanied by snapping and popping. Elkinal turned from the blaze and covered his daughter, forcing her to the floor. But, instead of being consumed from the fire, it quickly died, leaving them again in darkness save for the glow of the torches. Picking himself up, the fisherman went to where the fire was and saw that the black sand—or whatever it was—had disappeared. Left in its stead was the charred wood of the wooden planks, still smoking.

"It burned?" Serisa asked. "The sand burned?"

Elkinal just nodded, his mouth slightly agape. Finally he said, "I have an idea." Elkinal began cutting free each of the barrels from their bonds.

"Now," he said softly, "we stack them."

They worked quickly. Elkinal saw the purpose in his daughter's eyes as she understood what they were about.

"Will it blow the whole ship?" she asked.

"I, uh … I really don't know. If so, I hope not until after we make it out of here with Drailin."

Hurried footfall and concerned voices were heard above them. Elkinal froze.

"They must have found him," he said, not needing to be more specific about whom he meant. "We need to move!"

They had stacked nine barrels. With a tenth, Elkinal poured a long stream of the fire sand—*maybe that's what we'll call it*—back toward the staircase they had descended. It was maybe forty feet.

"Want to do the honors?" Elkinal asked with a grin despite his heart thudding hard against his chest.

"I don't care!" Serisa said. "We just have to get out of here fast!" She hesitated and looked back at the stack of barrels. "Yeah, actually, I do."

She grabbed the torch and threw it down. The fire sand flared to life but the flames—more like sparks—didn't move up the trail very fast.

"Is it going to work?" she asked.

Elkinal retrieved his sword from the deck and put it in the rope sling over his shoulder. "The slow burn gives us a little time, but I don't think we want to be here to find out what happens at the end."

They ran up the stairs, now less concerned about stealth than finding Drailin and getting off the ship with all haste. Elkinal started to round the corner and head up the next flight when Serisa grabbed his arm.

"This way," she said, pointing down the hallway in the opposite direction. "The dining hall is at the end of the hall."

Of course, Elkinal thought, realizing it must be the same entrance Serisa had been dragged out of by her now dead assailant.

They ran down the hallway, pointedly ignoring the cabin where Serisa had been rescued, and sprang though the entrance of the dining hall that had been converted to an arena. Elkinal immediately spotted Drailin, still unconscious in his cell. It was odd to have holding cells adjacent to the dining hall, unless you meant to torment your prisoners by starving them and making them watch as you feasted.

A single guard stood watch over his nephew and shouted in alarm. The man, dark haired and olive in his complexion like his shipmates, drew a scimitar and ran toward them. Elkinal retrieved his own from the crude rope sheath and brought it up to meet the enemy's blade just in time to keep his nose.

Serisa went to Drailin and tried to rouse him. "Drailin, get up! Drailin!" She found the bucket, rank with the smell of excrement, and dipped it in a large tank of water. When the water hit her cousin he awoke with a start, lashing out in reflex.

"Drailin! We're getting out of here!"

Elkinal knew he was in trouble. He had managed to win the other two confrontations due to surprise or circumstance, but now he faced an opponent who had room to move and who was skilled with the blade, unlike Elkinal. A fisherman had no need of such training. His movements were clumsy in comparison to his enemy's and too slow to return any attacks, being forced to do nothing but block.

Then came the fruition of their planned distraction. The boat rocked, skewing starboard, accompanied by a crack of thunder. The barrels of fire sand had done their work and the shock of it made Elkinal's assailant stumble with surprise. The breach in the man's focus proved lethal. Elkinal's sword found a way through his distracted defense and into his gut. The fisherman left it there, not paying the man another second of attention, and ran to the cell.

"It's locked!" Serisa said.

Elkinal looked back to the man, his scimitar still impaled in his stomach.

The keys have to be on him.

Amazingly, the man still stood, although he struggled. He was trying to uncap a vial that hung around his neck, bringing it close to his mouth with shaky hands. The look on the man's face was … snide? Whatever he was trying to do obviously was not going to be good.

Elkinal kicked his knees, buckling them, and then forced him down, snatching the vial from around his neck and throwing it aside. Blood spilled out when it hit the wall. He searched the man, feeling his clothes, arms, legs, and hips. Underneath a thick leather belt, Elkinal found what he sought. From above, he heard the yells of confusion and stampede of feet making their way toward the blaze at the bow of the ship.

He brought the key to the cell door, unlocked it, and grabbed his nephew by the shoulder, pulling him hard. "We have to move now!" Smoke started to make its way into the hallway whence he and Ser had come.

"Out the back!" Elkinal commanded, pointing to the door from where he had first spied Drailin sparring. They ran, nearly tripping over the still smoldering corpse Elkinal had killed, his face unrecognizable. The shattered lantern lay beside him. Serisa stifled a scream and kept moving.

Once on the quarterdeck, Elkinal saw the extent of the havoc he had created. The bowsprit, along with the jib boom, was completely blown away. Even though they now stood on the starboard side near the stern, he could imagine the gaping hole in the port bow. Black billowing smoke circled up into the night sky, obscuring the view of the stars.

"It's a long way down," Drailin mumbled as he looked over the railing. His left eye was badly damaged, the skin around it lacerated.

"We have to jump!" Elkinal said. "While they're still distracted. They will come looking for saboteurs before long."

The boy grunted with a sound that bespoke his feeling of numbness, as if accepting this fact as just one more aspect of his torture. He jumped. Elkinal grabbed his daughter's hand and they leaped together into the dark water below.

From his luxuriously appointed quarters, the Dark Diviner emerged, his robes flowing around him in the starry night. The screams and curses from the crew filled his ears as the smoke barreled upwards in a cyclone-like funnel, black with orange and red embers weaving through it.

Calmly, the Dark Diviner walked upon the capitol ship's deck, a clear irony to the frenzied state all around him. Men hauling water to the fire at the port bow and pulling burned bodies from the debris. Some screamed and writhed, some lay still with the stillness that only death can bring.

The heat of the blaze warmed his face as he closed the distance. The crew noticed him and one by one became silent, looking on the Dark Diviner to deliver them.

He would.

Gazing up to the empyrean firmament, he gathered what power second moon would bestow upon him. It was not as puissant as the power of first moon, but would suffice for this trifling matter.

The Dark Diviner extended his arms to the flames, hands in a cupping formation. Then, opening his mouth wide, he sucked in a sharp, short breath. The fire leaped from the ship's surface, leaving smoking and charred wood and debris behind, into his cupped hands. The blaze reduced in size as it gathered in his hands, becoming a small, smokeless ball of orange.

Bringing the fireball close, he whispered, *"Ontridari osk-lalune."*

The spherical fire launched from his hand heavenward, as if a miniature comet returning to its galactic home.

It was the light of first moon—in some way we could not understand—that we thought the Thoulden-sha harnessed his Influence and power. We could not have been more wrong.

—Prime Vicar Holden of the New Changrual Order,
Lectures on the Restoration of Confluence

EIGHTEEN

~THANNUEL~

Day 4 of 3rd Rising 393 A.U.

CALYN BUZZED WITH THE NEWS OF INVASION. Thannuel Kerr, newly appointed Lord of the Western Province, prepared to leave for Iskell, the capital of Senthara, where he would council with Prime Lord Parlan Wellyn and the other Lords of the Realm. More than a century had passed since Senthara was last invaded by forces whose lands were in the midst of cycling.

Lord Thannuel Kerr, only twenty-six years old, was young to have been appointed to lordship. But his father, Branton Kerr, suffered from some disease that the healers could not effectively treat. Last year, Branton had abdicated in favor of his son and still resided with them at Hold Kerr. The middle-aged lord did not fare well and his outlook was grim.

Thannuel sat with Moira, the love of his life since he was fourteen, since he had first met her at his hold with her parents and younger sister, Molina.

"What will happen?" Lady Kerr asked. "Will you be away in Iskell long?"

Thannuel was silent, packing his last provisions.

"Thannuel?"

"Hmm?" he grunted.

"Are you not hearing me? When will you return?"

"It will depend on what the Prime Lord and the council plan, but I shouldn't be gone for more than a couple span. A score of ships are already completed, more every day," Thannuel said.

"And you aren't going on one of them, right?"

Thannuel stopped what he was doing and looked up at Moira. He hadn't noticed the concern before that so clearly radiated from her. Coming to her, he took her hands in his and kissed her forehead.

"They don't send lords onto the field of battle, Moira. Not unless the situation is dire."

"But you're not a normal lord, Thannuel. I know you. You'll not simply stand apart from the fight. When have you ever been able to stand by when danger was close? In fact, you're likely to be the first one to set foot on those ships."

Thannuel sighed deeply as he looked down upon his wife.

"Promise me you won't go; promise you'll let the soldiers do their jobs and return here, to me," Moira said. She put her hand to her stomach longingly. Thannuel knew how she ached for a child.

For six years they had tried, to no avail. Every healer in the Realm prescribed different remedies and solutions, but none caused Moira's womb to quicken with child. She had wondered aloud many times if the Ancient Heavens had no children left to grant her or if she were in some way unworthy.

"My love, I won't be anywhere near the battle. I'm going to a war council to discuss strategy, nothing more. I assure you," Thannuel said. "I'm not even packed for such a long journey, see?" He held up two medium-sized bags, one in each hand.

"Wellyn will send you, I know it. How can he not? You are the most skilled with steel in all the Realm. I know you know this."

"Moira, I—"

"The Marishee? As if being sixteen when you defeated eight of them was not enough—"

"I wasn't the only one there—"

"You managed to disband their rebellion five years ago and end their sedition," Moira said. "No, husband, you have made yourself too valuable, I'm afraid."

The small pang of guilt that Thannuel carried with him suddenly flared to life, reminding him that Moira had almost been lost for his dealings with that rebellion.

A knock came at the door and Antious Roan popped his head in. Taking in the scene, he became embarrassed.

"Forgive me, my Lord, Lady Kerr," he said.

"Antious, don't be daft, come in!" Thannuel snapped. "We were just talking about you. Are we about ready?"

"Yes, Lord Kerr."

"Lieutenant, I'm going to demote you to kitchen duty if you don't stop with this 'my Lord' and 'Lord Kerr' ridiculousness."

"As you wish, *your Grace,*" Antious retorted with a smile.

"Antious," Moira asked, "are you ever going to marry her?"

"Yes, what's the holdup?" Thannuel asked.

Antious's face clouded. "It's not so simple," he grumbled.

"Of course it is. Kalisa loves you, you love her. Only lords' children's marriages are arranged anymore. You're under no obligation to anyone else. Why delay?"

"Try marrying the daughter of your commanding officer," Antious said. "It's not that easy."

Moira cracked a smile. "But you're an officer now. You left the enlisted ranks and started over. Wasn't that General Korin's concern? That his daughter would not marry an enlisted man?"

"I think that may have backfired on me. Kalisa now tells me her father can't respect a man who abandons his post."

Moira rolled her eyes. "You know he's just being a father. It's part of his job to be difficult when his daughter is involved. Thannuel, should you have a talk with General Korin?"

"I, uh … "

"No, thank you, Lady Kerr, but I'm certain that would make matters worse," Antious said sheepishly.

"Well, let's be off, then," Thannuel said, eager to change the subject.

Moira rose. Thannuel leaned in and kissed her.

"Promise me you won't go," she requested once more.

"I promise I'll come back. It won't be more than a couple span, don't worry."

"I'm not worried," Moira said, but Thannuel could hear the lie in her voice.

"Antious, the long-term provisions are packed?" Thannuel asked when they had exited the hold.

"Yes. I was discreet, as you directed," Antious answered. They came to the caravan of carriages, loaded down with supplies. Antious's platoon of fifty Arlethian soldiers stood at ease but came to attention at seeing their lieutenant and lord.

"Thank you. It's only a precaution."

"I don't want to have to face her when she finds out."

"We don't know if the Prime Lord will send me."

Antious stopped. "You're not really that naïve, are you?"

Thannuel did not answer.

"I have to go," Antious said. "It's my duty, but not yours. It's not required of you."

"I'm aware, but regardless, I'm certain Wellyn will ask me to go. I'm not sure how to say no."

"With your mouth, naturally."

Thannuel punched him in the arm good-naturedly. "Who will look after you if not me?"

"Will that brat be there?" Antious asked.

"You mean your future prime lord? What do you have against Emeron, anyway?"

"Nothing, I suppose. He's a spoiled louse, is all."

"He can't control to what family he was born. Besides, he can't be that bad. Didn't you have to study his military analysis at the academy? He's become something of a genius they say."

"Don't remind me," Antious groused. "I was actually impressed with his treatises until I remembered who authored them."

"Come on—"

"And he's not a military genius, by the way," Antious interrupted. "He just likes showing off. Trying to get him to focus on something for more than twenty minutes is something of a miracle."

Thannuel chuckled. "Yeah, that's Emeron. Always needing to have something occupying his mind. Ancients come, he's too scattered to hold a conversation with as of late."

"The Ancients aren't coming, Thannuel."

The Lord of the Western Province smiled as the platoon began to move out. "Your lack of belief in them causes you to take offense when someone swears by them? You're a walking irony, Antious."

Antious mumbled something inaudible.

"I think you're wrong, though," Thannuel said. "Someday, perhaps, they will come again."

"Perhaps," Antious replied.

NINETEEN
~THANNUEL~
Day 7 of 3rd Rising 393 A.U.

THANNUEL STEPPED IN THE COUNCIL HALL, his dark green cloak with his house's symbol draped around his shoulders. Large tapestries with illustrations of important historical events hung from the vaulted ceiling some thirty feet high. Thannuel passed by the large stone table that hosted the ministerial councils.

Two shipwrights stood before Prime Lord Wellyn, reporting on the best approach for increasing the Realm's naval presence. They seemed to shout more at each other than address the Prime Lord.

Thannuel knew one of them: Norvuld, a master shipwright from the Arlethian shipyards outside Aerikal on the west coast.

Finding Callum Hoyt, Lord of the Southern Province, leaning against the wall to his left, Thannuel walked over and stood next to him. Callum's son, Calder, flanked his father on the other side. Callum, all thought, would retire within the year and abdicate to Calder. Thannuel nodded in acknowledgement to Calder, a couple years younger than him.

"Lord Hoyt, what's going on?" Thannuel asked.

"Master Conny doesn't approve of your Arlethian shipwright's choice of wood for the ships," Lord Hoyt said.

Master Conny. The other shipwright Thannuel did not know. Across the room Thannuel noted the presence of Lord Erik Gonfrey of the Northern Province and Lord Grady Orion of the Eastern Province. General Korin, High Lord Marshal Hawkes, and two other lord marshals were also in attendance. And, to the right of the Granite Throne, sat Emeron Wellyn, not trying to hide his boredom.

"And what does it matter to you?" Norvuld asked. "You are free to make your ships from whatever you like. I'll be shaping my ships with whatever pleases me."

"You have to use the traditional hardwoods!" Conny shot back. "At least for the hulls! Come, man, you must see reason!"

"Just because triarch trees aren't 'traditional' does not mean they won't work," Norvuld said. "I've done it before. It's not as hard as oak but just as pliable as white cedar. It will work just fine. You've become boring in your middle age, do you know that?"

"This isn't a time for testing theories, old man! This is a time of war!" Conny shouted.

Parlan Wellyn finally broke in. "Master Norvuld, how many of your ships are completed of your requirement?"

"Of the ten ordered, four are complete, your Grace."

"And you cannot use a different wood?" Wellyn asked.

"We would never make the deadline your Grace imposed if we must start over. It will be difficult to meet our required complement as it is, but we will meet it. And the triarch ships will perform admirably, I guarantee it."

"My Lord," Conny cut in, "the wood is heavier and the ships will be slower than the rest of the fleet. It will cause breaks in formation or the fleet to move much slower than desired."

"No, it won't," Norvuld fired back at Conny. "When you've had forty-two years at the yards as a builder then you can spout off your own opinions. Until then, keep your trap shut about nautical matters, lad." Norvuld turned back to Wellyn. "I know a thing or two about design, my Lord. Arlethian trade secrets. You need not worry yourself on this matter. It will work just fine and I plan on captaining one of the ships personally."

Conny started to form a rebuttal on his tongue, but the Prime Lord motioned for silence. "Master Conny, I know your concerns are for the welfare of those we are sending into harm's way. This is noble of you. But, we cannot start over now lest we risk the operation being unduly delayed. In order for this preemptive strike to work, we must do it as quickly as possible."

"But, your Grace—"

"I will agree," Wellyn continued, "to use Master Norvuld's ships only for Arlethians. That should be well enough to sate your concerns."

Conny did not seem fully satisfied but lowered his head and nodded. As the two men walked away after being dismissed, Thannuel saw Norvuld cuff Conny on the head.

"What gives you the right after studying under me for ten years to start defying me in front of the Prime Lord? Just because you run the shipyards now at P'lor doesn't make you all knowing, does it, lad?" Norvuld scolded.

"Really? And your so-called 'Arlethian trade secrets' somehow never made it into my instruction? You just played the Prime Lord—"

"You're not an Arlethian, Conny. Why would I share them with you, apprentice or not?"

"Your head is full of feculence, as always. Nothing changes. When you croak, I'll have them bury you under my garden for fertilizer!"

The two argued all the way out of the council hall, leaving silence that felt out of place hanging in the air. A long tapered stone table, used for the ministerial councils, sat unoccupied.

Finally, Wellyn spoke: "Everyone take a chair."

The four lords, as well as Calder and Emeron, sat at the stone table. Wellyn came down from the throne and took a seat at the head. The four officers present waited until the Prime Lord was seated and then each took a chair. Sjoni'ah, the Archiver assigned to House Wellyn, stood just behind the Prime Lord, quietly observing and absorbing.

"My son has developed the strategy," Wellyn said. Everyone knew he spoke of the plan of a preemptive attack instead of waiting for the invasion to hit their shores. "He has discussed the battle plan with High Lord Marshal Hawkes, who agrees it has merit."

Hawkes nodded.

"I, however," the Prime Lord continued, "have some doubts."

"It will show them we are not afraid, Father," Emeron said. "We must hit back hard. If we simply wait here on the mainland, they will assume us cowering and weak."

"That in itself could be an advantage," Lord Gonfrey countered. "Let them underestimate us to their own peril."

"Even if it doesn't work, it will weaken their forces considerably for when they do attack the mainland," Lord Orion said. "From that view alone it's worthwhile."

"You don't believe it will succeed?" Wellyn asked.

Orion shrugged.

"It will work," Emeron said. "Father, I'm not being brash. I am certain, with the right insertion points, we can achieve a victory before they even come ashore here."

"We don't know the size or disposition of the enemy force," High Lord Marshal Hawkes said. His voice was gravelly, distorted with the years of shouting orders. Slightly shorter than average height, the High Lord Marshal made up every bit what he lacked in height by his thick muscular frame. "We have virtually no military intelligence on the situation. What we do know from the woman survivor who made it to P'lor is that they are called Orsarians and they have likely exterminated every citizen of the Runic Islands with extreme prejudice. Their ships are said to be swift and nearly silent, camouflaged in the night. These dark marauders, as they apparently call themselves, appear to be extremely adept in naval matters."

Hawkes stopped speaking but Thannuel could see the man was holding back. "Is there more?" he asked.

"Ailsa, the refugee survivor, she reported that these Orsarians were extremely clever but also brutal. They drink the blood of their captives in some kind of religious ritual, believing it gives them strength. The old and infirm, according to Ailsa, avoided this fate but were dragged into the sea and drowned."

Thannuel darkened at hearing this. His life had been dedicated to protecting people and lifting them up, Arlethian or not. He could not fathom what possessed men to do such evil to others. An anger started to germinate deep inside him.

"Who will lead the strike force?" Wellyn asked.

Hawkes squirmed in his seat, shifting his weight. "I have asked

General Korin to lead. I must remain and see to the larger preparations with the bulk of our armed forces here on Senthara, should our preemptive strike not succeed."

Everyone in the room could tell Hawkes was not pleased by having to miss this battle. Wellyn glanced at Thannuel and then just as quickly looked away. Thannuel did not miss the action.

"The Arlethian shipyards launch each completed ship from Aerikal's harbor and they sail around the south of the Schadar to P'lor," Wellyn said. "That takes almost a full day but progress is being made."

"Will they be ready?" Thannuel asked. "The departure date is only a half span from now and every day the enemy digs in deeper."

Lord Orion answered. "Current ship complement is thirty-six. Siege engines are being modified as we speak for naval use. Assuming the Aerikal yard can supply six more in time, as promised, we should have the full required fifty vessels plus a few smaller frigates."

"Norvuld will meet his quota," Thannuel assured him.

"Each ship will carry two hundred soldiers," Wellyn announced. "We are hopeful this force will be sufficient with surprise on our side."

"But again, we have little intelligence on the enemy force," Hawkes said.

"True," Emeron agreed, "but this also means they have little knowledge of us as well."

"We don't know that for sure," Thannuel countered.

Emeron looked at his friend. Though they were the same age, Thannuel still saw the boy he had snuck around with at royal balls and banquets, trying to find anything to cure the stuffy boredom of such events. That usually involved chasing girls of other noble houses present or pouring crates of hens over the banister into the dance hall. Emeron always had an attitude of jumping without looking, but nobility did that to a boy—providing a false feeling of immortality and personal importance. Thannuel reflected that it had not been many years ago that this attitude had grown roots in him. Thankfully, his father and Amnoch, with a little help from Antious, had beaten it out of him.

Despite Emeron's demonstrated brilliance in strategy while at the Erynx Military Academy, Thannuel wondered how much of this preemptive strike plan was simply the future prime lord trying to prove himself.

"Even if the attack is not successful," Emeron continued, "I have made provisions in the plan for a fast frigate to sail back to P'lor with first-hand information. We will be much better prepared to meet them on our own ground from this effort, regardless of its outcome."

"Why not let them come to us?" Lord Erik Gonfrey asked. He appeared to be in a perpetual state of agitation, but Thannuel had learned this was just his disposition. "There are very few landings available, your Grace. It would be relatively easy to defend."

Thannuel couldn't disagree with Gonfrey's analysis and saw that Wellyn had a difficult time countering it as well. However, he likely wanted to let his son handle these proceedings as part of his training for his eventual inheritance of the Granite Throne. If the plan succeeded, it would certainly be a boost to the confidence of the people when Emeron became prime lord.

"We are not here to debate what strategy to use, but to discuss how best to carry out the *chosen* strategy," Emeron countered, somewhat annoyed. "I am confident we can deal the enemy a decisive blow."

"Our troops are prepared?" Wellyn asked.

Hawkes looked to General Korin, cueing him. "Eight thousand

Senthary and two thousand wood-dwellers," Korin reported. "All provisions have been seen to and the men are all accounted for, currently encamped at Forden."

Hold Forden was the closest military installation to P'lor.

"Thank you, High Lord Marshal Hawkes, General Korin. I do not wish to burden your time any further," Wellyn said. The military leaders took the dismissal and exited the council hall.

"My Lord," Lord Orion began, "I wonder if we aren't using … well, all of our available resources?"

Thannuel's stomach clenched but Wellyn gave no reaction.

"Lord Hoyt," the Prime Lord said, "maybe young Calder would be more entertained elsewhere. The dance hall, perhaps. Lady Emberal is teaching the still eligible young ladies a dancing class right now in preparation for the ball next span. I think that would suit him just fine until we are done."

Callum looked at his son and motioned with his head, dismissing Calder. With a sigh of displeasure, Calder arose and made his way toward the dance hall.

When he was out of earshot, Wellyn said in a low tone, "Helsyans cannot be used in this effort."

Thannuel breathed a sigh of relief, the knot in his stomach loosening. He hated this secret, the secret that only provincial lords, a couple advisors, and the Prime Lord himself held. Obviously, the Prime Lord had seen fit to let his son also hold the secret. He glanced at Sjoni'ah, who observed unemotionally.

Helsyans. They were an ancient myth that Thannuel had shockingly been made aware of when he took on lordship of the West. Like all his peers at this council, he had taken an oath of silence regarding the Helsyan race—something all provincial lords, including his father, had done.

It wasn't fear that kept him silent on the existence of Helsyans, however. Their very existence was abominable to him, creatures of nothing more than hate and destruction. He kept his vow of silence only because he did not care to spread the knowledge of such evil in their world.

"But, my Lord," Orion protested, "we can lay these invaders to waste with just a few words—"

"That's not how it works," Wellyn answered. "In order for a harvest to be granted, I must know the identity of the one being given to the reaper, or the reaper must currently sense someone in their vicinity. Neither of those factors apply here."

"But perhaps you could delegate or allow someone else to bear the *urlenthi* temporarily—"

"No. Never," Wellyn said sternly, his hand moving to the center of his shirt, under which lay the gold amulet with the sigil of House Wellyn, a four-pointed star flare. Embedded in the back of the amulet was the Stone of Orlack, the *urlenthi*, which controlled the Helsyans, a milky white stone of strange create. "I will not surrender that responsibility to another." Left unsaid, though understood, was that fact that whoever controlled the Helsyans could control the Realm. This had been proven thoroughly in the Sentharian invasion when they fought against the Hardacheons.

"But there is a greater barrier to that plan," Wellyn continued, his tone softening. "Helsyans cannot cross water."

Thannuel raised a curious eyebrow. This was something he had not heard before.

"A narrow river or stream is tolerable, but a large body of water is impossible. They experience a sickness and loss of equilibrium that can kill them if exposure on the seas is sustained. They barely last an hour, if the legends are true, though I've never tested it. It seems part of their curse."

All were silent. Thannuel knew it would have saved the lives of many his countrymen if the reapers were to be used, but it just felt so wrong to use them, never mind their very existence feeling like an insult to life itself.

"I worry about this move," Gonfrey said, giving voice to his earlier protest. "We should wait for them to come to us. Then usage of the Helsyans would be an option."

"They will likely not expect our attack," Hoyt said. "It may be enough to send them running."

Thannuel found himself agreeing to the preemptive strike plan if it meant they would not have to use the Helsyans.

"They don't expect it because they know it would be foolish!" Gonfrey snapped.

"Your Grace, while I do not share the exuberant opposition Lord Gonfrey seems to be possessed of, he nevertheless has a point," Lord Orion said. "Without some significant advantage on our side, we may be going like a hummingbird into a nest of hornets. And, you've said we cannot use the reapers. I am forced to question what else we might have, besides surprise, that will give our forces a needed edge?"

"We have the Arlethians," Emeron answered in place of his father, nodding to Thannuel.

"Thank you, son, but I believe I'm fully capable of answering questions directed to me," Wellyn rebuked. "But he is right. Lord Kerr, I am inclined to know your disposition of the plan."

Orion bristled. It was no secret that he felt the wood-dwellers not a true part of the Realm. Such had been the case for many of House Orion over the centuries. Thannuel pretended not to notice the hostile body language from the Eastern Province's lord.

"We stand ready to follow and support your decisions, my Lord. While our greatest advantage is had when we are in our native forests," Thannuel said, "we of course maintain our speed and sensitivity no matter where we are. I have no doubt the wood-dweller regiment will serve well."

"Is General Korin the right person?" Wellyn asked Thannuel.

"He has been in the Arlethian military almost as long as I have been alive. If High Lord Marshal Hawkes believes him capable, then I cannot have any reservations. I believe the Sentharian forces will be emboldened by having an Arlethian commander."

Wellyn looked to be considering Thannuel's answer. "And, what of your willingness?"

"Your Grace?"

"Come now, Thannuel, you are perhaps the best swordsman in the Realm. Your abilities are needed to help this strike succeed. Surely you know this."

Thannuel sat silent, but did not let the silence swell too long. *Forgive me, Moira.* "I am prepared to do whatever your Grace requires of me."

"Excellent!" Emeron said. "I had slated you to lead a battalion on Fourth Island."

The presumption irritated Thannuel but did not surprise him. He glanced at the Prime Lord as Emeron went on about the insertion details. The Prime Lord looked apologetic as their eyes met, but also grateful.

"One thing," Thannuel said, interrupting Emeron without apology. "I will require Lieutenant Antious Roan in my battalion as a platoon commander. This is non-negotiable."

PART THREE

SAND, WAVES, AND BLOOD.

To kill Rehum is to kill a legion.

—Toth, Hardacheon Maker

TWENTY
~GENDAERI~
Day 12 of 3rd Rising 393 A.U.

GENDAERI RUSHED TO THE LOOKOUT POINT on the west side of the peak on Main Island with Pelnith right behind him. He arrived breathing heavy and wiped the sweat from his brow. Already high in the sky, the sunlight shimmered off the sea as he peered out.

"Where?" Gendaeri snapped.

"There!" the lookout reported.

The admiral squinted as he stared harder. In the foreground stood Fourth Island, and beyond that, he saw small interruptions in the golden light reflected on the top of the sea.

"Spyglass!" Gendaeri commanded, holding out his hand

without taking his eyes off the small dark flecks upon the water. The lookout handed over the small spyglass, a cone of rawhide rolled around a convex piece of glass at the larger end.

What he saw surprised him: an attack fleet of ships heading toward them. How would they have known they were here? Someone must have escaped, and the anger at his men's failure to secure all the coastlines burned inside his chest. Even then, the Dark Diviner had assured him they would be uninterrupted on these isles—he called them the Runic Islands in his tongue—as they gathered their forces. Gendaeri had witnessed his Influence, as he called it—what miracles lunar-enhanced blood of unbelievers could wield—but perhaps he was less divine than his title implied. It seemed the Underlander had decreed the first of their victories to be here.

With a grave look, he lowered the spyglass. They still had no sighting of their own reinforcements, who would be coming from the east. Immediately after securing the islands, the fleet's fastest ship was sent back to Orsari, a fifteen-day trip, to bring word and the rest of the dark marauder forces. That was thirty-one days ago.

Anything could have happened upon the open waters, he reminded himself. But his reinforcements would only be days away … if the message had made it back to his dying homeland.

Gendaeri handed the spyglass to Pelnith, his first officer.

"Crude make," Pelnith remarked. "These ships are not made for long voyage or battle, Admiral. Not like ours. In fact … I would say they were hurriedly built. I'm certain our ships are faster and more nimble. Shall I order our fleet to intercept?"

Gendaeri considered for several moments. "How many do you estimate are on the ships?"

Pelnith continued to peer through the lens. "No more than two hundred and fifty per ship, Admiral. Perhaps less. I would guess ten to twelve thousand in total. I'm certain our dark marauders can sink them to the ocean floor!"

Gendaeri liked Pelnith's optimism, but knew the man to be overreaching at times.

"I think not. We are already here, our defenses dug in. By the time we organized the fleet to respond, the battle would be in shallow water. No, let us make them come ashore, where we hold the advantage."

Pelnith looked as if he wanted to object, but held his tongue. *Good,* the admiral thought. *He still knows his place.* Pelnith had challenged Gendaeri for leadership of the fleet on their last voyage, a duel on the deck of the flagship. Gendaeri had savagely beaten Pelnith until he bled profusely and was barely conscious. Instead of killing him, the admiral wished to show his mercy. Pelnith's hands were bound and tied to a towline, and then he was thrown overboard. If he survived being dragged through the deep waters for a night, the blood from his wounds attracting all manner of sea-bound predators, then Gendaeri believed Pelnith would be worthy of forgiveness. In truth, the admiral fully expected his first officer to drown long before being devoured, but Pelnith had surprised him and survived being strung out as shark bait.

"Let each of our warriors take a second life into themselves," Gendaeri ordered. "We will double our numbers by the blood of their dead."

"It has already been prepared," Pelnith said.

Gendaeri opened a small vile that hung around his neck. It was filled with a dark, crimson fluid. Blood. Moon blood, to be sure, taken from unbelievers in full sight of first moon. The admiral threw his head back and swallowed the liquid, the surge of a second life filling him.

"Alert the Dark Diviner that he was wrong," Gendaeri said. "We shall indeed have a battle on these shores. Tell him to prepare."

Thannuel Kerr's feet silently hit the beach of Fourth Island, the westernmost of the four Runic Islands. He and those in his detachment had arrived under cover of darkness, although the light of the moon had not aided them in their desire for invisibility. He had no doubt that they had been seen and that an alarm had been raised throughout the islands before they even arrived onshore. General Korin had given his battalion the task of creating a beachhead for the Senthary forces that would follow on Fourth Island.

Thannuel had sent word by wing to Moira of his need to join the preemptive strike. He hated that he she was right, that Wellyn had asked him to go; mostly he regretted not being able to please his wife by staying off the front lines. *I promised her I would come back. I'd better at least be able to do that for her.*

Bamboo stalks were ubiquitous on these shores. Thannuel had never seen bamboo except for the swamp forests near the silver pools in the Eastern Province. And here, on the shores of the Runic Islands, he saw a cluster that was flowering, something that happened briefly only once a century or so. But there was also a wrongness he felt as he scanned the vacant beach, something that seemed off.

He halted, as did his men behind him. Five hundred Arlethians, a quarter of the total Arlethian regiment, were under his direct command. Antious Roan led a platoon, a fifty-man group, within Thannuel's battalion and came to his side.

"What is it?" Antious whispered.

Thannuel continued to scan the beach, unmoved. "The bamboo," Thannuel answered.

Antious swept his eyes left to right. "Yes, bamboo. And?"

"The shorter stalks … they don't look right."

A warm beach wind rustled through the high bamboo stalks and the soft sound of small waves crashed behind them, nothing in comparison to the monster swells that could hit the shores of Second and Third Islands during the dimming season. The bluish white light of first moon made the sand appear almost silver.

"My Lord, it's just bamboo—"

Something—a tremor—traveled through the ground. It was almost imperceptible but Thannuel sensed it. Looking to Antious, Thannuel could tell he did as well. Suddenly, a hand from below the wet sand reached up and grabbed his leg. Thannuel shouted in surprise despite himself. Other surprised shouts were heard as arms sprouted from the beach and attacked the wood-dwellers with swords and axes. Short bamboo stalks, now recognized as air tubes, were thrust aside as Orsarians arose in droves and rushed the wood-dwellers. It only took Thannuel a split second to gather himself and react with lethal reprisals.

He slashed his sword down, separating the Orsarian below him from his hand, followed by a downward thrust into the sand. A scream came from below and the sand darkened as blood sprouted around his blade like a small geyser. Thannuel heard the ten lieutenants, each in charge of a fifty-man platoon, shout orders and felt his men react with speed and efficiency. They retreated back several paces to where the bamboo grasses started, closer to the shoreline.

Hundreds of Orsarians had sprung up from the ground, covered in sand. Among them, the one-handed man Thannuel had just seconds ago impaled on his blade. His shirt had a dark stain that grew as he stood, blood draining from his wound, but the man appeared undaunted by his lethal gash.

The enemy appeared savage, like demons from the fathomless abyss, where the Ancients had sent the prior inhabitants of Vǎleira, Those Not Remembered. They charged the wood-dwellers, attempting to push them into the Sea of Albery with a great slaughter.

"Forward!" Thannuel ordered, answering the enemy's charge with one of his own. Thannuel sprinted to the man he had killed already once and with a powerful swing, nearly cut him in half at a diagonal angle through his torso. This time he stayed dead.

The Orsarian cries of battle turned to sounds of confusion as they witnessed the wood-dwellers advance with unnatural speed. Their confusion did not last long as they fell beneath the attacks of high velocity.

Thannuel lowered his shoulder and knocked down two enemy soldiers and brought his steel down with incredible force, taking them both in the face. Turning in a graceful spin before the last heartbeats of the two at his feet sounded, he cut another enemy across the abdomen. He parried blows from three attackers at once with dizzying speed before countering with his own attack that left each lifeless.

"Push!" he shouted. "Pound!"

Something bit at the back of Thannuel's arm, a grazing blow. He spun to see a mass of Orsarians behind him and his men. A few Arlethians were cut down in surprise from the rear assault.

They have surrounded us? How?

And then Thannuel saw there were no corpses on the sand, save for the one-armed man he had killed twice now. The several dozen that he and his men had felled were not there, but stood alive, now coming from behind. A moment of panic tugged at his mind.

Thannuel easily parried a blow from one who should have been bereft of life, his viscera hanging out from a low stomach wound. The enemy soldier became permanently still as Thannuel's sword found his heart.

What create is this darkness? Twice. They have to be killed twice.

He had no time to ponder further as another enemy ran toward him, a crossbow bolt protruding from his skull. It was not only strange but outright frightening. Perhaps these fiends were from the Fathomless Abyss.

Antious cut the man down before he reached Thannuel and spun on to the next man immediately. A skinny Orsarian soldier ran toward him, slashing dual scimitars with impressive dexterity. He was no match for wood-dweller speed, however, and Thannuel took him at the head. When the dead man's cranium hit the sand, its vibration felt similar to a coconut. The body showed no other wound and it stayed down.

"The head!" Thannuel roared. "Take off their heads or strike two lethal blows! Kill them twice!"

Antious was right beside him, swinging and slashing, killing those before him twice before moving to the next. Losses on their side were greater than expected due to the extra time and effort required to dispatch each enemy, but the Arlethians' discipline held and each platoon advanced with its officer in front. It was the way of the Arlethian officer.

To his forward left, Thannuel heard a crack in the air—something akin to boulders being slammed together—and saw a net ensnare four of his men. They fell, tangled in the mesh, as Orsarians rushed them. Thannuel threw his sword, taking a man in the square of his back, and pulled a short blade from his belt. Two other wood-dwellers sprinted toward their downed companions.

When he arrived after only moments, Thannuel let loose a volley of punches and debilitating strikes, sending three dark marauders to the ground, writhing in pain. They cried out for help but were cut short as Lord Kerr's short blade twice found each of their hearts in quick succession. The other two wood-dweller soldiers that had joined Thannuel's attack excused three more enemy combatants, but they were too late. The four Arlethians in the net were bloodied and still. One raised a hand, weakly.

"Take him back to the boat!" Thannuel ordered. "Bind his wounds with triarch leaves and return to the battlefield."

The vibrations of the battle were a chorus of chaos. For all the advantage an Arlethian gained by their sensitivity to vibrational signatures in the ground, it could prove a hindrance to them outside the forests of the Western Province as their ability to separate and identify vibrations lessened significantly without the help of speaking trees. The result was little more than a cacophony. Thannuel pushed the plethora of information that flowed to him through the earth toward the back of his mind and relied more on his sight and hearing for the time being.

Bladed boomerangs spun through the night air and caught a score of wood-dwellers in the head. Thannuel deflected one as it honed in on him, barely seeing its glimmer in the moonlight.

As the wood-dweller forces pressed forward, cutting down the Orsarian numbers, wooden posts sprang up from the ground with wire strung between them, creating a menacing fence that arrested their advance. Large barbs and hooks ornamented the wire. Several of Thannuel's men could not stop their momentum in time and ran into the sharp implements, slicing their skin and snaring several of them. Arrows cut the air amid the cries of the Arlethians.

"The ground!" Antious shouted. "Hit the deck!"

His platoon fell flat to the earth and others followed. The amount of weaponry and strategies employed by these Orsarians was unexpected and impressive. Thannuel's anger rose inside him, like a fire that raged in a dry grass field, spreading until it fully consumed him.

"Antious, we need to end this. Quickly." Arrows flew over their heads as they lay on the sand.

"Your orders, my Lord?"

"Take your platoon north on the beach with all speed, get behind their lines and flank the enemy."

Antious nodded and called to his men. They arose and sprinted north after the next volley of arrows.

"Push the posts!" Thannuel yelled.

He and scores of his men arose and put their weight against the wooden posts that were sunk not more than a foot in the sand. They came loose; the partition fell free and was soon trampled under the blurred advance of the wood-dweller force. It was only meant as a delay tactic, Thannuel knew, to allow the Orsarian archers a chance to cut down the odds against them. It had proven frustratingly effective.

Thannuel leaped into the enemy forces, his anger for his lost men raging, stoking his momentum greater as he handed out two deaths for every Orsarian in his reach. Within a minute's time, Thannuel felt the unmistakable signature of his closest friend charging into the left flank of the Orsarian dark marauders. The enemy screamed out in alarm and had no cunning devices or strategies to counter the attacks on two fronts from beings swifter than falcons. It was over in less than a minute.

"Well, that wasn't so bad," Antious said.

"We lost men," Thannuel told him.

"Yes, my Lord, perhaps a couple dozen."

"I know that's considered acceptable to a military mind, Antious, but it's not to me."

Antious nodded. "I just hope the other landing parties were as successful as we were."

Thannuel looked west, to the open sea, and saw Sentharian vessels anchored offshore with scores of smaller transport boats ushering thousands of soldiers ashore. Two thousand Sentharian men would join his battalion on the beach and move inland. The same strategy was being repeated on two of the other three islands, with double the number of soldiers allocated to Main Island. Two insertion points were designated for the largest of the Runic Islands, both overseen by General Korin. The resistance on Main Island was believed to be the heaviest. Third, or Pearl Island, was left out of the initial wave of counterattacks due to having no native population.

They warily moved inland about a quarter mile and stopped. The bodies were strung upside down, hanging from low branches, hands bound behind the back. Hundreds. All were pale, ghostly in appearance, and well into the decomposition process. Men, woman, children. All Senthary.

A healer came forward and inspected one of the bodies.

"He's been drained, my Lord. From the looks of it, they all have. A knife looks to have been stabbed under the collarbone, toward the heart."

Thannuel's lip sneered and his jaw quivered.

"The residual blood," the healer added somberly, "is not necrotic."

"Meaning what, healer?" Thannuel snapped, speaking harsher than he intended.

"These people were alive when they were exsanguinated—drained."

Thannuel did not try to hide his emotion, the anger that seized him. He felt the air charged with the same emotion from his men. ·

"Antious, have a squad take our wounded and dead back to our ship. Instruct Captain Norvuld to sail east of Fourth Island and anchor on the west of Main Island. We'll signal him to retrieve us when we've cleansed this island of its parasites."

Of all the Gyldenal, Master Norvuld was the meekest, I surmise. However, this should not be mistaken for weakness on his part; for none gave of themselves more willingly when called upon, even in the face of the greatest call.

—Memoirs of Våleira, section eight, 86th verse

TWENTY-ONE

~ANTIOUS~

Day 13 of 3rd Rising 393 A.U.

MORNING CAME QUICKLY as Antious and his platoon made their way to the beach of Main Island, debarking from Captain Norvuld's ship. Fourth Island had been eradicated completely, finding little further resistance after their initial landing.

Thannuel and Norvuld debriefed each other.

"From what we can tell, Lord Kerr, Second Island has also been retaken," Norvuld reported. "I have not heard directly from General

Korin, but reports are that the fighting here on Main Island has not gone as well. The enemy is entrenched in the mountain and is well fortified."

"We'll reconnoiter the west shoreline and start moving inward," Thannuel said. "Take your squadron around the north coast of Main Island and harass the enemy however you deem best."

"Yes, my Lord." Turning his head, Norvuld yelled to a boy, "Oy! You, castaway! Prepare to hoist anchor and send a flare to signal the other ships!"

"Castaway?" Thannuel asked.

"Aye, my Lord. Found him sequestered below deck, stealing rations. Won't tell me his name, so I just call him 'castaway' and put him to hard labor. Works hard, surprisingly."

"Did he not know we were headed to war?"

"I didn't say he was the most secure mooring, my Lord," Norvuld said with a grin.

"Lord Kerr," Antious interrupted, "we are ready to move out."

"Very good, Lieutenant. What is our count?" Thannuel had given Antious a battlefield commission to command lieutenant, a temporary position used only in the field.

"The battalion of five hundred is now diminished to four hundred and sixty-two, my Lord. Our attrition rate is less than ten percent, and while disheartening, is acceptable. The morale of the men is high. The Sentharian forces in our regiment have experienced no losses."

Antious saw his friend's demeanor cloud for a moment before clearing.

"Let's move out, Lieutenant," Thannuel said.

Antious hesitated. "My Lord, perhaps you would care to remain with Captain Norvuld and the fleet."

"Captain," Thannuel said, "I think Lieutenant Roan means to

keep me out of the way."

"It's only his duty, my young Lord," the captain responded.

Antious felt himself flush. "Lord Kerr, I'm certain I and the other platoons can take it from here."

"I have no doubt of that, Antious. Now, let's move out."

Antious saw the thirteen-ship squadron that had carried their regiment from Senthara to Fourth Island, and then again from Fourth to Main Island, depart northward. He marched up the beach, feeling the sand give way under his feet. He had never been to the Runic Islands, a destination for the wealthiest in society during the rising and high seasons, but did not see the appeal. Perhaps looking through the spectacles of war marred his perception of the islands, but he did not think he would ever be able to erase the nightmare he had witnessed from his mind. People strung up like hogs, drained of their blood, faces frozen forever in agony.

If Antious survived, he promised himself he would marry Kalisa straightaway, no matter the consequences. He was certain he may have to resign from the military, but if he could have the woman he loved, it would be a small price to pay in the end.

Dimming Light, if only Thannuel would see reason and stay back!

But he knew it was useless to argue further. Once he made his mind up, Thannuel was committed. It had always been like that, through childhood until now. His duty to protect the Realm as a soldier, to obey his lord as an Arlethian, and to protect Thannuel as his friend all swam inside him at once. Antious knew, though, that Thannuel would continue to stay with the army to protect him just as much as out of a desire to lead by example. Each would stand in front of the other without hesitation if it meant saving the other's life; such was their bond.

As the army of Arlethians and Senthary moved inland, they came to a forest. Antious instantly felt calmer, though these trees were short in comparison to the forests of the West. No triarch trees were found anywhere save the West, and these trees would not speak. Still, Antious's confidence increased as they stepped foot into the frondescence. The pulse of the soldiers with him radiated through the ground. He tried to focus on other pulses that might manifest themselves, staying sharp for enemy contact.

Ahead, he saw the forest thin a bit, maybe a meadow or clearing. The closer they came, the more uneasy Antious felt, his confident feeling from the forest waning.

Thannuel raised a hand, halting their movement. The Sentharian lord marshals followed suit and the whole regiment ceased. Obviously others shared his uneasy feeling. Thannuel moved ahead cautiously, every footstep silent.

The explosion came from his left, bodies flying in the air amid screams. More explosions followed, the ground rippling with the percussive booms that erupted all around them. Antious grabbed his sword tightly in reflex, his eyes searching for an enemy.

A fountain of soil and rock exploded to his right, almost directly under him, sending him through the air at high velocity. He hit a tree and fell to the ground with a ringing in his ears that drowned out all other ambient noise, even the screams of his dying men.

As he wiped the dirt from his eyes, he saw Thannuel dancing around a storm of debris. Explosions continued, still inaudible to him, though he felt them pulsing through the earth as he lay motionless, sending trees, rocks, and body parts into the air as if they were no more than pollen in a light breeze.

Minefield, his mind finally told him. The Orsarians buried explosive drums of some kind just beneath the surface of the earth. *But how are they detonating them? They must be close … unless they are triggered by weight,* he thought, too terrified to move.

Thannuel sprang from side to side, masterfully deflecting tree limbs and stone with his sword and dodging others. Another concussive pulse shot through the ground, one directly under where Thannuel had just landed, but the wood-dweller lord sprang up again immediately, barely touching the earth and too fast for the explosion to catch him. He looked as if a god, playing the game of lesser mortals. Antious could not help but feel awed at the natural grace and poise Thannuel displayed.

The ambush was effective and Antious's anger soon overcame his fear. *It has to be almost over.* The command lieutenant stood, forcing his knees to not buckle. Just as he found his footing, a dozen cracks sounded in the air. Familiar was their report but Antious remembered too late what they were to sound any warning. A multitude of large nets sailed through the air toward their front lines, but these were different than the one used on the beach of Fourth Island. They expanded larger as they swirled toward them, and Antious saw barbs and hooks laced throughout the mesh.

"No!" he screamed, not hearing his own voice above the ringing in his ears.

His warning was futile. The nets fell and ensnared scores of soldiers then were retracted at amazing speed, dragging their prey across the ground. Men screamed in surprise then agony as the barbs and hooks cut deep into them.

And then, his heart sank. Thannuel, his best friend from childhood and the lord of his people, never saw the net bearing down on him as he was distracted by avoiding flying debris from the explosions still thundering all around them. The net fell on him while in the air, in the middle of another evasive jump. Thannuel hit the ground face down and Antious desperately started to run toward him, ignoring all concern for his own safety. Their eyes met, and then Thannuel was gone, pulled at high speed by a tether attached to the net.

I can catch him!

The explosion rocked Antious and threw him back more than twenty feet.

"Thannuel!"

Antious hit the ground hard and his vision turned black.

Lo! The stars fall and the heavens burn! Azure hues give way to a red sky as clouds rimmed in fire spew black death to the earth below.

—*The Erynx Fragments*. Sample does not match any of the other fragments but is of particular note as it is written in the Hardacheon prophetic tense, one not easily translated into Sentharian.

TWENTY-TWO
~ANTIOUS~
Day 14 of 3rd Rising 393 A.U.

WHAT HE FELT when he awoke he was not sure, but the sensation felt something like small scabs being ripped off him, one by one. His arms, face, and torso. Vibrations muttered through him but he could not focus enough to make any sense of them. Eventually, sound returned to Antious Roan's ears and he heard a mix of pained outbursts, frantic voices, and yells for order. As he tried to open his eyes, he saw nothing. Not blackness, not blurred vision, not a bright expanse that unfolded forever. Nothing.

Panic rose in his chest and he sat up with a scream. Hands grabbed his shoulders and pushed him back down gently but firmly.

"Be still," a voice said. "It will hurt more if you struggle."

A sharp pain came again as something was plucked from his side, and then dwindled almost as quickly as it came on.

"What's happened?" he demanded. "Where am I? Why can't I see?" And then he remembered. The explosions, the nets.

"Thannuel! Where—"

"Gone," the voice said. Another stab of pain. "Lord Kerr is missing."

"What are you doing? If you intend to torture me you'll—"

"You are in a triage camp. I am a healer. Your body is riddled with shrapnel, metal and wood alike. It's likely there will be little scarring, thank the Ancients. We came across your regiment yesterday during our retreat … or, what was left of it."

"And my sight? My eyes … "

"Your eyes are intact," the healer said. "It is likely a temporary blindness from where you hit your head. Your skull is badly bruised, perhaps even a hairline fracture."

"You said yesterday," Antious realized. "I have been out for a day?"

"I'm not certain how long you were there before we found you," the healer admitted. "But at least a day, yes."

"How many?"

Antious thought he could sense the healer's confusion.

"How many are gone?"

"Including Lord Kerr, twenty-two are unaccounted for. Nineteen from your regiment survived," the healer answered.

Antious tried to speak, trying to calculate the losses. If what the healer said was true then over twenty-four hundred men were wiped out in a matter of minutes. Another piece of shrapnel was ripped free. Only then did Antious feel the press of something on his skin right where the pain had come from.

"Patches of triarch leaves," the healer said. "Small squares to cover your wounds. They have amazing healing properties and will—"

"I know," Antious said.

"Of course," the healer answered. "You are a wood-dweller. Forgive me, I'm used to having to defend the use of triarch leaves to those not of your province. After centuries I find it unbelievable that some still mistrust their virtues over silly superstitions."

"What of our other forces? General Korin?"

"The general is here, planning with what few officers are left."

Antious sat up. "When will my vision return?"

"I cannot say. Perhaps never, but I think that unlikely."

"Can you show me to General Korin?"

Antious sensed hesitation from the healer.

"Please," he said. "I must know the disposition of our forces."

"Very well," the healer replied. "But he is in a foul mood."

At least something is normal, he thought as he put his hand to the healer's shoulder to lead the way.

Antious felt others turn as he approached, looking at him. He must have appeared to be some kind of monster from all the wounds that peppered his body.

"Just ahead is the general," the healer told him. "I will leave you now. There are others I must see to."

Antious took his hand from the healer's shoulder and felt the man walk off.

"General Korin, permission to join your briefing, sir."

"Lieutenant, why are you not resting?" Korin asked.

"Forgive me, sir, but I cannot. How have we fared?"

"Poorly, I'm afraid," Korin said. "We are less than a thousand strong; of those, perhaps only two-thirds are battle-worthy. Now, if you're done debriefing me, I need to get back to planning our retreat."

"I was there. I saw him get taken," Antious said.

The general paused before he answered. "He was a good man, Lieutenant. His loss is felt by all, Arlethian and Senthary alike."

"He was alive."

Korin sighed. When he spoke, his voice was softer. "I know. But, it is not likely the case now."

"We have to go after him," Antious stated with calm nerves. "He is our lord."

"Lieutenant, I've been told your vision has been impaired, but the healers said nothing of your hearing. I am planning our retreat. This mission has served its purpose and softened the enemy. Their losses were at least twice ours."

"We have a duty to go after Lord Kerr, General Korin. We must rescue him."

"You forget yourself, *Lieutenant* Roan," Korin snapped. "Just because you cannot presently see the insignia of rank upon my breastplate does not change it." Softening only slightly, Korin said, "If I thought there was any chance of recovering Lord Kerr alive, I would go. But I have no expectation of this. He is dead, Antious. I cannot risk the lives of those few we have left on a suicide mission. Not only does military directive forbid it, I'm certain Lord Kerr would not wish more lives being lost in any such foolish attempt."

"Sir, I appeal to you as a citizen of Arlethia," Antious pleaded. "We must form a recon unit and infiltrate behind enemy lines to learn where they have taken Lord Kerr. I will—"

"You will do nothing!" Korin shouted. "You are relieved, Lieutenant. Confine yourself to this camp until ordered to move out."

Antious was speechless, but he did not falter in his resolve. The power of his oath sworn a decade prior had not lost any of its potency. What he did next would surprise him for years to come, as if watching someone else in the halls of his memory wearing his body.

"I resign my commission as an officer in the Arlethian army, General. I will operate outside the chain of command and lead a rescue party."

Though his vision had not returned, Antious knew the general had stood, indignation doubtless upon his face.

"Refusing an order in time of war is treason! Resigning your command is the same," Korin thundered. "You will be executed, Lieutenant. Is this what you desire? *I* do not wish this, but—"

"The only order I am refusing to follow, General, is to retreat. As I have resigned, you no longer have command over me. If you will insist on my execution, then let my attempt to rescue Lord Kerr suffice as you believe it to be suicidal regardless. If you disagree, I will still go. You will have to strike me down here and now in order to stop me. You may choose to dishonor the Arlethian warrior's creed, but I will not. *I am Arlethia,* and she is me. Are those not the words, General? Do we not all speak them? They are more than words, sir, they are a way of life! An ethos!"

General Korin's huffing was the only noise, save for some distant thunder. Antious had a difficult time distinguishing between the two sounds. Antious would not have been surprised to feel the penetration of steel in his chest, but the words the general spoke next were more painful.

"For the misguided love my daughter bears for you, I will

forgive this insubordination and grant you leave according to your desire ... on one condition. If you actually survive this death wish you seem to have, you are done with both the army and Kalisa. You will swear to never see my daughter again. You will rebuff her affection and not pursue her any longer. This is the price I require for sparing your life."

It was too much for Antious. How could he agree to this? He loved Thannuel and Kalisa differently but equally.

I will always come for you, Thannuel. I swear it. Always, no matter what may be in the way. I will come for you.

How could he live with heart being turned to ash? Or conversely, as an oath breaker? Was he to sacrifice his heart or his soul? He would not agree for his life, although Korin put it as such, but because he could not undo the oath he swore. In the end, he had given his love to Kalisa but, although he eagerly would have with her father's permission, Antious had not sworn himself to her. Korin could not stop him from always loving her. That would have to be enough.

"I accept your terms. Give me a small contingent of men and I will leave you to your retreat."

"No. I will not send men on your crazed mission, following a blind man," Korin told him. "But, you have leave to try and convince whomever you may to follow you. I will even leave you a ship, if any of the captains are willing to waste their time waiting for you."

Antious nodded. Light started to appear in his vision, blurry images before him without any discernable recognition ... but it was progress.

"Thank you," Antious said. "As I am all but dead to you, sir, I don't mind telling you that you are a bastard of the foulest of swine."

He might not be an officer in the Arlethian army any longer, but he still claimed the status of an Arlethian warrior. Just as Antious turned on his heel, he thought he saw the blurry formation of an impressed smile on General Korin's face.

I'm coming, Thannuel.

I tire of this game, Toth. Either kill me permanently or join me.

—Rehum

TWENTY-THREE
~NORVULD~
Day 14 of 3rd Rising 393 A.U.

CAPTAIN NORVULD SHOUTED COMMANDS amid the thunder and rain that poured all around his small fleet. The sea wielded unruly force when a tempest surged upon its surface, as if answering the sky's challenge, battling to show which could muster the most fury.

Lightning cracked the dark gray sky as Norvuld's ship crested a large wave, burying its jib boom deep in the sea before resurfacing. Salt water sprayed on the deck, thicker than the sheets of rain coating his crew. Several men vomited from the vessel being hurled to and fro in the storm but also from the rocking caused by a near constant bombardment of enemy ordnance, black smoothed rocks that cut through his ships like spears through fish.

"Return fire!" he shouted.

Catapults loosed, flinging their slower but larger projectiles in long, skyward arches. Some hit their targets, smashing through enemy hulls and decks alike, but most harmlessly hit the water. Norvuld cursed the poor accuracy of their weaponry as his men reloaded. Another flurry of small fires sprouted forth from an enemy ship, signaling a new barrage of incoming ordnance.

"Brace!" Captain Norvuld shouted.

Most of the ordnance missed, but some struck home. None seemingly on the lower decks, thank the Ancients.

"Ready the harpoon bow!"

Two men swiveled the harpoon bow—a modified large crossbow—into position while a third loaded a solid iron shaft a fist thick. This arrow was not sharpened at the end but left blunt, its only purpose to punch holes in things. It was ugly, but Norvuld prayed more accurate than the catapults were, especially on rough waters.

It took two men to crank the crossbow back but only one to steady and aim it.

"Release when ready!" Norvuld said.

After a few tense moments, the man squeezed the trigger and the bow's limbs, each six feet long, sprang forward and shot the iron arrow so fast that Norvuld lost track of it. From across the aqueous battlefield, he saw wood fly from the back of the closest enemy ship.

Burning Heavens, did we just take out their rudder?

The crew on the main deck cheered, and another volley of catapults were loosed. One of the crew, still jubilant with their strike, lost his head as the next barrage of black rocks slammed into them.

"Down!" Norvuld shouted.

He had seen General Korin's flare—a purple one—calling for an immediate evacuation. Of course, the Orsarians had seen the flare as well, turning their progress to the waypoint into a desperate race. Some of the Orsarian fleet had cut them off, engaging them. Likely their ground forces were also making their way overland to the fledgling Senthary and Arlethian remnants.

Dimming Light, you've let them know right where you are! Norvuld had complained, cursing the use of flares, seeming such a crude method of communication when one had become accustomed to conversing within the Light. Of course, triarch trees would be required for that, but his ships would have likely sufficed, assuming another member of the Gyldenal were present with at least a triarch leafling on the other end of the transmission.

Alas, we are stuck with archaic forms of communication that may prove our doom.

"Cast away, secure those moorings!" Norvuld yelled.

The dark-haired boy scrambled to do as commanded when a large wave rocked them to the starboard side, throwing two men overboard. He would not have believed his eyes if hadn't seen it for himself. The castaway boy stood sideways on the deck railing, defying gravity with alacrity, as if he were in the Arlethian forests. The ship righted itself and he continued onward to the wayward moorings, executing his task as if death had not just brushed up against him. The starboard rails he had just danced upon were slightly darker where the boy's feet had touched than the rest of the rail's length.

Could it be—

"Captain!" a crewmember shouted while pointing over the port bow. One of the Sentharian ships burst into flames, breaking apart. Men jumped from the burning wreck into the swirling depths, choosing to drown rather than to burn. Norvuld would have chosen the same, believing the sea to be a welcoming grave for one who had spent more time upon it than on land.

While still gazing in that direction, he saw several other Sentharian ships become tangled with enemy grappling hooks, Orsarian boarders swinging over to his countrymen's ships. The fleet was lightly crewed, almost all the soldiers having disembarked to the land war. A naval battle had not been conceived in the strategy, or at least not hoped for.

The harpoon bow fired again, this time an arrow with two prongs spread wide at the head. It struck its target and the central mast of one Orsarian vessel creaked loud enough to be heard over the storm's ambience as it toppled down, crashing onto the deck. Its sail covered a score of deck hands, trapping them for several moments.

"They're done!" Norvuld said. "Rudder fifteen degrees to the port. Focus on the boarding ships."

His ship turned swiftly and within a few moments had aligned itself with one of the enemy ships docked against a Sentharian vessel. A battle had ensued on the deck of the Sentharian ship, with more dark marauders coming across constantly. There was nothing he could do for the crew, but he could add a few water intakes in undesirable places on the Orsarian ship.

"Fire!"

His portside siege weapons loosed, punching torso-sized holes in the enemy vessel's hull. Noticing the new attack on their ship, the dark marauders ceased crossing the threshold to the Sentharian ship.

"Fire again, blast you! Don't stop!" Captain Norvuld commanded. "Their ordnance is unmanned! Fire!"

As the next cluster of purple-white lightning streaked across the sky, like veins in the forehead of an angry god, Norvuld's harpoon bow shot another bolt at merciless speed. Just as it struck the hull, lightning hit the arrow, effectively turning it into a fuse. The Orsarian ship broke apart from the ensuing blast, its quarterdeck ripping free from the rest of the ship and sinking aft first into the ocean. The remaining two-thirds of the ship soon followed.

Norvuld laughed. He couldn't help it.

"Take down the mast of that ship!" the captain commanded, pointing to the Sentharian ship. He could not risk the vessel being wrested away from Sentharian control and turned against his own fleet if the boarders could not be repelled. The dark marauders that had jumped from their ship would fight more fiercely now that their own ship had been destroyed, knowing there was nowhere to retreat.

As his ship turned starboard, a high-pitched buzzing sound whizzed past his head, followed by a splash off the port side. Smoke plumed from an enemy ship's recent volley to his right. They were close—too close. Norvuld's siege weapons could not get a proper angle fast enough to return fire before a second volley came their way.

"Cover!" Norvuld shouted.

The barrage riddled his ship. Men screamed from below deck as gaping holes were blown in his hull.

With his face down against the wet deck of triarch wood, Norvuld whispered, "Hold together, girl. Just a while longer."

He jumped up and grabbed the wheel. Gratefully, they still had their rudder.

"Return fire!" he shouted. Nothing. "I don't care if you've lost a limb or have a hole in your gut, crying for your mommy! You will man those catapults and return fire!"

Several men from below deck emerged, taking a position at the catapults, replacing those who had just died.

"Boy!" Norvuld shouted to the castaway. "Get down there and assist where you can. This is where you earn your return trip, lad."

The castaway disappeared as he submerged below deck. And then the rain lightened noticeably, turning Norvuld's attention upward. The sky was turning from a deep gray to a pale green. Clouds began to swirl.

"Oh no," Norvuld said to himself as his heart sank.

Just ahead of him, a spout funneled down from the sky to the ocean, howling its terrible song. It spun, faster and faster, gaining momentum like a raging bull, stirring the ocean into a cauldron of devastation. He felt the tide change as a massive whirlpool erupted into life.

Though his mind had been entirely focused in the moment, he broke his thoughts away from the battle momentarily, praying he would be able to return to *her*, if only to see her one last time … even if he had to go to that forsaken wasteland-of-a-forest near the glaciers to be with her.

Eight. That was all Antious Roan could convince to return with him in search of Thannuel. All eight were Arlethians; he didn't even bother approaching the Sentharian soldiers for assistance.

The rain was a welcome element to their task, as it would help camouflage their movements. To normal men, the rain would also help mask the sound of their approach, but wood-dwellers were naturally silent in step.

To the north, where Antious knew lay the ocean, he heard small cracks of thunder sounding, not unlike the sounds of the exploding mines that had blinded him. Reflexively, he turned toward the sounds but could not make anything out with his very limited and blurry vision.

"The naval battle," one of the eight reported, obviously noting where Antious gazed. "The Orsarian ships have siege weapons on their ships that spit fire and rocks. Tore apart some of our ships off the south insertion point of Main Island as Senthary troops disembarked. Scary as the fathomless abyss to watch."

Antious felt footsteps approaching from his squad's rear: a runner, not a wood-dweller, coming from the direction of the encamped Sentharian and Arlethian armies. Antious turned, his hand at his sword's hilt, cautious.

"Lieutenant! Sir!" called a man. "Lieutenant, I have a message from General Korin." He breathed heavily, obviously having exerted himself greatly to catch up to Antious's squad.

"It's not lieutenant anymore, messenger," Antious replied. He could only make out a dim outline of the man.

"Right, yes, sir, of course. The general gave me this to deliver to you." The courier extended his hand, bearing a folded piece of parchment. Antious felt for it, fumbling, finally grabbing it before the rain could soak the message beyond legibility and handed it to one of the volunteers to his left. The man read it.

"Seek him on Third Island. Scouts reported captives being taken in that direction."

Perhaps the hard general was not as unwilling to help as he led on. Turning to his men, Antious said, "We must secure a boat."

They arrived on the western shore of Third Island an hour later. Antious's arms were sore from the vigorous rowing. They had found two small rowboats that barely fit all his men and were weighed down heavily as they crossed the channel between Main Island and

Third. He looked up to the sky, but his vision had not improved. All he could see were the clouds, a strange green pallor.

"How much light is left?" he asked.

"It is overcast with clouds of strange create," a soldier answered. "Impossible to tell without the sun, but I would guess not more than a hand, probably less."

Antious nodded.

Pearl Island, as the Runics called it, was small in comparison to the others, but not much smaller than Second Island. After reaching the central part of the island, rife with all manner of exotic and tropical wildlife, Antious and his eight felt them. A large movement of people to the south, not more than a mile. The vibrations were muddled and Antious instinctively reached his hand out to a tree, putting it flush against the bark. He felt no connection to the forest and then remembered he was not in Arlethia. Trees did not speak on the Runic Islands. Feeling a little foolish, he slowly took his hand from the tree. The other soldiers looked at him not with scorn but understanding.

Of course. They would be wanting for the forests of our home as well.

They would have to get closer. With the innate silence of wood-dwellers of Arlethia, Antious and his men crept toward the source of the muddled pulsing. The ground dropped away into a hollow, covered in frondescence of the tropical forest. He knew they had arrived at a gathering of men but could not see well enough to make things out.

"What is it?" he whispered.

One of the soldiers, a Corporal Remel, described what he saw. Hanging upside down from branches, bound and gagged, were scores of men. Most wearing the uniforms of Senthara, less of Arlethia. Some were awake and struggling, screaming into their gags; others were still: unconscious or worse. More than a hundred enemy soldiers occupied the hollow, moving casually among the hanging men at the direction of a man dressed in loose-fitting black clothing. His pants were thin, tight at the waist but loose around the ankles save for the ends, which were drawn tight. His tunic was robe-like, several layers interwoven over one another with a gold colored belt over his waist. And, most curiously, he wore a turban around his head that also covered his face, except for the eyes.

Remel continued with his description of the scene: "The Orsarian dark marauders are going from one prisoner to the next with a long, thin knife, stabbing it under the collarbone at an angle toward the heart. They are collecting the blood as it shoots from the wound."

Antious's stomach turned and his anxiety peaked. If he were too late, he would charge them in a blood rage, striking down every one of them until he himself fell. It would be a fitting punishment for failing to keep his oath.

"Ancients, if you really do hear us, now would be a perfect time for some intervention," Antious muttered to himself.

A soldier grabbed his shoulder and pointed. "There!" he whispered.

Antious looked in the general direction the blurry hand indicated, but it was no use.

"Is he alive?" Antious asked.

"It's hard to tell. He's not moving, maybe just unconscious," the soldier reported. "Others near him are pale, but he still has his color. I think he is still alive, Lieutenant. But … "

"Yes?" Antious asked with his heart in his throat.

"He is badly wounded," Remel said. "His body is torn in many places and bloodied, torso naked."

The barbed net, Antious thought.

Above them, Antious could see the trees extended for a good height—or he thought he could. Using hand signals, he motioned for everyone to ascend the trees with all care. Neither he nor any wood-dweller needed keen vision to scale a tree with dexterity.

Thannuel, we just need to get Thannuel. This would be a fast and messy snatch and retreat operation, relying on their speed to outrun the Orsarians ... assuming they could even get to Thannuel. Antious lamented that they could not attempt to save anyone else. His mind told him it was logical that the Lord of the Western Province take priority; his heart told him the Dark can have the logic, for his oath to his best friend would compel him regardless of Thannuel's political station.

Cursed Heavens, give me my vision! And then, Antious remembered something: his advancement examination. The blindfold. Perhaps ... quickly, he untied one of the bandages from an arm wound and secured it around his head, covering his eyes. The blurry vision would only distract his concentration. The intended injustice General Korin had placed upon him during his test may prove a blessing after all.

He listened intently, felt. No vibrations from his men. They were in place, waiting for his command. The vibrations from the men below in the hollow reverberated in his bones, but he needed more movement in order to gauge things more properly.

Holding his breath, he stood up. Knowing what he must look like, his body bandaged and a bloody blindfold across his face, he decided to gamble.

"Hello?" he called out. "I can hear you ... where are you?"

He took a few steps forward and allowed himself to stumble. Immediately below him, men became alert and he felt their vibrations through the earth. His eyes were closed despite being blindfolded, helping to aid his theory. As men rushed him, scrambling up the bank, a curious thing happened. His mind, deep within the waters of concentration, began to portray outlines to him that vaguely resembled the shapes of people. The images dissolved slightly between footsteps, but rematerialized in his mind's eye every time a foot hit the ground. One of the soldiers slipped, and Antious saw a pulsing image of a man on his elbows and one knee before rising again. In the precious few seconds he had before they reached him, the outlines his mind portrayed became thicker, more defined.

"I got separated. What regiment are you?" he asked, trying to sound as innocent as he could despite knowing the Orsarians spoke a foreign tongue and could not understand him. A score of men were clambering up the bank. The vision in his mind wasn't perfect, but he could use it.

Just as two dark marauders brought themselves up from the bank, Antious smiled.

"Now!"

His men dropped from their perches above into the hollow. As he felt their lighter, fluid movements pulse through the ground, their outlines came to life in his mind and he smiled again. The two men before him did not have time to understand the situation before being struck down. Antious dispatched the head of the first and impaled the second, unsheathing his blade from the man's abdomen with a powerful kick that sent him sprawling back down the bank.

With a few quick strides forward, he jumped when he reached the edge of the bank and landed in the middle of the hollow.

"Free Thannuel!" he commanded. "Cut your way to him! Do not engage unless you have to."

His sight proved too tempting for the Orsarians, likely not believing what their eyes showed them—a ragged blind man standing in their center, challenging them. Antious knocked into a few hanging bodies as he maneuvered, swaying them. These were images his mind did not show him as they gave no discernable vibration, but he mentally marked where each one was as he touched it and his mind began mapping them for him, showing him a generic outline of a body suspended upside down.

The general may be a bastard, but I'll still thank him if I make it out of here.

Cries of challenge came from the enemies as they confronted him. He defended and countered, drawing upon his many years of training under Master Amnoch and the seemingly countless katas he had memorized. Not having the advantage of his natural sight seemed to enhance both his mental and muscle memory—or perhaps it simply forced him to rely more upon those things.

Weaving between the hanging bodies became easier, using them against the Orsarians as obstacles as he attacked with speed that they could not match. He felt the thud of one of his men hit the ground. He did not rise.

Antious put his steel to several more, felling them as he dashed around them. The killing felt right. Not good, right. That inner assurance propelled him, keeping him calm when he should have been anxious and afraid. But he had never actually felt more alive, never more—

"Antious."

The raspy, weak voice rang with familiarity. It came from close by, his mind mapping the direction just behind him to his left.

He turned in a blur of speed, reached out and felt a body.

"Thannuel!"

He climbed up Thannuel's inverted body like a rope and found the cord that bound his feet.

"Antious—"

"I'm occupied currently, highness! Curl your head up, now!"

Antious severed the cord and they fell to the ground the few feet that Thannuel had been hanging above it. Quickly, Antious came to his feet and cut Thannuel's bonds from his ankles and hands, managing to dispatch another Orsarian that tried to take advantage of his attention being diverted.

"Get up!" he said, but Thannuel did not move. Another one of Antious's men died and he felt the noose closing in around them. The enemy numbers should have been much less by now, should have—

"You have … to kill them twice, Antious."

He had forgotten. *Foolish!* The fear and anxiety that had so far been staved off started germinating inside Antious. Heaving his friend over his left shoulder, he shouted, "Retreat!"

The Dark Diviner watched the skirmish, far enough removed to be out of harm's way. These infiltrators had only come for one, for their leader. It did not surprise him; Arlethians were generally more tightly bound to one another than the Senthary. He supposed at one time he had been one of the Senthary, as much as genealogy and geography played a role in what one was.

Now, however, he belonged to no race—an unforeseen blessing brought on by his banishment. He was above such meaningless associations or cares, for Mari-shaden had plucked him from the world, aggrandizing him far above an otherwise base existence, destining him to be the one who freed the power trapped inside the moons. It had once flowed free on this land before the Ancients had risen, expelling the forbearers of the Influence he now cultivated, Those Not Remembered.

It had been decades, but the power he now wielded had been carefully harnessed, excavating it with care and tenderness from the blood of unbelievers. The Orsarians had accepted him, as had many of the Senthary years before. No matter his current title or what his adherents termed him, he knew he belonged to Mari-shaden, its chosen Thoulden-sha. As his power had grown, a melody had played in his mind, louder as the years passed. Discordant yet memorable all the same. Sometimes it was less prevalent in his mind, but always there. It occurred to him that hearing a constant motif in his mind, no matter its beauty, should have driven him mad. Rather, it comforted him, seemingly encouraging him, coaxing him forward. Most worldly pursuits and desires had become small to him as his Influence grew, the strivings of most men appearing as nothing more than childish.

They will all come to know Mari-shaden when the Resurgence is fulfilled. I am so close now!

One worldly desire he could not root out of himself was revenge. A blindfolded Arlethian soldier now carried Lord Kerr away. Perhaps the Thoulden-sha would have been impressed if it were not his prized possession escaping.

"Pursue and kill them all except Kerr. Bring him back that I might have his blood in the sight of the moons."

As the soldiers left in pursuit, he turned his attention back to the brewing storm over the ongoing naval battle.

Now you shall witness a few drops of power, a small taste of Mari-shaden.

"Strike sail!" Captain Norvuld shouted. His ship was being jerked and tossed and the wood groaned in protest. He could barely hear his voice above the tempest as they were sucked toward the vortex. Pointing to the sails, he gestured for them to be lowered. With wobbly legs, his crew responded with the determination he expected from them.

Easy now. Hold together, girl. The Light will sustain you.

As the sails came down, the ship steadied a bit with the wind's force mostly nullified, now only dealing with the massive currents beneath them. Norvuld spied other ships, both ally and enemy, toppling over or being torn apart as the world poured its wrath from above and raised fury from below.

"I'll take it from here," Norvuld said as he came to the wheel, relieving the helmsman.

"Aye, Captain."

Sails were no use for propulsion and he could not row the ship out of this squall. Of all his time on the waters of Våleira, he had never faced a battle such as this one. Behind him, he felt the light gait of the castaway boy approach. Over his shoulder, he saw the fear on the lad's face.

"You can't fight it," the captain said. "This kind of beast … you have to let it drag you along."

The boy was pale as he stared ahead, white-knuckled.

Blasted Night, you can't have me that easily.

Fighting the natural urge inside him to turn the wheel as far away from the whirlpool as possible, Captain Norvuld turned the rudder directly toward it and let the current draw him in.

"What are you doing?" the castaway cried.

Norvuld did not answer but focused on the water, his hands firmly gripping the helm. His crew shouted out in alarm as they drew closer to the downspout, urging the captain to wave off, but

Norvuld remained undeterred.

"Brace!" he yelled.

The ship shuddered as they entered the whirlpool, turbulent jolts throwing men several feet into the air. Norvuld almost lost his grip on the wheel and would have for certain gone overboard if not for the castaway grabbing him with one hand and the rail with the other. Again, the wood darkened where the lad had grabbed.

It is true, Norvuld marveled, his suspicions confirmed.

"Look!" the boy shouted, pointing aft. Norvuld turned and saw other ships, vessels he had made, following him into the whirlpool. The tornado still spun in its center, stirring the whirlpool faster. The triarch ships following him must have trust in him beyond reason.

This better work.

Turning the rudder enough to fight the current from sucking him down but not tear the ship apart, Norvuld circled the vortex.

"We have to get closer to the center," he shouted over the howl of the tornado and rushing of the ocean.

"We have to get dimming what?" the castaway asked. "Are you insane?"

The next turn, Norvuld angled the helm slightly inward, toward the center of the whirlpool. Their speed increased markedly, the centripetal force fighting Norvuld significantly at the helm.

"Boy! Come to me!"

The castaway scurried across the quarterdeck, risking the few steps without any hand hold, and grabbed the wheel below Norvuld's hands.

"When I give the word," Norvuld said, "We're going turn this wheel to port and shoot out of this. We should have enough velocity to do it."

"Should?" the boy asked, terror on his face.

"Listen, lad, you're never so alive as when you're dancing on death's threshold."

The boy shrugged and braced himself.

"Hoist sails!" At Norvuld's command, and to the crew's credit for not staging a mutiny at such a deranged order, the sails started to rise on the masts and immediately went violently taut, snapping several moorings.

"Now!"

With all the strength he and the boy could muster, they turned the wheel. The reverberations through the ship felt like an earthquake as the rudder fought the mighty current that sought to draw them down to unknown fathoms. With the unnatural gales catching and starting to tear his sails, his ship's velocity approached levels he was sure would rip her apart.

"Hold, girl! Hold!"

With a final push, they turned the helm enough. The ship shot forth at an angle as if a diving blue falcon of Iskell rising on a chasm gust, crested the lip of the watery vortex, and launched in to the air.

General Korin felt them coming. The Orsarians. While the Sentharian fleet had been making their way to the extraction point on the east shore of Main Island, a storm of strange create had materialized almost from nothing. Battling currents and winds, Norvuld and the other captains were forced to deal with attacks from Orsarian vessels simultaneously. Though his forces seemed to be prevailing, ironically thanks to the storm that had caught ally and enemy alike, they would never reach them in time.

He and his men formed ranks as best they could. Those able-bodied soldiers formed lines in front of the wounded still strong enough to hold a weapon. Senthary and Arlethian alike were intermingled into a single body. There was no point in separating the races, as was typical in joint military operations, with so few left.

Barely six hundred, Korin thought. *Some three hundred wounded.* Most of those could still at least hold a sword or spear. They had a few short archers, but not nearly enough. From the ground's pulse, he could feel what he guessed to be more than double their own numbers.

"Men," he said, facing his soldiers, "I do not have words to embolden you. I do not make speeches. Those who have served around me for any time know me to be a hard person. I will only say that I want to live, and I want you to live. If you will fight for the person standing next to you, we have our best chance of survival. Even then, we will likely die. So, let each man here vow to take at least one of these vile miscreants with him before joining the Light. This final act will echo in service to your families and country for ages."

Through the trees, Korin saw them come. The dark marauders—a most fitting name for them, he had decided—advanced without much organization. Seeing Korin's small band looking beleaguered and weary sent the enemy into a frenzy.

"Kill them twice!" Korin said as he raised his blade.

Admiral Gendaeri had led the search for their enemy. Some were extremely fast, he had observed, obviously blessed by the Underlander with their abilities. Arlethians, the Dark Diviner had called them, warning of their innate abilities of speed and vibrational acuteness, but they were of no consequence in the end against the ingenuity of his forces.

He pointed. "There!"

He had found them. They were north on the eastern shore of Main Island, a perfect harbor for escaping. But his naval forces had intercepted the enemy ships and the Dark Diviner added his power to the fight. It angered Gendaeri to lose so many ships, but his people, his entire nation, were not far off now.

He charged the enemy band with the rest of his men, joining in the jubilant cries of assured victory. The second life provided by the Underlander from his Dark Diviner had truly been the catalyst for their victory, but the admiral chose to believe in what he could understand and explain, preferring to credit his forces' overwhelming numbers and ingenuity with weaponry, but then cursed remembering that most of the advanced weaponry had been revealed to them by the Dark Diviner.

Coming within striking distance, Gendaeri marveled at the discipline of the enemy. Though they were close enough to make out minute details upon their faces, they still stood in ranks. And then, the enemy erupted in action, dodging his soldiers' attacks and countering before many realized what had happened. There was awe inside him as he witnessed their retaliations, seeing these beings of incredible swiftness up close for the first time. It would have been enough to make any enemy turn and retreat, causing a rout, but the assurance of living through mortal wounds pushed his men forward.

One of his dark marauders was impaled on a spear and after only a second or two, Gendaeri saw his second life kick in and retaliate with a killing blow of his own, spear still impaled through his abdomen. Others attacked with full zeal while arrows stuck from eyes and throats, the wounds not affecting them as their second life took over.

One of these Arlethians bore some insignia on his breastplate that Gendaeri intuited to be of high rank. If that was not enough indication, the man fought with ruthlessness, striking down his men with two mortal wounds, sometimes more, before most could even block.

Their leader, no doubt. Finally.

Gendaeri threw a spear but the man dodged it effortlessly, as if he had expected the attack. Not stopping his movement toward the enemy leader, Gendaeri drew his scimitars, one in each hand.

As the sounds of battle coalesced in the air, the two clashed together. The Arlethian was faster and skilled, but Gendaeri was younger and stronger. He could feel it when their blades met, the way the Arlethian gave slightly under the power of his blow.

Other soldiers came between them, separating their engagement. Gendaeri now faced two enemies, but neither moved with the speed of Arlethians. The confrontation lasted less than a minute before he dispatched them both; but the Arlethian leader, having dealt out similar fates to a few more of his dark marauders, immediately met him again. He could see his opponent was wounded slightly, favoring one leg. A stream of red worked its way down his left leg. Gendaeri smiled.

Wielding his scimitars and slashing them with a fluidity that caused the Arlethian's face to register fear and respect, Gendaeri spun into the man, using his back and hips like a battering ram. He felt the cold steel enter his lower left side, through his abdomen and into his hip, deep and low. The pain was searing but he continued to twist his body before the Arlethian could retrieve his blade for a second blow, forcing the man to lose his grip on the hilt. The blow of his body sent the Arlethian stumbling back, swordless.

Cold came upon him, spreading through him. They said this is how it felt, those who had experienced their second life, but for all the mental preparation, nothing could help him cope with the fear that accompanied his temporary death.

Something might be wrong! What if it does not work?

He came to one knee as the cold spread and his vision turned dark. The beating of his heart, thudding hard against his chest, slowed.

I am lost …

Before a full second had passed, heat shot through Gendaeri and he felt his heart restart, racing like a stampede of wild horses. His vision exploded back to life and the man before him, the Arlethian leader, was trying to get up, his leg obviously badly injured.

Gendaeri withdrew the sword from his side, feeling its cold metal exit his flesh, and tossed it aside.

"When you meet the Underlander," Admiral Gendaeri said, knowing the man could not understand his words, "tell him who sent you to him."

He came down on the Arlethian with both scimitars, seeking his chest. With a feral yell, however, the man twisted his body, raising his wounded leg up high across his chest, almost as if curling into a fetal position. Gendaeri's blades pierced his thigh completely and the man screamed, the veins in his neck bulging. Before he saw the blow, Gendaeri felt something like iron strike the side of his temple. A metal wristband that extended up the Arlethian's forearm had struck with surprising force from the wounded man. Rotating his hips, the scimitars still embedded in him, the Arlethian brought his uninjured right leg up and over Gendaeri's face before he could counter, coming down hard on his neck. His head was now pinned down in a clamp between the Arlethian's legs.

Gendaeri screamed as the man squeezed his legs, turning his screams to gasps, cutting off his air supply. The pain the Arlethian must be enduring to flex the muscles in his wounded leg had to be excruciating, beyond what could be consciously borne. And then, Gendaeri's surprise knew no bounds as he saw the man, with a trembling and bloodied hand, reach down and pull free one of the scimitars from his own thigh. Blood shot forth from the narrow wound, but the Arlethian paid it no attention.

This time there was no coldness, only darkness, as Gendaeri's own scimitar pierced his skull. The last thing he consciously felt was the thump of the curved sword's hilt striking his head, ceasing the blade's penetration, followed by the sound of the hilt being snapped from the blade as the Arlethian violently twisted the scimitar.

Roan stumbled through the thick of the forest with Thannuel barely conscious over his shoulder. His speed was severely hindered and if it were not for his wood-dweller reflexes, he would have gone down a half-dozen times already.

"Lieutenant, let me carry Lord Kerr," Remel said. "It will be faster with your hindrance."

It was logical, but Antious could not let go now that he had Thannuel. He shook his head. "Run ahead of me. I'll follow your vibrations, stepping where you step."

As he traced Corporal Remel's vibrational signatures, he felt the other five wood-dweller soldiers behind him, engaging and hindering the small horde of Orsarians that pursued them, buying time for their escape. Antious lost their pulses in his mind's eye one by one as they became overwhelmed.

Bless you, men, for your sacrifices.

Finally, they broke free from the forest into an opening. The sound of waves filled his ears and the scent of salt water his nostrils.

"The beach?" he asked Remel.

"The eastern shore, yes."

"Is there a boat? A ship?"

"North," Remel said. "I see several Orsarian frigates anchored close to shore. They almost blend in with the black sands of this small island. We could swim to them."

They'd never be able to sail a frigate with just two people. The problem would be further compounded if they met any resistance upon boarding one of the frigates. Antious's arm, shoulder and back ached from the punishment he was putting his body through and his muscles started to spasm.

"We need another way," Antious said hurriedly, feeling the Orsarians getting closer. Sand was perhaps the most difficult medium to accurately sense vibrational signatures through, but the stampede of dark marauders came to him clear enough. He did not sense his other men, who had run interference, any longer.

Remel spun around, obviously searching and thinking. "South, there's a narrow strip of land that extends into—"

The corporal's words were interrupted by a *thunk* and Antious sensed his body crumple to the beach.

"Corporal! Remel!" Antious knelt down to the man and found a spear protruding from Remel's neck, its broad head adorned with four jagged blades. The soldier bled out in silence.

He would have escaped if I had not asked him to come. They all would have.

Within seconds, the vibrations of Antious's pursuers were strong enough so that his mind began to once again project to him the rough outlines of those approaching: scores of them.

Another spear hurtled toward him, but Antious sensed this, seeing the portrayal of a blank man in his mind mimic the stance and follow-through of a spear throw. With only milliseconds to spare, he ducked, avoiding impalement. But it really didn't matter now, did it?

Backing up until the shore break washed around his feet, Antious gently put Thannuel down and knelt beside him. The cold, wet sand felt good against his aching muscles.

"I'm sorry, my friend. I am not strong enough. I tried."

The Orsarians arrived and started to encircle Antious, still kneeling. He continued to feel the waves washing up around his legs, so he knew he was still alive.

"Trust yourself," Thannuel said in a weak voice, surprising him.

"You're awake? Best if you were not, I'm afraid."

"I trust you, Antious. Trust yourself. You will find a way."

Antious Roan saw no way out, no way forward. "I hope you can float, Thannuel."

I will decipher the complexities of your harmonic identity. Then, I will remake you as mine—for all things have a song.

—Noxmyra, Mother of Helsya

TWENTY-FOUR

~ELKINAL~

Day 14 of 3rd Rising 393 A.U.

ELKINAL SAT WITH HIS DAUGHTER, Serisa, and nephew, Drailin, in one of the crew's quarters of a frigate off Pearl Island. They had swum here after escaping from a massive ship over a cycle ago, an explosive distraction covering their passage. With all the frigates here abandoned, the enemy sailors all long disembarked to the land, they had their choice of dwellings. Besides, this would be the last place anyone would search for refugees.

The rations they had found were barely suitable for consumption, but they fished and harvested oysters under the cover of night. Fresh water was the biggest problem they had for sustenance. As a solution, they boiled the seawater and placed a metal plate at an angle above the pot, causing the steam to condense upon the metal. Driblets of water then ran down the underside of the metal plate into an awaiting basin. A tedious process, and the water tasted terrible, but it did sustain them.

Drailin's bruises had almost completely healed but puffy pink scar tissue around his left eye would likely remain the rest of his life from not being properly tended to. Fortunately, the boy had not suffered any vision loss.

Serisa's wounds, however, were deeper. She did not speak of her time as a captive. In fact, they had tried to avoid the topic altogether. The three of them lived relatively quiet lives, an ironic peace, while the battle for their homeland raged. Elkinal thought of it as sleeping in the eye of a hurricane. Eventually, they would be rousted from their temporary quarters as the storm found them; but for now, they enjoyed having free rein on an enemy ship.

Elkinal had the water duty shift. He emerged above deck, a large bucket in his hand secured to a chain. He always went to the port side of the frigate, the view being unmolested by the other invader vessels anchored along the island on the starboard side. And if that was not enough for despair to set in, the eastern harbor of Second Island, also visible from the starboard view, contained a greater number of invader ships, including the large one upon which he had created an immense amount of destruction. Elkinal wondered about that at times, how the ship hadn't sustained more damage. He believed it might have been permanently crippled from his sabotage, but it remained afloat, proudly defying him. He had long ceased disturbing his peace by glancing northward. It seemed that was a different age, another lifetime, despite the reminder every morning when he awoke in an Orsarian bunk.

Elkinal brought the bucket up and was about to drop it over the side when he heard voices. Shouts. Instinctively, he squatted behind the railing. Two men sprang from the trees. No, three. One was draped over the shoulder of another. They wore uniforms of some create, obviously soldiers, and obviously not Orsarians. He had seen enough of their kind to know. Even with a wounded man, they moved impressively fast.

Wood-dwellers? Elkinal didn't know for sure, having never visited the mainland, but it made sense if the legends of their speed were true. And then another group, much larger, emerged from the trees.

Suddenly, one of the wood-dwellers took a spear to the throat and crumpled down. It was an impossible throw, made from over forty boat lengths. The remaining wood-dweller soldier put his burden down on the sand close to the shoreline and knelt. Elkinal squinted in the fading light ... was he blindfolded? Just as Elkinal believed he had given up, the blindfolded Arlethian rose with a burst of energy—a blur to Elkinal's eyes—and dragged his companion into the ocean.

The war had once again found him; it was just a matter of time. He had witnessed the first death of his countrymen in this confrontation, his stepbrother Lomand, and he did not wish to see more—not if he could help it. But angry tides take him, he would not stand by idly.

He dropped the bucket to the deck and ran below with a speed approaching reckless, falling more than stepping down the stairs. Dashing through the narrow girth of the berth deck quarters, he found his daughter and nephew.

"Quickly! Come with me!" Elkinal exclaimed.

Concern immediately registered on Serisa's face and Drailin stood sharply, hitting his head on a low beam.

"What's happening? Are we in trouble?" the girl asked.

"I don't have time to explain, Ser," her father answered. "Follow me."

They started moving with all haste.

"This isn't the way to the upper deck, Uncle," Drailin observed. "If we need to escape—"

"We're not going to the upper deck."

"Then where—"

"The *thunder* deck," Elkinal said.

Antious did not know what he was thinking. He slogged waist deep in water, cutting through the waves and dragging Thannuel behind him, trying his best keep him on his back.

The Orsarians were coming, following him into the surf. He knew this because he lost their vibrational signatures completely as they did, not able to feel them in the water. In reflex, he opened his eyes and removed his blindfold. He could make nothing definitive out in his murky vision besides different colored blotches that were moving toward him.

"This might be a good time for your Ancients to intervene!" Antious shouted at Thannuel. "Or for you to miraculously heal!"

Antious heard the splashes of men getting closer.

"Come on, Thannuel! I need you!"

With an obviously colossal effort, Thannuel rolled over and started to swim. Too weak to dive below the waves, Antious pushed him through. Thannuel's strokes were slow and anemic, as if he were demonstrating to children how to swim in slow motion. His legs barely kicked.

A blood-chilling cry came upon Antious and he felt something blunt smack the back of his head. He almost lost consciousness until an increased amount of light filled his vision, shocking him alert. It was almost blinding but his eyes refocused in a few moments. Whatever had been wrong in his head had been smacked back into place. Literally.

He turned in time to block a blow from a scimitar and return the attack, stabbing the man twice in the chest. The man with the mace, who had kindly though violently returned his vision, received a blow at the top of his cranium, splitting his skull asunder. He ducked the next blow from another enemy, pulling himself under the water and slashing at legs before resurfacing, then struck another man in the throat and stomach. It took twice as long to kill these bastards, but the water at least caused them a small hindrance.

Having let go of Thannuel to defend himself, Antious spied him drifting back toward shore, not able to fight the waves. Several Orsarians fell on him.

"No!" Antious cried.

But they weren't killing him. They were grabbing him, carrying him. Thannuel tried to free himself but was easily subdued by a volley of punches to his face and chest.

Why? Antious thought.

"Thannuel!" Antious was pulled from his ankles, an enemy having approached from below. With a powerful thrust, he kicked the man's face and resurfaced like a bolt, nearly coming completely free from the chest-deep water, and came down on the man, impaling his back with his steel while the Orsarian was still submerged. Next, Antious put his foot on the man, ripping free his sword but holding his attacker down. Drowning would be his second death.

"Thannuel, I can't get to you!" He parried another sword and dodged a spear as another wave crashed into him. They had almost extricated Thannuel from the water. "Fight! Ancient Heavens, fight!"

A loud boom filled the air and a plume of sand shot into the air just south of them. All stopped. Antious looked to the closest ship, the provenance of the sound, and saw smoke billowing from a square hole in the ship's hull.

A second boom reported and this time the plume erupted much closer, splashing in the shallow waters of the beach.

In the battle's lull, Antious dove and started swimming frantically for his lord and friend.

"Do you know what you're doing?" Serisa asked her father. "Of course, I'm secretly a thunder weapon expert and am familiar with all manner of incendiary siege engines," Elkinal answered with a short temper. He adjusted the height of the metal tube by turning a threaded column at the tube's rear, raising the backend and lowering the flared mouth a few degrees.

"Drailin, load another ball with more fire sand, quickly!"

The boy had already gone into action before Elkinal had spoken. He worked with impressive efficiency.

"Ser, ready with the—"

"Torch, got it," she said.

"Ready!" Drailin reported, putting a new wick in the vent. "This is *so* fun!"

"Fire!" Elkinal ordered, and Serisa lit the wick.

They all covered their ears for the third shot. The thunder weapon again shattered the silence, the air seeming to ripple around them, and this time, the projectile hit a group of half a dozen or so Orsarians. Body parts and screams filled the air.

"That's for my father, you sons of whores!" Drailin shouted.

Serisa looked abashed. "Drailin, I can't believe—"

"Reload!" Elkinal commanded.

The boy is right. I haven't had this much fun in a long, long time.

"Who's firing?" Thannuel asked, one arm cradling his left ribs.

"Does it matter? They're not firing at us!"

Thannuel felt Antious encircle his torso as they hurriedly made their way toward the enemy ship that had unexpectedly aided them.

"You're heavier than dead weight, *your grace,*" Antious said.

Thannuel smiled. "Sorry, mop boy." He could barely feel his legs under him and he was dizzy, likely from the loss of blood. His skin stung from the salt water in his wounds, like a hundred leaches on him.

"Like an idiot, I knew you'd come," Thannuel said. "You proved me right. Don't you know when something is a lost cause, Lieutenant?"

He grimaced as they waded through the ocean, fighting the waves of water and pain. Another shot sounded, almost deafening as they closed the distance to the black-hulled ship.

"No, Lord Kerr, apparently not," Antious replied.

"I'm glad," Thannuel said.

*Some have incorrectly called Entropy a distortion to the nature of things;
but it is the Lumenatis that dares to distort Entropy's natural reign.*

—From *"Våleira's Noctuary."* Record considered apocryphal.

TWENTY-FIVE
~THANNUEL~
Day 15 of 3rd Rising 393 A.U.

THANNUEL'S HEAD POUNDED from dehydration. He lay in Captain Norvuld's quarters a day after their narrow escape on Pearl Island, not completely sure how he had gotten there. He and Antious owed their lives to three Runics who had been hiding within an enemy ship. When Thannuel had tried to thank them, one of the trio—he couldn't remember who in his state, but he thought it was the girl—instead thanked him for providing them the best entertainment of their lives. He learned they had suffered much during the first days after the dark marauders landed.

The wounds on Thannuel's torso and back were deep gouges from where the barbs of the net had dug into his skin. From what he could tell, it didn't look like they had been removed with any sign of concern.

"I can't imagine the pain that must have caused you, Lord Kerr," Antious said. "I'm sorry I was not fast enough to spare you that agony."

"To be truthful, Lieutenant, I don't remember much," Thannuel admitted.

"Not lieutenant, Lord Kerr. General Korin ordered me not to come after you, so I resigned. It only seemed logical."

Thannuel managed a smile. "Well, Lieutenant, I do not accept your resignation. You are promoted to captain. Please resume your duties."

"Lord Kerr, that's not what—"

"Relax, Captain, you'll work it out."

"Lord Kerr, I seek a word with you in private," Norvuld said. He nodded and the others who attended to him left. Antious stayed behind.

Looking at Antious, Norvuld said, "Captain Roan, it's quite sensitive in nature, I'm afraid."

Antious still did not move, looking at Thannuel.

"It's okay, Antious." Reluctantly, Antious left the captain's quarters.

"Our fleet does not fare terribly well, I'm afraid," Captain Norvuld reported. "A whirlpool created by the Ancient Dark arose and wreaked havoc upon our ships. The only good news is that much of the enemy fleet has also been destroyed … at least those that had engaged us on the way to pick up General Korin. The Orsarians remain heavily entrenched upon Main Island, however."

"Where is General Korin?" Thannuel asked.

"Gravely wounded, I'm afraid, beyond healing. We were intercepted, as I mentioned, by Orsarian ships and the Ancient Dark's meddling. We escaped the whirlpool, along with several of our triarch ships, but were too late to aid the general. The dark marauders' land forces arrived first and the remnants of our armies were not fully prepared and were nearly overrun."

This news saddened Thannuel. Seeing his concern, Norvuld added, "If it's any consolation, when we finally arrived, we had to drag the general from the beach with what few survivors were left. He was cutting the head off every Orsarian, screaming and cursing in a rage. He appeared quite mad, actually."

"How many ships do we have left?" Thannuel asked.

"Twenty-one."

Less than half the fleet? "And able-bodied men?"

Norvuld shrugged. "A few hundred perhaps, maybe less. And before you ask about the enemy's strength, I have no idea since we did not know how many they started with. But, they still have scores of ships, my Lord."

"Could we escape back to P'lor?" Thannuel asked.

"Unlikely. The ships we still have are lightly crewed; many should probably be scuttled. The Orsarian ships are a great deal faster than our own, regardless. I admit a bit of angry jealousy on my part. I do hope to be able to examine the design of one ship rather than blowing every one we see to smithereens."

"And, they know they have us trapped," Thannuel surmised. "This is why we're not under attack currently?"

"I would guess we are no longer a threat to them, especially with what's on the horizon."

Thannuel looked questioningly at the master shipwright.

"Come above deck," Norvuld said. "You will see."

Thannuel stared toward the eastern horizon. Disbelief raced through him.

"How many?" Thannuel asked.

"More than the stars." Norvuld shrugged. "Four hundred ships at least, large enough to carry four to five hundred souls each. Maybe more."

"These people have been searching for decades," Thannuel said. "There's no other possibility. To be this prepared … that many ships … this might be their entire civilization."

"Aye," Norvuld agreed. "At least one hundred thousand souls are there. Likely, my Lord, many more."

"How long until they make landfall?"

"Sometime during first moon."

The desperateness of the situation seized Thannuel's heart.

"If we don't find a way out of here before they get too close," Norvuld added, "we're done."

"You said we could not escape. Aren't we already lost?"

The old shipwright smiled. "Escape is not the only option, Lord Kerr. If, that is, you are prepared."

Thannuel followed Norvuld back below deck to his quarters.

"Prepared for what?"

Norvuld opened a trunk and reached his hand inside. It came out holding a sword roughly four feet long with a dark blade. Thannuel looked up with curiosity, his head still pounding.

"Jarwynian ore?" he asked.

"Aye," Norvuld said.

"I've handled these blades once before. Master Amnoch has one, in fact. They are lighter and stronger than anything I've ever wielded. You could spend a lifetime saving up for one of these. How did you get it?"

"They are not so rare," Norvuld said. "Not in our circles." The captain offered the sword to Thannuel and the Lord of the Western Province accepted it.

"Master Norvuld, I'm in no condition currently to take this." Despite his physical condition, the sword felt amazing to him as his hand wrapped around the hilt. "When did you acquire this?"

"This sword has never had an owner. It was made specifically for you."

"For *me*? How can that be? Who—"

"We are in all walks of life, Lord Kerr," Norvuld explained. "Some shipwrights, some fishers, some craftsmen, some miners, some even in the Prime Lord's court. This blade was provided to me for you, should the occasion arise. And, it has."

Thannuel did not follow.

"To you," Norvuld continued, "the ability to speak with trees, feel vibrations, move with incredible speed are all simply parts of being a wood-dweller. However, young lord, this is not entirely accurate. You see, these abilities have more to do with *who* you are from, rather than *where* you are from. And Jarwynian ore ... yes, it has some special properties. Lightweight, incredibly strong yet flexible. But to a *Light Shepherd*, one who can harness sparks of the Living Light, it can be so much more."

"Forgive me, Master Norvuld, but if this would normally make sense it is not now," Thannuel said, feeling his head. "I'm certain I just need some rest."

"Well, we haven't time for that, Lord Kerr. Do you remember when you first started recycling friction?"

Thannuel's astonishment could not be hidden. *I know this word ...* The memory of raiding the Thoulden-sha's hold, of facing

Muhktar in the narrows, came back to him.

Do others know of this? he wondered.

"It was likely in that alley when you were sixteen. When the Marishee first attacked you," Norvuld said. "You were able to scale building walls and jump from them with strength and ability that normally should not have been yours, despite being a wood-dweller."

"How did you know that?"

"One of us was there that night, observing. In fact," Norvuld admitted, "we had been observing you for several cycles by that time."

Thannuel grew wary, an image of an elderly looking man in an elm tree entering his mind. The man had *spoken* to him somehow … in his mind. "Master Norvuld, I know you to be a gifted shipwright at the Aerikal yards. What are you trying to tell me? Why was I being watched?"

"It's as I've said, young lord. We are in all walks of life. Even your father's Hold Guard."

Thannuel stood up. "Amnoch is a spy?"

Norvuld tipped his head. "Master Amnoch is one of us, yes. Spy is perhaps too strong a word."

"Who are you?" Thannuel asked, eyes narrowing.

"I, Lord Kerr, am a member of the *Gyldenal,* a Warrior of Light. And you are a Light Shepherd, though you do not know it."

"The Gyldenal are long extinct, if they were even real!" Thannuel yelled. The throbbing in his head increased. "We don't have time for this!"

"That is," Norvuld agreed, "what we have worked hard to perpetuate. We must remain clandestine in order for our mission to have its greatest chance for success."

Thannuel forced himself to listen. Though skeptical, he knew Master Norvuld to be a sober man.

"With a weapon forged of Jarwynian ore," Norvuld continued, "you can store the Light you draw from the forest, from the trees. The Light itself is the reason we can feel what we do through the forest. It thrives in the forest, hidden there long ago by the Ancients … or more specifically, by those who were not part of The Turning Away."

Thannuel stumbled, catching himself on Norvuld's bedpost. The Jarwynian sword fell to the floor.

"Master Norvuld," he said weakly, "I've lost a lot of blood. I need time to heal, time we do not have. Good steel in my hands is largely useless for now. I'm not sure it would make a difference in anyone's hands now."

"Certainly not mine. The Light's gifts to me are not with steel. I was never blessed in that area. But one such as yourself, yes, the results can be … impressive."

"I believe in the Ancients, Norvuld." Thannuel sat down upon the bed. "But, it looks more like we'll be going to them sooner then they return to us."

"Did you wonder about these ships?" Norvuld asked. "Why I made them of triarch wood? It's not been used before, to my knowledge, other than by myself in some limited experiments."

Thannuel shrugged. "I just assumed it must have been a way to bring a little bit of home with us into the battlefield."

"You believe this war we're engaged in is for land, for survival against another aggressor," Norvuld said. "I don't blame you. That's what it no doubt appears to everyone else, even to the Orsarians, to be sure." The master shipwright paused. "However, it is and always has been much greater. The Ancient Dark seeks to overrun the Living Light, the Lumenatis, which we have protected for over four millennia."

"You're right," Thannuel said. "I think this is simply about land

and the Orsarians are here because theirs has cycled. At some point, we will have to do the same."

"No. For if Arlethia ever cycles, we have already lost."

"All lands eventually cycle, Master Norvuld."

"Not so, my Lord. Not Arlethia. For what lies in Tavaniah Forest is the heart of sentient life in all Våleira. If Arlethia ever began to cycle, the lands of the world would never be reborn."

Something hit Thannuel, something he had known but just taken for granted. "Arlethia has never cycled," he said, more to himself.

Norvuld nodded. "The Ancient Dark seeks the Lumenatis, to extinguish it and the Light it sends forth into the world, the Light that renews and sustains."

"What does this have to do with the Orsarians?"

"Not with them specifically, but more the one who leads them. You have had dealings with him before … "

"I have never met any Orsarian before this war."

"Their leader," Norvuld said, looking straight into Thannuel's eyes, "is not an Orsarian. He was once of the Senthary."

When Thannuel had been captured, he spent most of that time unconscious, a mercy from the pain he had endured from the nets used to capture him and many others. Hanging upside down, his head pounding from blood pressure and dehydration, he had blurry images of other captives also in the same predicament. Orsarians wove between them, speaking in their foreign tongue. They seemed to always move past him, to another prisoner, draining them instead. He hadn't wondered why that was then, but did now. As he rummaged through the upside down distorted memories in his mind, he focused on one man who always stood far off. Dressed in loose-fitting black pants and a robe-like tunic with a turban. The posture, the air of superiority … it was more than a commanding officer, Thannuel realized. It was the bearing and demeanor of one who thought himself a god.

"The Thoulden-sha!"

Norvuld nodded. "Aye. He escaped when his rebellion failed. Fortunate for us, he was hasty and rash in his decisions, acting before he was ready … before he had full command of the Ancient Dark."

"And he does now?" Thannuel asked.

"Unlikely. But, his power and fluency of Dark Influence has increased dramatically. He can control the tides and weather in his vicinity, as we have already seen. The tempest we barely survived was not natural."

"Nor is the fact that our enemies require two mortal blows to bring them down, save for decapitating them."

"Yes, a second life," Norvuld said. "The Ancient Dark does have power. It grants this to those who ultimately serve its purpose, even if they are unaware of it."

"But the Thoulden-sha seemed to follow a different belief system altogether," Thannuel said, confused. "He was always babbling about some Mari-shaden and the power trapped in the moons; never about the Ancient Dark."

"No matter the names, Lord Kerr, the fruits are the answer. Do one's beliefs lead to life and cultivation of knowledge and the sustaining of Light, or to the destruction and decadence of all we know, causing Darkness? There are many ways to access the Ancient Dark, my Lord. It is not specific in its requirements." Norvuld paused. "But, I think you might recognize Mari-shaden if translated properly."

"It is not just some gibberish?"

"Unfortunately, it is not. Rather, it comes from the roots of the Feylan people."

"Who?"

"They are the ancestors of the Senthary. Languages morph through time, Lord Kerr. To the Feylan, Mari meant mother. Shaden, well that's a little tougher, but one among us, very familiar with the Hardacheon Age, believes this is a variant of Chardantien, which roughly means 'joy through endless night'."

Thannuel's face came alive with understanding, recalling the stories of his youth. "The Dark Mother?"

"Aye, my Lord. This Thoulden-sha is a prophet of the Dark Mother, of Noxmyra. Mari-shaden is simply a different name for her in a mixture of tongues. Through time, she has worked through those who are open to her Influence, striving to prepare the way for her return. And, you, Lord Kerr, may have the capacity to bring about the return of the Ancients."

"What? Come on, Master Norvuld! I admit there are some startling events happening, not the least of which is that new fleet from the east, but I'm not one of the Ancients!"

"No, but perhaps you are unaware of the importance of your lineage, of your family's place that was once among the Ancients."

Thannuel squinted in confusion. "How would anyone know such a thing?"

"We are keepers of knowledge, Lord Kerr, including many records preceding The Turning Away. Those are mostly fragments and incomplete, I'm afraid, but we do have the records of the Kerr family."

"Why?"

"Because, my Lord, your bloodline is chiefly responsible for bringing the Ancients to Våleira and in casting out the previous inhabitants, wielders of great Influence of the Ancient Dark. The ones called Those Not Remembered. Your line has always ruled, long before it was known as Kerr."

"What then? Who were we?" Thannuel asked.

"Your bloodline is from the Kiarra Clan. And, my Lord, the Dark Mother has not forgotten.

"Now, there are great ones among us," Norvuld continued. "Those who have great capacity for Light … but none that can extract the Living Light and restore it whence it has been hidden."

"Why was it hidden?"

Instead of answering, Norvuld grabbed a triarch leafling from the same trunk that had contained the Jarwynian sword.

"My use of the Light is somewhat limited," Norvuld explained. "Most of us protect the knowledge of the Living Light, allowing us increased access to it as we conform our lives to the ways of the Ancients … or as best as we can. Few of us can utilize the Light in conjunction with friction, as I suspect you can."

"You mentioned friction before. I still don't understand this."

"Every emotion, Lord Kerr, produces energy," Norvuld said. "Just like rubbing two sticks together creates heat. That heat *is* energy. In a very similar way, the emotions within us create energy, what we term *friction*. That energy can be captured and recycled, directed."

This made more sense to Thannuel, lining up with his insights that came to him in the narrows years ago.

"Can you do this?" he asked.

Norvuld shook his head. "I've never been able to capture it. I am too block-headed, she tells me."

"She?"

"Not important." Norvuld waved him off. "You'll meet her someday, I am sure. What is important, Lord Kerr, is what I can do for you now. But, take heed; I can only do this once. The rest of the Light you will need if we are to overcome the Dark against us."

Master Norvuld brought his hand with the triarch leafling to

Thannuel's face. He gently pressed and said, "*Mylendia Shaul.*"

Warmth spread through Thannuel's body, his plethora of wounds tingling. He raised a hand, seeing the wounds there and on his arm seal, becoming scabless thin lines where the barbs and hooks of the Orsarian nets had ripped him. The feeling of weakness inside him fled, a healthy strength replacing it, and his skin's paleness abated, being restored to its natural hue.

The quarters he and Master Norvuld occupied became darker as Thannuel was healed, the wood turning from a lighter brown to a more gray appearance, as if it were decades old and not been treated against decay.

"Okay," Thannuel said with amazement. "I think I'm willing to hear some more."

Norvuld put the sword back in Thannuel's hands. "I think, perhaps, it will come to you more naturally as you wield this blade."

Again, Thannuel accepted the sword. It was indeed made for *him.* A perfect length of steel and a hilt that seemed to mold to his hand at his touch. As he raised the sword, it felt like nothing more than his arm—natural—as if his arm were simply extended, such was the feel of control.

"What will the rest of you do?" Thannuel asked.

"Oh, I do have a plan. It's a faint hope, but a hope at least. The remaining ships of our fleet and I have requisitioned as much of the explosive powder and artillery as possible from the enemy frigates around Pearl Island. Elkinal and his family were most eager to help and remain so. Their story is quite remarkable actually."

"Another time," Thannuel said. "Where should we start?"

"Perhaps General Korin can best answer that. But there is one promise I will require of you, Lord Kerr." Norvuld paused.

"What kind of promise?"

"One I hope you will not have to keep," Norvuld said.

TWENTY-SIX

~THANNUEL~

Day 16 of 3rd Rising 393 A.U.

ON A BED OF TRIARCH LEAVES, General Korin lay wrapped in bandages. Antious joined Thannuel for this visit.

"How is he?" Thannuel asked a healer.

"Not well, my Lord."

"There's nothing you can do?"

The healer shook his head. "The wounds on his limbs, even the mangled left thigh, would be recoverable. But the general took several blows to his midsection that were not attended to soon enough. I'm amazed he has lasted this long, my Lord."

Thannuel nodded to the healer and approached Korin.

"My Lord," he said weakly, trying to sit up.

"No," Thannuel said, putting a hand to his shoulder. "Rest, General Korin. You have won your battle. The Light awaits you with warmth and peace for your loyalty and dedication."

"I see that rascal friend of yours was right," Korin said, turning his eyes to Antious. "I should have come for you … not assumed you were lost. Betrayed you, my Lord."

A thin line of red streamed down the corner of Korin's mouth as he coughed.

"No, General, you did what you thought was right. My father always said you were a rock. A hard man but also impenetrable in your convictions."

"I fought him," Korin said with effort. "Their leader."

Immediately Thannuel thought of the Thoulden-sha, but he was on Third Island.

"Their military leader?" Thannuel asked.

Korin nodded. "He is dead, my Lord. Their forces cannot be many more, not after their last assault on us. They lost every man, Lord Kerr. My men … "

The dying general coughed again, trying to clear his throat from the blood pooling inside him.

" … they stood. Wounded and afraid, they stood."

"General, do you have intelligence on the whereabouts of the remaining enemy forces?" Thannuel asked.

"Other than on Main Island, I do not. But they are without their leader. Regardless, retreat is all we have left for now."

Thannuel knew this was not completely true on either account, but did not contradict the general.

"It is enough, General Korin. Captain Roan and I, along with what few we have left, will take it from here."

"Captain?" Korin asked, turning toward Antious. "So, you passed your advancement exam after all." Korin pursed his lips and nearly smiled. And then, resignation came upon his face.

"I have been hard on you, Captain. You will forgive a father his shortcomings when it comes to his youngest daughter."

"Sir, I hold no contempt for you," Antious said. Thannuel could see the emotion on his friend's face.

He really does admire him, no matter how harsh his treatment has been.

"I regret my earlier words," Antious added.

"No, you don't, son. I *am* a bastard," Korin said. "But, I cannot think of a more worthy match for my daughter." Korin grimaced in pain, his face contorting.

"You will have to be patient with her," he went on. "She takes after her father in many areas. But she loves you, Antious. She always has, ever since she was ten, Ancients take me."

"I love her, General Korin. Everything I have done was in hopes of having her as mine with your approval."

Korin was fading. His face turned paler and breathing became shallower. "You had my approval when you put Lord Kerr on his back." A weak smile tried but failed to appear on his face. "I am proud to call you a son."

Antious's jaw quivered as he looked at his commanding officer. "I will love her loyally. Forever."

"I know." And then the general said no more, his eyes glazing over.

"He is gone to the Light," the healer said.

Thannuel turned to his best friend. "Are you with me, Antious?"

Antious's emotion glistened in his eyes as they met Thannuel's. "Always."

Thannuel felt the hilt of the new sword at his hip. "Then let us finish this."

TWENTY-SEVEN
~THE THOULDEN-SHA~
Day 16 of 3rd Rising 393 A.U.

THE THOULDEN-SHA, MARI-SHADEN'S CHOSEN ORACLE, stepped on the black sand beach of Third Island. The remainder of the Orsarian forces were on the largest island, how many left he did not know. Fifty followed him now. They only had their scimitars and one net cannon left as the enemy had taken most of their ships from this island, leaving them stranded. It mattered little, however.

Once upon Senthara, others will come to my side, heed my call. His mind circled back five years ago, to his encounter with the Helsyan. *They must be freed and stand with me, with Mari-shaden to bring about the Resurgence.* This had become an integral part of his strategy after meeting the Helsyan and knowing him to be related to Mari-shaden.

Despite the interruption from yesterday, in which Kerr had escaped, the Oracle had still harvested the blood of dozens of unbelievers in sight of full first moon, including many Arlethians. The power that surged inside him proved that the Resurgence was near completion. He had limited control of the elements, but enough.

Soon, the power of Mari-shaden will fill me and my followers to overflowing, bringing immortality and total control of the world.

Up to this point, a second life was all that could be conjured, giving his men a needed edge against the Arlethian warriors. It was a fairly recent addition to his growing pantheon of power, but only a mere stepping-stone to full immortality.

One more cycle, the Thoulden-sha thought. *Three span from now, at the next full first moon, I shall set Mari-shaden free with the blood of the cursed Thannuel Kerr, undoing the blasphemy of the Ancients.*

Through a vision, the Thoulden-sha had seen that Mari-shaden's power could only be completely unleashed with the sacrifice of those that trapped its power so long ago, expelling Those Not Remembered from this world. While the so-called Ancients no longer existed, the Arlethians were the closest by lineage and principle. The sacrifice of many Arlethians last night had brought the Resurgence so near; he could taste it in the air he breathed. Kiarra blood would be needed as the finale. The Oracle salivated heavily in anticipation of Thannuel as the ultimate sacrifice, knowing this last one would be the most succulent of all.

What better way to unleash Mari-shaden back into the world than by the death of him who nearly destroyed me?

And then, the Thoulden-sha would begin his assault on

Senthara with a host of immortal dark marauders behind him. In fact, he thought he would walk there rather than sail.

Perhaps a precursor, he thought, desiring to display his growing abilities.

As he stepped into the water, the shore break washed over his feet, up to his ankles. As the waves receded, the undertow took the sand from beneath his feet, forming small craters that his feet settled into as the next waves came.

Then, suddenly, the next wave came in and circled around him, not touching his feet at all. It parted around him like prey giving a predator a wide berth. Another step forward and the water parted again. The sand under his bare feet was dry, for when he commanded the water to divide asunder, *all* the water obeyed, including that which had clung to the individual grains of black sand, leaving them dried out like the sands on the upper parts of the beach.

The Orsarians fell in line behind him, single file, as they walked through the Sea of Albery to Main Island on dry ground.

As Thannuel and Antious exited Captain Norvuld's ship they encountered the survivors of their strike force. The men were tired and worn. This beach, the eastern shoreline of Main Island, was about halfway up the coastline. To the east, Second Island could be seen. To the west, the single peak that pierced the clouds filled Thannuel's vision.

An Arlethian command sergeant approached and saluted. "Lord Kerr, Captain Roan, I am Command Sergeant Glimon. We have re-formed ranks and assimilated into a single unit. At present, I am the highest ranking enlisted soldier, and so have assumed temporary field command, as it may please you, Lord Kerr."

"Sergeant, who is the officer in charge?" Captain Roan asked.

"May I ask after General Korin?"

Antious shook his head.

"Then, Captain, you are the only officer present and accounted for. The unit is yours," Glimon said.

"How many?" Thannuel asked.

"My Lord, at present we are two hundred and seventy-one strong, counting the big guy twice." Glimon motioned to a tall and thick man who easily stood a head and a half taller than any other present and half as thick again in the shoulders than the broadest-chested man among them.

It's no wonder he has survived, Thannuel thought.

"Very well," he said. "Men, we have little time. All of you have seen what hovers against the horizon. Captain Norvuld tells me we cannot outrun the Orsarian ships and so we are forced to continue here. We have two options: hide or fight. For my part, and with the aid of the Ancient Heavens, I choose to engage the enemy until they or we become extinct."

"Every man made his choice when they enlisted in the army, Lord Kerr," Glimon said. "Whether Arlethian or Senthary, we have all pledged to place ourselves between any enemy and our home. Nothing has changed."

The soldiers wore grim expressions but were resolute.

They believe we will all die, Thannuel realized. *Perhaps they are right.*

"Your orders, Lord Kerr?" Antious asked.

"What do you suggest, Captain?"

"My Lord, the enemy is most likely sequestered in the caves at the north side of the mountain, doubtless waiting for their reinforcements."

"How do we know this?"

Glimon summoned a slender man forward from the ranks.

"This is Corporal Teagan. He is a scout," Antious reported. "Corporal, advise Lord Kerr of what you were able to recon."

Teagan saluted Antious and then bowed to Thannuel. "My Lord, the Orsarian ships are mostly anchored off the northeast coast of the island. From there, it's only an hour's walk inland to a series of caves. Elkinal has advised us that these were once mined for ore, but the veins ran out long ago. I didn't dare to get too close, Lord Kerr."

The corporal almost looked ashamed that his report did not contain more detail.

"There's no use in gaining detailed intel if you're not around to report it," Thannuel told him. "You were wise."

Turning to Antious, he said, "Captain, take your unit with all haste to those caves. As has been the case this entire conflict, we do not know the enemy's numbers, but you can be assured you are outnumbered. It is imperative that we distract the remaining dark marauders long enough for Captain Norvuld to execute his plan."

"Yes, my Lord. If I may, Lord Kerr, where will you be?"

Thannuel looked southeast, toward Pearl Island. He could see distortions in the air, light bending unnaturally. It was small and would not be recognized by a glance. More, he could *feel* the darkness approaching, almost like gravity that pulled on his soul rather than his body.

"Dealing with what should have ended five years ago," he said.

Captain Norvuld tied his shoulder-length hair back as he readied his ship, passing the word of their plan along to the other captains of the triarch ships. They were aligning themselves side to side, facing the oncoming fleet from the east. Beside him stood the castaway boy.

"Will it work?" he asked.

Norvuld shrugged. "Maybe." He tousled the lad's obsidian hair. "You're not worried, are you?"

"Aye, I am. So are you, I can see it," the boy said.

"Can you? And where did you learn to read emotions, then?"

The boy looked down. "Mostly just know what worry looks like, from seeing my own face."

"What does a young lad from Helving know of worry?"

The castaway looked up sharply.

"Ah, there's the worried look you must be speaking about," Norvuld said. "It's your accent, lad. Gives you away. It's no secret where you're from."

Norvuld could see the deep distress on the boy's face, as if he had been caught.

"What are you hiding from?" the master shipwright asked. "You *are* running from something, aren't you?"

"I don't want to talk about it! Have I not earned my place here? Isn't that enough?"

Norvuld looked back to the approaching fleet. "Aye, you've earned your keep. And whatever you're running from will eventually find you. It's inevitable."

"No, he won't find me. I made sure of that."

"I see," Norvuld said. "I see."

After a few moments of silence the captain asked, "Well, are you going to make me call you 'boy' or 'castaway' for the rest of your life?"

The boy huffed, scrunching his face in thought. Finally, he seemed to come to a decision.

"Aiden," he said. "My name is Aiden."

"I'm pleased to meet you, young Aiden. If we make it through this, I'll see to it you get an apprenticeship at the Aerikal yards. It's a good future, good honest work."

"If we survive, Captain Norvuld, I don't think I'll want to set foot on another ship again."

Despite himself, Norvuld chuckled. "I couldn't blame you if that was your decision."

Just then, the ship's color changed, the wood planks under their feet growing darker, the masts and rails showing the same effect. Norvuld looked to the ships on either side of him and saw the same occurrence.

"What's happening?" Aiden asked.

"I'll tell you when you're older, lad. Don't be concerned about that. Let's turn our attention there." Norvuld pointed east. "Hoist sails, raise anchor!" he shouted. The crew responded with the spryness he demanded of them.

"What? Just because I know your first name now somehow relieves you from your duties?" Norvuld asked Aiden. "You're still a castaway. I won't think twice about throwing you overboard if you've lost your inclination to work."

"Aye, Captain!" Aiden shouted and jumped down from the quarterdeck to join the crew.

Captain Antious Roan stood at a low elevation on the north side of the mountain, directly above the caves Teagan had indicated. The Arlethian portion of his detachment had taken a circuitous route, heading up the mountain and around, while their Sentharian counterparts had made their way in a direct path, taking them through towns and villages that had been abandoned.

No guards, Antious noted. *Either brilliant or stupid.* Choosing to not post guards would make a predator force, such as his, pass right by this place. However, the Orsarians were not hiding, but believed *his* forces to be in hiding. Antious settled on the latter summation of his prey.

There were only two caves. Assuming there was no outlet on the other side of the caves—a piece of intelligence that Antious lacked—their plan would work. He gave the signal to the Sentharian soldiers on the ground. Immediately, the men began to stack wood in large piles several yards into each of the two cave mouths along with kindling. One man used a flint and striker to set the woodpiles ablaze.

Now we wait.

Lord Thannuel Kerr waited alone on the southeast beach of Main Island for the Thoulden-sha. He held the sword of dark Jarwynian ore in his hand, a triarch leafling between the palm and hilt. The master shipwright had said it would feel natural to draw in the Light, almost like speaking through a tree in his native forests. Once it was drawn in, he would be able to direct that power through his blade, the specialized ore acting like a conductor of sorts ... or so the legends had said, anyway. Norvuld admitted he really did not have firsthand knowledge of this ability, but that it *should* come naturally to Thannuel.

"Should?" Thannuel had asked.

"Your intentions matter, Lord Kerr," Norvuld answered. "If you have lived your life in accordance with the principles of the Ancients, or what we know of them, you will be able to harness the Light."

"And if I can't 'harness' the Light, as you say?"

"Run," Norvuld had responded. "Now get off my ship, my Lord. I have work to do."

The leafling provided enough of a connection to the triarch wood of Norvuld's ships. He could *feel* the vibrations of the men on them, as if they were here beside him. His sensitivity was as keen as if he stood in an Arlethian forest even now, not on a sandy beach.

How am I supposed to draw in the Light? he wondered. *How can—*

His mind caught on something Norvuld had said. *Speaking* through *a tree.* That seemed significant to him suddenly. *We say speaking* with *a tree when putting our hands to a trunk to increase our senses through the forest. Norvuld said 'through'* ...

Could the channel go both ways?

He did not have much time. The water in front of him split, forming an uncanny tunnel, fish flopping on the ground and sea crustceans becoming visible that were moments before hidden by their natural aqueous habitat. In the middle of the tunnel, the Thoulden-sha came into view with scores of Orsarians in his wake.

Thannuel tried to connect with the triarch wood in the ships through the leafling, the way he would by putting his hand flush against the bark of a tree. It was there, the connection, but elusive, slippery in his mind. His tension increased as the Thoulden-sha grew nearer and Thannuel tried again, willing the channel to open to him. He could not grasp it, still only feeling the same increased sensitivity he always had when holding a triarch leafling.

Ancients come! What must I do? The Thoulden-sha set foot on the beach wearing a broad smile. The face covering of his turban had been discarded.

Through, speaking through … Instead of opening a channel to receive information, Thannuel attempted to send a message through the connection. His mind hit a barrier. *If there's a barrier, there is something on the other side. There's no other purpose for a blockade!* He pushed with his mind, trying to break through, to open the channel both ways, but the barrier seemed impenetrable.

"Why, Lord Kerr, you're sweating," the Thoulden-sha said with mock concern. "Does my presence trouble you so?"

The Orsarians formed a circle around him.

You do not need to push, his mind told him. *There is no barrier.*

And then he saw it. No, felt it. The barrier was an illusion, built by his lifelong misunderstanding that the channel only flowed one way. Once this understanding settled in his mind, he felt the Living Light, sparks of the Lumenatis, within the triarch wood. His understanding expanded as he saw new perspectives, new possibilities. Most relevant, new currents of power.

I am a current.

Thannuel drew in the Light and his sword began to hum.

Captain Norvuld and his seven remaining triarch ships, along with eleven of the Senthary ships, led a charge toward the massive Orsarian fleet that approached. Roughly thirty Orsarian frigates they had liberated and crewed to the barest necessity followed.

Norvuld looked up to the sails, taut from the afternoon breeze, and sighed.

"Sails should be white," he muttered.

Under his orders his crew, and those of the other ships, had dyed their sails black.

Perhaps it will give us enough time. He silently argued with himself about the validity of his plan, wondering if he shouldn't relieve himself of duty for this crazy stunt.

"We're low to the water," Aiden observed. "We have brought on board more of the Orsarian fire powder and balls than could ever be used. The ship herself is basically a floating barrel of disaster waiting to happen!"

"Aye," Norvuld said. "Loaded down heavily. We'll be slow moving, I'm afraid."

"But, we won't be able to maneuver then."

"If the Ancient Heavens are paying attention, lad, we won't have to."

Norvuld looked aft, peering between the ships in his wake. *Where is he? Elkinal should be underway by now ...*

The capitol ship came into view, towering above the horizon as it left Second Island's harbor.

There you are, Elkinal.

With all sails deployed on four masts, Norvuld counted seven sails on the middle two masts and four on the forward. The rear mast wasn't visible to take a count, but he guessed it would hold at least three. Its hull was higher above the water than most mizzenmasts of Norvuld's ships and wider than any three Orsarian frigates.

"To be borne down on by that leviathan would make even the Dark Mother flee in fear," Norvuld whispered. "Well, Elkinal, seems you're going to get your shot to complete what you started."

Elkinal had never before sailed more than a skiff. The Orsarian capitol ship felt like a floating town, able to lodge more people than any village of the Runic Islands. He and a score of sailors had easily secured the vessel, rooting out the skeleton crew that had been left behind to guard it. Even with their crew complement of twenty plus himself, Serisa, and Drailin, they barely had enough hands to man all the stations.

It seems like such a waste, he mused.

As they departed from Second Island's harbor, the lumbering gait of the ship felt like slow motion as they watched the repaired jib boom languidly rock up and down against the horizon. Elkinal looked over the side to the water below just to make sure they were actually moving. Serisa joined him at the rail.

"What are you looking at?"

"The wake, Ser," Elkinal replied. "We're moving a lot faster than it feels like."

"I almost feel dizzy looking down from this height."

"What, it doesn't bring back fond memories of jumping for our lives?"

Serisa looked down and Elkinal realized his mistake.

"I'm sorry, Ser. I didn't mean to drag out other memories of this ship. You didn't need to come."

"I know," she said. "I wanted to, though. Just felt like I could get past it all better by coming along."

Elkinal smiled. "It is going to be something to see." Turning his head, he yelled, "Is that escape boat secure?"

"I think so!" Drailin yelled back. He had been testing its release mechanism with several of the crew, ensuring its pulleys and ropes were in working order and familiarizing themselves with the system.

"Because, it would *really* be terrible for that to fail after all this trouble!" Elkinal said.

"It's secure, Uncle. It will probably work."

"Probably?"

Drailin looked at the sailors with him. They all shrugged. "Yup, probably," was all Drailin could say.

"It'll work," Serisa assured him.

"How do you know?" her father asked.

"Because if it doesn't, we're dead."

"Still, it seems like such a waste, to use this magnificent beast in such a manner."

"I think it's a perfect use, actually."

"I have no doubt, Ser. I have no doubt."

"All right, you're my first officer now," Captain Norvuld said. "Got it?"

"What all does a first officer do?" Aiden asked.

"Whatever's he's told, of course. And, he passes orders along to the crew and ensures they are carried out. He also carries something of the captain's belongings."

Norvuld unsheathed his short blade from his hip and extended it to Aiden. It was a dark metal.

"It's not hard to use one of these," Norvuld started to explain. "It's just a matter of—"

"Oh, I know how to use this," Aiden assured him. The boy felt its edge, dragging his thumb across the blade. "You never run your finger up and down the edge, only across, left to right. The rougher it is, the sharper the blade."

"Aye," Norvuld said. This had elicited other questions, but he did not voice them now.

Aiden sheathed the short blade. "So, what order should I pass on?"

"It's time to fan the fleet out. We need about a dozen or more approaching enemy ships between each of our own. The crew knows what to do, they just need the word. Think you can handle that?"

Aiden took a few steps toward the bow of their ship, putting himself in front of the helm. "Oi! Listen up, ya waterlogged, ninny bastards! We'll be spreading out from the other ships, as previously designed, hear? Any man not pulling his weight or cowering before the task at hand will be tossed to the sharks after I spit in his eye! Now, see to it before lashings and other morale-increasing activities ensue!"

The crewmembers, all four of them, stared in slack-jawed bewilderment at the thirteen-year-old castaway. Aiden turned on his heel and went back to the helm.

"How'd I do, Captain?"

Norvuld placed a hand on Aiden's shoulder. "You're a natural, lad."

"Will the Orsarians actually believe us to be them? Won't they wonder why we're heading out to meet them?"

Norvuld had considered this but decided it was a risk that could only be managed, not eliminated. "We just need them to believe it long enough to get between them."

As they came closer in to the enemy fleet, Norvuld started making out individual classes of ships: frigates, galleys, cruisers, dreadnoughts and others Norvuld was unfamiliar with. None held a candle to the grandeur of the capitol ship.

She must have been one of a kind, he thought. *The Thoulden-sha certainly has a way of propping himself up wherever he goes.*

Norvuld's stomach was in knots as they were about to breach the line that divided his fleet from the oncoming Orsarian ships.

"It's time," he said. "Order the crew to abandon ship in the skiff."

"And you?" Aiden asked.

"I'll light the fuse. Be right behind you."

Below deck, Norvuld inspected the tons of fire powder and ordnance that had been brought aboard from the scores of enemy ships they had looted. The barrels and crates he had to crawl and squeeze through were so tightly packed that he almost got himself stuck on a few occasions. Everything looked to be in order. Above, he heard his four-man crew and Aiden getting ready to let the escape boat down.

Now, where is that fuse ...

He stepped in a puddle of water.

Blasted Night, what's this? It was ironic to wonder about water on a ship, but there should not be any water here, not below deck. He made his way through the maze of explosive packages and heard running water, like a small stream. Though it was too dark to see anything, he knew what was happening. Not surprising that the hull's integrity had been compromised with all that his ship had been through. The leak was slow but had pooled enough over the past day to be several inches. Regardless, all seemed dry enough to still carry out his intended purpose.

As he backed out of the narrow cavern of crates and barrels, he found the fuse—soaked beyond use.

Ancients come! Why now?

There was no use laying a trail of powder out, as it would have to go through water to get to the stored pulverulence.

He dashed back up the narrow staircase above deck to check his time. Perhaps there was enough remaining to rearrange some barrels and—no, they were almost there. He could nearly make out the faces of the Orsarians on the decks of their ships.

"Captain!" Aiden called. "We must go!"

Norvuld looked out at the other ships in his fleet. Some were already intermingled with the enemy fleet. He caught sight of more than a score of skiffs and other small craft in the sea, hastily making their way back toward land. No doubt the Orsarians had also seen them, as men were pointing and drawing attention to the fleeing smaller boats. Though Norvuld did not speak their tongue, it was not hard to intuit the concerned timbre of those voices.

We are out of time.

Turning to the crew at the muster station, he ordered, "Deploy the skiff! Leave! I will have to detonate the ordnance from here. Quickly, there's no time!"

"What?" Aiden said. "No blasted way we're leaving without you!"

"You have your orders! Men, detain the first officer and deploy that skiff!"

The four crew members grabbed Aiden and dragged him into the escape boat. The boy kicked and screamed, cursed and fought, but the larger men overpowered him.

"Aiden," Norvuld said in a calm voice that somehow cut through the boy's protests and curses. The wind blew his salt and pepper hair, whipping his ponytail over his shoulder. "Aiden, lad, listen to me. 'Twill be all right, son. Find Lord Kerr with all haste, likely on Third Island. He'll look after you now."

"The Burning Heavens he will!" Aiden cried. "You're not doing this!"

"I'll find you in the Light, Aiden of Helving." Turning to the other crewmembers, Norvuld said sternly, "Cast off!"

The lines were cut and he heard the small boat hit the water's surface. Immediately, he ran to the helm and turned the wheel starboard ten degrees. His ship was pointed directly toward the closest Orsarian vessel, a dreadnaoght.

The triarch wood felt rough under his touch as he held the wheel, appearing darker than its natural color. That was the purpose, he knew, to make the Living Light available, should it be needed. Still, it saddened him a little to see his ship in what appeared to be decades of decay. He knew it wouldn't matter now.

He said farewell silently to his life-long love, and prayed a portion of his Light would be permitted to somehow be with her after he was gone. He was not sure how this could be possible, but had enough faith in the Living Light to believe it were possible. Eventually. Somehow.

Lighting a candle, Norvuld quickly made his way below deck. In the distance, he could hear Aiden still yelling for him.

"All right, girl, let's bring light to these dark marauders."

Captain Antious Roan fell upon the Orsarian soldiers as they came out from the caves, coughing and vomiting, rubbing at their eyes. It had been nearly two hours and the Sentharian soldiers had kept the fires stoked high, burning as much dead foliage and kindling as possible to create more smoke. Others had palmetto branches so large in size that two men were required to hold them and fan the smoke constantly into the caves.

Antious's men meted out death without discrimination. It lasted less than ten minutes before the caves stopped spewing out dark marauders.

"Glimon!" Antious shouted. "How many?"

"No losses, sir!"

"How many of the enemy is there?" Antious clarified. "This can't be all."

"I'd say less than two hundred lie here, Captain."

Antious considered for several moments. "Extinguish the fires. We'll need to search them out."

"As you say, Captain; but, sir, there's no way anyone survived that. If they didn't come out by now, they're dead."

"You're probably right, Sergeant. All the same, we'll still search."

After an hour of letting the smoke clear from the caves, Antious and his unit tied wet cloths around their mouths and entered the caves. In the light of torches, they came upon several groups of Orsarians sprawled on the ground. Eyes bulged and bodies lay in painfully contorted positions, the evidence of dying twice. Some open mouths leaked wispy smoke trails into the air.

"There are maybe fifty, not more than sixty here," Glimon said with surprise. "Perhaps they were really hiding if this is all they had left."

"It can't be," Antious muttered. "It has to be a trick."

"I don't think so, sir. When they attacked us on the beach with General Korin while we waited for our exfiltration, they had two thousand roughly. They all died, including their leader. Their losses before that had been much more than double our own, adding up to well more than twenty, maybe even thirty thousand. Judging by the number of ships they had anchored off various points of the islands, they could not have had more than that."

"Could this actually be the end?" Antious asked, more to himself.

In answer, the ground started to tremble. Antious and several others lost their footing and fell to the rocky ground. The shaking continued and a large section of the cave's roof dislodged. As it came loose, Antious, still down, put his hands over his head. Instead of getting crushed, he heard a loud grunt above him.

"Thank you, Merrick," Glimon said in a shaky voice. "That was close."

Antious looked up to see the man whom Glimon had counted as two men, Merrick, standing over him.

"It is heavy, Command Sergeant," Merrick grunted. "Perhaps you could thank me later and escort the captain out."

"Gladly." Glimon grabbed Antious's shoulder. "Time to go, sir!"

Thannuel saw the Thoulden-sha standing by idly, calmly watching as the dark marauders with him—his new breed of Marishee—attacked. Most came at him with dual-wielded scimitars, the choice more often than not for the Orsarians rather than the long sword his people favored.

The low hum of his sword sounded in the air as he raised it in defense. The pulsing of dozens of enemies came to him through the sandy ground and he split his mind in two, the way he had when he was sixteen. But he was facing only two Marishee then. Skilled as they had been, the current circumstances would prove far more challenging.

With the first part of his mind, he countered the strikes levied against him with a torrent of speed and efficiency. With the second part, he analyzed every foe that engaged him, trying to find weaknesses. Several presented themselves, but there was too little time between attacks to take advantage of them, so constant was the barrage from the Orsarians. His movements of defense were one fluid motion, his body never remaining in the same place for more than a microsecond.

At least Master Amnoch would be proud.

Frustration found him, making his moves more anxious. It would have cost him if the frustration had stayed within him longer, but Thannuel remembered the words of Master Norvuld. Emotion. Friction. *Energy.*

Without much thought, the second part of his mind captured the frustration and saw the energy it had created: only a small pool.

That energy, he heard Norvuld's words in his memory, *can be captured and recycled, directed.*

It did not take long for the word to come to him.

"Relitha."

Instantly, the frustration friction came under his control, waiting to be directed. The ease of it … so much different than when he faced Muhktar in the narrows where the friction flowed in feral currents. He had been barely able to stand against it as he mentally plunged into the rushing power. But now …

The word, *Relitha* … where had it come from?

Reflex, he said in his mind. The small pool of energy funneled into his muscles and joints, increasing the speed of his reflexes to a degree that allowed him to counterattack. A handful of decapitations occurred in as many seconds, whittling down his opponents. But more filled in the gaps with every dead marauder. Only four or five could face him at once with any effectiveness before they began to trip over one another, which helped Thannuel;

but he would tire eventually. He needed a greater impact against his foes, something that would bring down many at once.

As if on command, the needed word came into his mind. He ducked the next group of volleys and thrust his sword down into the ground.

"Welkaira!"

A shockwave of energy burst out from him, as some of the Living Light within him shot through his sword of Jarwynian ore. Orsarians close to him were thrown back several feet, stunned but not harmed. The usage of the Light's Influence should have had a greater effect; he could feel it but not quite grasp it. Thannuel used the time the shockwave had bought him to dispatch those who had been thrown down.

A lesser portion of Light was in him now but he still felt more within him, waiting to be used. The connection he felt to the triarch ships was still strong through the leafling in his hand and he drew in more, filling himself to capacity again. His sword's humming increased as he channeled some of the Influence into it.

Around Thannuel lay twelve dead dark marauders, most headless. The remaining enemy, though still greatly outnumbering him, paused with uncertainty. The blood tainted the sand crimson, sinking into it and leaving abstract shapes behind. Occasional waves washed up far enough to wash the stains away, leaving new trails of red that streamed toward the water as the waves receded.

The Thoulden-sha laughed.

"You laugh as your followers die?" Thannuel asked. "You have always seen this as a game, I presume."

"Yes, a game of high intrigue and even higher stakes, Lord Kerr," the Thoulden-sha answered. "We are pitted against each other, you and I. But this need not be. Be part of the Resurgence and witness ..."

As the Thoulden-sha spoke, Thannuel felt him try to reach into him, the way he had tried years past in the narrows near Dispa, but he easily blocked the intrusion, the Living Light inside him making the Thoulden-sha's attempt ineffective. It was not a powerful surge, almost as if he did not expect to succeed, more like ...

A distraction.

Movement, from behind the Thoulden-sha. Thannuel could feel something but it was muddled. The steps were light and slow, deliberate. He could not hear the Thoulden-sha's rambling as he focused more intently. The vibrations came from the Orsarians behind the Thoulden-sha; they were doing something ... *moving* something.

Suddenly, the Thoulden-sha threw himself face first to the ground as the air shuttered with a crack. Thannuel thought he could almost see the air shimmer before him. Smoke billowed just above the Thoulden-sha, followed by a net twisting and swirling through the air directly toward Thannuel.

The velocity of the net's flight, at such close proximity, was too great for the Lord of the Western Province to dodge completely. Instinct propelled him in his reaction, feeling the Light within him prompt his movements. As a split second of fear came upon him, it was captured almost before he even realized it had been there, and recycled effortlessly to increase his mental fortitude in preparation for the bladed net's strike. The word shot in to his mind as the net's tentacles reached him.

Faerathm!

Thannuel swung his sword in a large arc, starting from the ground behind him and ending with the tip of his blade in the sand in front of him with such velocity that he stumbled at the end of his swing. The net that started to collapse around him had been cut in half, the severed ends of metal links red hot and smoking as the smell of smoldering metal permeated the air. Two barbs had found his left shoulder but he hadn't even felt the pain until he saw them. Though the wounds were deep gouges their sting felt far away, faded, as if old wounds. Nonchalantly, he ripped them from his shoulder.

Drawing in more Light from the leafling's connection to the triarch ships, he put his dark blade against his left shoulder, feeling the power surging in him, and said, *"Mylendia Shaul."* The wounds sealed, leaving only trickles of blood on his flesh.

If the Orsarians were hesitant before, they were terrified now after seeing Thannuel's display of power and began talking amongst themselves in frantic tones.

Suddenly, Thannuel stumbled—something wrong. He felt as if a boulder had just hit him in the chest, knocking the wind from him. Immediately after, he felt starved, as if a famine violently swept through him. It took him several moments to realize what had happened: his connection to the triarch ships had been severed.

Aiden fought the two crewmembers holding him down while the other two rowed the skiff as fast as they could away from the Orsarian fleet.

"There's still time!" he shouted. "We can go back and get him!"

"You heard the captain, boy," one of them snapped.

"Get off me!" Aiden commanded. "I'm the first officer!"

"And your captain gave you an order that you didn't follow."

"That's because he's mad, you stupid bastard! Turn around! We can still save him—!"

The first explosion commanded their attention to the north,

The ship, one of the commandeered Orsarian vessels, turned into a ball of fire and sent flaming bolides streaming through air. Most harmlessly hit the water's surface, but several found their way to enemy ships, cutting through sails and landing on decks, spreading the fire. Several more explosions followed and cheers from other crews, in their own skiffs, were heard as the ocean turned angry from the blasts.

Wake hit Aiden's boat and the men holding him shifted to catch themselves. The castaway boy did not hesitate, kicking one in the face and biting the arm of the other. Amid curses, he found himself free and jumped overboard.

"Don't be stupid, lad, get back here!"

But Aiden dove beneath the surface and swam hard for Norvuld's ship, kicking fiercely and pulling his arms through the water. He surfaced for air but it was immediately knocked from him as the triarch ship he sought exploded, the shock wave slamming into him. Three enemy ships that were in the immediate vicinity were now in flames with one of them, the closest, breaking apart rapidly and sinking.

He tried to scream, to cry out for Norvuld, but his voice failed him in the chaos. It would have been futile regardless. The majestic storm of fire and destruction was deafening as it spewed high and wide. Aiden dove again, this time for protection, as debris began to rain around him.

When he dared to resurface, his lungs begging for air, he saw the first line in the enemy fleet completely in disarray, vessels burning and men jumping overboard. But beyond that, he saw the remainder of the Orsarian fleet relatively unaffected. They had inflicted great damage, it was true, but deeper lines of the fleet were now alerted to the ploy and had begun to fan out. Some could not avoid the floating blazes and succumbed to the fire; but others navigated around, changing course.

Aiden saw that Elkinal, aboard the capitol ship, was pushing his way through the wrecks, trying to get to at least the second line of ships. Some other vessels, those of his fleet that had not yet detonated, followed in Elkinal's path. But the Orsarians were wise to the deception and moved away as fast as they could.

I don't think so, Aiden thought and took a deep breath. He swam, putting his determination into his strokes. Before long, though, he felt strong hands lift him up and haul him back aboard his skiff.

"You'll never catch them, boy," one said—the man he had kicked.

"Let me go!" Aiden yelled. "I will!"

"No, you won't. But *we* might be able to."

They obviously saw the question on Aiden's face.

"Seems the captain is dead," one of the oarsmen said. "By rights, I think that puts you in charge as first officer."

"Move over!" he said to one of the men at an oar. The man complied and Aiden began to vigorously row to the closest enemy ship. As he did, the wood of the oar darkened under his hand, as did the wood below his feet.

What is this? he wondered.

"I need help!" the man at the other oar shouted. "I can't keep up with him. We're turning off course."

Aiden's rowing was deep and swift, more so than should be possible for a boy of thirteen. A second man came to the opposite oar and the two men worked it together, countering Aiden's strong paddling and turning the boat toward its target. They navigated through the floating debris and came alongside the black-hulled invader vessel. Spears were thrown from the ship, but the wood-dwellers easily dodged them. One buried its head in the skiff's floorboards and was deftly returned to its owner by one of the crewmembers, sending it through the Orsarian's neck.

When they were just ahead of the ship's center, Aiden jumped up from his station. The ship started pulling past the skiff, now just coasting, and Aiden stepped gingerly along the side of the boat. He jumped, launching himself nearly six feet above the skiff and rammed his short blade into the Orsarian ship's hull. The blade bit and held. He felt the other crewmembers follow suit as they scrambled up the hull, reaching the railing of the ship.

Aiden was not sure what to do when he arrived on the deck of the enemy ship. The other four Arlethian sailors went to work, engaging the Orsarian crew. Their natural speed, despite being outside the forests of the West, was too much for the invaders, who cut them down and threw them overboard. Below deck, Aiden could feel the vibrations of scores of men.

These are just the sailors, he realized. Below deck were the soldiers, and they were making their way up. They did not have much time.

Time to do what? he asked himself frantically.

An open hatch mid-ship revealed several crates, mostly full of provisions of some kind or another. But one crate, with a picture of what looked like fire, was full of glass spheres, small enough to fit inside the hand like an apple. Inside the globes, Aiden saw two different colored powders, separated by another piece of glass through the middle of the sphere. Intermixed within the powder of each hemisphere were jagged pieces of what looked like metal, bone, and bits of glass.

I wonder …

Aiden grabbed one and threw it across the ship, right where the soldiers were emerging from below deck. A small explosion erupted as the glass broke and the powders violently mixed, sending a few men flying, accompanied by screams. More soldiers emerged, looking confused by the bloodied sight of their compatriots. Aiden helped them understand with another volley, this time throwing two of the explosive spheres in quick succession.

He felt no remorse for dealing out this punishment. Though not the first time he had killed, it was much easier this time, not being closely related to the enemy.

Perhaps you were right, Father. Killing can be as easy as breathing.

The ships avoiding the chaos Norvuld's fleet had purchased with their own vessels were tightly packed as they executed evasive maneuvers. Aiden scanned the seascape and saw the capitol ship nearly through the first line of ships, all smoldering.

Elkinal is almost in position. We have to stop these ships!

Figuring all the Orsarian ships would have a similar cache of explosives, an idea sprang to his mind. Aiden gathered half a dozen explosive spheres and started climbing the mast, toward the crow's nest. All the time he had swung from the Furlop trees of his home village of Helving, with their long tendrils of strong, white moss hanging over daunting cliffs, was about to prove helpful.

"Get back to the skiff!" he shouted to his crew.

Serisa watched, standing on the bow of the escape boat, as the massive capitol ship sailed toward its prey, impossible to stop now. She had lit the fuse, taking that honor to herself. Behind her in the skiff, her father, Elkinal, and Drailin worked the oars frantically. She turned amid their calls for help, as two other crewmen joined them at the oars.

Around them, burning hulks smoldered and sank, cries of men sounded, many of them on fire and jumping from their ravaged ships. Another ship exploded, spreading the fiery wrath. Debris and corpses littered the water.

"Row, angry tides!" Elkinal commanded.

"I am!" Drailin exclaimed.

"Well, row harder!"

"I'm going as fast as I can, Uncle!"

Serisa turned her head back to the capitol ship, watching it get smaller, foot by foot. She didn't feel any of the concern her father and cousin were filled with.

The closer the better.

She wanted to see, to feel, the destruction of her former prison, to watch it decimate those who sought to violate her home, who had violated—no, she would not think of it. She prayed the Ancient Heavens would allow her nightmares to be obliterated along with the capitol ship, having turned it to a weapon for good, a vanguard for redemption.

It felt like a cool wind at first when the time came, but quickly turned hot, then scalding as the gales of the explosions slammed into her, like an avalanche of fury. But it was not painful, not something she retreated from. Purifying. She closed her eyes. It passed quickly, rushing past her and dissipating.

The ocean's surface slopped with the concussion, almost tossing them from the skiff. Several waves washed up over the side, the cool water shocking after the heat she had just experienced. As she opened her eyes and scanned the incredible scene before her, she spied roughly only a couple dozen Orsarian ships not in flames. Those few were turning away as fast as they could, in full retreat.

Serisa looked back at her father and cousin. They held firm to the sides of the boat, bracing themselves. She saw the concern and tension in them.

"Don't worry," she said. "It's gone now."

The concussive booms turned Thannuel's attention east, over the water, and he understood why he had lost his connection to the Light of the triarch ships. Filling his view were balls of fire expanding on the sea's surface, one detonation after another. Thannuel felt each explosion deep in his chest, their force great despite the distance being close to a mile out to sea.

Burning debris followed by trails of smoke screamed through the air, great flaming projectiles, landing on other ships in the vicinity of the exploding vessels. The horizon began to turn a shade of orange, as if the sun were setting in the east. He thought he spied someone jumping from ship to ship, mast to mast, as if dancing on the large plumes of smoke that spiraled heavenward. It looked like a boy, like …

The castaway, he realized. *Why … something must have gone wrong. Master Norvuld … where is he?*

Explosions followed on each ship where the boy landed before immediately leaping to another vessel, running across the yards that held the sails as if they were branches of their native forests.

The finale came when the capitol ship, a mammoth among warships, exploded in the middle of the oncoming Orsarian fleet. Enhancing his vision with captured friction, he saw several of the enemy ships get reduced to splinters by the force of the explosion itself, being completely destroyed before the tendrils of fire had time to reach out. When they did, they were far reaching, setting alight scores of black-hulled ships. Through the air, he saw the castaway fly aimlessly, blown by the force of the blast. After only a few moments, Thannuel felt the breeze from the capitol ship's blast.

I'll find him, Norvuld, he silently promised, his mind returning to the vow he had given the master shipwright.

The Sea of Albery became unruly with the dozens of detonations on its surface, and angry waves began making their way to the beaches of the Second and Third Islands. Soon after, Thannuel saw enemy ships that had caught fire begin to explode. Though their blasts were smaller in comparison, they were still effective in causing many of the other Orsarian vessels to catch fire. Drifting out of control, other ships crashed into one another, spreading the blaze further. The chain reaction was masterful.

From what Thannuel could tell, the entire Orsarian fleet was set in disarray. Many Orsarians jumped from their burning wrecks, struggling to find debris to hang on to. Those ships unaffected began to turn away from the Runic Islands.

Master Norvuld, I didn't know you enjoyed playing with fire so much. You're a genius.

"No!" the Thoulden-sha screamed at the first explosion. He watched the daisy chain of fire leap across the water, from one ship to the next, not able to react. The dark marauders around him also watched, dumbfounded. He searched for the answer, straining to hear the comforting and empowering melody in his mind, but Mari-shaden's voice was drowned out by the percussive symphony of ruin before him.

"So," he said, turning back to Thannuel, "it is fire you wish to wield."

His enemy, this descendent of the Kiarra Clan, turned and faced him. The look on Thannuel's face was one of confidence, one that said he knew he had won.

"You've lost!" Thannuel shouted. "It is over!"

The Thoulden-sha did not answer. He felt for the destructive powers that he could manifest, for the elements that Mari-shaden had thus far granted him control over. Deep, very deep, beneath the ground, beneath the ocean floor, he found them. The Thoulden-sha pulled with his mind.

As the ground began to shake, several fissures manifested on the beach around them and crawled inland for miles. And then, with a fury that defied description, the mountain on Main Island erupted, spewing comets of fire in all directions. That changed as the Thoulden-sha honed his focus, turning the trajectory of the magma toward Thannuel.

"I will turn this entire island into my altar, Kiarra."

Antious sprinted with all speed through the island, jumping over rivers of flowing lava and bouncing off trees, propelling himself at bursts of speed only diving falcons could match. The lava seemed to flow unnaturally fast, but Antious had to admit he had never tried to outrun a volcano before. The cloud of ash began to thicken at the peak of the volcano, blocking out the evening sun with its translucent haze.

The rest of his unit he had commanded to depart toward the closest beach and swim out if they needed to in order to escape. He, however, was dashing toward Thannuel, several leagues away from the caves at the north end of the island.

A ledge with a sharp drop-off of roughly a hundred feet had turned into a bright red lava fall, pooling and continuing its flow far below. There was no other way down except for backtracking, but that might cause him to be too late to help his friend.

Perhaps he already was.

Parting the flow of lava below, he spied a rock. It looked large enough … he hoped. The heat of the molten river caused his eyes to water. Backing up several paces, Antious Roan ran toward the edge at full sprint and leaped.

A drop of one hundred feet in the forests of Arlethia to the ground was certainly doable. The nimbleness of his race and light-footed step allowed them to land with dexterity upon the forest floor. Landing on a rock in the middle of liquid fire, however, was a different story.

Antious hit hard and rolled before catching himself. His ankle throbbed but he could still move it. Sprained, not broken. Smelling burning leather, he inspected his boots but they were intact. His scabbard, however, was not. Several inches of it had sunk into the lava as he rolled, turning it to char. The tip of his sword was exposed, glowing red, dripping with the lava.

Antious removed his belt that held the scabbard and, without unsheathing his sword, smashed it down on the rock. The tip bent.

Fallen Ancients!

It had lost its strength, as he feared. He struck it repeatedly against the rock, bending the weakened metal over and over from side to side until it broke off. The weapon had been shortened by nearly five inches and Antious cursed again. It would have to do. He fastened his belt and scabbard back around his waist and sheathed his shortened sword.

Turning his attention back to his other problem—standing on an island in the middle of a river of fire with a rising tide—the captain saw several other rocks, most too small for two feet, protruding above the lava's surface.

Brilliant, he thought as memories of the pedestal jousting games at Therrium Academy when he was eleven came back to him. His adrenaline and pain from his ankle had kept him from realizing that his skin was starting to burn. Looking down, he saw his arm hair curling and withering away, like a candlewick with no wax. His hands were red from pushing himself up after rolling on the rock, several blisters forming on a few fingers, and the soles of his feet felt like they were being cooked inside his boots.

"Burning Heavens, time to move!"

Holding his breath, he jumped to the closest rock and landed with one foot, immediately launching to the next stepping-stone. As he landed on the second, sharp pain shot through his ankle and he nearly tumbled into the lava. Only adrenaline kept him on his foot as he waved his arms and leg to regain his balance. With immense concentration and strength, he bent his wounded leg and sprang forward, launching one-legged to the next stepping-stone. He landed on his good leg this time and sprang the remaining several feet to shore, crumpling to the ground and holding his pulsing ankle. His pants smoldered, boots blackened from the heat.

"You're no good to him if you can't get to him!" he cursed himself between gritted teeth.

The ground shook again and a renewed volley of terrible ash and molten meteors sailed through the sky. As he stood, the punishment he had put his ankle through came back to him with a vengeance. It could sustain no weight without lancing pain shooting up his leg into his hip—truly debilitating.

His field medical training started coming back to him as he forced himself to think. He didn't dare take his boot off, knowing that exercise would only cause him more pain. Instead, Antious unsheathed his sword and shoved its now blunted end into the ground. Next, he sat down and took the ruined scabbard, placing it along the outside of his ankle. With his belt, he lashed the thick leather scabbard against his ankle, weaving the belt around his heel, under the arch of his foot and around his calf. The belt barely had enough length to make it back to the buckle, but it was too short to allow Antious to latch it down.

Taking several deep breaths, he pulled the end of the belt with all his might, cinching it tighter. The agony was too much for him to contain and he screamed but did not relent. With only conviction driving him forward, he finally pulled the belt tight enough to latch the buckle. He clamped it down hard and released his hold, allowing himself to fall back on the ground for a few seconds of rest.

In his pain-induced stillness, he thought of Kalisa. What was she doing now? Was she laughing? Praying for him and her father?

One of us must survive. For her, one of us must. Korin was dead. That left the burden of survival upon his back. Reaching up, he found his sword's hilt and used it as a crutch to stand up. He hobbled on his right leg, too afraid to put weight on his left. Slowly, he tested his splint by letting his left leg rest on the earth. Throbbing, but no sharp pain. A little more weight … still good. And then he shifted his weight so that it was even between both legs, standing shoulder width apart. A small twinge was there, but bearable.

"All right then," he muttered. "Limping or crawling, I will make it to you, Thannuel."

Thannuel dodged the flaming rocks that the Thoulden-sha hurled at him. They came barreling down from the sky, out of the mountain's peak. Gelatinous, semi-solid hunks of molten rock and crystalized minerals. Some landed in shallow water, shooting spouts of steam in the air as the waves crashed around them. Some were small, the size that could fit into a hand; others were boulders the size of small ships.

Thannuel's wood-dweller sensitivity was useless in sensing the vector of the natural ordnance raining down all around him, only able to feel the impacts once they hit. He relied on his eyes and hearing to warn him and his reflexes to dodge.

The smaller debris, pebble-sized flecks of fire, struck him in several places and burned pockmarks into his skin. He did not have time to brush them away before needing to yet again dive and roll, evading another bombardment.

How was he able to do this?

He captured the friction of his wonder and fear, feeding it into his muscles and mind, increasing his stamina and reflexes. Screams from several of the remaining Orsarians found his ears as they became collateral damage from their Dark Diviner's attacks.

Thannuel dropped the leafling that was between his palm and sword in his evasive moves. Even though it held no more advantage for him, he still felt a loss. One of the ground fissures tripped him as he landed, and he rolled over to see a molten rock half his size racing toward him from above. It whistled as it hurled down, picking up velocity well beyond the natural effect gravity should have had on it.

"Thannuel!"

He heard his name sound through the air: Antious's voice, a timbre of extreme trepidation laced through it.

In complete reflex, Thannuel raised his sword to defend himself, his muscles reacting with the ingrained motion when danger presented itself, despite the futility of the action. Anger flared inside Thannuel, begging for escape, an outlet.

You promised you would come back! He could almost hear

Moira demanding it of him. *You promised!*

The very moment the rock came into contact with the Jarwynian blade, Thannuel felt it flex infinitesimally.

"Vrathia!" The anger, the wrath, within him flowed at the speed of light into his blade and into the rock. It exploded, sending molten debris in all directions.

"Thannuel!" came Antious's call again.

Thannuel stood up, shaken but unharmed. Smoke curled up from his clothes. He saw his best friend, a hundred feet or so off, limping toward him. The barrage ceased for a few moments and Thannuel looked back to the Thoulden-sha. There was amazement on his face but it quickly fled, morphing to determination.

As Antious reached Thannuel's side, he said, "You should be dead … how?"

Instead of answering the captain's question, Thannuel asked, "What did you do to yourself, my friend? And that's a terrible looking splint. In fact, you look terrible altogether. Don't ever become a healer, you're no good at it."

Then, seeing Antious's sword with its jagged blunt end, Thannuel was about to say something but Antious interrupted him. "It's a marvelous story, my Lord, I assure you. Maybe I'll even tell you about it someday."

"Fair enough," Thannuel said. "Care to lend a hand here?"

"I thought you'd never ask," Antious answered with a smile.

"Excellent. You deal with the dark marauders. I'll handle that," Thannuel said, pointing toward the Thoulden-sha.

"You always get the more fun parts."

Still limping, Antious dashed around the Thoulden-sha and engaged the score of Orsarians, too quick, even injured, for them to deal with.

"You *have* lost!" Thannuel shouted. "Your fleet is in ruins and turning around, fleeing!"

"They were only a means to an end, young lord," the Thoulden-sha answered. "They are not indispensable. Others await my arrival, those that are hideous to most but exquisite in beauty to Mari-shaden."

Others?

Behind the Thoulden-sha, Antious had felled two of the dark marauders and snatched up their swords, wielding two scimitars more deftly than the Orsarians who made them did. He fought in a cat-like stance, placing almost all his weight on his uninjured right leg.

"If you will not yield, you will be destroyed!" Thannuel warned.

"You have become powerful, Lord Kerr, beyond simple skills with a blade. Regardless, you cannot withstand the full power of Mari-shaden."

"The Ancient Dark is only strong when Light is not present. Even the dimmest spark is enough to penetrate the thickest night!"

In answer, the Thoulden-sha raised his arms to the sky. His lips moved but Thannuel could not hear what he said. The air temperature changed, decreasing drastically, and the ocean began to steam. Heavy snowflakes started swirling around them, becoming thicker, coalescing together in mid-air. Before many moments had passed they shaped themselves into shards, hardening, and began flying toward Thannuel.

Simultaneously, the volcano's fury returned, the sound of explosions streaming through the air along with another barrage of flaming meteors. Thannuel's mind struggled to move his body to dodge the ice shards and fiery debris fast enough, but even with his mind split into two independent spheres, the task proved immense.

As several ice daggers came too close and fast for him to dodge, he was forced to expend more of his limited Light.

Welkaira!

The shockwave turned them away, making them inert, but the barrage intensified. Lava started filling the fissures, flowing into the Sea of Albery and making him focus on one more peril. The familiar feeling of stress building in his mind rose to the surface, the same sensation that happened ten years ago, when he first discovered he could split his mind.

Is it possible? he wondered.

A third region in his mind formed out of necessity, ripping its way free. The feeling of trying to consciously deal with three independent spheres brought on a wave of dizziness and dropped him to his knees in a fetal position, shaking.

Antious Roan spun as he engaged more than a dozen of dark marauders at once. The freezing air had at first seemed a blessing to his scorched skin, but his fingers lost some of their dexterity as the temperature continued to drop. Fortunately, this change hindered his opponents as well.

Having a scimitar in each hand, he let the enemy come to him. And come they did, from all sides. Their vibrational signatures were already muted due to the loose sand he now fought on, but was exacerbated by the constant bombardment of volcanic rocks striking the beach. Nevertheless, Antious was lethal to those who came for him.

He dodged a blow, letting the man's momentum carry him forward and into another Orsarian. He only had enough time to kill him once before needing to block a slew of oncoming strikes. With his left ankle throbbing but not screaming in pain, he kept most of his weight upon his right leg as he danced.

Movement is life.

Ducking yet another strike, he rolled across the beach and leg-swept a man before he had a chance to bring his sword down on him. Once on his back next to him, Antious inverted his grip on one scimitar and stabbed the man twice in the heart before it could beat once.

He scrambled back up to his feet and was again immediately swarmed by several more dark marauders.

Their determination is insatiable!

Antious jumped and pushed off the chest of the closest Orsarian, pushing him to the ground and launching himself a few feet higher. He landed on the shoulders of another, but before the man could react, Antious grabbed the hair at the crown of his head and jumped down behind him, snapping the man's head back so far that his eyes met Antious's.

I wonder, Antious started to think, but saw the man begin to come back to life, despite the broken neck.

Fine!

The Arlethian captain decapitated the man, obliging him his second death, and simultaneously raised his other scimitar above his head, parallel to the ground, blocking a blow from behind. Down on one knee, Antious spun, taking the offending man in his stomach, and then with the blade he had used to block, his neck.

Obviously feeling they might not best him with the blade, several dark marauders rushed him at once. He stabbed and slashed, but they still came, pinning him to the ground and holding him down. Antious struggled mightily, but could not free himself. Another enemy stood over him with a blade. It started to fall toward his chest.

Desperate, only one thing crossed his mind. Antious turned his head left and sucked in a large mouthful of black sand. The man holding his left arm received a blast of black sand in his face and eyes as Antious exhaled with all his might. The flinch was enough and Antious freed his arm, grabbed the man's jaw, and brought his head over his chest in time to meet the blade seeking to impale him.

Any time you feel like helping, Thannuel, would be welcome.

Several ice shards impaled Thannuel, striking his arms and hands. Blood mixed with the ice as it melted from the heat of his body and the magma. He didn't dare use more Light with only limited amounts remaining. The impact of the volcano's projectiles jolted his frame as they hit mere feet from him.

The Thoulden-sha spun as he hurled more daggers of ice, making throwing motions with his arms, though he did not touch the frozen shards. Thannuel focused the first part of his mind there, blocking and batting away the volleys with impressive speed despite his injured arms. Spinning his sword nearly as fast as a hummingbird's wings, he battered and chopped the unnatural lethal bodkins. Still, several got past his defenses. The second part of his mind, coordinating with the first, pulled him from the magma projectiles when they came too close, analyzing and predicting trajectories. But the third part of his mind remained wild, not in sync. It searched for something—something it knew was there but somehow could not find.

A narrow fault opened up under Thannuel, ripping through the ground like a streak of lightning and causing him to stumble. He recovered quickly but an ice shard got through his defenses, nearly impaling his head as it grazed his eyebrow, drawing a new river of blood that coursed down his eye. A smoking boulder cracking with red veins crashed down just in front of him, the energy from its impact hurling Thannuel back, and he lost his sword. He hit hard.

Finally, Thannuel gained enough grasp on his mental faculties to think somewhat coherently. Blood ran down his arms where the ice had penetrated him but had already melted away. Hot sand sprayed against the right side of his face from the impact of another volcanic rock.

His mind spun, not able to refocus the disparate pieces. The rain of ice shards and magma lessened as Thannuel rolled over on his side, his body reeling.

His hand, coated in sand and blood, reached for his sword. He was reminded that the triarch leafling he had held between his palm and the hilt was gone.

It doesn't matter. The ships are gone, no more Light to harness.

Still, Thannuel felt a deep loss, not having anything of Arlethia left, no connection to home. The third partition of his mind raged, like a man drowning only an inch below the water but unable to surface.

It's so close, his mind told him … but he did not understand his thoughts.

"You are not fluent enough in your powers, Lord Kerr!" the Thoulden-sha taunted. "I have spent decades refining and cultivating Mari-shaden's powers. You are a mere child, a babe, searching for his mother's breast, not yet understanding what you are!"

Thannuel found his sword; the regret of losing the leafling provided a small bit of friction that he recycled, but not enough.

I'm sorry, Moira.

iden heard muted voices, disturbing the best sleep he'd received in years, maybe his entire life. He willed them to be silent but the voices remained, sounding as if they were calling out to someone, searching. His mind started to surface from his all-too-short hibernation, lethargically rousing itself from dormancy.

They were cold, his blankets, and his bed firmer than he remembered. In fact, he became more uncomfortable as the seconds passed. Somehow he had lost his pillow, replaced by something that felt like rope and splinters, and his hair was wet. His whole body was wet, shivering, in fact.

"Aiden!" came the call, sounding in his ears like thunder as his mind snapped back into focus. His eyes shot open.

He drifted in the ocean, floating on a hodgepodge of debris, almost completely face down. The lower half of his body dangled off the debris and floated in the ocean, cocking the concoction at an upward angle slightly, mercifully keeping his head a few inches above the water. His legs tingled from the chill as night approached, feeling almost completely numb.

"Aiden, boy, reach out!"

It was one of his shipmates, the one he had bitten. He leaned over the side of the skiff, arm outstretched.

"Come on, reach!" the man called, waving his hand.

Water lapped up over the edge of the debris Aiden floated on, splashing him in the face. The salt water burned his nose. As he reached out, his weight shifted and the debris pile upended, causing Aiden to slide. Too weak to arrest his descent, he slid into the deep, the cold and dark engulfing him. The thought to go search for Norvuld, to join his captain in the depths, crossed his mind.

A beefy hand found him, pulling him up by the hair at the crown of his head.

"Gotcha!" he heard his shipmate say as he surfaced, spluttering briny water.

Another man grabbed him and they hauled him aboard the boat like a wet dog.

"You should have let me go," Aiden rasped.

"No dimming way, lad. You're our captain now." The men gave him a sad smile.

"And if your captain had commanded you to let him sink to the bottom?" Aiden asked.

The man shrugged. "I suppose we would have mutinied, overruling your order, and saved you anyway."

"But you obeyed Captain Norvuld when he gave basically the same command."

"That was different," another shipmate said. "His death had meaning. Yours would not have."

Aiden couldn't resist a smile as he lay on the floor of the skiff. "I was right," he said. "You're all bastards.

"The ships? The enemy fleet?" he asked.

"Done. Gone," came the answer. "You were amazing, lad. Whatever you did caused enough havoc to distract the crews of those vessels, keeping them close enough to the capitol ship's blast radius. Very few Orsarian ships were unaffected and those have fled."

"Where to now, Captain?" asked another.

Aiden thought it really didn't matter and was about to say as much when he remembered Norvuld's words. They hadn't been spoken with urgency, but as he heard them play again in his mind, they *felt* urgent.

"Third Island," he said. "And be quick about it."

Thannuel stood, using his sword of Jarwynian ore to raise himself. His posture was skewed, not being able to stand up fully from the pain of his wounds. Using the last bit of Light in his sword, he healed his most serious wounds and stood straighter.

"Maybe you're right, Thoulden-sha," Thannuel admitted. "Maybe I am still a child; but if so, it will be a child that shall bring you and the Ancient Dark to extinction."

"You have nothing left, Kiarra. I see it in you. But witness, first moon will soon rise, lending the trapped powers of Mari-shaden to me. Indeed, the Resurgence is so near. If you fall here rather than upon an altar at next cycle's full first moon, it is no loss. I believe your father's blood will serve just as well."

Fear. Rage. The two emotions circulated through him, powerfully conjured. He felt their currents pulsing inside, the friction being strong and deep. Capturing it took intense concentration and mental fortitude, requiring his whole mind to tame the stampede of fast racing friction. Thannuel redirected the friction to all of his senses, forcing his wounded body to operate at inhuman levels—levels that could take too much in retribution. Thannuel raised his sword.

"Very well, Lord Kerr." The Thoulden-sha shrugged. "Let it end."

The assault was an unbridled, feral intrusion into Thannuel's core, into his soul. His sword, forged of Jarwynian ore, was no protection as the Thoulden-sha's attack penetrated him, seemingly sending white-hot pain through every nerve ending in his body, every pain receptor. He screamed as he felt capillaries in his left eye burst from the mental attack being levied against him.

"Thannuel!" he heard Antious call, still engaged in his own battle.

He looked up, past the Thoulden-sha to his friend. Antious moved gracefully, using basic but reliable movements against his many foes. Thannuel recognized the many katas he drew from. Antious's style had always been straightforward, trusting the rudiments of combat rather than more fancy and advanced tactics.

The Orsarians stopped suddenly, standing around Antious but not attacking. Thannuel could see the confusion on his friend's face as he stood wary, looking from man to man. As one, each of the remaining Orsarians—seven if Thannuel could see them all—raised their scimitars in the exact same motion, each taking the exact same stance. Their movements were in sync, like perfect reflections of one another. It was then that Thannuel saw the Thoulden-sha's expression, his face grimacing and a line of red coming from one nostril.

"Antious!" Thannuel yelled in a pained voice. "Antious, they are being controlled—"

The warning came too late. The synchronization of the attack was perfectly executed, each Orsarian seemingly a limb to a greater body and mind. Thannuel saw the shock on his friend's face as they converged on him, all the while the Thoulden-sha not loosening his grasp on him.

"How do you think," the Thoulden-sha taunted with a strained voice, "that I knew every inch of the narrows around Dispa, Lord Kerr?"

A shudder went through the Thoulden-sha's face as it contorted with effort. "Or divined the Orsarian language in a matter of moments?"

Another grimace on the Thoulden-sha's face and Thannuel tried to push through his pain and rise, but he was thwarted by another wave of Dark Influence pounding him. Antious dodged, jumping and flipping through the air, blocking and parrying. Two of the now-mindless dark marauders lost their heads; another took two mortal blows, both to the chest in rapid succession.

"Mari-shaden's gifts to me as her oracle are far reaching. To think I cannot recognize, analyze and overcome such predictable tactics!"

The Orsarians' movements changed, shifting in strange motions. With a quivering upper lip, the Thoulden-sha's expression turned to a ravenous sneer. Thannuel saw it coming, observing from the outside as Antious struggled to adapt to the alien motions of his opponents.

"*Antious!*"

"*There!*" the Thoulden-sha said, seething.

"No!" Thannuel yelled. "Antious!" His protests were cut short as his throat constricted. He tried to advance to his friend but the pain increased, immobilizing him and sending him to a knee.

The curved sword skewered Antious's upper right breast and protruded out his back. He stumbled backward and the dark marauder let go of the handle. A look of disbelief filled Antious's eyes as he brought his hand to the wound, touching the blood that escaped the gash. The remaining four Orsarians waited, each standing with the same posture as the other, their bodies still slaves to the Thoulden-sha's Influence. Antious looked at Thannuel, acceptance and regret in his eyes, as if saying, *It's all up to you now.*

The son of a janitor and night watchman, the boy who had become Thannuel's best friend, nodded in goodbye.

Time seemed to stand still for Thannuel.

"*No!*" His voice was hoarse, teeming with pain and anger, but Thannuel could not capture the frictions with his mind and body so overwhelmed.

"Wretched and archaic!" The Thoulden-sha spoke with a smile, but it lasted only a moment. He could not hide his shock when, instead of falling to the black sand and expelling his last breath, Antious attacked too fast for the Thoulden-sha to force his minions to react. All four heads hit the beach. Then, so did Antious.

Stay with me, Antious! Please!

Now kneeling, Thannuel held a hand to his head. He forced the first part of his mind to recognize and accept the pain he felt, funneling it all there, containing it. With the second part, he tried to capture the frictions inside him. Most of them sped past, like raging rapids, too powerful to contain; but he did catch some, finally. He reinforced his bones, joints, muscles, tendons, sinews, attempting to hold himself together as the pressure from the Thoulden-sha's attacks increased, feeling as if he were being crushed and ripped apart simultaneously. But the reserves of friction inside him were limited and too shallow to sustain him.

Friction alone isn't enough, he sensed. *I need Light.*

Blood trickled from his nose and ears, and he knew his skull would crack and his heart explode any second. His hand hit the sand as he hunched over, struggling to still keep himself from collapsing. Under his touch and beneath the sand, he felt something—a familiar texture and shape.

Instinctively, he grabbed the triarch leafling, the same he had lost, like a lifeline, and brought it up. All its leaves were charred and dead save for one that still had a patch of green surrounded by burned edges. Thannuel placed it in the palm of his hand, knowing it was just a comfort to him in his final moments.

The third part of his mind, clawing and scratching, immediately fell into sync as it found a link. It was small, faint, but getting closer. A pulse, a heartbeat that he first felt when he was sixteen in a time of desperate need.

But all the ships were destroyed. I saw them ...

Thannuel looked left, east, and saw five people approaching in a small boat—a boat made of triarch wood.

He sucked in all the Light, greedily absorbing it into himself.

"What?" the Thoulden-sha said, feeling his grasp on Thannuel become slippery.

The Light coursed through Thannuel, pulsing and pounding, combining with his friction and restoring him enough to rebuff the Thoulden-sha's assault; but the limited amount of Light would not last long.

"I told you, Thoulden-sha," Thannuel said. "It only takes a spark."

Ignoring the pain of dozens of wounds and skin searing, Lord Thannuel Kerr funneled the remaining stored friction he contained to strength and threw his sword. Just before it left his hand, he poured all the Light of the triarch boat into the sword and whispered, *"Faerathm."*

The humming Jarwynian blade flew through the air like a spear, small blue flames springing to life around it, leaving a trail of smoke in its wake. It struck the Thoulden-sha in the chest and flames began spreading out from the wound, consuming the oracle. He screamed as the flames leaped from his mouth, the fire spreading both inside and out.

Thannuel stumbled to the collapsing pile of human combustion and touched the sword's hilt. The vibration of its humming was still present, still pouring its power into the Thoulden-sha.

Vrathia!

The Thoulden-sha's screams changed tenor, becoming unrecognizable as human as his body twisted and contorted in ways nature never intended it to, folding over on itself. His flesh burned from the fire, bones pulverized from the weaponized wrath. It was not long before he ceased writhing on the ground, his remains heaped in an unnatural position as they smoldered.

Deciding to not leave anything to chance, Thannuel used the remaining Light in the blade to check for a pulse.

Welkaira!

As he thought the ancient word, his hand still on the sword's hilt, the Thoulden-sha's body flew apart into half a dozen pieces, the shockwave having its genesis at the point of the sword's impact in his now charred chest.

The volcano's tempest quieted and the air's chill normalized. Scores of ice shards, larger than most short blades and staked in the sand near him, decorated the black beach.

Thannuel looked up to see Antious on the ground, not moving. He sprinted to his friend's side.

"Antious! Speak!" Thannuel slapped Antious's cheek, then twice more.

"That hurts," Antious said weakly, opening his eyes.

The skiff landed and the men hauled it up the beach to secure it. The castaway boy was with them.

"Master Norvuld!" Thannuel cried out. "Where ... where is he?"

The boy shook his head, sadness upon his countenance.

Thannuel had hoped Norvuld could heal Antious, the way he had done for him on his ship. But there was no Light left to draw upon regardless. His friend's breathing was becoming shallower, his skin paler.

"Stay alive!" Thannuel commanded. "You will stay alive! Do you hear me?"

"You'll need to apologize to Kalisa for me," Antious said. "I meant to survive ... for her."

"Don't say that!" Thannuel shouted. He turned away, not

wanting to let his friend see his face as he tried to hold back his grief.

Please, Ancient Heavens!

"I would do it again," Antious said, "even knowing this is how it would end. I would do it again."

The castaway and other four men approached and knelt around them.

"Is there anything we can do, my Lord?" one of them asked.

Thannuel just shook his head, not hiding his tears now, until he saw a short blade on the castaway's hip. The blade was pewter colored.

"Where did you get that?" Thannuel asked.

"Captain Norvuld gave it to Aiden when he made him first officer," one of the men answered.

Aiden, Thannuel thought. *Finally gave up your name.*

"Aiden," Thannuel said, "is this true? Norvuld gave it to you?"

The boy looked wary but only hesitated a moment. "Aye."

Thannuel held out a hand. "Please, may I see it?"

The hesitation was a little longer this time, but Aiden took it from his belt and handed it over. As soon as Thannuel's hand touched the blade, he felt the stored Light within it. Gazing meaningfully at Aiden, Thannuel understood why Norvuld had made him promise to look after the young boy.

He doesn't know what he is, Thannuel realized, looking at Aiden.

"Antious, this is going to hurt, my friend," Thannuel said.

With a quick pull, Thannuel extricated the scimitar from Antious's right breast. Despite the searing pain, Antious barely reacted as the steel left him. He was fading, his eyes barely open.

Thannuel took the short blade of Jarwynian make and pushed the tip gently into the open wound.

"Mylendia Shaul."

The Lord of the Western Province felt the Light leave the infused blade, entering Antious's body. A moment passed before Antious's eyes shot wide open.

TWENTY-EIGHT

~ANTIOUS~

Day 21 of 3rd Rising 393 A.U.

CAPTAIN ANTIOUS ROAN reported to High Lord Marshal Hawkes and Prime Lord Parlan Wellyn in Iskell. Emeron Wellyn was also present along with High Vicar Rehum Tarylgen, the Changrual Monastery's preceptor. Among the two hundred and seventy-one surviving Realm soldiers, he was the only officer. The duty of reporting on the battle had fallen squarely on his shoulders.

He told of the Thoulden-sha's return after being banished from the Realm, having led the Orsarians to their lands; the deaths of General Korin and Captain Norvuld; the destruction of the Orsarian fleet and their turning away from the islands; and the eventual death of the Thoulden-sha at Thannuel's hands. Much of what he did not understand—Thannuel's miraculous display of ... Influence, he guessed was the only proper word—did not make its way into his report. He would ponder more on this in the years to come.

"It sounds fairly straightforward, Captain," Prime Lord Wellyn said. "In fact, we may have overestimated them, it seems, if ten thousand of our soldiers were able to deal them such a decisive blow."

Straightforward, Antious inwardly mused. *It must seem that way to an outsider, to one who has never stood on the edge of this life and the next.* Antious decided to bite his tongue.

Turning to his son, the Prime Lord said, "Congratulations, Emeron. Seems your strategy did indeed prove effective. Word of you as the architect of the strategy will be spread throughout the Realm."

Rehum Tarylgen looked displeased with Antious's report. "Captain, I have heard rumors of strange things, weather and other anomalies that many have tried but failed to explain."

"We did encounter storms of ironic timing," Antious said, shifting his weight. His left ankle was still a little tender. "And a volcanic eruption was certainly less than desirable, preceptor. The cloud of ash and smoke that lingers over Main Island has made it uninhabitable for the time, though the other islands remain intact. Even still, I've been told that many islanders, those who survived, are choosing to move to the mainland."

"Did you bring back the body of the Thoulden-sha?" Tarylgen asked. "Perhaps I could—"

"Given to the sea," Antious interrupted.

The disappointment on Tarylgen's face struck Antious as odd, but perhaps it wasn't strange for one of the Changrual Order to want to study someone who served the Ancient Dark, even if it was just the remains. But then Antious reminded himself there was no Ancient Dark or Living Light or …

There is something, he admitted silently. *What I saw—*

"Captain Roan, you are a hero of the Realm," Prime Lord Wellyn said, interrupting his thoughts. "Please accept our deepest gratitude for your service, as well as for those we lost. The Granite Throne will honor their sacrifices forever."

He found Kalisa waiting for him outside the Prime Lord's council chambers. She stared at him with her typical piercing look.

"I'm sorry," Antious said, but she held up her hand and looked away.

"Were you there?" she asked.

"At the end, yes. He spoke of you."

Kalisa shut her eyes, squeezing back the tears, still refusing to look at him.

"You should know," Antious said carefully, "that while he was heavily outnumbered, he defeated their military leader, taking out all but the very last of their forces."

Kalisa wiped away a disobedient tear and looked sternly at Antious. "Of course he did!" But then her brave façade cracked, her lower lip quivered, and the tears fell freely.

Antious came to her gently, not sure if he dared to touch her, but she leaned into him, her head fitting in the crook of his neck.

"Kalisa," Antious began, "I promised your father I would love you forever. I intend to do that."

"Did he order you to?"

"Just about."

A silence for a few minutes held.

"What do you intend to do about that?" Kalisa asked.

"Marry you, of course."

"Is that you asking?"

"Do I need to?"

"It's always nice," Kalisa said.

Antious faced the woman he loved fully and took her hands in his. "Kalisa Korin, I could never survive this life without you by my side. If you will have me, I promise to protect and honor you, to make you laugh, and to always find my way back to you. Will you marry me, Kalisa?"

"Yes!" she said, this time with joyful tears coming to her eyes. She did not stem their flow as she kissed him over and over.

"You forgot one thing," she said, finally pulling back from him.

"Which was?"

"You forgot to promise children."

Antious Roan suddenly felt fear like never before in his life. "Kids?"

In a dark corner of the throne room, Maynard had listened to the report given by the wood-dweller soldier. He and his Helsyan brethren had all been summoned from hibernation. Though the bearer of the Stone of Orlack had not told them why, it was obvious that Wellyn had been preparing for something, taking precautions. Overhearing the report by the Arlethian scum, Maynard now understood.

If the Orsarians had made landfall upon mainland Senthara, we would have been unleashed. Only the water that separated the mainland from the Runic Islands had kept them from the confrontation, it being a curb against them, part of the Light's curse upon his race.

He sorrowed for the loss of opportunity to be placed under a *dahlrak*, likely many. Wellyn would not risk them being discovered by the general populace, and would have used them discreetly, as always. Still, it had been many years since receiving a Charge and he ached to be of service.

But something even more troubling had caught his attention. Somehow the Thoulden-sha, with whom he had been Charged years ago, had led the Orsarians to Senthara. Maynard had feared this enigma, who had erased the effects of the *dahlrak* once pronounced upon him by the *urlenthi,* swiping it aside like nothing more than an old garment, had perished when Wellyn quelled his rebellion. Learning, however, that he had survived only to be defeated again, this time permanently, anguished Maynard's soul.

The Thoulden-sha was to free him, all of his kind. He had felt the words burn inside him like fire when the Thoulden-sha promised this; but now, those words were only ashes of loss and regret inside him.

How could an Arlethian defeat him when I could not even lift an arm against him? he wondered. *Helsya shall not rise again and be forever lost if we cannot break our obeisance to the Stone.*

Something else would come, he thought. Some other way. He felt it as assuredly as he breathed the North's nearly frozen air. The Light's curse upon them could not last forever.

Something is coming, he knew. The faith in this feeling was likely the only thing that kept him from sinking into despair, becoming a mindless slave to the *urlenthi's* will. He had seen that before, others of his kind becoming a lifeless shell until being granted a harvest. He committed to himself that this would not be him, that he'd search out his dreams for more meaning and prepare his brethren as best he could.

The Thoulden-sha spoke of a Resurgence, he remembered. It had seemed nonsensical to him at the time. *Perhaps it had something to do with reclaiming Helsya, wherever the ancient land has been hidden,* he reasoned.

This thought stayed with Maynard as he exited Hold Wellyn, pulling his hood over his head and making his way back to the Kail. Yes, it made more sense to him as he pondered, giving reason to why he could not fulfill his Charge against the Thoulden-sha. *The Dark cannot fight itself.*

He doubted the Thoulden-sha had known what the Resurgence truly was, only that he was a part in it. Maynard truly believed, however, that it would take a Helsyan to reclaim Helsya, not some Oracle of the Ancient Dark. It was his clan, after all, that had devotedly embraced the Dark Mother above all others before The Turning Away … before their cursing.

Someday, one shall rise from among us and crush the urlenthi, freeing us, and reclaim our hidden land of Helsya.

ʃʃ\\Ʀ

Thannuel had been tempted to go straight home, to Hold Kerr, and sweep Moira into his arms, but he felt another priority deep within him. He had personally visited the families of the eight soldiers that had accompanied Antious to rescue him, conveying his condolences and endless gratitude for the giving of their lives for his.

"I would never have asked it of them," he told each of the families. "I cannot take back their sacrifices, nor do I suspect they would want me to; but I can and will honor them, not just as a lord, but as a fellow Arlethian. They embodied the Arlethian Warrior's Creed to the fullest, proving they were truly Arlethia."

Once the triarch ships had been lost, no Living Light had remained to harness. The worst of his injuries he had healed when he returned to the Western Province, drawing in some of the Living Light from the sentient trees. But those that were superficial and most visible, he maintained as he visited the families.

It wouldn't do to show up without the signs of battle. They must know that I fought with their sons.

Now, as he approached his home late in the evening, he clutched the triarch leafling in a satchel slung over his shoulder and made a connection with the forest. He drew in more Light, marveling at how natural it felt despite his short time with his expanded understanding, and spoke softly.

"Mylendia Shaul."

The warmth spread through him and the wounds that would have left scars for life disappeared, leaving no evidence of their former presence. He would not allow his wife to see the punishment he had endured, but feared the punishment he would yet endure upon being reunited with her.

As he stared at the gates that would lead him onto the hold grounds, Thannuel hesitated. There was something near … some*one* near.

"I can feel it," he said. "I'm not sure how."

Master Amnoch stepped out from behind a cluster of woven trees, their trunks intermingling together, forming a beautiful tapestry that ascended over a hundred feet before melting into the frondescent canopy.

"You feel my current, Lord Kerr," Amnoch said. "The spark of life granted to all by the Lumenatis."

"It's faint," Thannuel replied. "Almost like a vibrational pulse, similar but different. I don't understand it."

"My Lord, I doubt there are any that fully do. It's said that only the Ancients could see the currents of Living Light in others. Our abilities to sense and feel vibrations, though seemingly wondrous to those who are not wood-dwellers, are crude shadows of the abilities the Ancients once had."

Thannuel pondered this for a few moments. "It's not something I see," he admitted. "It was like someone whispered to me that you were here; like an awareness that even with your eyes closed you know which way is down."

Amnoch nodded. "I have heard of it described similarly, but only by one other."

"You cannot feel it?" Thannuel asked.

"No," Amnoch said, shaking his head. "And even what you feel is far from the sensitivity the Ancients felt. The records we have speak of being able to *see* and discern the tendrils of life all around you."

Thannuel felt inward. It disappointed him that he only felt Amnoch's current and then felt slightly ashamed that he had vainly hoped he was more powerful. But then, he did sense another current, one younger than him.

"The boy," he said. "He is near?"

"Yes," Amnoch answered. "Out of earshot, just inside the gate. He arrived bearing your message two days past. He has been well looked after."

"And Lady Kerr ... she does not know he is here?"

"Just as you commanded, Lord Kerr."

Thannuel nodded and pursed his lips. "And my father?"

Amnoch looked down. "He does not fare well, my Lord. I fear he will join the Light before long."

Thannuel could see the true sadness in Master Amnoch's

countenance. And then something dawned on him.

"You're only staying for him."

Still looking down, Amnoch nodded. "I must return to the Tavaniah Forest once he passes. That could still be some time; your father is a fighter. But once he does, my time here is done, Lord Kerr."

"Who will take your place?" Thannuel asked, suddenly feeling vulnerable at the thought of losing his teacher and mentor. "I had thought—"

"Quit quibbling, my Lord," Amnoch scolded. "It hurts my ears." Then the Master of the Hold Guard smiled. "I'll be around, my Lord. But my oath to the Gyldenal transcends everything else. You will understand, when you're ready. Besides, I think you could benefit for a time by being your own Master of the Hold Guard. Eventually, the right person will come along."

Thannuel still felt melancholy about the prospect of Amnoch leaving, especially coinciding with his father's inevitable passing; but he knew Amnoch was doing what he felt was right.

"One more thing, Lord Kerr," Amnoch said. "I know Archivers are neutral—or supposedly so—but you cannot be too careful with your new … understandings. Be extremely careful around him. The Gyldenal's existence must remain clandestine, at least for now."

"For now?"

Amnoch nodded slowly. "Evrin, the Keeper of the Living Light, sees something coming."

Thannuel's mind drifted back to the first encounter he had with the Marishee in the streets of Calyn. *The old man in the tree who … spoke to me through my mind.* "Who is he?"

"You will meet him again when you are ready, my Lord."

"What does he see coming?"

"He does not say … or, at least, not completely. There's a

parasitic Influence in the Light, he calls it, but does not say more. Honestly, I don't think even he knows how to describe it more than that."

Thannuel nodded, though he didn't really understand.

"Please let my father know I have returned and will see him after I see Lady Kerr."

"About that," Amnoch said, "I have only one piece of advice if you want to survive that encounter: move your feet!"

ᛋᛁᛉ

Lady Moira Kerr felt Thannuel's footsteps come into the hold, cross the courtyard, and enter their bedroom. As soon as her husband crossed the threshold, she slapped him.

Thannuel accepted the blow. He had his sheathed sword and a bag slung over his shoulder. Moira's lip quivered and tears spilled down her cheeks.

"I wanted to come back earlier," Thannuel said. "I really tried—"

"Shut up," Moira said. She stood fidgeting, not sure if she should slap him again or kiss him.

"I promised I would come back."

"Oh, Thannuel," she whimpered and crushed him with a full body hug, wrapping her arms around his neck and legs around his hips. She heard his sword and the bag hit the floor and felt his strong arms wrap around her, his hands lacing in between her straight ebony hair.

"Hold me," she whispered. "Just hold me."

After all too short of an eternity, Thannuel whispered, "I have a surprise for you."

Letting Moira down, he turned over his left shoulder, looked toward their bedroom door that led to the courtyard and motioned with his hand.

"Don't be shy," Thannuel coaxed.

Into sight walked a boy, early in his adolescence, with shaggy black hair. He bowed slightly to Lady Kerr.

"Moira, this young man is Aiden. He is one of the many brave sailors who served with Master Norvuld and made a significant contribution to our victory."

She looked questioningly at her husband.

"I made a promise to Master Norvuld," Thannuel said. "One that I am both sad and happy to have to keep."

Moira understood as she looked into Thannuel's eyes, at least on some level. She saw the purity within him, the absolute noble conviction of heart that shone through his eyes, the same she had loved since the first time she met him.

"He'll be staying," she said. It was not a question. She went to the shy-looking boy and hugged him with a mother's tenderness.

"Welcome to Hold Kerr, Aiden."

EPILOGUE

Day 24 of 1ˢᵗ low 396 A.U.

"DO YOU HAVE TO GO?" Moira asked.

"I do," Thannuel said.

"I don't understand why. What's in the Tavaniah Forest? Men chase nothing but ghost stories there."

"Something I must do, my love. I would not go if I did not feel I had to. Can you trust me?"

Moira rubbed her rounded belly. "Of course. I just don't want you to miss it."

"The twins aren't due for several span yet," Thannuel replied. "Don't worry, I'll be back in five or six days."

"I remember the last time I heard something like that," she said.

"Three years, and you still won't forgive me?" Thannuel smiled disarmingly. "I'm not going off to some war *this* time, Lady Kerr."

"I never know with you."

"Come here."

Moira came to him and they embraced. Thannuel felt his wife's womb jump as it pressed between them. He knelt down and put his hands lovingly on her stomach.

I wish you could have been here to see them born, Father. But then, he felt that the Living Light would allow Branton Kerr to look in on the blessed event when it happened. Master Amnoch thought it would be so, having said as much when he left to go back to the Tavaniah shortly after Branton had been buried in the sepulcher below Hold Kerr, joining his forefathers.

"Are you sure?" Thannuel asked. "A boy and a girl?"

"Yes," Moira said with a loving smile.

"The healers don't even know that. How can you tell?"

Thannuel felt Moira's hand run through his hair as he rested his forehead on her belly. "I just know," she said softly.

"You wait for me, my little ones," he whispered. Then he kissed Moira's stomach. "That's for you, Hedron. And this," he placed a second kiss, "is for you, my little Reign."

Evrin waited in the Tavaniah Forest for Lord Kerr. It had been over three years since Master Norvuld had introduced him to the Gyldenal, but they had never called on him, waiting instead for him to seek them out.

Perhaps Amnoch is right, he mused. *Perhaps. It would be fitting for one of the Kiarra Clan's lineage.*

He and the Gyldenal had waited for several millennia to find one who had the capacity to draw out the Lumenatis from the forest and restore it to the world. Evrin himself had been in search of him for more than a thousand years. The Ancients who had not followed after Noxmyra and the Ancient Dark had concealed it there during The Turning Away.

Master Amnoch believed Thannuel might be the one they had waited for, but Evrin remained cautious. Thannuel had indeed displayed promise thirteen years ago as Evrin watched him from an elm tree in the Calyn Gardens, giving him a slight mental nudge; and again with the defeat of the Thoulden-sha in the Runic Islands.

The rise of the Thoulden-sha troubled Evrin. It showed the Ancient Dark's power was growing in the world, its Influence extending.

The tide. The parasite.

The Gyldenal had found no lands in the rebirthing cycle for the past four decades. Norvuld and others had searched extensively. Only decay seemed to prevail in Våleira. The few remaining civilizations outside Senthara would soon die out unless they found their way to Senthara.

But those who come will not come in peace, he lamented. His eyes turned north, to the Northern Province, beyond to the glaciers, and felt the whispers of warning in the forest as his mind's eye traveled even further. *Yes. They will come. They must.* The Ancient Dark's Influence upon the hearts of those in the world had buried itself deep. *The Living Light's Influence is only strong when others live after the Ancients.* One of the main reasons, he knew, that the Lumenatis had dimmed.

Evrin, Light Shepherd and oldest living person in the world, felt Thannuel's approach. The sword Master Norvuld had provided him with hung at his side, a thick cloak draped around his shoulders, and hair that looked like the dimming season's leaves as the gentle breeze tousled it framed this impressive man.

The Lord of the Western Province stopped and peered around the meadow. Evrin saw the recognition of another's presence in

Thannuel's eyes.

Very good, Evrin thought. Thannuel wouldn't be able to see him, as Evrin took in all the light around him, making himself invisible; nor could Thannuel sense him from vibrational pulses, as Evrin stood perfectly still. Yet, he could tell Thannuel knew he was there.

"I am a current," Thannuel spoke. He waited for a moment. "I am a current … " he repeated.

Evrin saw no need to delay any further. He allowed the light to find him, becoming visible to Lord Kerr. Startlement followed by recognition flowed over Thannuel's face.

Yes, you know me, Thannuel.

"I am a current of friction and Light," Evrin answered the ancient greeting, "a spark against the Ancient Dark that cannot be extinguished, a beam of the Lumenatis. Welcome, Lord Kerr, to the Gyldenal."

THE END OF
ALTAR OF INFLUENCE
THE ORSARIAN WAR
A PRELUDE TO THE DYING LANDS CHRONICLE

ACKNOWLEDGMENTS

To my family and friends who have enthusiastically supported me in my writing, I thank you sincerely. To Mike Sirota, for lending his experience as a successful author and eyes as an editor. To my daughters, without whose insistence on original bedtime stories, I may have never have forced myself to conjure up new worlds. To Jed, Seth, and Nate for once again encouraging me to keep going and dive deeper in my development of the world of Våleira. To John Avon, for your amazing ability to capture the visual essence of my words. To Michael Kramer, for giving voice and life to this story. Finally, to Kristen, my wonderful wife, for believing in me without fail. There's never a day that goes by when I don't count myself fortunate with you by my side.

ABOUT THE AUTHOR

Jacob Cooper is an award-winning, #1 bestselling epic fantasy author. In addition to writing *The Dying Lands Chronicle*, his works have been included in several anthologies alongside other high-profile authors. His first effort, *Moon Monsters*, was written when he faked sickness one day in first grade to stay home and write. This story received the acclaim of his parents and sits in a black 3-ringed binder somewhere in their basement. Aside from writing, Jacob is an accomplished percussionist, pianist, and composer. He enjoys power sports on land and water, as well as spending time with his family.

www.circleofreign.com

Facebook.com/jacobcooperCOR
@AuthorJacobCooper